THE STORIES WE TELL

THE STORIES WE TELL

A Homefront Mystery

First published by Level Best Books/Historia 2021

AUTHOR PHOTO CREDIT: Erin McClain Studio

First edition

ISBN: 978-1-953789-16-7

Cover art by Level Best Designs

This book was professionally typeset on Reedsy.
Find out more at reedsy.com

Praise for THE STORIES WE TELL

"Betty Ahern is still honing her detective skills in Liz Milliron's second Homefront Mystery, but she's shaping up beautifully despite opposition at home and the demands of that pesky day job, building planes. *The Stories We Tell* has its dark side, but Buffalo's First Ward in 1942 is still a world of warmth and charm, where Betty's honour, loyalty, and sheer moxie are guaranteed to win the day."—Catriona McPherson, multi-award-winning author of the Dandy Gilver Mysteries

"Liz Milliron delivers an affectionate and unexpected glimpse of WWII era Buffalo through the eyes of her determined and spunky sleuth."—Jessica Ellicott, author of the Beryl and Edwina Mysteries

"A refreshingly different take on WWII with a homefront drama involving Polish exiles in Buffalo and an appealingly gutsy Irish American heroine (who reminds me of my own Molly Murphy)."—Rhys Bowen, *NYT* and #1 Kindle bestselling author of the Royal Spyness and Molly Murphy series as well as internationally bestselling stand-alone novels

Chapter One

December 1, 1942

Buffalo, NY

Pop once told me that people tell stories about themselves all the time. About who they are, where they come from, why they did a particular thing. It's a way of coping, he said, and of making sense of their lives. I guess it works. I mean, I've done it. Why not other people?

'Cept sometimes the stories aren't true.

Emilia Brewka, "Emmie" to us girls at Bell Airplane, set down her spoon, her soft brown eyes wide. "I just don't think she died natural, Betty."

I peered at her over my cup of coffee. Emmie was what Mom called "peasant stock." Not that she was poor, least not any more than the rest of us. But she had a sturdy build and a rounded face usually wearing a broad smile. I always thought Emmie looked like a grown-up version of Shirley Temple with her curly hair, rosy cheeks, and big grin. Right now, that friendly face was creased, her eyes lit with worry, mouth in a definite upside-down U.

Emmie Brewka was not happy.

I set down my cup. "What do you mean?"

She sniffed. "The doc said she died of a heart attack. Baloney. *Babcia* didn't have a bad heart. Back in Poland, she and *Dziadek* worked hard. Him in the fields, she as a maid up at the big house. When they came to the States, back in '05, he got a job working the blast furnace at Bethlehem and she did laundry and cleaning for the rich folks. She raised seven kids and worked twelve hours a day. Does that sound like a woman with a weak heart?"

"No."

"When I talked to her a week ago, she was all set to start the Christmas baking. Yesterday she has a heart attack." Emmie shook her head, brown curls bouncing. "Not natural."

"Got it." I took another drink, mostly to give myself time to think. This stuff was better than the chicory I had at home, but I had a flash of memory, the wonderful roasted taste of the coffee at the German American club. Heaven. "Why're you telling me all this?"

Her cup clattered against the saucer as she set it down. "'Cause you're the one who figures things out, ain't ya? I mean, that's the word at Bell."

She had a point. Since October, I'd solved two murders, busted open some black market activity, and uncovered sabotage at Bell. After that, girls had been bringing me all sorts of problems. For a small fee, I had found some missing jewelry, followed a couple sneaky boyfriends before they shipped out, and even located a lost cat. This, however, smelled like a different thing. How was I supposed to prove a poor old lady hadn't died a peaceful, God-fearing death? I didn't know any doctors.

But I did know Detective Sam MacKinnon of the Buffalo Police. "Did anyone call the cops after your grandma died?"

"No." Emmie finished her coffee. "I wanted to, but Mama said not to be silly, I'd be wasting their time."

Darn it. No cops prob'ly meant no autopsy. "Let's say you're right. Who would want to kill her, your grandma? She have any enemies?"

"Not that I can think of." Emmie leaned forward. "But ain't that what you're s'posed to find out? As a detective, I mean."

I drained my cup. Too bad I couldn't take some home. "It would help if I had a clue or two to start with. Heck, that's the first thing Sam Spade, or even the police, ask when someone's murdered."

"I'll try and think, but far as I know *Babcia* got along with everybody. Well, enough they didn't want to kill her. I mean, I'm sure she argued with lots of people throughout her life. She was over seventy, after all." Emmie bit her lip. “But she gave cookies to all the kids in the neighborhood, ’specially at Christmas. She took care of babies and gave gifts to new mothers. Far as I know, everybody in our neighborhood liked her.”

“Emmie, this doesn’t sound like murder to me.”

“Betty, please. I’m telling you, it don’t feel right. She didn’t just die. Something happened.”

I blew out a breath. “Fine, I’ll ask some questions. We’ll see where we go from there.”

Emmie’s frown turned into a dopey smile. “Oh, thank you.”

I’d started cases with less, but not many. This one didn’t seem likely to go anywhere. “Right, let’s talk dough. What can you pay? I don’t do this for free, you know.” I didn’t charge much. Anne Linden had paid me fifty bucks, more than a week’s salary, but most of the girls who came to me for help had a fraction of that. I’d done jobs for fifty cents. It was about helping, not robbing, people.

Emmie pulled out a frayed change purse, threads loose from the once-colorful birds embroidered on the sides. “I don’t got a lot. I’ve scraped together five dollars, is that enough?”

Ouch. That had to be all her money, and Christmas was right around the corner. “Tell you what. Give me a dollar. If I don’t find anything, I’ll give you back fifty cents and we’re square. If I do, we’ll talk.” I could go to two movies on fifty cents. If I went to the Sunday special, I could get some candy bars and pop, too. Not bad for asking some questions.

Emmie handed over a crumpled, dirty bill. “Thanks.”

I pocketed the cash and glanced at the morning *Courier-Express* I’d picked up on the way to my meeting with Emmie. “Did you see? The Polish government-in-exile is gonna be in Buffalo tomorrow and Thursday.” I wiggled out of the booth.

Emmie followed. “It’s big news in my neighborhood. Everybody’s excited, ’specially *Babcia.* She was gonna go downtown and see ’em arrive. She always spoke Polish when she got excited. I must’ve misunderstood her though ’cause she kept saying ‘I cannot wait to see him. He has to know.’” Emmie chuckled. “Imagine, my gramma knowing a member of the Polish government. Ridiculous!"

I stopped dead in my tracks. "She does? Who?"

Emmie turned. "Oh, I don't think that's what she meant. She only ever said 'him.' Is that important?"

"It might be." The story Emmie told me before didn't make me think murder. But if Mrs. Brewka knew someone in the Polish government, she expressed a desire to see this person, and then she turned up dead, well, that was a whole 'nother story.

Emmie gave me a sheepish grin. "Forget it. For all I know, she was talkin' about someone in the neighborhood, maybe telling 'em about the government visit."

We left the coffee shop and a frosty wind caught the ends of my scarf. I wrapped it around my neck and tugged my knitted cap down over my ears. The mild temperatures of November were long gone, replaced by the normal Buffalo cold. Lake Erie was iron gray, and the smell of snow was in the air. No gulls whirled overhead. They had the sense to beat it for warmer homes. "I'll talk to you in a week. Sooner if I find anything." I pulled on my mittens.

Next to me, Emmie had put on her own winter gear, so wrapped up she looked like a rounded ball of wool. "Thanks, Betty. I appreciate you trying." She headed off to catch her bus.

I watched her go. Find a killer who might not exist. No problem. How hard could that be?

* * *

After leaving Emmie, I hopped a bus downtown, then hoofed it to police headquarters. The wind swirled around the streets, making the whole area a series of windy tunnels. I tried burying my face in my muffler, but by the time I reached my destination, my nose was colder than an ice cube and redder than Uncle Teddy's when he'd had too much whiskey. Even my thick woolen mittens weren't enough to keep my fingers warm. The heat of the building was a blessing.

My luck held. Detective MacKinnon was in and came down to the lobby to meet me. "Miss Ahern, it's a pleasure to see you, although I'm more than a bit surprised. What brings you downtown on such a blustery day?"

"I thought we were past all that 'miss' stuff."

He shook his head. "This is a professional setting. What do you want?"

I breathed on my hands and rubbed them together. "Who said I wanted anything?"

"Why else would you come to police HQ?"

I'd helped Detective MacKinnon solve two murders in the last two months. He might not see it that way, but I had. And he was right. 'Cept to see him, I had zero business downtown. City Hall was a nice building if you were into architecture, which I wasn't. Most of the storefronts were on Main Street, not that I had much money for shopping. It was too blasted cold to be strolling around anyway. "Okay, okay. It's about a case."

"A case? I can't divulge information about an ongoing investigation, you know that."

"Not one of your cases. It's mine. A girl I work with, well, her grandma died, and she's suspicious."

"Ah, one of your...private investigations."

His tone put my back up. Sam knew better, least he should. He didn't crack wise about me being a private dick, but he didn't act like he took it completely serious, either. "Yeah, one of my investigations. You got something to say about it?"

"Not at all." His mouth twitched, like he was fighting a smile. "What's the grandmother's name?"

I pulled a scrap of paper out of my coat pocket. "Pelagia Brewka. Wife of Rudolph Brewka. Her maiden name is Ferchow. You got any information on her?"

"I'll have to check. You stay right here." He disappeared.

I amused myself watching the cops come and go. Some were in regular clothes, some wore uniforms. Most of 'em didn't spare me a glance, but a few shot puzzled looks my way. I was sure they were wondering what a girl was doing hanging around Court Street by herself. I mean, what business could I possibly have? But none of 'em spoke to me, so I kept my yap shut.

Detective MacKinnon returned maybe five minutes later. "No reports on a Pelagia Ferchow Brewka."

"Nothing, not even 'found in bed dead'?"

"Nothing." He took a pack of smokes out, shook one out, lit it, and inhaled.

"No autopsy?"

He blew out a steady stream of smoke. "A death certificate was filed. It was signed by a doctor. Cause of death is listed as heart failure." Now he did grin. "Were you hoping for something more exciting?"

"Well, the girl who hired me, Emmie, is sure her grandma didn't die of a heart attack like they said." I bit my lip. "Wouldn't an autopsy show that?"

"It would," said Sam. "But she died at home, in her sleep, with her son in the next room. The family didn't even call the police. There's no reason to perform an autopsy. It's not an unattended death and you can hardly say a seventy-year-old woman dying is unexpected."

"Guess not."

"I only looked for the death certificate because you said the woman died. She did. Of natural causes."

I deflated a little. Which was silly, because not every death in Buffalo could be suspicious. Old people died, even when their granddaughters thought they had perfectly good tickers.

I thanked him, bundled myself up, and went back out into the biting December wind. Guess I owed Emmie fifty cents.

Chapter Two

The next morning, I relayed the details of Emmie's "case" to Dot while we rode the bus to work out in Wheatfield.

She scrunched up her forehead. "That's all she said?" Dorothy Kilbride had been one of my partners in detecting since the very beginning, when I hunted down Mr. Lippincott's murderer last October. "What did Lee say?" Our friend, Liam Tillotson, had helped us in November. He pretended it was to keep me out of trouble 'cause he'd made his friend Tom Flannery, who happened to be my fiancé, a promise. But I knew, or at least I suspected, Dot was just as important a reason for Lee to keep a finger in whatever she and I were up to.

"I didn't tell Lee anything. I didn't see a point." I tightened my muffler around my throat. The air on the bus wasn't much warmer than outside.

"Not much to go on." Dot's voice through the wool of her own winter trappings sounded muffled. "Detective MacKinnon wasn't any help?"

"Nope." I rubbed a patch of window clear so I could stare at the brown grass peeping through the snow cover. "'Cept to say there's no police report and no autopsy. He did look at the death certificate. It's sad, but the old lady died of a heart attack."

"What are you gonna do?"

"Give Emmie back her fifty cents, say I'm sorry about her grandmother, and move on to the next case. What else can I do?"

"Nothing. I'm surprised Emmie was so certain her grandma was murdered though. You'd think she'd rather have it be a heart attack instead of a crime, wouldn't you?"

"I guess. I can sorta see why she's gonna be disappointed, though."

Dot's mouth formed a perfect "o," visible even under her scarf, and her sweet pinup girl face turned a perfect picture of surprise. "You can?"

"Sure. Murder's not great. But there'd be some logic there. She'd be dead for a reason. A heart attack no one saw coming? That's awful random and pointless." That was prob'ly what Emmie wanted, logic. "But Emmie couldn't give me suspects, or a motive, or anything. She'll have to make her peace with this as an act of God and move on."

Dot made a noise of assent and picked at a fraying string on her mittens. "Did you know the Polish government is in Buffalo for the next two days?"

"Yeah, I saw it in the paper." The Polish government-in-exile, those who claimed to be the real representatives, not the stooges put in office by the Nazis, were making a stop in Buffalo to raise money and make speeches about the conditions in Poland. "I guess it's 'cause of the Polish population in the city."

"My folks had a big fight about it," Dot said.

"Really? Why?"

"Ma said we didn't need to be hosting a group the Nazis were against. Buffalo was already a big enough target 'cause of the war production." Dot rolled her eyes. "Dad said Hitler was at war with the entire United States, and a group of dissident politicians wasn't likely to make him think one city is a better target than another. Besides, the Poles were visiting a lot of places, not just Buffalo."

I had to agree with Mr. Kilbride. Turning away the exiled Polish leaders wasn't gonna make Adolf call off the fighting. Dot's words jogged loose a thought. "There is one thing that interests me."

"What?"

"Emmie said her grandma got real excited when she learned they'd be in town. She kept saying she was going to see him, that he had to know."

"Him who? Know what?"

"I dunno, Emmie only said 'him.' It's not likely her grandma was talking about the president or any other bigwig, is it?"

Dot shrugged. "Maybe they're cousins or something and she wants to tell him about her life here in Buffalo."

"If they are, Emmie didn't tell me about it." What were the chances of a family relationship? Slim, but I decided to ask Emmie.

"Why is that important anyway?"

The bus turned into the Bell parking lot and I gathered my things. "Mrs. Brewka talked about wanting to see a member of the government, to tell him something. Then she dies."

Dot followed me. "That's what makes it fishy."

"Exactly." We stowed our stuff, punched in, and got to work.

When I finally caught up with Emmie at lunch, she denied knowing anything. "I don't think so. No one in our family even has the same last name as any of the government men." She picked at the crust of her baloney on white. "I s'pose it's possible, though. I can ask Dad. I mean, Polish families are pretty big so maybe it's a second cousin or something." She took a bite of her sandwich. "Then that's it? She really died of a heart attack?"

"Looks like. I'm sorry, Emmie. I know you wanted something bigger." I packed up the remains of my lunch. "I didn't bring the money, but I'll get it to you tomorrow. And hey, let me know what your pop says, okay? I don't know that it means anything, but I'm curious."

Emmie swept up her own trash, face glum. "It's okay, Betty. Thanks for looking into it."

I watched her walk away. Maybe I'd missed something. But what? The only thing I could see is this connection to the government and that was slim. "Don't be a dope, Betty," I said under my breath. "Not every dead person in Buffalo got murdered."

Chapter Three

Thursday morning, I walked into our kitchen where Mom and Pop were arguing. "It's a black mark for the city," Pop said.

"Now, Joe, don't you think you're making a mountain out of a molehill?" Mom used her soothing voice, the one she used when she was calming down one of the menfolk.

"Hardly. Buffalo is hosting a foreign government—"

"A government in rebellion."

"It doesn't matter." Pop huffed. "Those men are recognized by Roosevelt as leaders of the Polish people."

"Good morning," I said, breaking into the conversation. "What's the hubbub?"

Mom turned to me and handed over my lunch pail. "It's nothing."

"Nothing? Mary, I tell you—"

"Hush, Joseph." She fixed him with a stern look and held out his lunch as well. "One of the junior secretaries for the Poles is missing, at least according to the morning *Courier-Express*. I'm sure they'll find him. He'll probably stagger into work later today, half-drunk after a rousing night with his fellow countrymen. Isn't that what men do at these kinds of parties, drink?" Mom sniffed. She wasn't a teetotaler, but she didn't think much of men who let liquor get in the way of their work.

I inspected the contents of my pail. "How junior?"

"The paper made it sound like he's not very high up in the ranks at all." Mom sighed. "Baloney on white, same as yesterday. That's what we have. If you don't like it, you can go back to making your own lunch."

CHAPTER THREE

Last month, Mom had been pretty clear she didn't like me working at Bell. Her decision to make my sandwich and stuff while she took care of Pop was a huge step. "No, ma'am, just curious. So this guy," I turned her attention away from my food inspection, "when did he go missing?"

Pop shrugged on his heavy coat. "Last night, but they aren't sure of the exact time. I tell you, if he doesn't turn up today, it'll give the city a black eye. After all, a missing foreign national, however junior, is big news." He kissed Mom and pecked me on the cheek. "I'm off. Have a good day, both of you."

The kitchen door closed with a thunk and I turned back to Mom. "How do they know he's missing?"

She held out my coat. "He didn't return to the hotel after the party last night, according to his roommate, who called the police. They are looking for him. You'd better get going, Betty. You miss that bus and it's a long walk to Wheatfield."

* * *

I wasn't able to look at a paper until that afternoon when I found a copy of the *Courier* on the bus. I riffled the pages.

"You never read the paper," Dot said. "What're you looking for?"

"Something Mom and Pop mentioned this morning." I turned a page. "Here it is."

The story about the secretary wasn't very big. Josef Pyrut, junior undersecretary to a minor member of the Polish government, had not been found. His roommate had reported him missing late last night. Police were asking for people with information to get in touch.

Dot craned her neck to read the story. "Why are you interested in an almost nobody with the Polish government?"

"I dunno. It feels fishy."

"Fishy how?"

"Emmie's grandmother said she would get to see 'him.' Isn't it more likely that she was gonna see this guy, Pyrut, than what's-his-name, the president?"

"Raczkiewicz," Dot said. "Don't look so surprised. My dad has Polish friends at work and he's interested in the politics. Anyway, to answer your question, yes, I can see some Polish bubba from Buffalo meeting up with a minor secretary better than I can see her talking to the president. But that assumes 'him' means someone in the Polish government, which is a pretty big leap. Are you sure she meant Pyrut?"

"No." I folded the paper. The story had gone on to say the entire group had gone to dinner at some swanky house party hosted by one of the prominent families in Buffalo. The dinner had included some Delaware Park residents and money had been collected, donations to the Polish resistance. Josef Pyrut had left the party earlier in the evening before the rest of the group, but not returned to his hotel. The police couldn't find him, but the government group was leaving today anyway.

"What's the big deal?" Dot rolled her peepers. "This guy is way too young, anyway. He wouldn't even have been alive when Emmie's grandparents emigrated."

"I dunno. It's prob'ly nothing. Guess I'm just suspicious. Philip Marlowe would be." I drummed my fingers on my knee. "Course you're right. There's no connection at all." It was definitely a coincidence.

Then why did the story make the hairs on my neck stand up?

Chapter Four

Friday at lunch, I tracked down Emmie. "Your fifty cents. Again, sorry I couldn't find out more." I dropped the coins in her pudgy hand.

"That's okay. You tried." She turned to go, then stopped and faced me again. "Oh, remember how you were asking me about *Babcia,* and if she knew anybody in the Polish government?"

"Yeah, you said you didn't know, but prob'ly not."

"I know." She nodded, brown hair swinging. "But I was wrong."

"You were?" If Emmie's grandma was related to the Polish president, I was the next MGM pinup girl.

"Did you read about that missing secretary?"

"Yeah. What was his name again?"

"Josef Pyrut. But him being missing isn't my point."

I waited, but Emmie didn't say anything. "So who is he?"

"It turns out *Babcia* has relations named Pyrut. Dad told me last night." She huffed a laugh. "I never really believed 'him' meant someone in the exiled government. I was sure I misunderstood her, or at most she was talkin' about one of our neighbors. Think of it, I might have relatives in the Polish resistance." She glanced at the clock. "I gotta go. See ya later Betty."

I watched her back as she walked away. A grandmother dead of apparently natural causes was not a big story. A missing junior member of a visiting government? Slightly bigger story.

The two of them possibly being related, however distantly?

Nick and Nora Charles would most certainly look into that.

* * *

After I got home that night, I gathered with Lee and Dot behind my house. I knelt on the frigid ground, cold seeping through the knees of my work pants, to stuff a worn blanket into a box. "Do I hafta go over this again?" I asked.

Dot held Cat, the stray I'd adopted—or, more accurately, that had adopted me. She stroked his head while he closed his eyes and nuzzled her hand, soaking up the attention. "Tell me again what you're doing?"

"I'm thinking there might be a connection between Emmie's grandmother and this missing secretary."

Dot pointed at the box. "No, that."

"Oh for the love of..." I blew out a breath that instantly sparkled on the air and tucked a stray lock of hair under my knit cap. "It's a house for Cat."

Lee ashed his cigarette, the glowing end the only hint of warmth on the evening air. "Betty, he's a cat. He'll find somewhere warm to stay. You don't hafta do that."

I shot him what I hoped was a dirty look. "You tell that to my little sister." Mary Kate had cornered me as soon as I got home and we'd had this exact talk with me playing Lee's part. She'd clutched the raggedy blanket and fixed her big, sad eyes on me, insisting that Cat would freeze if we didn't provide a warm hole for him. I'd given in, of course.

Lee took a drag on his gasper. "No way."

"Coward." I fluffed the blanket a bit. Then I stood and took Cat into my arms. "Okay, bub. That's as good as it gets around here. You can stay or scram, doesn't matter to me." I'd miss the rascal if he left, but I wasn't gonna tell him that.

Cat meowed, leapt down, and wormed his way into the box with a flick of his gray tail.

"Guess he likes it," said Dot, brushing cat hair from her coat. "Now what about this guy no one can find?"

Finally, a return to business. "It's too much of a coincidence for my liking." I dusted snow from my knees.

"What's your beef?" Lee spoke, smoke swirling from his mouth.

I faced him. "Emmie said this Josef Pyrut might be a cousin or something of her grandma's. At least her father told her they have relatives with the same last name. That's my problem."

Dot bit her lower lip. "Because…"

"Two members of the same family, however distantly related, are dead or missing?" I fought the urge to be sarcastic. "Nope, don't buy it, not as a coincidence."

"But we don't *know* anything happened to Josef. Maybe he decided he liked Buffalo better than wherever he was before."

Lee pointed the glowing cigarette at me. "She's got a point, Betty."

"Yes, she does." I clapped my mittened hands together and snow flew, icy sparkles glowing from the nearby streetlight. "But we won't know for sure until we ask around, will we?"

Chapter Five

Luckily, the following day was one of my free Saturdays. Normally, I'd take off for the cinema to catch the latest Flash Gordon installment before Mom heaped extra chores on me. Today, I volunteered to take care of the laundry.

Mom narrowed her eyes. "Why are you suddenly keen on washing dirty clothes?"

I grasped the basket in her hands. "No reason in particular. It's too cold to walk to the theater. I figured I'd stay and help you. But if you don't want me to, I'll do something else."

I could tell her suspicions were not eased by my glib excuse, but she let me take the clothes. "Fine. Remember, not too much starch when you iron your father's dress shirts."

"Yes, ma'am." The truth was, I could do the wash and comb the papers at the same time. Maybe if I helped around the house more, my folks would let up when it came to rules and my detective work would go easier.

My first task was to build a timeline from the Polish government's arrival to Josef's disappearance. I knew when Mrs. Brewka had died from her granddaughter. That had happened November thirtieth, two days before the Poles arrived in the city.

I stuffed a couple copies of the *Courier-Express* under the dirty laundry and picked my way down the basement steps. Although we hung our clothes to dry, outside when the weather was good, downstairs when it wasn't, we were lucky enough to own a washing machine. Pop bought it with some bonus money he'd gotten from his job at Bethlehem Steel a couple years ago, making Mom the envy of her friends, most of whom used the neighborhood laundromat, 'specially since war production had stopped washing machines from being built. Being alone in the basement suited my detecting purposes for the day.

I tugged the chain to light the single bulb. I sorted the clothes at top speed, loaded the machine, tossed in the soap, hooked up the hoses, and turned it on. Then I set about searching through newspapers.

The Polish government had arrived in the city last Wednesday, December 2nd. The first day was spent in meetings, glad-handing local Polish leaders, and touring the Polish district up near Fillmore Avenue, including the Broadway Market. That evening, the group was treated to a fancy dinner at the Delaware Park home of Sebastian Witkop, a wealthy Buffalo resident who'd made his money through savvy investments in the twenties. He'd managed to keep most of it after the crash, but whatever he'd lost he made up for by investing big in Buffalo's booming industries, namely Bethlehem Steel. According to the paper, Witkop was sympathetic to the plight of the Poles and their treatment at the hands of the Nazis.

The machine clunked behind me as I finished with one paper and moved on. Mom's voice echoed down the stairs and froze me in my spot. "Elizabeth, are you doing okay down there?"

"Yes, ma'am. A couple of these shirts are stained pretty bad, though," I hollered back, thinking fast. I needed to keep her upstairs.

"Do you need help?"

The last thing I needed was Mom to come downstairs to check on me and blow my whole plan. "No, I'll be fine. You do whatever you need to do and I'll take care of everything down here."

"Well, when you're done, I need help peeling potatoes for dinner."

Luckily, there wasn't much more to the story in the paper. The party at Witkop's lasted well into the night, according to the article in the Society pages. Most of the press on December 3rd was given over to yakking about what the government officials had done before departing the city. The disappearance of Josef Pyrut, reported around midnight, was squashed into a small story buried in the News section. An even smaller follow-up story appeared the next day, December 4th. All it said was that Pyrut was still missing, and the investigation continued. The police had no reason to suspect foul play.

I folded the papers. I pulled the stop on the washer, poured in water for the rinse, and started it again. Time to build more goodwill by peeling spuds. I'd come down and wring the clothes out later.

As I mounted the stairs, my mind churned. Maybe Josef had taken off on a lark, enjoying the offerings of the local Polish community.

Then again, maybe not.

I wasn't sure how I was gonna find out, but I would.

Chapter Six

We went to early Mass at Our Lady of Perpetual Help on Sunday morning, like always. There, I lit my usual candles, one for Sean, my older brother, and one for Tom. We hadn't heard from either of them in a while. Tom was with the 1st Armored Division in North Africa. Sean was on the *USS Washington* in the South Pacific. They were never far from my mind, and I said daily prayers for their safety. Even if the papers didn't think there was anything to report, folks at home longed for some word their loved ones were okay, if not exactly safe. No letters was not good, but no telegrams was better.

After church, I hightailed it over to Dot's to fill her in on what I'd learned from my search yesterday. Cat followed me.

"Witkop survived the crash? That's pretty impressive," Dot said as she stroked Cat's head.

"Yep." I studied the notes in my hand. "Funny. Pop's never mentioned that name before." Then again, he didn't know everyone at the Steel, and I doubted a man who lived in the flashy part of Buffalo worked in the coke ovens.

"Well, just 'cause he invested in Bethlehem doesn't mean he's in management."

Cat trotted over to bat at my mitten. I gave him a scratch behind the ears, best I could. With the temperature near freezing, I wasn't gonna take off my mittens, even for a cute gray feline with cream swirls, no matter how much he asked. "Wanna check them out? We could catch the bus if we leave now."

"Betty, we'd stick out like sore thumbs over there."

She wasn't trying to be difficult. When we'd cased Kaisertown last month, blending in wasn't a problem. It was a working-class neighborhood, like the First Ward. German, not Irish, but that was the only difference.

Delaware Park was a different story. Big houses, big lawns, and fancy cars. There was a big park designed by Frederick Olmstead that included a copy of Michelangelo's David, a large fountain, and a statue of some Civil War general on a horse. The art gallery was nearby and you could see one of the houses by that famous architect guy. All around were the homes of Buffalo's heads of industry. Two girls from the First Ward had no business there.

"There is one way," I said.

Dot frowned, puzzled. "One way what?"

"One way we'd fit right in with all of the flash."

"Oh? How's that?" Disbelief dripped from her voice. "You gonna steal us a couple of fancy dresses?"

"No, we'll be dressed like we always are. We'll be invisible."

"How do you figure?"

I could picture the sly grin on my face. "Because nobody pays attention to the help."

Dot's mouth opened and closed.

Off to Delaware Park we went, dressed in plain clothes and holding bundles of laundry we snitched from our houses. Who would question, or even notice, two girls hauling the wash out for their employer?

Sure enough, when we got there, the first thing we did was pass an older gentleman holding the paper. He didn't even step aside for us. Two little boys with their nanny pointed, but she was too worried about keeping track of the kids to bother with us. I paused on the sidewalk. "This is it."

The house was grand by my standards, big white columns and a sweeping drive. Compared to the ones on either side, though, it was on the small side. The Witkops had cabbage, but not more than their neighbors.

Dot shifted the bundle in her arms. "Now what, Sherlock? You figure on ringing the bell?"

I snorted. Truth was, I didn't quite know what our next step was. A lot depended on what we found. I checked the area. It was quiet. The gas ration kept the expensive cars in their garages, and the cold weather had sent the birds packing. A few pigeons looked for scraps along the sidewalk, but even they seemed to know they were low-class. The leafless trees swayed in the icy breeze, a few dry leaves skittering down the pavement.

Aside from those we'd seen, there were no people. They were either out for their Sunday visits, at church, or tucked in their warm homes. I brushed a strand of hair from my forehead.

A door slammed and suddenly, the sound of a lilting voice raised in song reached us. The tune was "Danny Boy," an Irish ballad. I looked around for the singer.

Dot nodded at the Wikops' house. "Back there."

I moved so I could see 'round to the back. Sure enough, a girl about my age strolled through the yard, a bowl of food scraps on her hip. A kitchen maid on the way out to the compost heap? I hefted my laundry and trotted her way. "'Scuse me. Hey, excuse me!"

She stopped and faced me. "Can I help you?" Her voice held a trace of a brogue, like my grandma's had. Up close, freckles dotted her nose and cheeks, which had turned red in the cold. Her breath steamed before her. Her eyes were green as clover and her red hair was swept back into a knot, but the strands around her face curled, making me think of the glorious mass that hair would be if she let it down. Just like Maureen O'Hara in the poster for *How Green Was My Valley*. This girl wore a plain black coat and mittens, but the skirt of the dress underneath the coat was soft blue and I could tell she had a crisp white apron over it all. Definitely a kitchen maid.

I set down my bundle and caught my breath. "Do you work here?"

"Depends on what you mean by here."

I waved at the Witkops' house. "For the family who lives here."

Her eyes narrowed. "Why should I tell you?"

"Good question," Dot muttered, shifting the laundry in her arms.

I thought fast. "My friend and I were walking by with the laundry and admired the house."

"It be Sunday. You can't take the wash anywhere on the Lord's day."

I heard Dot mumble. I had forgotten the day of the week. A stupid mistake.

Dot piped up. "That's what I told her."

"Carrying the wash wasn't the best idea." I nudged the bundle with my toe. "I thought looking like servants would make us less noticeable. Daydreaming about being rich, I s'pose."

Her peepers stayed slits. "Then why are you talking to me?"

"I figured if you worked here, you'd know everything that goes on. You'd be able to give us the real dope about what it's like." I extended my hand. "I'm Betty McDowell, by the way. And this here is Dorothy Fitzpatrick." I borrowed the last names of some of my neighbors. You know, just in case the girl mentioned us to someone.

Dot waved.

The girl's face softened. "Irish?"

"We live over in the First Ward." No sense lying about that. Fortunately, the First Ward was big enough to be both specific and vague at the same time. "My grandma came from Ireland a bunch of years ago. You?"

"My name is Bridget Innes. I came with me mum and pa when I was a wee girl." Our shared heritage had eased the suspicion and Bridget smiled, showing a slight gap in her front teeth.

I glanced at Dot, who remained silent, clearly leaving the yarn-telling to me. "Isn't this the Witkop house?"

"Yes. I think they be a Polish family, but I'm not sure."

Polish? "How can you tell?"

"Some of the art, it's by Polish artists, and Mr. Witkop said they're family pieces." She shrugged. "Of course, it could also be they like art from Poland."

I glanced around. How long would Bridget chat? "I read in the paper they held a flashy party for the Polish government."

"Oh, aye." Bridget nodded. "It kept us hopping. I never saw Mrs. Witkop so fussy or Cook in such a lather, making all those Polish dishes."

"Did you meet that man who's missing, the secretary?"

Bridget's face creased in thought. "Oh, aye. Saucy boy, he came into the kitchen to steal bites." She giggled. "Cook chased him out with a spoon and left gravy on his shirt. He laughed."

"Did you see him sneak out or anything?"

The questions had crossed a line, I could tell by the frown that appeared on her face. "I didn't see that. Are you a copper or something?"

"No, no." I waved my hands and beside me I heard Dot hissing. "I'm not police. I read about it in the paper is all. My pop tells me I'm too curious for my own good."

I'd roused Bridget's suspicions again, that much was plain from the look on her puss.

"Thanks for the chat." I turned to my friend, now a cherubic picture of innocence. "C'mon, Dorothy. We'd better get back with this laundry. Have a good day." I tossed the last words over my shoulder as we hot-footed it down the sidewalk.

Out of sight of the Witkops' Dot dropped her load on the sidewalk to rest after our hasty retreat. "Brilliant, Betty. Now she knows our names and where we live."

"Relax, I bet she won't say anything. I only gave her our first names. Heck, I can think of at least three more Dorothys and that's before I really try." I gazed behind us.

"This visit was a bust. Worst of all, I gotta take these clothes home and re-wash them. Look, there's a smear of soot from the bus." She pointed at the black mark. "Ma will tan my hide if she sees that."

I hefted my bundle. "Oh, I don't think it was a bust. I think Josef left the party early and what's more, Bridget saw him."

"How d'you reckon?"

"She said 'I didn't see that' when I asked. Not 'no,' or 'I don't know.' My bet is she saw him and he asked her not to tell. Question is why." I looked up at the sky, where the sun was on its way down. "That's a puzzle for another day. I'll figure out how to crack it."

Dot lifted her bundle. "Well, if the answer involves carting clothes all over Buffalo, count me out."

Chapter Seven

As the bus rumbled to Wheatfield on Monday morning, I scanned the paper. A small story on page three caught my eye. "Holy jeepers!"

Dot's eyes popped open. "What?"

"They found Josef Pyrut."

"What was he doing?"

"I dunno, but it's gonna be hard to figure out."

"Why?"

"He's dead." Dot's mouth fell open in an "o" that would have been comical under other circumstances. She listened while I read. "Polish junior undersecretary Josef Pyrut was found dead late Sunday evening in an alley off Fillmore Avenue. Mr. Pyrut's body was discovered by a local resident when he put out his trash for the evening."

Dot chewed her lip. "Fillmore? But he was at the Witkops' party, right? He musta gone from Delaware Park to Polonia. You think he took the bus?"

"I don't know." I scanned the rest of the story, but it didn't say much more. "Reading between the lines, I don't think the cops know, either. How would a visiting foreigner know how to get from Delaware Park to over to Fillmore Avenue? I mean, he'd have to know where to get the bus, which one to take, and that line goes right through Canisius College. I'm sure he wouldn't have been seen."

"Maybe he walked."

"But would he know the route? Plus that's gotta take at least an hour on foot. How cold was it last Thursday?"

Dot shivered. “Cold enough.”

“Exactly.” I snapped the paper and folded it. It wasn’t far from the Witkops’ house to Fillmore if you drove, but that was even less likely. A guy who’d only been in the city a couple of days, and prob’ly didn’t speak our lingo, would have a tough go.

Morbid curiosity got the best of Dot. “Did the police say how he died?”

“They think he was mugged, although his wallet was left behind. Prob’ly because he didn’t have any American money, only Polish. That isn’t easily spent in Buffalo. Unless that’s all they took.”

The bus shuddered to a stop, and the doors opened, letting in a gush of cold air. We exited and hurried to the main building to clock in. In the locker room, we stashed our lunch pails and coats, then hurried across the yard to the massive assembly line building.

The line creaked to life and the half-assembled planes began their trip through the various stations. Dot shook her head. “The whole thing sounds a little weird to me. I mean, I can see something happening at one of the political stops, or even someone attacking the whole group as they left the party. But a junior secretary? And in a different part of the city?”

“Remember, Emmie said her grandma might have been some kind of distant cousin to the Pyruts. Maybe Josef was trying to track them down.”

“Do they even live near Fillmore?”

A fuselage stopped in front of me and I signed my name on the back of the instrument panel in my hands, something we girls did as we assembled the planes. Prob’ly no one would ever see ’em, but it gave us a sense of accomplishment, like an artist signing his work. “I don’t know,” I said after I bolted on the panel and the plane moved to the next stop. “I’ll ask at lunch.”

“’Course that means he’d have to know he was related to Mrs. Brewka. And where to find her.”

“Exactly.” I attached another panel. “The cops might think it was a mugging, but no private dick in Hollywood would buy that story and neither do I.”

* * *

I tracked Emmie down at lunch. Her family lived on Fougeron Street, not far from Fillmore. "Daddy only told me that *Babcia*'s family was related to some Pyruts, but he didn't mention Josef," she said when I asked.

"How did he know about the Pyrut family?"

She blinked. "I never thought of that. I'd have to ask him."

"Do that and tell me what he says, okay?"

She agreed, and I went back to work.

By the time I clocked out and got back to the First Ward, it was four-thirty and the sun was low in the sky. The wind had died, but it was bitterly cold, the kind that penetrated my heavy work pants and wormed its way through the wool of my mittens. Piles of snow dotted the street, but the air didn't have that smell I associated with more. I paused.

Dot was ten feet away from me before she realized I'd stopped. "What?" she asked. "Let's go, I'm cold."

"I think I'm gonna swing by police headquarters and talk to Detective MacKinnon again." I considered taking off my mittens to light a smoke, but decided it wasn't worth getting my fingers cold.

"Okay." Dot drew out the word, and it was clear to me that she was humoring me. "Don't you think maybe you're making a bigger deal of this than it is? Not everything is a crime."

"Sometimes it is."

She threw up her hands. "Fine. Be that way. I'm not gonna go with you to see the cops and don't expect me to cover for you with your folks. See you tomorrow." She stomped off.

I knew I was being stubborn, maybe unreasonably so. But I had a tingly feeling on my neck, the same one that I'd had on my last two big cases, when I was sure there was some fact staying just out of reach.

It was near full-on dark by the time I reached downtown. I saw Sam MacKinnon leaving the building as I double-timed it up the sidewalk. "Detective! Hey, wait up."

He squinted in my direction and his peepers widened when he recognized me. "Miss Ahern. I told you. There is nothing suspicious about Mrs. Brewka's death."

"I'm not here about her. Well, not directly. What can you tell me about Josef Pyrut?"

He stuffed his hands in the pockets of his overcoat. "You read the *Courier*, I'm sure. What more is there to tell?"

"Oh c'mon, Sam. Don't feed me that malarkey."

He sighed.

"First-name basis, remember?"

He closed his eyes, then opened them. "There's a coffee shop across the street. It's too cold to hang around outside."

I hesitated. "You buying?"

"It would look bad for a member of the Buffalo Police Department to be accepting favors from the public. So yes, it's on me."

"Then lead on."

Fifteen minutes later we were tucked into a booth in the shop, cups of real coffee steaming in thick white ceramic diner mugs in front of us. "Tell me about Josef Pyrut," I said and blew on my java.

"Not much to tell." He sipped from his cup. "Josef Anatol Pyrut, age thirty-four. Attached to the Polish government-in-exile as a junior undersecretary to one of the ministers who was under the Prime Minister."

"Not very close to the big cheeses."

"No. Pyrut was originally from Jablonna, Poland. It's a town outside Warsaw. He came to Buffalo as part of the political tour, attended some events in the Polish neighborhood, and went to a party hosted by Sebastian Witkop on the night of December second. He was reported missing by his roommate, Absalon Kafel, around midnight. We found his body yesterday, the victim of an apparent mugging."

"The story in the paper said his wallet was on him. Isn't that strange for a mugging?"

"Not if the only things in it were his war ID and a Polish coin. If he had any American cash, it was gone." He took another drink.

I eyed him. I'd gotten to know Sam MacKinnon pretty well on my last two big cases. "You're holding back. Spill."

He rotated his mug. "He had his watch, a very fine, gold pocket watch, and a pinky ring. Nothing too fancy, but gold with a little chip of black stone in it. The wallet was made of good leather."

"All things that a street thief would take."

"Correct."

I pondered his words. "Then why's it being called a mugging?"

"I don't know. Maybe because the body was dumped in an alley. Maybe the higher-ups think his death would be an embarrassment to the Poles." He drained his mug.

I'd lost interest in my coffee. "Maybe it's a cover up."

"Possibly." He pushed aside his mug. "All I know is my hands are tied."

"Why?"

"The department says Mr. Pyrut was the unfortunate victim of a mugging. Unless we find a similar crime, the chances of us actually solving the case are slim."

I stared at the cold brown liquid in front of me. "You don't buy it."

"No, I don't. At least, I have more questions that I'd like answered." He ticked them off on his fingers. "Why did the suspect leave behind the valuables? How did the victim get from Mr. Witkop's house in Delaware Park to Fillmore Avenue? He was a stranger in Buffalo, or so we've been told. Who did he meet?"

The same questions I'd had. "Did you know he was possibly related to Pelagia Brewka?"

He blinked. "I did not."

I told him what I'd learned from Emmie.

"Huh." MacKinnon leaned back. "But Mrs. Brewka didn't know a Josef?"

"She never mentioned him by name." I tapped the table. "But get this." I told him about Pelagia's desire to talk to "him" and how I thought she meant Josef.

"What do you think she wanted to talk about?"

"That's what we gotta find out, Detective."

He spread his hands. "I told you, I can't do anything. One death was ruled natural causes, the other is a probably never-to-be-solved mugging. I have other things to do."

I slugged down my cold coffee. It made my tongue curl, but I liked the visual, at least in my mind. “Lucky for you I don’t.”

Chapter Eight

Needless to say, I caught hell when I got home after my meeting with Sam. Mom was beside herself with worry, and even Pop wasn't too happy. I didn't make things any better when I remained vague about where I'd been, saying only that I'd been "held up."

"They don't get it, Cat," I said as I put out his chipped saucer the following morning before I headed to Bell. It held a little milk and some scraps I'd filched from last night's dinner. "I can't be a detective and be home by five every night. Private dicks don't keep regular hours."

Meow. Cat blinked.

"Of course I'm gonna keep doing it. I gotta figure out how to convince them it's a good idea. Maybe someday I'll even have my own office." I pictured the frosted glass door with my name painted on it. Where, I didn't know, but it was gonna happen. Someplace swell, like on Main Street or maybe near City Hall. "I need a name for my agency, though. I can't be plain old Betty Ahern, Detective."

Meow, Cat replied and attacked the slivers of meat.

Lee came around the corner. "You talking to the cat again?"

"He's better company than some people," I said, flinging a ball of slushy snow.

"Hey," he yelped. "Watch it. And you better not be talking about me."

"No, not you. Why aren't you at work?" I was pretty sure Lee oughta be at General Motors, where he made engines, by now. Like Bell, GM didn't stop for anything.

"I told 'em I'd be in a little late today," he said. "Had to take Anna to the doctor to see about her cough. Mom's got enough to do and Dad, well..." Lee trailed off.

"He's not getting any better?"

Lee's face darkened. "He'd be a lot better if he'd lay off the sauce."

I knew Lee'd found half a dozen empty whiskey bottles in their trash last week. His dad had been coming home from work late all November. The family thought he'd been pulling overtime.

He had. Just not at work.

I skipped away from the topic. "Walk with me to the bus stop?"

"Sure." He fell into step beside me. Every other step was a hitch, the result of his bum leg, the same injury that kept him outta the service. Not for the first time, I wondered how Lee felt about that. He'd never talked about it, 'cept when he'd come back from the recruiting station with his 4F designation. "Not even fit to be a dishwasher," he'd said. But when so many of the neighborhood boys had gone overseas, it had to be on his mind. The only thing he'd ever said to me was, "Billy McClusky and I finally have something in common," when Billy was sent home because of his asthma.

Despite the limp, Lee had no problem keeping pace with me. Dot was waiting when we arrived at the stop. "Hey, Lee."

He blushed, or maybe it was the cold, but his cheeks were apple red. "What's shaking, Dot?"

It was like being in some dumb romantic flick. No wonder I preferred detective pictures. "Anyway," I said, breaking the silence. "You wanna hear what I learned about Josef Pyrut?" I recapped my conversation with Sam.

"That's not a lot," Dot said, her voice doubtful.

"You're sure MacKinnon has doubts?" Lee asked.

"That's what he said." I craned my neck, watching for the bus.

"Then what do you figure is your next move?" He lit a cigarette.

"I gotta find out more about Pyrut. I mean, besides what's been in the paper. He left that party for a reason. Did he meet someone? Maybe he had a friend in Buffalo no one knows about. Were the Pyruts and the Ferchows definitely related, and did he know about Pelagia?"

A bus came into view. It was Lee's. He hefted his lunch pail. "For that matter, what's the deal with Pelagia?"

Dot scrunched up her face. "How do you mean?"

"Where did she come from, what's her story?"

I thought. "You think that's important?"

"Sure do. Look. You think she wanted to see Pyrut, right?"

I nodded.

"Why? I mean, why him? She coulda talked to someone right here in Buffalo, someone in her immediate family, a whole bunch of people. But she was excited to see some stranger. Plus, I think it'd be easier to find out about her."

The bus stopped, belching black smoke and giving the crisp air a dirty diesel scent. "How do you figure that?"

The doors whooshed open and Lee put his good leg on the stairs. "Don't you work with her granddaughter?"

* * *

I cornered Emmie in the lunchroom. "I need to know about your grandmother."

She paused as she unwrapped her sandwich. "*Babcia*? Why? I thought you said she had a heart attack, that the police said she died of natural causes?"

"Here's the thing. Now I believe she wanted to see the guy who might have been a distant cousin of hers."

She took a bite. "Josef Pyrut? The one who was mugged?" she asked around a mouthful of baloney and bread.

I ignored the bad manners and mushy mess. "Yes. I need to know about him, too, but learning about your grandmother might help with that."

She considered this and swallowed. "That makes sense. What do you want to know?"

"You said she was a maid and your grandpa was a field worker. When did they get to America?"

Emmie thought a moment. "I don't know exactly when they immigrated. She came from the Prussian-controlled portion of Poland, though. *Dziadek* was a field worker for a big landowner."

"Like a, what do you call 'em? A slave?"

"You mean a serf? No, they got rid of those a long time ago. From the stories *Dziadek* told though, the conditions were barely better than serfdom 'cause the landowners could take whatever they wanted, whenever they wanted. Anyway, *Babcia* would have worked the land with him, but she was pretty. The lady of the house picked her as a personal maid. You know, do the laundry, help her get dressed, all that guff."

I could picture it. A big sweeping country house with a lord and lady dressed in ridiculous clothes. Why not choose a pretty country girl, poor as dirt, to help out? Although I doubted they paid well. "They must've gotten tired of that arrangement if they came to America."

Emmie took another bite. Mercifully, she chewed and swallowed before she continued. "*Dziadek* heard about all the factories in America, how easy it was to get work and such. So he and *Babcia* came here. Eventually they made it to Buffalo and *Dziadek* got a job with Bethlehem Steel. This was the early days, you understand."

"Gotcha." It was unlikely anything had happened here in Buffalo that would help me. "Did they ever talk about the old country?"

"Not *Dziadek*. He was all about being here. Nothing good came from Poland, he said. When the Nazis invaded, he was sad, but he said it wasn't surprising because the Polish people were sheep. But *Babcia* talked about the big house all the time. She'd tell stories of the art, the grand parties, the fancy food. According to her, a lot of the furnishings in the house were French."

"What did she mean?"

Emmie scrunched up her face in concentration, a bit of her tongue sticking out. "The Germans had a war with France, I think. Yeah, France. The Polish sided with the French. To punish the Poles, the Germans took a lot from the people. Made them work hard, took their stuff, you know."

I didn't, but Lee would. He was the history buff. I made a note to ask him later.

"Go on."

"Anyway, that's why a lot of the fancy things were from France. Although. . ."

When she didn't continue, I prompted her. "Yes?"

"She told me something once. About how the landowner got a lot of money and valuables from the Germans. Gold and stuff. It all got swept aside after the war. But I dunno. Sometimes she rambled, *Babcia*, especially when she was talking about the old country. I have no idea how many of the stories were true and how many were just that, stories."

"What was the name of this family?"

"I don't...wait. Witkowski. That was it. Yeah, now it comes back to me. The family was Polish, but they'd sided with the Germans, so they were allowed to keep their trinkets. But *Babcia* always hinted they'd gotten most of their wealth by ratting out their neighbors to the Germans. That was it."

I jotted it all down in a pocket notebook. "Now tell me about right before your grandma died. Is there anything that happened to make you suspicious? Any strange guests, or packages, or letters?"

"Not really. *Babcia* was excited for the season. Thanksgiving and Christmas were her favorite holidays because she got to see all her friends and family and she baked up a storm. About the only odd thing is, she got this really pretty box full of peppermint candy. She said it was a gift, but not who gave it to her."

"That doesn't seem all that strange."

"Yeah, but all her friends are old Polish ladies. They give handmade gifts. This was a blue box with a white ribbon. It obviously came from a store and that's not usual." She glanced at the clock. "Is that it? I want to pee before we get back on the line."

"Yeah, yeah. I'm good for now. I'll let you know if I have any more questions."

"Thanks, Betty. I know this is kind of a wild goose chase, but I 'preciate you taking it seriously. When d'you think you'll be done?"

"I'll give you the solution for a Christmas present." I waved, and she walked away, beaming.

Pelagia had worked in a rich guy's house. A Polish man who'd maybe gotten wealthy by telling tales about his neighbors. Had that been what Pelagia wanted to tell her possibly long-lost relative? Now that she maybe had ties to someone in the Polish government, had she wanted to right a long-ago wrong?

That all made sense. But it didn't explain how she'd gotten in touch with Josef or why he'd ended up dead. Or who had sent her a pretty store-bought box of candy just days before she died.

Chapter Nine

After dinner, I stood at the sink washing dishes and thinking. There had to be a way to trace someone's family. There just had to be. Didn't people do this all the time? "That's what someone needs to invent," I said under my breath.

Pop came into the kitchen. "What does someone need to invent?"

I rinsed the plate I held. "Some way of researching family trees. It's all word of mouth." I set the dish rag aside and dried my hands. "How would you do it, Pop? If you wanted to know all the way back to when your family lived in Ireland, who your relatives were and where they came from?"

He put his pipe between his teeth, struck a match, and puffed it to life. "I'd talk to my mother, for starters. Then my dad, then I'd move on to my grandparents. I might talk to my aunts and uncles."

It would be effective, but slow. "Say all those people are dead. Then what?"

He exhaled a fragrant cloud of smoke. "Why all this interest in family history? We came from Ireland. It was miserable. The end."

"It's not for me."

"Oh?"

"It's a girl at work." I pulled the plug on the sink and the water chugged down the drain. Then I dried my hands again and took a seat at the table.

Pop sat across from me. "What girl?"

"Her name is Emilia Brewka. We call her Emmie." I traced a pattern on the scrubbed wooden table. "Her family is Polish. She knows her grandparents came to America and ended up in Buffalo in the early 1900s. Her grandpa worked at Bethlehem Steel when it first started."

He nodded and smoke drifted up around his head, leaving a warm, comforting scent in the air. "Common enough. A lot of immigrants went to work in the factories when they emigrated. American industry was booming. Jobs were plentiful." He paused. "I take it that isn't enough for you."

"Uh-uh." I leaned my chin on my fist. "I need to know about the family when they were in Poland."

"What for?"

"Emmie's asked me to look into something. Turns out her pop told her they might be related to that Polish secretary."

"Hmm." Pop smoked for a moment. "Why don't you ask her grandmother?"

"She's dead. She died last week."

"That would be a problem." He puffed. "What about her grandfather?"

"Also dead. And it was her grandmother's family that had the connection." I stood, went to the fridge and opened the door. There was a little of the day's milk left, so I poured some into a glass. "I'm kinda in a jam on this."

"Is there any more of that milk?" Pop nodded toward the glass in my hand. "What about family records?"

I got a second glass and emptied the milk bottle into it. "What kind?"

"Oh, families keep all sorts of personal histories." He took the glass. "Everything from plain old sheets of paper recording births, deaths, and marriages to histories written in books. My best friend when I was growing up had a family Bible that was passed from the eldest child to the next eldest child. His family tree was in there going back at least six generations."

"Really?" Emmie hadn't mentioned such a thing, but I'd ask tomorrow.

"Yep." Pop finished his milk, rinsed the glass and set it on the drying rack. "Now what's this about? I know you said this girl asked you to look into something. What is it?"

I told him about Emmie and her suspicions about her grandmother. Then I finished my milk and washed my glass.

Pop headed for the living room. He picked up the evening paper and sat in his favorite chair.

I looked at the front-page headlines, which were all about some English attack in France and a little about the launching of the new U.S. battleship, the *New Jersey*. "Anything about Tom or Sean?"

"I don't think the *Courier* follows them specially." He chuckled. "But, no, they don't mention the 1st Armored or the *Washington*."

That was a relief. I said a silent Hail Mary in thanks.

Pop turned another page. "You really think there's a connection between the Emmie's grandmother and this Pyrut fellow?"

His words stirred doubt in my mind. How could they be connected? "I…I don't know."

Pop examined me over the newspaper. "I know you fancy yourself a detective, my darling girl. That's all well and good. But don't go making trouble where there isn't any, you understand me?"

I stood and kissed him on the forehead. "Yes, sir."

Chapter Ten

I asked Emmie about the family records first thing Wednesday morning as we stood in line for the time clock.

"A family Bible?" she asked as she punched her card.

"Yeah." I clocked in and followed her to the locker room. "Or any book, really. Just somewhere you might have written down a family tree. You know who was born when, the dates of marriages, when people died, that kind of stuff."

She hung her coat, turned to me, and said, "I don't know if Daddy has such a thing. But I can ask him."

"Swell. Let me know."

Until I got the results, I was stalled on Pelagia. I had to change up my game. That's what Sam Spade would do. If I couldn't find out more on the Brewka family, I'd tackle the other end and find out all I could about Josef Pyrut.

"How?" Dot asked when I told her.

"First, I go back to the papers. I didn't read those stories real close. Maybe there's info there to dig out."

"And if there isn't?"

I fitted in the instrument panel I held. "I got one more source."

Dot straightened from where she'd been screwing in another panel. "Lemme guess. You're gonna write the Polish government."

"Don't be a sap." I paused to sign my name to the back of the panel and attach it. "Detective MacKinnon."

The chain pulled the dollies along until a new plane stopped in front of us. "You think he'll tell you anything more than he already has?"

"Worth a shot. I s'pose I should also find out what I can about the Polish government. The one that came through Buffalo, not the one the Nazis put in. That should be a lot easier."

Dot brushed a curl from her forehead. "Who're you gonna talk to for that? Your pop?"

"Nope. I'm gonna consult my history and politics expert."

"Who's that?"

I winked. "Lee. Wanna come?"

* * *

I didn't doubt that Lee could give me the scoop about the Polish government-in-exile. He was a nut about history, politics, and current events. He would bore the pants off me if I let him. Maybe it was because he couldn't get into the Army, but he prob'ly knew as much about the war, in Europe and in the Pacific, as Roosevelt. Just in case he got mulish, I made a quick stop at the local bakery and bought a sweet bun.

Despite some hemming and hawing, Dot came with me. By the time we reached the Tillotson house, Lee was home from GM, although he was still in his work clothes. "Gimme a minute," he said. "Have a seat in the living room. Mom's not here, she's up at the church. Dad is...out."

Dot and I exchanged a look. Out drinking.

Less than five minutes later, Lee returned. "Now what are you two up to?"

"Who said we were up to anything?" I gave him a wide-eyed look. I held out the bag. "I should be hurt. And here I brought you a present, too."

He took the bag and looked inside. "If you were thinking that bringing me a goodie would make me less suspicious, you were wrong. Only way you'd spend the cabbage on a treat would be 'cause you want something. What is it?"

"Just information. Honest." That was the problem with being friends with a guy for almost twenty years. He knew me better than just about anyone, maybe even better than my fiancé.

"'Bout what?" he said, mouth full of sweet bun.

"What do you know about the Polish government? The exiled one."

"Since when have you ever been interested in current events or politics? Beyond the daily war news, of course. We're all interested in that." His peepers narrowed in a shrewd gaze. "This got anything to do with that dead guy? Don't tell me you're getting mixed up in crime again."

I tried for an innocent expression. "Maybe I'm just curious and I know you've got all the dope."

I must have failed, because he snorted. "Yeah, sure."

"Okay, fine." I decided to be straight with him. "It kinda has to do with Josef Pyrut. He's the stiff. I'm waiting on Emmie to see if she has a family tree. I hoped she'd be able to give me the skinny immediately, but I gotta wait. I can't just sit on my hands, so I'm trying to find out what I can about him. I figured the exiled government would be a good place to start."

"That makes sense. But why're you so bent out of shape about a guy who was mugged?"

"I'm not sure he was." I told him what I'd learned from Detective MacKinnon, about Josef's stuff not being stolen. "I can understand leaving foreign money. But jewelry and a good leather wallet?"

Lee licked sugar off his fingers. "Okay, brief lesson on the Polish government-in-exile. If nothing else, you'll learn something for the day."

Dot giggled. "You sound like my dad. You oughta been a schoolteacher, Lee."

He made a face. "No way. I remember what I was like as a kid. If I had to teach me, I'd go nuts."

"Are you two finished?" I asked and poked Dot in the side.

"Sorry, Betty." But she gave Lee a grin.

A flash of surprise passed over his face, then he turned to me. "Germany invaded Poland in September 1939. A lot of Poles fled the country and some of 'em formed a government, what they said is the real Polish government. The president is a guy named Raczkiewicz."

"Are they? The real government?" Dot asked.

"Well, depends on who you ask," Lee replied. "They've been recognized by the Allies. Of course, the Nazis would disagree, and if Raczkiewicz and his buddies went back to Poland, Hitler would have them arrested, maybe even killed."

"Then they're just a bunch of guys without power? Why would Roosevelt and Churchill recognize that as a government?"

Lee sat back and stretched out his bum leg. "They are still connected to the Polish Underground State, the resistance movement. The U.S. and England definitely want them on the side of the good guys. Nobody's ever sure about the Soviets and what they want. Anyway, it's set up like any old government, which means they've got a president, and ministers, and secretaries, the works. If I understand the news stories right, Pyrut was a junior undersecretary to one of Raczkiewicz's secretaries or ministers or whatever."

"You said Raczkiewicz is the president?" I asked. Lee nodded, and I continued. "Would Josef have contact with him?"

"Prob'ly in some way," Lee said. "Least I would think so."

"And they could share secrets?" Dot asked.

"I s'pose, although I can't see the president sharing any big secrets with a junior undersecretary."

I thought a moment. Maybe there was something Pelagia wanted to tell the president, knew she'd never get such a chance, and decided to spill to her distant cousin instead, hoping it would make its way to Raczkiewicz. "Would he tell his boss anything, 'specially if it was important?"

Lee raised his eyebrows. "Like what? What could an old woman who has been here since the turn of the century tell a young man in the exiled government that was so important? Important enough to get her killed, as you seem to think it did."

"I dunno. But let's say a woman who immigrated from Poland years ago knew...something she thought was important about either people still in Poland or someone who'd left. She still felt some loyalty to the Poles. If she told Josef, would he tell Raczkiewicz?"

Lee puzzled it over and spread his hands. "Maybe. I guess if it was a big enough deal, yeah. He might not talk to the President directly, but he'd know how to get the information up the chain. Especially if it was critical to the government or to the resistance movement. What're you thinking?"

"I don't know that Pelagia actually talked to her maybe-cousin. But if she did, or if someone thought she did, and what she said was really bad, that's a motive for murder. It coulda been something about a member of the government or a person high in the resistance."

"Like they aren't really loyal to the exiled Poles?" Dot asked.

"Could be." I rested my chin on my hands. "Except I've tried to figure out where Pyrut was and when during his visit and I don't see where he'd slip out to see some old Polish immigrant who's lived in American for forty years."

"'Specially since she was dead," said Dot.

I shook my head. "He wouldn't know that. He's been traveling, and I doubt they put Buffalo obituaries in national newspapers."

Lee shot a look at the clock on the wall. "I gotta make dinner for the girls. Tell you what, you bring over what you have tomorrow night and we'll look at it together. I still got all the newspapers. I'll put them aside, so Ma doesn't throw them out."

I chucked him on the shoulder. "Thanks, Lee. You're a pal."

He crumpled up the bag and smirked. "Oh, I'm not doing this for free. You'd better bring another sweet bun when you come over or the deal's off."

Chapter Eleven

When I arrived at Bell on Wednesday morning, I was glad to have a day full of nothing but P39 assembly to worry about. Progress on my case was zilch. Waiting on other people meant I couldn't move. It was like being stuck on the corner of Main and Ferry, hoping for a break in the traffic so I could cross the street. Patience wasn't my strong suit, but an impatient private detective prob'ly wasn't a very good one.

As I trudged across the yard to the main assembly building, Emmie caught up with me. Her breath puffed in front of her. "There you are. I've been looking all over for ya."

I carefully stubbed out my cigarette. With over half left, I could finish it later. "What's buzzin' Emmie?"

"I asked Daddy about the family Bible, like you said."

My heart thumped. Progress at last. "What did he say?"

"I've got good news, bad news, more good news, and more bad news."

She had more info than the *Courier-Express* evening edition. "Shoot."

"Good news is that we do have one. *Babcia* inherited it from her mother back in Poland. It's been kept up for over a hundred years, according to Daddy." Emmie's cheeks glowed pink in the cold morning air.

"The whole family or just your grandmother and her direct relatives?"

"Daddy is pretty sure it's the whole family. Aunts, uncles, cousins...the whole lot of 'em."

Just what I needed. "Perfect. Can I see it? I promise to take real good care of it."

"Well." She drew out the word and looked away, scuffing her shoe on the pavement. "That's the bad news. Daddy doesn't have the book."

"Where is it then? Surely your grandma wouldn't throw away something like that when she got to America."

Emmie's peepers widened to the size of saucers. "Oh no, nothing like that. It's only...Daddy isn't the oldest child in the family. That would be my Uncle Stan. That's my other good news. He does have it."

"He doesn't live in Buffalo?"

"He sure does. In fact, his house is only two blocks away from ours."

I didn't understand her. If her uncle only lived a couple houses away, she could walk over and get the Bible. Even if she didn't go until after she got home from work, it wouldn't take more'n fifteen minutes. "Then can you go get it? Or ask your pop to talk to his brother?"

Emmie lifted her hands in a helpless gesture. "That's the big problem. Uncle Stan and Daddy haven't talked for over twenty years."

I whistled. Brothers who didn't talk? That was unheard of in Irish families. Then again, maybe not. The Irish could hold grudges, but I didn't know anybody with a family like that. Not like folks from the First Ward couldn't fight like the dickens. My own two little brothers, Jimmy and Michael, went at it all the time. Of course, they also made up lickety-split. "That's some fight. What could possibly keep them apart for so long?"

Emmie's cheeks got redder. "I don't know the whole story 'cause my folks won't tell me much. But what I do know is that Ma was all set to marry Uncle Stan. A week before the wedding, she jilted him and ran away with Daddy instead. *Babcia* and *Dziadek* were furious, but forgave Daddy eventually, after my older brother was born. That was twenty-three years ago."

"Lemme guess, Uncle Stan is still mad." In a way, I didn't blame him. I tried to imagine how I'd feel if Tom broke it off with me and married Mary Kate instead. Yeah, I'd be steamed.

"That's why Daddy can't get the Bible."

My last source of information, so close and, at the same time, it might as well have been back in Poland. "Well, darn."

"I'm real sorry, Betty." Emmie twisted her hands. "Is it that important?"

"I was hoping to find out if your grandmother's family was related to the Pyruts. If I could prove they were related, then I could look into whether or not they wrote to each other and arranged to meet. I know he slipped away from the party up at Witkops' in Delaware Park the night before he died."

"But *Babcia* was dead by the time the government got to Buffalo."

"He might not have known that. He prob'ly didn't."

Emmie pursed her lips. "Uncle Stan and I sort of get along. I mean, I saw him a couple times at *Babcia*'s house when she lived on her own and he didn't cuss me out or nothing. Uncle Stan wanted *Babcia* to move in with his family, but she wouldn't go. She didn't like how he cut off his brother. Anyway, I can try and see if he'll loan me the Bible."

"Swell. I gotta get to work. Make sure you tell your uncle it's important and I promise I'll be real careful with it."

"Sure thing, Betty. Say," Emmie paused. "D'you think you can get Uncle Stan and Daddy to talk again if you find out what *Babcia* wanted to say to Mr. Pyrut?"

"I dunno, but I think restoring family unity is outside the job you've hired me for."

* * *

That night, I gobbled down dinner under the stern eye of my mother. "Elizabeth Anne, what on earth are you doing?"

"Sorry." I patted my mouth. "I only get so much time at work and I eat fast so I can go have a smoke. I guess it's become a habit. Eating fast, I mean."

She sniffed. "Slow down and chew before you swallow. Lord knows we don't have a lot of food, but no one's going to take it away from you."

"Yes, ma'am."

After dinner, Mom left for her Ladies of Charity meeting and Pop went to the living room with pipe and paper. Mary Kate and I stayed in the kitchen to wash up. As soon as my folks were out of sight, I turned to my sister. "I need a favor."

She grinned. "Can I clean up without you and cover for you with Pop while you go out?"

I stared.

"You're predictable, Betty. I'd complain about always having to do your share of the chores, but you make it worth my time in treats."

I ran to get my coat and mittens. "You're a gem, Mary Kate. I'll buy you something next time I go to Broadway Market."

She waved me off.

I stuffed my timeline in my pocket and jogged over to Lee's house. "Good evening, Mrs. Tillotson."

"Hello, Betty." She smiled, but there were huge purple smudges under her eyes and a few extra lines around her mouth. "I imagine you're looking for Liam. He's in the kitchen." She stepped back to let me in.

"I didn't interrupt your dinner, did I?"

"No, dear." She held out her hand for my coat and hung it on a peg in the hallway. "It was a cold supper for us tonight. Something is wrong with the oven. Liam's taking a look at it. His father is...not available."

Not here or drunk? I didn't want to know. Lee was prob'ly better suited to fixing things anyway, what with his work at General Motors. Still, a man should take care of his family, like Pop did. That duty seemed to be falling to an eighteen-year-old in the Tillotson house. No wonder Lee looked ashamed every time mention of his dad came up.

I found Lee kneeling down with his butt sticking out of the oven. A thin plume of smoke rose from the lit cigarette in an ashtray on the counter, and a steady stream of cursing came from the oven. "Anything I can help you with?" I asked as I put my timeline on the table.

He held out his hand behind him. "Hand me a screwdriver."

"Straight or Phillips?"

"Phillips, the medium one."

I put the appropriate tool in his hand. "What's wrong?"

"I think I've narrowed it down to the heating element. Pilot light is on, but the oven don't heat up." He backed out, shut the oven door, and wiped his greasy hands on a rag that was almost as dirty. "Maybe the old man can be trusted with a simple task. Prob'ly not, though. Hopefully I can get one tomorrow. Otherwise it's cold suppers for a while and I don't want Anna and Emma to go through that." He picked up and drew on his lit smoke.

I knew he was talking about his little sisters, thirteen and ten. "You got the cabbage for that?"

He nodded and crushed out the gasper. "I got paid yesterday." He stood and put the tools in a battered red box. "What do you want?"

I held up my paper. "You told me to bring this over so we could look at it. It's the timeline for Josef Pyrut's activities the night he died."

"Right, I forgot." He hefted the toolbox. "C'mon, we'll go in the basement. The girls won't bother us there. They don't like the noise and flame from the furnace."

Downstairs, he put the tools on a shelf and led me to a battered table where he'd stacked some newspapers. "These are all from the day before the Polish visit to yesterday. December first through the ninth. I figure that ought to cover it." He took my notes, laid them on the table, and started comparing them. After a while he stood and scratched his head. "I don't see where you missed anything."

"This is what I'm really interested in, right here." I tapped a point on the schedule. "I think he left the party at the Witkops' around nine o'clock the night of the second."

"How can you be sure?"

I told him about Bridget, the maid from the Witkops'. "She didn't come right out and say she saw him, but I got my suspicions. I think she *did*, and he asked her not to say anything."

Lee hmphed. "Where'd he go and who'd he see? 'Cause he saw someone, that's for sure. He didn't mug himself."

"No." I nibbled a fingernail. "We gotta go back to Delaware Park."

Lee raised his eyebrows. "Now?"

"Yeah. I gotta talk to Bridget again and get her to come clean." I glanced up at him. "You don't have to come. I doubt I'm gonna get in trouble up where the swells live."

He restacked the newspapers. "Nah, I'll go. I gotta get out of this house before he gets home."

No need to ask who "he" was. I'd never seen such anger on Lee's face. If Mr. Tillotson could see his son now, he'd stop his boozing. "Is he at work or somewhere else?"

"I'm not sure where he is, but it's not his job. Come on."

Lee hollered to his mother that he was going out for a while and we walked to the bus stop. Lee might be my oldest friend, but I didn't want to pry. At the same time, if he needed blood, I'd open a vein. "Lee, about your pop. What can I do?"

"Turn Buffalo into a dry city?" He barked a laugh, took off his cap, and rubbed his head. "It wouldn't work. Bastard would prob'ly go to Canada."

I hesitated again, but decided to push on. Some conversations were easier to have in the dark. "What happened? He wasn't drinking this past summer."

"No." Lee blew out a breath. "He got injured at work last August. Something in his back. I think it was hurting real bad and whatever the doc gave him didn't work, so he started hitting the bottle. At first it was just so's he could sleep at night. Then he started taking a flask to work so he could take a nip whenever it got to be too much. He started drinking earlier and earlier."

Mr. Tillotson worked at GM, same as his son. "And now he does it all the time," I finished.

Lee scuffed the ground and nodded.

"Did he lose his job?"

"I think the guys at the plant are covering for him. Because he's been there so long, you know? He must be holding it together at work well enough, but once he gets home, he just sits in a dark room and drinks. Ma throws out at least two empty pint bottles every day. Damn war." He pounded a nearby post. "Can't buy sugar, but you can get as much whiskey as you like."

I touched his arm. "We'll figure something out."

He looked at me, then off into the distance. "It's not your problem, Betty."

"You're my friend. Your problems are mine." I chucked him on the shoulder. "Besides, I owe you. I did ruin your Army career with that tire swing trick when we were kids."

"Well, there is that." Lee put his cap back on. "Tell me again who you want to see?"

"Bridget Innes. She's a maid for the Witkops. I hope she's working tonight."

The bus puffed up. We got on and settled in the first empty seat. As it drove, I tried to come up with my approach. I could embellish my lie or go with the truth. I decided a lot depended on Bridget and what she said.

We reached Delaware Park and strolled toward the Witkops' mansion. Lee whistled through his teeth. "Imagine living here. Bet these folks aren't scraping for sugar, or living off beans and bread."

"War time rations apply to everyone, Lee."

"Yeah, but from the looks of it, I bet they apply to some people more than others."

I couldn't figure out the tone of his voice, not quite anger, but not disgust either. More like resignation. "Here we are."

The lights from the Witkop house glowed through the front windows. We sneaked around back. The yard was deserted, footprints through the snow giving evidence of many trips back and forth. I knew from my last visit that the compost heap had to be back there somewhere in the gathering gloom.

"Now what?" Lee asked, his breath fogging up the air.

"Lemme think." I paused. "If she doesn't come out soon, we'll knock."

"On the front door?"

"No dummy, the kitchen door there." I pointed. "If the cook answers, we can say we're friends of Bridget's and we need to talk to her."

Lee shook his head, but he jammed his hands in his jacket pocket. After five minutes, no one had come out of the house. I screwed up my courage. "Here goes." I walked up to the back door and knocked. No answer. I tried again, but no answer.

Lee came up beside me. "Stop being so timid." He pounded on the door. At least that's what it sounded like.

An irritated voice rose behind it. "Just a blessed minute! I don't got all night to be answering doors." A few moments later, the door flew open to reveal a stout woman in a gravy-stained apron, flour on her hands. "Stop all this racket! Who are you and what do you want?"

Lee tipped his head in my direction, indicating it was my show from this point. "I'm Betty, this is Lee. We're friends of Bridget's. Is she here? We'd like to talk to her."

"Oh, you would, would you?" The woman crossed her arms in front of her generous bosom. She regarded us for a long moment, then called over her shoulder, "Bridget! Come here, you Irish moppet."

Bridget appeared, a towel in one hand and a dish in the other. "Yes, Mrs. Leggettt?"

"These two say they're friends of yours."

Her eyes widened a touch and a flash of recognition passed over her puss. "Aye, that's Betty."

The cook yanked the towel from Bridget's hands. "Well for God's sake, get out there, find out what they want, and get back to your work, girl. Mr. Witkop ain't paying you to be a social butterfly." She pushed Bridget outside and slammed the door. The light from the kitchen window was all that kept us from being plunged into total darkness.

Bridget wheeled on us. "You've got some nerve, coming here and dragging me out." Anger made her brogue thicker. "Jesus, Mary, and Joseph, what now?"

I held up my mittened hands and made a flash decision. "I didn't tell the exact truth the last time I was here." Bridget's peepers flared in anger and I hurried on. "Yes, my name is Betty, yes, I live in the First Ward. This is my pal, Lee."

He touched his cap.

I went on. "The thing is, I'm a private detective. I'm trying to find out what happened to Josef Pyrut 'cause I don't think he died in a simple mugging. I need to know if he left the party, the one Mr. Witkop threw for the Poles, and I need to know when."

"I told you, I didn't see anything and I don't know nothing about it." She turned to go back inside.

I touched her arm. "Please. I think you do. I think you saw him leave, and he asked you to keep quiet. Am I right?"

She didn't respond, but her face paled.

"Look, I don't know why he didn't want the others to know. I promise

I'm not gonna get you in trouble, although I don't know why you would. Unless..." An idea popped in my head. "Unless you weren't supposed to be wherever it was when you saw him and that's what would get you in trouble."

Bridget clamped her mouth shut, a mulish look on her face.

Lee glanced at me. "Maybe you were kissing a boy, sneaking a few quiet moments while everyone's attention was on the party?" he asked.

She blushed, and turned a fierce gaze on him, but still didn't say anything.

The kitchen door opened and a young man came out. "Bridget? Are these people giving you trouble? Mrs. Leggett said they just showed up out of nowhere."

I studied the newcomer in the light. He was about twenty, maybe a little older, dark hair that had been slicked back, and dressed in evening clothes, like a younger Clark Gable without the mustache. His eyes were dark pools, but could have been any color from deep blue to brown. His upper lip was marred by a small scar. I wondered briefly why he was here, in a Delaware Park mansion, and not overseas. Maybe he was another 4F.

"It's nothing, Paul," Bridget said. "They were just leaving."

I focused on him. "We're looking for information about Josef Pyrut. Maybe you saw him the night of the party? When did he leave?"

Paul lifted an eyebrow in disdain. "I don't bother with things like that. Come along, Bridget." He took the Irish girl's hand.

A woman appeared at the back door. She wasn't wearing an evening gown, but her dress was fancier than day wear. Her diamond necklace and earrings told me this was no servant. "Paul, what are you doing out here? Your father and I aren't finished talking to you." She spotted Lee and me, and Bridget. "Who are these people? And why are you out in the dark with the staff?"

"No one, Mother. No one important. They are the ones who came to see Bridget. I'm sending them on their way," he said.

She sniffed. "Well, get back inside. Now." She turned and left.

My opportunity was slipping away. "Were you cuddled up with Bridget that night? Is that why she won't admit to seeing Josef? Would it mean admitting she was making whoopee with you instead of working? Sounds to me your mom thinks it's a regular thing for you."

Bridget hissed, but Paul merely laughed. "You're out of your league, girl. First Ward, you said? You don't belong here in Delaware Park. I suggest you go back to your people before I call the police. Good night." He guided Bridget inside and shut the door.

"C'mon, let's get outta here before he calls the cops." Lee tugged down his cap. Halfway to the bus stop, he asked, "Who was that? Pretty flash suit he had on."

"I dunno, I didn't see him last time. But his puss looked familiar." I thought and snapped my fingers. "He was in the paper, one of the pictures from the party. That was Witkop's son, Paul. That stinker, he was eavesdropping."

"How d'ya know that?"

"He knew I was from the First Ward. I told ya, I didn't talk to him."

Lee nodded. "Or Bridget told him about you."

The bus was about to pull away and we were able to hop on. This time we took seats away from any other passengers. "Might be. Why's he not in the service? Daddy pay someone to keep him out or is he unfit?" Lee asked.

"I don't know," I replied. Paul was a handsome devil, standing in his evening dress, apparently immune to the cold. He'd had a hold over Bridget, too. I'd bet anything he and Bridget had been snuggled down in some quiet corner, and Josef had interrupted them in his exit. If Paul was Witkop's son, what would the old man say about his boy kissing the help? Nothing good, I'd expect, 'specially if they weren't being discreet. Was that what was keeping them mum?

Or was it something else?

Chapter Twelve

First thing I did Friday morning was dig out the papers from the previous week and scour the society pages. There he was, Paul Witkop, a big smile plastered on his face in every picture, standing next to his pop, visiting dignitaries, and the socialites who had come to the party for the Poles.

Every picture 'cept one.

In it, Paul was sandwiched between his dad, Josef Pyrut, and a man the caption said was the Polish president, Raczkiewicz. No toothy smile here. Instead, his lips barely curved, and he stood ramrod straight. His father's arm wrapped around him, as did Pyrut's, but his were at his sides. It was clear to me that Paul wanted to be anywhere but this scene. But who made him feel that way?

I saw the woman from last night, too. Her name was Eleanor Witkop, and she was often standing with her husband, but never touching. Her smiles were more genuine, less posed, when she was alone, husband and son not in sight.

I walked off to the bus stop with thoughts whirling through my head. Why was Paul so unhappy in that snap? Did he want to go back to his Irish cutie? Maybe he was tired.

Or maybe it was something else. I suddenly wondered if *he* had left the party and, if so, had he left with Josef Pyrut or did Josef follow later? He'd put his arm around Paul. It suggested the two were friends, at least Josef thought so. Paul's stiff look suggested he didn't feel the same toward Josef.

And why was his mother so unhappy with the men in her family? She'd certainly been steamed to find Paul standing with Bridget last night. Was that it? But what did that have to do with Sebastian Witkop?

Dot waited for me, all bundled up against the cold. "It's not good if you've started talking to yourself," she said through her muffler. "Did who leave with Josef?"

I took a drag on my cigarette. I hadn't realized I'd asked the question aloud. "Paul Witkop."

"Why d'you care?"

I told her about my venture to Delaware Park last night with Lee. "He didn't want Bridget to talk to us. And remember, she said, 'I didn't see that.'" I blew out a steady stream of smoke. "I don't think she'd cover for a total stranger. But her boss's cutie-pie son? I can see that. I met Paul's mother, too. I don't think she's fond of her husband and son." I told her about the pictures.

"Huh." Above the wool, Dot's eyes shone with dubious light. "You know, I been wondering. Why would Witkop host the Poles?"

"He's a fan." I ashed the smoke. "You want to raise money, you go where the rich people are. 'Specially the ones who are sympathetic to your cause."

"I get that. Here's the thing." Dot looked around, but we were alone and the bus was nowhere in sight. "Witkop isn't a Polish name, right?"

I thought about it. "I wouldn't think so. Sounds more English to me. Who cares? There are a lot of people who don't like Hitler. They might be willing to give dough to anyone who was on the opposite side."

"I s'pose." Dot paused. "The family Emmie said her grandmother worked for. You know, the one back in Poland. You told me their name was Witkowski."

The meaning of her words took a second to work through my brain, as though it too were half frozen, like my toes. "They changed their name."

The bus arrived. We took seats in the back, away from any people. "I admit it's a stretch. Witkop, Witkowski, the only thing they have in common is Witk. But think about it." She tapped her palm. "Your family is fleeing their homeland. Maybe you don't want to be recognized or maybe you just want a fresh start."

"Could be you just want to fit in," I continued, puffing on my dwindling cigarette. "Immigrants do change their names. Perfect way to blend in to the new country."

Dot shot me a knowing look. "Perfect way to get away from something in the old one, too."

"Huh." She was right. "It raises a few questions though."

"How do we find out?"

I leaned back. "That and why they'd do it in the first place. And what, if anything, does it have to do with Pelagia Brewka and Josef Pyrut?"

* * *

As soon as we got off the bus and into the Bell compound, Emmie ran up to us. She held an enormous leather-bound book in her hands, the cover dark from age. "Got it."

I blinked. "Got...the Bible?"

"Yep." She held it out. "Uncle Stan wasn't too keen on giving it to me 'cause he thought Daddy wanted it. But I explained it was a private project of mine. I wanted to trace *Babcia*'s ancestry. He loaned it to me as long as I promised I wouldn't let Daddy look at it. Isn't that dumb?"

"It's swell." I took the book. "I mean swell that you got it, not Uncle Stan's conditions."

"You'll be careful, right?" Emmie bit her lip.

"As if it were a relic from one of the saints." I turned the book over in my hands and looked inside. The back pages contained the information I wanted, generations of birth, death, and marriage information from Pelagia's family, all written in wobbly, cramped writing. The enormity of the task hit me. "You haven't looked at this, have you? I mean, it's a lot of names and the writing is tiny. It would be great if you could give me a starting point."

"'S'matter of fact I did." Emmie took the book back and ran her finger down the columns. "Here," she tapped the page. "This is where I saw the name Pyrut, but I didn't have time to read all the details."

"That's great." I patted my pockets, looking for something to use as a bookmark.

Dot removed a bobby pin from her hair. "Will this work?" she asked, correctly interpreting my need.

"Perfect." I took the pin and clipped it to the page. "I'll look at this tonight. Thanks again, Emmie. And thank your uncle for me."

"I'll do that later." She grinned. "If I tell Uncle Stan I'm looking for *Babcia*'s murderer, he'll think I've gone 'round the bend. See ya." She scampered off.

I wanted to dig right into the family history, but work first.

"You want help tonight?" Dot asked as we made our way to the administration building so's we could punch in and stow our coats.

"Yes," I said. "And bring some scraps for Cat. I'm out."

Chapter Thirteen

I suggested we go to Lee's house after dinner since his was the quietest. Two girls didn't make as much noise as two boys, and his parents weren't likely to bother us. If his pop was even home. He let us in without a question. I think he was glad of the company. I laid the Bible on his kitchen table and gingerly opened the cover.

"Are you sure that thing won't fall to pieces if one of us sneezes?" Dot asked as she bent over the pages.

I turned the end page to the family tree. "No, so don't do that."

Lee leaned over my other side. "The writing's awfully small."

"Yes." I shoved him a little to let more light fall on the book. "I doubt it's the same person for all the entries. After all, it goes back generations. But their writing had one thing in common. Size."

"I have a magnifying glass. Or at least Anna does." Lee sat down and pulled out a cigarette. "You want it?"

"That'd be swell." I batted his hand away. "Don't light that thing here! Ash falls off it and, bam! This book will go up in flames."

He put away the smoke. "All right, all right. Don't snap your cap." He pushed away from the table. "Lemme get the glass."

After he left, Dot turned to me. "That wasn't very nice."

"What?"

"Getting mad at Lee like that. It's just a cigarette."

I closed my eyes. "I'm not mad at him. This book doesn't belong to me, and I don't want it damaged. It's a family heirloom for the Brewkas."

Dot sniffed. "You coulda said it nicer."

I doubted Lee had been offended, not really, but I said nothing. He returned in a few minutes later, an old-fashioned magnifying glass in hand, the kind Sherlock Holmes used in the movies.

He handed it to me. "I don't know how well it works. Anna got it for collecting cereal box tops or something like that."

"Feels a little cheesy, but anything to save my eyes." I glanced at Dot. "Sorry for busting your chops over the cigarette."

He waved me off. "Don't sweat it. Let's see if the Brewkas and the Pyruts are related, shall we?"

I nudged Dot, but she refused to look at me. I held the glass over the script. Despite being a mail-in toy, it worked pretty well.

It took a while, but eventually Dot saw it. "There."

"Where?" I asked, stopping the steady movement of my hand.

"There." She tapped a page. "I think I saw the name Pyrut."

I repositioned the glass to where her finger pointed. Sure enough, some past female Brewka had married a Pyrut. And eventually had a son named Josef. As I examined the earlier records, I saw where Pelagia Ferchow had married into the family.

"There it is." Lee moved over to the sink and lit a cigarette. "Old lady Brewka was related to the Pyruts."

"Don't call her that," I said as I continued to read. "Her name was Pelagia. At least you could call her Mrs. Brewka."

He shrugged. "If you insist."

Dot continued to trace the names. "They're related, Josef and Pelagia, but not by blood. By marriage. And if I'm right, they'd be something like third cousins. Not a real close relationship."

"No." I rubbed my eyes. "The more I think about it, this doesn't prove anything."

Dot looked up. "What d'ya mean?"

"Think about it. Josef is the same as the English name Joseph, right? It's not uncommon. There are probably thousands of Josefs in Poland. And for all we know, Pyrut is as common there as Smith is here." My shoulders sagged. "We were hoping this would prove a relationship between Pelagia and our Josef Pyrut, but honestly? I don't think it does. And let's say that they are related. Everybody involved is dead."

We stood in silence for a moment. Then Lee tapped the ash from his smoke in the sink. "Does it matter?"

I stared at him. "Of course it matters! Without the family connection, Pelagia has no reason to contact Josef. If she even did, which we also don't know."

"I think you're overcomplicating things," Lee said. I sputtered, and he held up his hands. "No, listen. This Bible proves that Pelagia does have a distant relation named Josef Pyrut, even if it's just by marriage, right?"

"Right," Dot said, drawing out the word, clearly as confused as I was where Lee was going.

"Okay. Pelagia sees the name Josef Pyrut in the paper. She doesn't know if it's her cousin, or whatever he is, or not, but she might not care." He pointed at me with his cigarette.

I thought I saw his idea swirling through the smoke. "You think she'd contact him anyway, maybe to find out if he *was* her cousin."

"Exactly." Lee nodded. "Even if he isn't, this Josef Pyrut is in the Polish government. If she had information, I bet she'd tell him even if it turned out he was some other Pyrut and not her kin."

I rolled the idea around in my head. "You might have a point." I closed the book. "Let's say you're right. Pelagia wrote to our Josef Pyrut, to find out if they were related or maybe just 'cause he had the same name. She has information and plans to meet him when he comes to Buffalo. I buy it. Just one problem."

My friends looked at each other, then me. Dot spoke. "What is it?"

I shut the book and put it away. "How're we gonna find out?"

Chapter Fourteen

I returned the Bible, which I'd wrapped in brown paper, to Emmie on Saturday morning. "Thanks for letting me read this."

"Was it helpful?"

I told her about our discovery last night.

She placed the book in her locker. "Then *Babcia* was related to Josef Pyrut."

"She's related to *a* Josef Pyrut. We don't know it's the same guy who's dead, and I don't know how I'm gonna find out. Not like I can write the Polish government." I turned to get to my station, then paused. I faced Emmie again and asked, "Hey, what was the name of that family your grandma worked for? The one back in Poland?"

Emmie shut the locker. "Witkowski. I wonder if they're still there." She wrapped her arms around herself. "Does this mean you're at a dead end?"

"I wouldn't say that, not yet. I'll let you know. Thanks again, Emmie." This time I really did head for the assembly building, dawdling as I crossed the courtyard, my thoughts a muddle.

Witkowski. Witkop. Two wealthy families. Dot was right. The names were awfully close. What were the chances it was the same family? Pop told me once the number one reason immigrants changed their names was to blend in and sound more English when they arrived at Ellis Island. Witkop was nice and generic. It could be a name from anywhere. People might assume it was English, especially if the family spoke without an accent. I'd seen it happen before, the name changing. Had it happened again?

I shared my thoughts with Dot when I got to the production line. "I told you, it sounds reasonable to me," she said, after thinking a moment. "The more I think about it, the more I believe they must be hiding something."

"How do you figure?"

"If the family was rich, who'd care what their name was? I can see changing it if you wanted to, say, get a job and you thought having an ethnic name would work against you. But if you already have the cabbage? What's the point? Simple. You don't want people to find you."

"Makes sense."

"Thanks." Dot glowed with satisfaction.

My hands moved through familiar patterns, working on the plane in front of me, while my mind was free to ponder this latest hunch. "He committed a crime. A serious one."

"How d'you figure?"

"Witkowski didn't just want to leave Poland. He wanted to start over, but keep the cash. He decides to hide in plain sight, change his name to something English-sounding, and that, as they say, is that."

Dot frowned. "What kind of crime?"

"Maybe his money isn't so clean."

Her puss wrinkled as her frown deepened. "I don't get it."

I stepped back and let the chain pull the next plane into place. "Emmie already told us, remember? The Witkowskis were German sympathizers. That's why they got to keep their stuff. What if they helped the Germans with other things, too?"

* * *

That evening, as I washed the dinner dishes, I continued to think about the puzzle in front of me. The more I thought about it, the more likely it seemed that Witkop and Witkowski were the same. But it wasn't like I could walk up, talk to the elder Witkop and say, "'Scuse me. Did you change your name when you immigrated and also, would you mind telling me why? Was it because your pop was a German sympathizer back in Poland?" I couldn't even ask Paul. One, he prob'ly wouldn't tell me, and, two, he might not even know.

'Course, maybe he would. The elder Witkop, that is. Paul had already met me and I got the feeling he didn't take too kindly to me harassing Bridget. But his father, he'd never met Betty Ahern. I'd have to come up with a good story. Some version of the truth would prob'ly work best.

Oh Tom, what would you think of me now? I hadn't heard from him in weeks and his last letter led me to think he was still in North Africa. I knew one part of the division, something called Combat Command B, had attacked the Germans on December 3rd and had sustained a counterattack on December 6th, but I didn't know how or if that affected Tom. I'd tried to keep busy with Emmie's case to distract me, but now, standing at the sink, my thoughts wandered to the hot desert of North Africa and my fiancé.

Pop entered the kitchen, paper in hand and his pipe between his teeth. "You're taking an awful long time with the washing up."

"Just thinking." I glanced at the paper. "What's the news?"

He shook his head. "Looks like Rommel is running before the Brits." He paused and took his pipe from his mouth. "Don't be alarmed, Betty, but CCB of the 1st Armored encountered the Jerries at a place called Bedja yesterday. There aren't a lot of details yet, but it doesn't look good."

A plate splashed as I dropped it into the sink.

He placed his hands on my shoulders. "Now, now. I told you not to be fussed. I talked to Mrs. Flannery. She hasn't heard anything about Tom. No telegrams, no letters, nothing. He may not even be with CCB."

"But he might be. You can't write a letter when the enemy is shooting at you."

"You're right." Pop rubbed my shoulders. "But worrying won't help him or you or any of us. You say an extra prayer tonight, light your candles at church tomorrow. God will watch over him."

I turned back to the dishes. Life without Tom? I couldn't even imagine.

Pop shook out his paper. "Tell me about your day. What about your case?"

Just like Pop to try and keep me in good spirits. I snuck a look at him and when I saw him reading, I dashed the tears from my eyes so he wouldn't notice. "Oh, Bell's pretty quiet. You know, we build planes, they fly 'em off. Nothing like last month."

"And the case?" He turned a page.

"It's…interesting." I pulled the plug on the sink, dried my hands, and took a seat at the table. I proceeded to tell him all about Emmie and her grandmother, and also the connection between the Brewkas and Pyruts. "I can't prove any of my suspicions, though. I don't know how. Writing Ellis Island will take forever and not like I can just put in a long-distance call to where ever the Polish government is now. Or write them. Besides, would they even know?"

"True." Pop laid the paper on the table, then rummaged in the fridge for the last of the milk.

"Um, don't drink all of that," I said. "Please?"

He turned to me. "Why on earth not? It'll be bad by tomorrow."

I took a deep breath. "It's for Cat. Part of his dinner."

It took Pop a moment to understand me. "Are you feeding that stray I've seen hanging around? The gray one?"

"With the cream-colored swirls? Yeah. Just scraps, though," I added hastily once I saw his eyes widen. "I'm not taking anything we could still eat or using our food coupons or nothing."

"I'd expect that out of Mary Kate, but you? Will wonders never cease?" He put the milk bottle back and sat down. "Then Josef Pyrut is a dead end?" he asked, returning to the previous conversation.

"For now, yeah."

"Then what are you going to do next? Or are you throwing in the towel?"

"Not hardly. Most Polish are Catholic, right?"

He puffed on his pipe. "I believe so, yes. Why?"

"There's this family, the Witkops. I think they may be the same as the one Pelagia Brewka worked for in Poland." I sketched out my reasoning and he nodded along as he listened. "I figure I'll go to church tomorrow and see if Mr. Witkop is there. Maybe he'll talk to me. It'd most likely be St. Stanislaus, don't you think?"

"That's the Polish area church, but if he's changed his name and is denying his heritage, trying to blend in as you say, he's more likely to attend one of the churches closer to Delaware Park, like St. Mark's or Blessed Trinity. My guess would be St. Mark's." He narrowed his eyes. "Do you mean to tell me you're going to interrupt worship in the house of God just to track down a man and ask a question?"

"I'd wait for after the Mass." Pop was understanding, but he had his limits. "And 'course I'd go to Mass with the family first, as usual." Pop relaxed a bit. Besides, even detectives went to church, right? "That means I gotta visit at two extra churches and I don't even know when the Mass times are." The size of my task teased me. It'd take half a day to ride the bus between all these places. Besides St. Mark's and Blessed Trinity, there was at least one other church near Delaware Park, I was pretty sure.

Pop patted my hand and rose. "Try St. Stanislaus first, late morning. Most churches have a service then. Even when a family changes their name, they may need a connection to the old country. Religion can provide that. If you strike out there, go to St. Mark's. It's closest to where the Witkops live. The priest at St. Stanislaus may even be able to provide you with Mass times."

"Wish there was a paper that listed all this info," I said, grumbling a little. But only a little, because Pop's advice, as always, was good.

"Someday, my darling girl. Someday." He took a step toward the door, stopped, and turned. "One other thing?"

"Yes?"

"Don't let your mother see you taking food from the fridge to feed a stray cat, scraps or not." He winked.

I tried to suppress a grin and failed. "Yes, sir."

Chapter Fifteen

Right before I left Our Lady of Perpetual Help on Sunday morning, I spoke to Father O'Connor. He told me the pastor at St. Stanislaus was Father Tryka and they had a late morning Mass at eleven. I lit two candles on my way out of church as usual, and said an extra Hail Mary for Tom. There still wasn't a lot of news about the 1st Armored, but I'd learned one thing. If the news was good, it was out quick. If it wasn't, well, it could take a while.

After we returned home, Mary Kate and I made breakfast for the family. The boys inhaled their food and ran out into the frosty sunshine to play. I was able to slow them down long enough to put on hats, scarves, and mittens. There wasn't much snow on the ground, but it was cold enough they'd freeze their fingers off in no time. I hoped they wouldn't do something stupid, like the flagpole-licking dare I'd caught them at last week.

I went to the living room where Pop read the paper, gently puffing on his pipe, while Mom mended a pair of trousers. "I think I'm gonna go see if Dot wants to take a walk. Do we need anything? I can stop at the Broadway Market or somewhere while I'm out."

Mom looked up. "Whatever do you want to go out in the cold for?"

I clasped my hands. "I need to get some fresh air. You know, I worked all last week and who knows when it'll snow again. Might as well get out in the sun while it's here."

She clucked her tongue. "I could use help with the mending, you know."

Mary Kate put aside her comic. "I can do that. I'd like to."

"See?" I pointed at my sister. "You have a helper, one who's better with a needle than I am. I promise, I'll be home in plenty of time to give you a hand with dinner."

Pop took his pipe from his mouth and examined it. "Let her go, Mary. She's right. We could be under six feet of snow by this time next week. She should get some exercise while she can." He went back to reading his paper.

Mom sighed. "Your father has spoken. Make sure you bundle up."

"Yes, ma'am." I sped out of the room before either of them could change their minds. I made sure my muffler was wrapped tight around my neck, tugged on my mittens and pulled my cap over my ears. Then I hoofed it down the street to Dot's. The bright sun glittered off a heavy frost that sparkled like diamonds on the metal garbage cans, even into the late morning. The sun was throwing a lot of light, but not much heat. I was glad for my winter things. *Tom, you aren't missing this. Or are you?* I was sure it was a lot hotter wherever he was.

Dot answered her door a minute after I knocked. "What's up?"

"I'm gonna make a visit to St. Stanislaus. You wanna go with me?"

"I can't." Dot cast a look back into the house. "Ma drafted me to help in the kitchen all day." She bit her lip. "Believe me, I'd rather go with you."

"I thought you liked baking."

"I do, but Ma's so particular. Nothing I do for her is 'just right' and it drives me nuts." She stepped out and pulled the door most of the way shut. "What's at St. Stanislaus?"

"I hope the priest over there knows something about the Witkop family."

Dot lifted an eyebrow. "Like if they really changed their name?"

"That or more. If the people at St. Stan's don't know anything about it, I'll try St. Mark's. Pop says that's the closest one to Delaware Park."

Mrs. Kilbride's voice cut the air. "Dorothy, where are you?"

Dot rolled her peepers. "I gotta go. Let me know what you learn?"

"Absolutely. And chin up, the baking will be over before you know it." Dot went back into her house. At least she'd be warm.

I waited about ten minutes for a ride. It was mostly a straight shot to St. Stanislaus, down South Park and up Fillmore. I got off at the corner of Fillmore and Peckham Street As I looked down Peckham, I could see the church a block away, a crowd of parishioners out front. Mass had to have just ended.

I strolled up to the church, greeting women in somber-colored coats, some of whom wore the traditional Polish head scarves called "babushkas." The priest was by the front door, dressed for Advent in purple vestments over his black clothes, the white of his collar peeking out. They were nice vestments, too, heavy on the gold thread and embroidery. His breath steamed in front of his face, cheeks red as apples from the cold. How did he stand it? "'Scuse me, Father?" I called as he shook a man's hand and turned to go inside.

He paused and looked back. "Yes?"

I hurried up. "Sorry for busting in on you. My name's Betty Ahern. I hoped I could talk to you."

He opened the door. "Certainly. But come inside. I can't feel my fingers."

We entered the narthex, what most folks would call the lobby, then went through the main doors into the nave. I dipped my fingers in the holy water and made the sign of the cross while I genuflected toward the altar and tabernacle.

The priest smiled. "You're Catholic."

"Yes, Father. I go to Our Lady of Perpetual Help."

"First Ward. Ahern, you said your name was? Irish?"

"Yes, Father. I live over on Mackinaw Street."

He took a seat in one of the back pews and I sat in the one across the aisle. "You're a bit out of your neighborhood. You said you wanted to talk to me?"

"Are you Father Tryka?"

"That's me. What can I do for you?"

"Do you know if either of these men is a parishioner here?" I held out the newspaper photo. "This one is Sebastian Witkop. This other is his son, Paul."

He studied the photo. "I don't think I've seen them. Where do they live?"

"Up in Delaware Park."

Father Tryka gave me the picture. "It would be quite a ways to travel for church. You'd be better off asking at St. Mark's."

"I know that's closer, but I think the family is Polish and I wondered if that might make them come to St. Stanislaus to worship."

"May I see that again?" He took a second look at the snap. "You said the family name is Witkop. That's not Polish."

"I understand. I believe they changed it. You know, when they came through Ellis Island."

"Hmm." His forehead puckered as he thought. "No, I can't say as I've ever seen either of these two at a Mass here. Now, that's not to say they've never been here. But I'm pretty familiar with our regular parishioners and I'm certain these two aren't in that group. No one in our congregation has the kind of money it takes to live in Delaware Park."

"Thanks, Father. It was worth a shot." I stood and put the picture in my pocket. "You don't happen to know the priest or Mass times at St. Mark's, do you?"

He followed me back to the narthex. "The priest at St. Mark's is new, I'm not familiar with his name. But the late Mass there is twelve-fifteen. I take it that it's important you find these two men?"

"Yeah, it relates to a..." I almost said murder investigation, but decided not to. "I'm trying to track down some information for a friend of mine. She's Polish and she thinks her grandmother might have known the Witkops. She's dead, the grandmother, so my friend can't ask her."

Father Tryka's gaze turned shrewd. "Why isn't your friend tracking them down?"

"She's shy. She asked me to do it for her." Emmie really wasn't shy, but she had asked me. I hoped God would forgive the little white lie, 'specially as I was talking to a priest.

"I see. There are several other churches near Delaware Park, you know."

"Yeah, but St. Mark's is as good a place to start as any." I stuck out my hand. "Thank you for your time and have a good day."

On my way out, I lit two of the candles by the door. I'd already done so at church this morning, but you couldn't have too many prayers these days. Then I tugged on my mittens, walked out, and headed back to the bus stop. One church down, who knew how many more to go.

Chapter Sixteen

Monday morning found me irritable and distracted. Dot knew better than to talk to me on the bus to work. The news was in about Bedja, and it wasn't good. The Germans had pierced the lines and the 1st Armored Division's CCB had sustained heavy losses. All I could hope was that Tom was safe, either because he hadn't been in the fighting or because he'd escaped without injury. I mentally recited a few Hail Marys to make myself feel better.

I was on my second cigarette of the morning before Dot screwed up the courage to say anything. "You read the news I s'pose."

"Yeah."

"Any word from Tom?"

"Nah." I blew out a stream of smoke. "If he was involved, he wouldn't have had time to write before the battle. If he wasn't involved, he might be busy with something else. Pop talked to the Flannerys and they haven't received a telegram."

"Well, that's good, right?"

"Better than getting one, that's for sure. I can only say a prayer that he's okay and he'll write me soon."

Dot paused. "You have any luck with the churches yesterday? You know, finding the Witkops?"

"No." I ashed my cigarette. "I went to St. Stanislaus, but nothing doing. Then I squeezed in a quick visit to St. Mark's, but the priest there didn't recognize them, either. After that, I had to go home."

"Maybe they go to another church. Are those the only ones close to the

Witkop house?"

"No, I figured they were the most likely ones, though."

Dot chewed at her lip. "Could also be they don't go to church at all."

I swatted her shoulder. "I've told you at least a dozen times, stop making ground meat of your lip. Anyway, that's another possibility. Or they could be some other religion, not Catholic. Pop told me most Polish are, but not all. The next best Catholic possibility is Blessed Trinity."

Dot thought this over. "You gonna try again next Sunday?"

"Unless I get a better idea, yes."

"I'll go with you next time. I'll come up with some kind of story."

"Thanks." I watched the dead grasses roll by out of the window. The trees bent in the wind, and the morning was cold as the dickens, but little snow was on the ground. "Bridget."

Dot blinked. "The Witkops' maid? What about her?"

"I have to talk to her again. Alone and away from the house."

"You've tried. What makes you think she'll talk now, no matter where she is?"

I faced Dot and stabbed the air with my cigarette. "That girl knows something. About the Witkops or about Josef, or...I don't know. But it's important. The question is, how do I get at her? If I go to the house, chances are I'll run into Paul and he'll stop me. Or she'll be too scared to talk. No, it's gotta be somewhere safe."

"How about the Broadway Market?"

The Market was a great gathering place, with a variety of ethnic shops, and lots of people. It was good for meetings and innocent conversation. But there was a problem. "I don't know if she does the shopping. If she does, I don't know when or even if she goes to Broadway."

"If the Witkops are Polish like you think, isn't that the best place to go for their sausages and stuff?"

It was a good point. But I'd still have to figure out when. "It's no good. I can't tail her like Philip Marlowe. I have to work. And like I said, I don't even know if she does the shopping. She's a maid."

"Could be she helps the cook," Dot said. She was trying and I loved her for it. "We're off this Saturday, right? It's a possibility. Definitely worth trying."

"Let's keep it in mind. I don't want to wait that long if I don't have to." I ground out my cigarette and wondered whether I should have a third. Nah. No use going through the whole pack on a single trip.

"She's definitely Irish, right?" Dot asked after a moment.

"Oh yeah. With her accent, she may even have gotten here recently."

"But I don't recall if she told us where she lived."

I thought back to our meetings with Bridget. "No, she didn't say. Why?"

"Well, if she's Irish, there's a good chance she lives in the First Ward, right?"

"I guess, yeah. Unless she lives in over at the Witkops' house."

Dot shifted in her seat. "If this was Ireland or someplace else in Europe, I'd think that might be the case. But aside from the really big houses in New York City, I'm not sure that's common here, especially in Buffalo."

"You think we should search close to home?"

"Yes. Ask at Our Lady of Perpetual Help." She held up her hands. "I know what you're gonna say. You've never seen her there. She could go to a different service. Or maybe she changes each week based on when she has to work."

"Fair enough. I can go with Mom when she goes to her Ladies of Charity meeting this week and ask the others if they've seen her. Irish girl with red hair and an accent, she ought to be memorable. I'll ask Father O'Connor, too."

"I think that's smart." The bus rumbled into the Bell parking lot. We gathered our things and got off. It belched black smoke as it drove off and we headed for the main building. "We should go back to the Witkops' place, too," Dot added.

I stopped dead in my tracks. "Didn't I just say I don't want to talk to her there again?"

"Yes." Dot didn't turn or stop. "I don't want to talk to her, though."

I jogged to catch up. "Who do you want to see then, the cook?"

"No." She pulled her time card out and punched it. Then she faced me. "I think we need to talk to Paul Witkop."

* * *

My first reaction to Dot's statement had been "no way." I was pretty sure the person Bridget was most afraid of was Paul. What made her think he'd talk to two girls from the streets, especially after the last time? But she kept on it. "Yes, I know. You said he acted pretty confident the night you and Lee saw him. But that's the thing. It's pretty clear to me he thinks he's better than us. That's why it might be a good idea to corner him. Could be that he'll be so eager to show how superior he is, he'll say something that'll give the whole store away."

I continued to resist, but finally had to admit she had a point. We agreed we'd visit the Witkops at some point, but I wasn't sure when. I had plans that night. I was gonna go work with the Ladies of Charity.

"You want to do what?" Mom asked when I told her I was going with her to the church after dinner. Her eyes narrowed. "What for? None of your friends will be there, it's mostly older women."

"Mom, you read the news. I'm going out of my mind thinking about Tom. If I'm helping you, I'll be doing something, not sitting at home, fretting."

"All right." She shook a finger in my face. "But you better not be using this as an excuse for something else. This is serious work, helping those poor boys overseas. You mind yourself in front of the ladies."

I made a note to myself to sit far enough away that she wouldn't be able to hear me. I'd bet none of the detectives in the pictures had to work around their mothers this way. "Yes, ma'am."

We arrived at the church by seven that night. Several older women were already there, chatting as they worked. I took a seat near two I knew from the neighborhood, Mrs. Gurley and Mrs. O'Toole. "Good evening. Is there space for me here?"

Mrs. Gurley moved over. "Of course, Betty. I'm so happy you could join us. How is work at Bell?"

"Oh, not too bad. They keep us hopping, of course. But you get in a rhythm, like this." I waved my hand at the room, now full of women sorting papers, cans, and balls of foil and rubber bands.

"Have you made a lot of friends there?" she asked.

"Oh yeah. Not all the girls are from the First Ward. I get to talk to all sorts from all over Buffalo. Sometimes we meet up during lunch or outside of the plant."

Mrs. O'Toole sniffed. "Girls in pants, working in factories. It wouldn't have happened in my day."

I figured Mrs. O'Toole was at least sixty, maybe older. She'd have been past mothering when the Great War happened. "Things are different now, I s'pose," I said.

"How so?"

"Well." I bundled together a stack of paper. "There aren't many men around to do the jobs, are there? With all the tanks and planes and jeeps and stuff needed, if the women didn't work, stuff wouldn't get built. That's not good for our boys, right? Seems to me, women have always been involved in wars and doing what needs to be done. Back in the Civil War, who made the bandages or tended the farms while the men were off fighting?"

Mrs. O'Toole blushed. "Women."

"Right. The U.S. doesn't need me to do those things. What I can do is help make sure the army has the planes, or tanks, or whatever they need. It's my duty as an American, as well as a sister to a sailor, right?"

Mrs. Gurley patted my shoulder. "Good for you, Betty. Frankly, I see all these young women and I wish I was twenty again. It must be terribly exciting."

"Yes, it can be. But mostly it's the same work every day, all very routine." I looked around the room and wondered how to slide my inquiries into the conversation. "There are a lot of people here tonight."

"Yes," Mrs. Gurley said, as she sorted a box full of cans. "Seems like we have more every week."

"Are they all from the First Ward?"

"Mostly." She picked up another box.

"There are never any strangers here?"

Mrs. O'Toole looked up. "Why do you want to know?"

"Oh, just curious. It's my first time, see." Perhaps I hadn't been as slick as

I thought. Nick Charles would've done it better.

But my answer seemed to satisfy Mrs. O'Toole. "Yes, most of the ladies are from the neighborhood. Sometimes they bring their children, too."

Drat. "Then you never see strangers?"

"No, well, rarely. Although Mrs. McMahon brought her sister's girl, two weeks ago, wasn't it?"

Mrs. Gurley thought. "About that. Nice girl, a little plain."

No one would describe Bridget as plain. "Anyone else?" I asked.

Mrs. O'Toole tapped the bundle in front of her. "Mrs. Shaughnessy brought her second cousin. Such an overbite on that child."

I thought about Bridget's teeth. White and straight with a little gap, but no overbite.

"Oh, and Mrs. Biggs brought a visitor just this past weekend, remember?" Mrs. Gurley said. "The family recently moved in next to her. I'd say the girl was about sixteen or so. Lovely blue eyes she had."

Too young. The prospect of finding Bridget in the First Ward was slipping away. "If that's all—"

Mrs. Gurley spoke. "There was that girl last week. Remember her, Eileen?"

"Oh, you mean the Irish girl? Red hair, green eyes?"

My heart leapt. But that was a pretty thin description.

Mrs. O'Toole thought a moment. "Oh yes, I know the one you're talking about. Young, maybe mid-twenties. Such a lovely accent, it reminded me of my grandmother. She was visiting friends around here, wasn't she?"

Mrs. Gurley moved on to sorting some rubber. "That's right. She's a maid to one of the moneyed families in Delaware Park. Live-in, I think she said, but she had come to see some old family acquaintances and wanted to help. She said she might not be American, but she lived here now, and would do her part to support our boys, even if most of the people in Ireland were neutral. What a wonderful sentiment." She looked up. "What was her name again?"

"Bridget," Mrs. O'Toole replied. "Bridget Innes."

She'd been here and she lived with the Witkops. I was sure my face was red, and I hoped Mrs. Gurley and Mrs. O'Toole thought it was from the stuffiness of the room. "I wonder if it's the same Bridget I met a couple days ago. Who was she with?"

The ladies exchanged looks. "Sheila Donohue," Mrs. Gurley said.

"No, that wasn't it." Mrs. O'Toole shook her head. "I think it was Elizabeth Hanley."

"Don't be daft, Elizabeth hasn't been here in ages. It was definitely Sheila," retorted Mrs. Gurley.

Mrs. O'Toole bristled. "Don't call me daft. Elizabeth was here just last week, you old biddy. I—"

I cut off the argument. "Oh, don't worry about it. She prob'ly wasn't even the same person. Would you pass me that box of paper so I can bind it up?"

Mrs. Gurley did, but I could tell she was biting her tongue, prob'ly so hard she was leaving teeth marks.

I didn't really care. I knew both the Hanleys and the Donohues. Finding out which of them was friends with Bridget would be a snap.

Chapter Seventeen

I brought Dot up to speed Tuesday morning on our way to work. "What makes you think either the Hanleys or the Donohues will talk to you?" she asked.

"Why wouldn't they?" I pulled my coat tight against the cold.

"I don't think the Donohues will fuss. They're all real nice. But I know Marjorie Hanley and she's a terrible snob. She thinks she's a cut above everyone else in the neighborhood. I can see her not talkin' to you just because it'll make you mad."

I knew Mrs. Hanley, too. She henpecked her poor husband half to death. If Mr. Hanley said the sky was blue, she'd snap and tell him it was pink and get him to agree. Her three sons had gone off to war. Two of them had died fighting Rommel in North Africa. The third was somewhere in the Pacific. She was always at church sayin' how brave they were. That is, when she wasn't railing against Roosevelt, about how if he were a decent human he'd send her only boy back to her. 'Cept she didn't have anything on the Sullivan family from Iowa. They'd had five boys on board the *Juneau*, which had been torpedoed by the Japanese last month. The government wasn't saying anything about survivors, but there'd been so little information in the news that things couldn't be good. But we didn't say that to Mrs. Hanley.

She also liked to drop big names, as if she knew them personally. Everybody else in the First Ward knew she read the society pages then gabbed about what she'd learned. The other ladies felt bad for her 'cause of her sons, so they let her.

"That's true," I said to Dot. "On the other hand, imagine her knowing she's friends with someone who's connected to a Delaware Park family, even if it is as a servant. That's something she'd want to brag about."

"You might be right." Dot burrowed into her coat. "You going after work?"

"Yep. Mom's not gonna be home because she's volunteering with the Red Cross, so no problems there. Pop won't mind."

"Want some company?"

I shot her a look. "Won't your folks be upset?"

"Nah." Dot's mischievous grin was just visible. "Dad's up at the Knights of Columbus and Ma is going to be at the Red Cross, too. They won't be home until late." Dot's parents made Mom look permissive and easy-going.

"Swell. We'll go as soon as we get home."

I was on my way to the assembly building when Emmie cornered me. "Betty. Any news about *Babcia*?"

"Nothing yet, at least nothing I haven't already told you."

"Then the investigation's over? After all, anyone in the Polish government is long gone."

"Cheer up." I patted her arm. The forlorn look on her face made me want to lift her spirits. "I got a lead on a maid in the Witkops' house who might be able to help."

Her expression brightened. "Thanks, Betty. You're the best."

The memory of the hopeful look on Emmie's puss fortified me against the cold as Dot and I got off the bus in the First Ward. "Who do you want to visit first?" I asked Dot.

The stop was at the corner of Louisiana and South Park, and Dot looked up and down Louisiana. "The Donohues," she said. "Not only is Mrs. Donohue likely to be nicer, they live closer."

The Donohue house was over on Alabama Street, between Miami and South Park, only a block away. It didn't look much different than mine, a neat, square building without much of a front yard. The only difference was Mrs. Donohue had two stars in the window instead of just one. She answered my knock within a few seconds. "Betty Ahern and Dot Kilbride," she said when she saw us, her apple-red cheeks glowing above a warm grin marred by two missing teeth. "Come in, come in. Lord it's cold! Give me your things. Can I get you anything? Tea or hot chocolate maybe?"

"No ma'm," I said. "We don't want to trouble you. It's just we have a simple question."

Mrs. Donohue bustled to the kitchen. "Certainly, my dear. Are you sure you don't want anything? Maybe a quick bite? Working in that factory must leave you with quite an appetite." She set out a chipped blue plate with a couple rolls on it and a bit of margarine.

"If you insist." I wasn't hungry, but Mom and Pop had drilled manners into me. I took a roll. "I'm looking for someone, a girl by the name of Bridget Innes. Last night, someone at the Ladies of Charity told me you might know her."

Mrs. Donohue settled her stout bum in a kitchen chair. I took the one opposite and waved at Dot to sit next to me. "Innes, Innes. No, I can't say as the name is familiar. What does she look like?"

"Red hair, freckles, green eyes, and a little gap in her teeth. Oh, and she has an Irish accent." I nibbled my roll. It was stale. Not from this week's ration.

"You'd think that would make her memorable." Mrs. Donohue's forehead wrinkled as she thought. "No, sorry dears. I can't say as I know her. Betty, how is your mother? Have you heard from your brother lately?"

Dot was right. Mrs. Donohue was much friendlier than Mrs. Hanley. Good for the purposes of asking questions, but it made it hard to get in and out of the house quickly. We spent nearly an hour talking about our parents, my brother Sean, her sons, the state of the war in general, and Buffalo politics before we were able to escape to the frigid air outside.

"Lord!" Dot blew out a breath. "I thought she was gonna talk all night."

"She's all alone," I said. "Both her sons are overseas and her husband died last summer, I think. We should've expected it."

"You still want to talk to the Hanleys?"

I glanced at my wristwatch. It was nearly five and the sun was close to completely set. "Yes. I don't know when we'll get another chance."

"Meaning a time when my folks are out and your Mom is busy." Dot grinned.

"Exactly. Let's go."

Our pace was brisk as we set down Alabama. The Hanleys lived down near the First Ward Community Center on Hamburg Street. Once we got there, we stood outside, taking in the light from the front window and the front of the house. Unlike the neighbors, who had Christmas decorations up that had obviously been handmade, the Hanleys' decorations were store bought. 'Cept not from a nice place like Hens and Kelly. More like the five and dime.

Dot clucked her tongue. "Tacky."

"Don't say anything." I knocked. "Or if you must, they are the most gorgeous things you've ever seen."

She shook her head at the sad evergreen wreath on the door. "I hope she doesn't ask. I don't think I can lie that good."

Mrs. Hanley answered the door after my second knock. "What do you want?" she asked.

"Evening, Mrs. Hanley. Can we come in?" I waved at Dot. "It won't take but a minute, but it's real cold out here. I don't want you to catch chill."

"Oh, I suppose." Mrs. Hanley held the door open barely long enough for us to get inside then shut it with a snap. "Quick, tell me what you need. Supper's on and I don't want to burn it."

While I hadn't expected the same welcome as at the Donohue house, I thought she'd be friendlier than this. "What nice Christmas decorations. We were admiring them before we knocked. Weren't we, Dot?" I stepped back and trod on Dot's foot.

"Ow, wha—yes, we were," she said. "Just beautiful."

"Well, thank you," Mrs. Hanley said, unbending a little. "You said you wanted something?"

"Yes. Fact is, Mrs. Hanley, I'm looking for someone and I think you're just the person to help." The way to this woman's heart was flattery, so I laid it on thick. "After all, you know just about everybody."

She preened a little. "I am familiar with most anybody in Buffalo who's worth knowing. Why just the other day—"

She knew them all right. From reading the paper. "I'm sorry to interrupt you, Mrs. Hanley," I said in a voice sugary enough to give me a toothache, "but I don't want to take up too much of your time."

"Oh." She was obviously disappointed to not yak about her "connections," but she had mentioned supper. "Yes?"

"I'm looking for a girl named Bridget Innes. She's a maid to the Witkop family. You know, the ones in Delaware Park who hosted the party for the Poles when they were here earlier this month. I know if anybody could help me, it would be you."

"Of course I know the Witkops. What a wonderful event." Mrs. Hanley permitted herself a small smile. "Innes, Innes. Bridget Innes. No, it doesn't ring a bell." She wandered off toward the kitchen.

She was gonna make me work for it. I motioned to Dot and we followed. The kitchen boasted a strong smell of onions and not much else. A sorry looking loaf of bread rested on the counter.

Instead of reprimanding us for following, Mrs. Hanley bent to open the oven door and spooned thin gravy over a tiny cut of meat.

"Are you sure?" I asked "I mean, if anyone knows someone connected to a Delaware Park family, you must. I felt sure you were the exact person to talk to."

"You are right, of course." She straightened and shut the oven. "That party at the Witkops', it was *divine*. Their cook must have worked for days, simply days. All those complicated dishes. The ladies' clothes were simply amazing and the men, so handsome. And the artwork in the house, so lovely."

All of which was easily learned from the snaps in the paper. But I played along. "I can't believe you don't know Bridget. I was just down at the Ladies of Charity with Mom, and the women down there were certain she was a guest of yours and not too long ago."

"Bridget you said the name was? No, it definitely doesn't mean anything to me." Mrs. Hanley pursed her lips. She sliced the loaf. "I can't imagine why they'd think that. No, I don't think I know any of the household help, my dear. A woman like Mrs. Witkop must employ so many maids, honestly, I can't even imagine."

I couldn't think why Mrs. Hanley wouldn't admit to knowing Bridget.

Then it hit me. She wouldn't admit to knowing the servants, only the rich folks. I'd have to think of another way to approach her. "I must be wrong, then. Mrs. Gurley and Mrs. O'Toole were sure you knew Bridget. Maybe they were thinking of another Irish girl who works for a wealthy family. I'm sorry to bother you."

"Oh, that's quite all right. Do you mind seeing yourself out?"

"Marjorie? When will supper be ready?" Mr. Hanley came into the kitchen and started at the sight of Dot and me. "Hullo. Dot Kilbride and Betty Ahern, right? I didn't know you were visiting." He turned to his wife. "Are they staying for supper?"

"No, sir," I replied. "I mean, yes, that's us and no, we aren't staying. We're looking for someone and we hoped Mrs. Hanley could help us."

"Looking for someone?" Mr. Hanley turned a puzzled expression from his wife, who'd gone silent and still, to us. "Who?"

"Nobody, just a hired girl from one of the rich families. Like I spend a lot of time bothering over that, what with your lazy body to take care of," Mrs. Hanley said in a clipped voice. "Betty and Dot were just leaving. Goodbye, girls."

It was a clear dismissal. Drat. The entry of Mr. Hanley sure had soured his wife's mood. "Thanks for the help, Mrs. Hanley." I tilted my head toward the door, indicating to Dot we needed to go.

"I'll see them out," said Mr. Hanley.

"Anything to get you out of my kitchen," Mrs. Hanley waved us out.

On the way to the front, Mr. Hanley said, "You said you are looking for someone?"

"Yes," I said. "It's a girl named Bridget Innes. She works for the Witkop family up in Delaware Park."

"She has red hair and green eyes," added Dot. "Oh, and an Irish accent."

Mr. Hanley pondered this a moment. "Sounds like a girl who Marjorie talked about when she got home from the Ladies of Charity meeting. Last week I think it was. No more than the week before."

Eureka! "You sure?" I asked.

"Quite sure." Mr. Hanley beamed. "Come to think of it, I saw her myself. I stopped by the meeting to drop off some discarded rubber from work. The girl said she knew Marjorie's grandmother's people back in Ireland. Very nice, she was. You're right, she works as a maid for the Witkops. Live in, I believe she said. So happy to find people she knew here. She's all by herself, poor lass."

The visit hadn't been a bust after all. "If you can get Bridget a message, that would be swell."

Mr. Hanley opened the door. "I'm not sure I'll be back at the Ladies of Charity this week, but I can try. Maybe I'll ask Marjorie to do it. What's the message?"

I hoped Mr. Hanley would find time 'cause I was fairly sure Mrs. Hanley didn't do anything her husband suggested, at least not willingly. "Would you please tell her that Betty would like to talk to her, soon as she has the opportunity, and I'm willing to buy her a cup of tea and a muffin for her time." If that offer didn't get her out of Delaware Park, I wasn't sure what would.

Chapter Eighteen

Wednesday morning brought a drop in the temperature plus a brisk wind. I wondered if I could transfer to a Bell factory somewhere warmer, like Florida. The air was dry and icy, and the cold cut right through my many layers of clothes. At least there wasn't any snow. Then again, I'd rather have mounds of white stuff up to my thighs and a temperature closure to thirty than the biting air.

Dot and I didn't talk much on the ride to work. We were too busy keeping our scarves tightly wound around our faces. When the bus deposited us at Bell, we scurried to the time clock then to the assembly building, which was blessedly warm despite the large space. Or maybe it just felt that way after being outside.

"Whew! I bet it isn't this cold in the Arctic," Dot said. "Almost makes me envious of the guys in North Africa. Least they're warm."

"Yeah." I tucked a grease pencil behind my ear and made sure all my tools were ready for use. "It's grand. Except for the tanks and the shelling, that is."

Dot bit her lip. "I'm sorry, Betty. I didn't think. I'm sure you'd rather Tom be here with you."

I waved her off. "Forget it, I'm in a mood." The assembly line clanked to life.

Dot watched a fuselage travel toward her and stop. "You think Bridget will send an answer?"

"A better question is whether Mr. Hanley will let her know I want to meet her." I twisted the electrical wires for the instrument panel.

At that moment, Emmie passed me. "Psst. Betty. I have somethin' for ya."

She handed me an envelope that contained two sheets of paper and glanced around. Prob'ly looking for Mr. Satterwaite, who'd like nothing more than to catch us passing notes when we should be working.

He was nowhere to be seen, so I laid down my tools and took the paper. "What is it?"

"A letter *Babcia* wrote. The mail returned it yesterday. I can't think why it took so long, but it did."

I was tempted to brush it off, but I realized Emmie wouldn't bother me with any old letter. "Who's it to?"

"Josef Pyrut, the Polish undersecretary."

I whistled and unfolded the sheet.

Dot, who stood on the other side of the assembly line ignored the plane in front of her and craned her neck. "What's it say?"

"Dunno. It's in Polish."

Emmie brushed back her curls. "That's the actual letter. I asked Daddy to translate it. Look at the second sheet. I figured you'd want both." She squeaked. "Here comes Mr. Satterwaite. Quick, hide it. I'll talk to you later." She hurried back to her place before she was caught.

I folded the paper and put it in my pocket. "Look sharp, Dot." I picked up my tools and went back to work.

Moments later, Mr. Satterwaite stalked over. "Miss Ahern, Miss Kilbride. Is everything all right over here? I thought I saw you talking to Miss Brewka. Were you passing notes?"

Dot focused on the fuselage looking like the perfect worker. I hefted a wrench. "No, sir Mr. Satterwaite. Everything's swell. You must've been mistaken."

He sniffed. "I'm watching you, Miss Ahern. I won't have you disrupting my shifts, like last month." He turned and stomped off with as much outrage as he could, considering his pudgy frame.

I shook my head and went back to work. Did he not remember my role in all that or did he not want to remember?

I wasn't able to read Pelagia's letter until lunch. I unpacked my sandwich and apple, and scanned the spidery writing. The only words I recognized were "Josef Pyrut" and "Pelagia Brewka." I turned over the envelope. "No wonder this was returned."

"Why's that?" Dot asked, leaning over to read from her seat next to me.

"The address. Pelagia addressed it to City Hall here in Buffalo, but sent it directly to Josef." The words Return to Sender were stamped across the address. "They prob'ly spent a couple of days trying to figure out if he worked here in Buffalo before sending it back."

"What's it say?"

I set aside the Polish to focus on the second sheet. It was written in a much stronger handwriting and had to be Mr. Brewka's. I'd seen Emmie's writing and it was tiny. He hadn't dictated his work. I cleared my throat and read.

> *Dear Mr. Josef Pyrut. You don't know me, but there is the chance we are related. My name is Pelagia Brewka. Before I married, my last name was Ferchow. My parents are from near Breslau. In my family tree, there is a Josef Pyrut. He may be you or not, but I am presuming on the relation to ask a favor. There is a man here in Buffalo. He calls himself Sebastian Witkop, but he strongly resembles a man I worked for back in Poland. He was a child, but I worked for his father. His name there was Sebastian Witkowski.*

Dot, who now hung on my arm, set down her lunch. "Hah, he did change his name. At least Mrs. Brewka thought so. She recognized him 'cause he looks like his dad." Her crow of excitement drew looks from the other girls.

"Yeah, yeah. Shhh. Let me finish." I shook her off.

This man, Witkowski, he has money. He says he earned it through investments, at least that's what the papers say. I believe differently. If you would be willing to meet me, I would like to talk to you. I believe it has meaning for the Polish resistance now, and is something you should be aware of especially as I read you are to be received at Witkowski's house for a party when you arrive in Buffalo. Please let me know as soon as you can by return post if you can see me. Respectfully, Pelagia Ferchow Brewka

I flipped the paper over. There was no writing on the back. I checked the original letter, but nothing was there, either.

"That's it? What was the information?" Dot asked and grabbed the letter out of my hands.

"She doesn't say." I picked up the second half of my sandwich and chewed thoughtfully. "When we talked to Bridget, she said there was a lot of Polish art in the house. If Witkop really is Witkowski, that makes sense. He brought it to Buffalo. Which means he prob'ly had dough back in Poland."

Dot handed back the letter. "But Lee said a lot of the Poles were, not serfs, but not landowners, either. I mean, they worked the farms, but the money and goods went to the rich folks. Then the Germans came and took it all away because of the war with the French. So why'd he have money?"

I took the sheets, folded them up, and put them back in my pocket. "It's like we thought. The older Witkowski was friendly with the Germans. And that's why he did it."

"What's why?"

I studied the rest of my lunch. "Why he changed his last name. Nobody would care if he was Polish once he got to the States. And it's not a particularly hard name to pronounce."

Dot blinked her eyes, expression perplexed. "He wanted to fit in? Sound more English? Break with his life in the Old World?"

"Could be." I demolished the rest of my sandwich in two bites. "There's another reason. He was trying to hide."

"I s'pose. From who, though?"

I gathered up my trash. "And why?"

* * *

After dinner, I ran down the street to show Pelagia's letter to Lee. I ran not just 'cause I was in a hurry, but 'cause I was sure if I stood still I'd freeze in that spot and not thaw until April.

Lee brought me to the kitchen, where he smoked and read. "Yowza," he said when he finished.

"She knew something embarrassing to old Witkop, that's for sure." I took back the paper. "And she wanted the exiled government to know. She thought it was important."

"Was she related to Pyrut?" Lee nodded at the letter.

"I don't think it mattered." I read the letter for the dozenth time. "She didn't know, but she might have been and she hoped that possibility was enough to get Josef to agree to meet."

"Do you think he did? Is that why he left the party, to meet Pelagia?"

I paused a moment. "She was dead by then, remember? Besides, the letter never reached him, did it? How would he have known she wanted to meet? No, I don't think the two were in touch. He left that party for another reason."

Lee inhaled, then blew out a stream of smoke. "Too bad she didn't say what it was about."

"Sure would make things easier." I drummed my fingers on the scrubbed table-top. "It had to be something about Witkop-Witkowski. She mentions him by name. My guess is that it was about how he really got his money." I drummed them again.

Lee set his cigarette in an ashtray. "Lemme see that envelope again."

I handed it over.

He peered at the slit edge. "This was opened before it was returned."

I leaned in. "How can you tell?"

"Here." He pointed at the ragged edge, which was slightly shiny. "That's clear cellophane tape. Someone at City Hall opened this and sealed it back up before it was returned."

"At least someone did it before it got to Emmie." I took the envelope and sat back down. "I wonder why she didn't mention that."

"Maybe she didn't think it was important." He picked up his smoke.

I turned the envelope over in my hands. An open letter brought an unknown person into the mix. "It coulda been opened 'cause they were trying to find out who Josef Pyrut was. Nothing more."

"We should try and find out," Dot said.

She was right. Rats. How would I do that? I put the thought aside for the moment. "Emmie told me they came from the Prussian part of Poland."

"Prussia punished the Poles for supporting France in the Franco-Prussian War," Lee said, stabbing the air with his cigarette.

He was such a history nut. "What if…"

"Yeah?"

"Do you think this Witkowski, I dunno, worked for the Prussians in some way?"

"How?"

"Maybe he informed on his neighbors, or passed on information about the French to the Prussians, or…something like that. It's dumb to think he had military intelligence, or that kind of dope."

Lee puffed. "Not so dumb. If the Polish were supportive of the French, maybe they knew stuff about troop movements, that kind of thing. If the other Poles didn't know Witkop-Witkowski was really on the side of the Prussians, they might've told him and he passed it on to the invaders. They might have rewarded him with money, art, or valuables."

"Yeah, maybe things they'd taken from other Poles." I rubbed my forehead. "But who cares about that? It was years ago. All those folks are prob'ly long dead by now. "

We sat in silence. Then Lee said, "What if he's up to it again?"

I sat up straight. "You mean the Nazis? Don't be a sap, he doesn't know anything about the U.S. military, does he?"

"Maybe not." He stubbed his cigarette out in the dregs of chicory in a nearby cup. "But he could be giving them other things, like money. And remember, Buffalo's a big manufacturing spot, what with GM and the steel production, and even Bell. He could be stealing designs for the planes and passing that information."

Lee's words hit me like a hammer. The info he talked about was just as valuable as numbers of soldiers, tanks, and ships. I opened my mouth, then shut it again.

"I don't think I've ever seen you speechless." He got up from the table and took the dirty cup to the sink. "Anyway, it sure does make it likely Emmie is right. Her grandmother was murdered."

I stood and picked up a towel to dry the dishes. "The killer knew she was gonna spill the beans to Josef and got to her?"

"Or he was afraid she already had. That's why he had to kill Pyrut, too."

"That means Sebastian knew about Pelagia's letter and was able to intercept it."

"I admit it's a tricky point. 'Course that might be why the letter was opened. He might have friends in City Hall who found out for him. Heck, he prob'ly does." He glanced at me. "You don't have to help, I'll just leave them in the rack."

"I don't mind." We worked in silence. I mulled over Lee's words. Pelagia had died before the Polish government got to town. That meant her killer was local. Another point in favor of Witkop-Witkowski's guilt. If he somehow knew Pelagia had written the letter, but he didn't know if Josef had gotten it, so he had to die, too. "We still don't—"

"Lee!" Mr. Tillotson stumbled into the kitchen, face red. "Boy, what have you done with my whiskey?" He was drunk. Not only was he staggering and slurring his words, he reeked of booze.

Lee dropped the cup he'd been washing into to the sink, where it landed with a splash. "You've had enough, Dad." He moved so he was between his pop and me.

"The hell I have. That bottle was two-thirds full. Where is it?"

"I don't know."

"Liar. You poured it out, didn't you, you ungrateful, little..." Mr. Tillotson pushed his son, but his balance was so bad he was the one who staggered, not Lee.

I grabbed my coat. "I should go." Lee would not want me witnessing this.

"Good idea. We'll finish our talk later," he said, not looking at me.

Mr. Tillotson took a few unsteady steps in my direction. "Now who is this pretty lassie? Don't go, sweetheart. I'll open a new bottle, and you and I can share a dram, what do you say?"

Lee maneuvered to stay between us. "That's Betty Ahern, Dad. You know her. She's leaving."

Mr. Tillotson blinked like an owl. "Scared away another one, huh? You sissy. Nothing but a mama's boy, clinging to her skirts. Did breaking that leg take away your manhood?"

"Enough." Lee's voice was hard, but I could see the shine of tears in his eyes. "Betty, scram. Use the back door."

"I said stay!" Mr. Tillotson roared and tried to push past Lee. When he couldn't, he swung a meaty fist, completely missed, and stumbled, crashing into the stove.

"Betty, get out!"

I didn't need to be told a fourth time. I grabbed my things and scrambled outside. Behind me, I could hear the rumble of Mr. Tillotson's voice, and Lee's quieter voice, its tone just as harsh. I didn't think about the cold as I pulled on my coat and mittens, and walked home.

Oh, Lee, I thought. My poor friend. This was one case I couldn't solve.

Chapter Nineteen

I worked Thursday, but I couldn't tell you what I did. I moved through the day without paying attention to the tasks, which earned me two reprimands from Mr. Satterwaite, including a threat to dock my pay, which I knew was mostly guff. He liked to pretend he had more authority than he did, slinking around with his slicked-back Boris Karloff hair. But I always thought of him more as a slapstick cartoon villain. Annoying, comical, but not all that threatening.

On the way home, Dot's normally cheerful pinup girl smile was all the more noticeable since it was missing. I'd told her about Pelagia's letter and the incident last night at the Tillotson house. While she had been properly puzzled by what Pelagia could possibly have known, Lee's situation really brought her down. "D'ya think we should go see Lee when we get home?"

My answer was immediate. "He'd be embarrassed and get mad at us. If we go, we have to talk about something other than his pop."

"Betty—"

"He won't thank us for gettin' nosy. Until recently, he hadn't talked much about his pop's drinking. I only saw it last night 'cause I was in the house. I'm pretty sure a good bit of Lee's anger came from that."

"You don't want to help him?"

My gaze snapped from the cold, gray landscape to her and I bristled. "'Course I want to help him. But I can't stop his pop from being a swigger. Lee's stubborn and he's proud. He's got moxie. When he's ready for help, he'll ask. Until then, we keep our lips zipped. Got it?"

She nodded, a little glum. After a moment, she asked, "What are you gonna do about Pelagia's letter?"

I rubbed my temple. "I dunno. It's clear now she knew something that could at least hurt the Witkop reputation. Maybe more. But unless she left that hidden somewhere, I'll never be able to discover exactly what." Except, it all brought me back to the same point. Who really cared about something that might've happened over fifty years ago?

Dot pressed her lips together and said nothing.

"Bridget."

Dot tilted her head to the side. "Huh? We were talking about Pelagia."

"Yes, but she's dead and we can't talk to her. That's what Bridget knows, whatever Pelagia had on the Witkops. It all makes sense. That time we saw her with the son, what was his name?"

"Paul."

I snapped my fingers, not a very impressive gesture while I wore mittens. "She looked like a cat on a hot roof while he was in the room. She knows about him and his family, she saw Josef get involved, and she's all twitchy as a result. I bet he's threatened her." I thought a moment. "I wonder why he's not in the service."

"4F?"

"Or his daddy paid someone off." The thought turned my stomach.

Dot shook her head. "Unless Bridget talks to you, how are you s'posed to know for sure?"

I slumped in my seat. Dot had hit the nail on the head. I had to convince Bridget to spill the beans, all my theories were for nothing. One of the tough-guy detectives would intimidate her into talking, but I didn't think that was the right move. I needed the finesse of Nick Charles in my approach.

If she didn't send me a note soon, I'd go back to Delaware Park.

The sun had set over Lake Erie and the air was cold enough to freeze bare flesh in minutes. There was no sign of Cat. Smart animal that he was, he had prob'ly holed up in his box or in some other warm spot to spend the night. Inside the house, I unwound my muffler and headed for the kitchen, and the sound of two female voices. Mom had company.

"Hey Mom, what's—" I broke off at the sight of Mrs. Hanley. "Hello, Mrs.

Hanley. What brings you over on such a cold night?"

Mom stood and took the cups from the table. "She came to see you."

Me? But the only reason Mrs. Hanley would see me was… "Did Mr. Hanley give Bridget my message?"

Mrs. Hanley sniffed. "No, I did. She said she'd meet you at the soda shop on the corner of South Park and Sidway tomorrow at seven. At night, of course, as she won't be able to get away from the family until after dinner."

And I would be at work in the morning. "That's swell, Mrs. Hanley. Thank you for your help." Now I would find out some of the skinny on the Witkops.

Mrs. Hanley rose and slipped on her coat. "I'll see you next week, Mary." She glanced at me. "As I told you, I'd keep a close eye on this girl. She's set herself up for trouble with all the questions." She buttoned up and left the room with a dramatic huff.

Mom said nothing as she rinsed the cups and put them in the drying rack. "How was work?" she asked, back to me.

"Fine." I wrinkled my forehead. "You aren't gonna ask what that was about or reprimand me or anything?"

She dried the counter, then turned to wipe the table. "The day I take Marjorie Hanley's advice about how to raise my children will be a sad day indeed."

I smothered a smile.

"I'm sorry about her boys, of course, but the whole neighborhood knows they were on a bad path. The Army was the best thing that ever happened to them. Lord knows they needed a firm hand, and they weren't going to find it at home, not with a mother who doted on them and a father who's been henpecked half to death." She folded the towel. "But what *was* that about? I didn't know you talked to Mrs. Hanley."

"Not as a daily event." I emptied my lunch pail, rinsed it in the remaining soapy water, and put it next to the coffee cups. "She knows someone I need to talk to is all. I asked her husband to pass a message. I guess she didn't want him to do it."

"For one of your…investigations?"

I turned, expecting to see a disapproving frown on Mom's face. Instead her face wore an expression of resignation, as if I was one of the boys and had gotten into something she didn't quite approve of, but knew she couldn't stop. "Yes." I studied her. "What? You look funny."

She sighed, came over and brushed aside a lock of my hair that had come loose. "You do seem determined to break tradition, Betty."

"What tradition?"

"Of what a girl is supposed to be like. You should be getting married, raising a family, maybe buying a nice house. With any luck, Tom would get a job at the steel plant and you could afford to live in one of the suburbs. Hamburg, maybe."

I huffed a laugh. "The war kinda interrupted that, Mom. Not me."

"I know. But this detecting. Is it necessary?"

"Necessary?" I thought a moment. "No, I s'pose not. But Mom, I've helped folks. Maybe not in big ways, 'cept for that whole sabotage thing at Bell of course, but little stuff. And I like doin' it."

She crossed her arms. "You do seem to be good at it."

"Does this mean you and Pop will lift my curfew?" I could barely hope.

"Oh no. Just because I can't stop you from doing this, doesn't mean you can go gallivanting around at all hours of the night."

Rats. It was worth a shot.

"Just promise me one thing," she said.

"Yeah?"

"Don't become one of those hard-drinking men from the movies. I'd have to draw the line at that."

I wrapped my arms around her shoulders and planted a kiss on her cheek. "Promise."

Chapter Twenty

Friday was another day that passed in a blur. I went to work, I made planes, but I couldn't have told you much more than that. As we got off the bus in the First Ward and walked toward home, Dot shivered next to me. "What time are you meeting Bridget?"

It was another night where the cold cut right through my clothes, helped along by a brisk wind off the lake. Christmas was fast approaching and I wondered if baby Jesus had had to deal with cold like this. Wasn't the Holy Land in the desert? Wouldn't it be warm there? "Seven. I can't believe Mom didn't fuss more about it when Mrs. Hanley came last night to tell me."

"Neither can I."

Dot tucked her mittened hands under her armpits. "You want company?"

"D'ya think you can get out? What will your parents say?"

"I'll tell 'em I'm going Christmas shopping. 'Course that means I'll have to really go. You buy presents for your family yet?"

"Some." I'd sent Tom two good pairs of socks a couple of weeks ago. His last letter had mentioned how he didn't have enough and was always doing wash. I had model airplanes for the boys and a set of the newest sewing patterns for Mary Kate. I'd been setting aside a portion of my pocket money for a month, saving up to buy Pop some good tobacco for his pipe and a nice set of handkerchiefs for Mom. I finally had enough dough to pick them up this weekend. But I hadn't come up with anything for Lee or Dot yet. "What do you want for Christmas?"

"An end to the war and all the rationing."

"You can't buy that with S&H Green Stamps."

She giggled.

"I'm serious, what do you want?"

"A new lipstick. Mine is just about out and with all my paycheck going to my parents, I can't buy a new one."

A lipstick was possible. "Well, you be a good girl and maybe Santa Claus will bring you one." I elbowed her. "Back to business. If you can get away tonight that would be good. Why don't I stop at your house and we'll go together? A story that you're going shopping might be better if you have a friend with you."

"Good idea. I'll see you later."

* * *

I went to Dot's house about quarter 'til seven, giving us plenty of time to hoof it to the soda shop. "Is it going to warm up any time soon?" she asked, her breath a frosty cloud in front of her, despite her scarf.

"Don't talk, I think it makes it worse." I looked at the buildings. "Here we are."

Once inside, we went to the counter and each bought a Coke. Bridget wasn't there yet, so we picked a table and waited.

A little after seven, an older lady entered the shop. I stared when she spotted us and made a beeline for our table. "You're Betty, aren't you? I saw you through the window the day you met Bridget."

"Yes, that's me. This is Dot, I mean Dorothy. Where's Bridget?"

"She won't be coming." The woman unwound her wrap. "May I sit?"

"Sure." I waved at the seat across the table. "What do you mean she isn't coming?"

"Does this place serve coffee? I could use a warm drink." She looked over at the soda jerk at the counter. "Young man, may I please have a cup of coffee?"

"Yep, but I don't wait tables. You gotta come and get it." He pulled a coffee pot from the machine and filled a cup.

By now the woman had taken off her coat, revealing a stout middle to go with her graying hair and kind face. She reminded me of Marjorie Main, who played Bogie's mother in *Dead End* and who always played that type. She tried to hang her stuff, but first dropped her gloves and scarf, then her coat as she juggled them and attempted to open a change purse.

"I'll get your joe," I said.

The woman removed some money from the blue pouch. "Thank you."

I took the coins, went to the counter, and got the coffee from the soda jerk. Then I returned to the table. "Now what about Bridget?" I asked as I set the cup and saucer in front of her. "I forgot to ask if you wanted sugar or milk."

"No, black is fine." She took a sip and closed her eyes, obviously savoring the taste. "It is so nice to taste real coffee. Even working for a moneyed family like the Witkops, some things you just can't get."

I restrained myself from grabbing the woman and shaking her.

Dot must've sensed my growing frustration, 'cause she laid a hand on my arm. "I'm sorry, but who are you? I missed your name."

The woman didn't speak. Then she set down the cup and patted her mouth with a napkin. "So silly of me. I'm Mildred Janson. I'm the housekeeper at the Witkop house."

"You were saying about Bridget, that she's not coming? Did something or someone get in her way?"

"In a manner of speaking." Mildred took another drink. She had to be stalling. Then she continued. "I'm sorry to say Bridget is dead." Her eyes glistened and she busied herself with her coffee.

"What?" Dot yelped.

"When did that happen?" I asked. "She was fit as a fiddle when I saw her last week. Some people I know said she was at a Ladies of Charity meeting Friday and she was healthy as a horse."

"It was very sudden." Mildred toyed with her cup. "It happened this morning. First thing I do when I arrive at the house is arrange for breakfast for the family, then eat with the live-in staff." She took an oversized handkerchief out of her purse and blew her nose.

"You don't live at the house with the Witkops?"

"No. Bridget does, but I leave after the dinner things are washed up at night." She dabbed her eyes and took a deep breath. "I'm sorry, I didn't think I'd get this emotional."

I patted her hand.

Mildred sniffed and continued. "This morning we were lucky to have eggs and toast with a bit of jam. Then I asked Cook to brew a cup of tea for Bridget. She doesn't drink coffee. She spooned in her sugar and milk, like she always did, but she complained of the taste. She said it was bitter, no matter how much sugar she used, so she poured it down the drain. What a waste."

I had to agree with her. Using a lot of sugar was bad enough. Pouring it down the sink was almost a crime.

"Two hours later, we were washing the last of the breakfast things, then... oh, it was dreadful." She shuddered at the memory. "She fell to the floor, and screamed and twitched something awful. I thought she was having a seizure. It happened a few times. She sort of went rigid and I could tell she was in a great deal of pain. I called for Mr. Charles, our butler, but by the time he arrived the poor girl was dead." Mildred dabbed at the tears leaking from her eyes. "Terrible it was. Just terrible." She blew her nose and patted at her cheeks.

The description of Bridget's death tickled a memory in my head, but I couldn't pin it down. "Did you call an ambulance or anything?"

Mildred composed herself and nodded. "Mr. Charles did. Of course they couldn't do anything, but here's the funny thing. The ambulance men called the police soon after they arrived."

Dot and I exchanged a look. "The cops?"

"Yes." Mildred nodded vigorously. "They asked us all sorts of questions. Who drank tea, was it loose or bagged, who used sugar, and whatnot. They were quite interested in the servant's sugar bowl. I believe they took it with them. Then they had all sorts of questions about who uses it."

"And? What did you tell 'em?"

"Bridget is the only one of us who uses sugar," Mildred said. "Mr. Charles and I have mostly stopped drinking coffee at the house. Neither of us can bear the taste, even sweetened. The family, of course, uses a completely different set of tea and coffee things, so they have their own sugar bowl, with cubes and tongs."

The police suspected something and the sugar played into it. I was sure of it.

"Oh, one other thing."

"Yes?" Dot asked, while I tried to pin down the thought teasing the edges of my brain.

"They were very interested in whether we had any rat poison in the house. Of course we don't keep that sort of thing in the kitchen. I insist anything dangerous stay in the garden shed." Mildred puffed up. "I will not have any of that in the kitchen, and that's a fact. It's much too easy for it to be confused with something else. 'Mark my words, Mr. Charles,' I told him one day when he tried storing it in the pantry, 'you leave that in the kitchen and someone's bound to become ill.' Then I told him—"

"Yes, yes," I said, interrupting what I was sure could become a long, drawn out speech. "Do you have rat poison?"

"Of course. I just told you, we keep it in the shed." Mildred took a sip of coffee. "It reminded me of a scene in one of those books, the mysteries that woman writes."

"Agatha Christie?" Dot asked. At my look of surprise, she muttered, "Ma likes to read 'em at night before bed."

"Yes, that's her." Mildred shook her head. "Oh such horrible deaths some of those people have. But poor Bridget, well, it reminded me of Mrs. Christie's writing." Her eyes glistened again, and she once again dabbed with the giant hankie.

Of course I'd heard of Mrs. Christie, even if I didn't read. I knew she used poison in a lot of her books. I had to talk to Detective MacKinnon. This wasn't something they'd be able to brush off as an accident, that I was sure of. The sound of Mildred's voice brought me out of my thoughts.

"Bridget told me last night she was going to meet you," Mildred was saying, with a catch in her voice. "I thought the least I could do was come tell you what happened, so you didn't think she'd changed her mind. She was always a very reliable girl."

I tapped my glass. "Did she say why she was coming?"

"Only that you'd asked to see her. Oh, and she had decided to tell you."

"Tell me what?"

Mildred shrugged her broad shoulders. "She didn't say." She pressed the hankie to her mouth.

Darn it. After I moment, I asked, "What kind of girl was Bridget? You said reliable, but was she a gossip or a sneak?" Not a gossip, or else she would've told Mildred what she was gonna say, but I had to ask.

"Neither. She was a hard worker, never complained, no matter what the task. Whether she had to clean the toilets or scrub the floors, it was all the same. She sang the most beautiful songs as she worked." Mildred sighed, dabbed her eyes again, and stared in to the bottom of her now-empty cup. "She used to say anything she had to do here was better than grubbing the dirt back in Ireland."

Maybe I was a cynic, but Mildred's reactions looked staged, like how she *thought* a person would react to the death of someone she knew, instead of a genuine feeling. I kept that opinion to myself, but resolved to ask Sam MacKinnon about it later.

"Then you had no complaints about her?" Dot asked. Her expression and dubious tone of voice said she had a lot of trouble swallowing the image of Bridget as an Irish angel. Or maybe she also suspected the quality of the housekeeper's grief.

Instantly, the tears dried and any sorrow evaporated from Mildred's face. "Well," she drew out the word, "I don't like speaking ill of the dead."

"But?" I prompted.

She paused, maybe thinking on how much to say. It was clear to me she *was* a bit of a gossip. The kind of witness a private dick liked to talk to. "She could be a bit too saucy with the master, if you know what I mean."

"Mr. Witkop?"

"No, his son. Mr. Paul. Not that he behaved much better. He'd pinch her bottom and oh, such cheeky retorts she'd give him! A couple of times I found them in the pantry, or in the downstairs butler's closet, her hair all mussed, apron askew. Obviously gone in for a secret cuddle and kiss." Mildred's voice was indignant. "A nice girl, Bridget was, but not in the same class as Mr. Paul. And it was horrible of him to lead her on, if you ask me."

I'd been right. Chances were Bridget had been with Paul the night of the party. "Do you know why Mr. Paul wasn't drafted? Most young men have been."

Mildred drew herself up. "I wouldn't know."

"What can you tell me about the visitors from the beginning of the month?"

She eyed her empty cup.

"Would you like another cup of coffee?" I asked, as I dug some coins out of my pocket.

She pushed the cup across the table. "Don't mind if I do."

Dot kept our guest entertained while I ordered another cup of java. "She can talk, can't she?" the soda jerk said as he handed me the steaming brown liquid.

"That she does," I said and returned to the table. "Here you go. Now, what about those visitors?"

Mildred sipped. "It was a big to-do. The work involved, my stars. All these strange dishes. Mr. Witkop gave Cook and me the recipes, all written on little pieces of paper. So old, some of them, it was hard to read the writing. I could barely see the ingredients to make the shopping list."

"Really?" Old recipes brought from Poland, maybe? Pelagia might have been right.

"Yes. 'Be careful of those, Miss Janson,' he told me. Well, I was as careful as I could be. So complicated some of them, meats I could only find from the Polish butchers at the Broadway Market. I did wonder where they came from." She drank. "Anyway, the guests were quite nice people. Not many of them spoke English, but they were all very polite. Mr. Paul and one of the young men seemed to hit it off quite well. At least, they talked a lot."

My breath quickened, and I felt Dot quivering beside me. "Which one?"

"Oh, let me see." Mildred tapped her lips. "Yes, the one who went missing, the secretary. What was his name now? Joseph, I think."

"Josef," Dot said. "Josef Pyrut."

Mildred snapped her fingers. "Yes, that's the one. So many drinks they shared. Clear liquid in little glasses."

I thought a moment. "Vodka?"

"I don't know. Mr. Witkop had it brought in special."

I tapped the table. "Josef, he stayed for the whole party?"

"Oh no." Mildred leaned in. "He left early, I'd say around nine o'clock. His boss was ever so angry. I couldn't understand the words, mind you, because he was speaking Polish, but his tone was all too clear. He scolded Bridget something fierce. As if the girl had anything to do with the young man disappearing. Although she did look guilty, her nice starched apron all wrinkled and her hair coming out of her cap. Maybe she was up for a little cuddling with more than Mr. Paul." She *tsked*. "What a shame Mr. Paul had to go to bed early. Not well, he said. Probably all that drinking."

"He did?" Dot blurted out. "Are you sure he went to bed?"

"Well," Mildred huffed. "That's a pretty picture. Accusing Mr. Paul of lying. And him such a nice young man. You don't know the half of it." She puffed up her chest. "I didn't follow him to bed. But he went up the stairs, and I didn't see him all the rest of the night. What else could he have done?"

"We didn't mean to accuse him of lying," I said, trying to soothe her. "Josef left around nine, Bridget looked like she'd been sneaking some hanky-panky, and Mr. Paul went to bed early? Do I have that right?"

"That's what I said." Mildred looked at the clock. "Lordy, look at the time. I must get back." She squeezed herself out of her chair and gathered her things. "I have chores before bed, I can't sit around chatting all night." She sniffed, as though we'd been the ones keeping her out. "I had to do my Christian duty by Bridget though, poor girl." She pulled out her hankie and sniffed again. "Good night to you." She bustled out.

"She didn't even say thank you for the coffee," Dot said in disgust. "Josef left around nine, huh? You think that's what Bridget was gonna tell you?"

"That and maybe more."

"Do you think Paul really went to bed, or was that an excuse so he could sneak out?"

"No self-respecting detective would buy his story without seeing him tucked in. Maybe not even then." I slipped on my coat and things, and headed for the door. "My money is on him sneaking out to meet Josef. And not for anything good."

Dot followed. "Is it just me, or was that woman a bit strange?"

"How so?"

"When she talked about Bridget." Dot tugged on her mittens. "First she was all upset, then she acted like she had a bit of juicy gossip. Then it was as if she remembered she was supposed to be mourning. Weird."

"It was not just you."

"What do you think happened to Bridget?"

The cold outside stole my breath and I had to take a moment before I answered. "I don't know. But the one thing I am sure of is that she didn't die of a heart attack."

Chapter Twenty-One

I had the nineteenth off, one of my alternate Saturdays. For all the good it would do me. Pelagia was dead. Josef Pyrut, dead. Now Bridget Innes. Was there anyone left to help me?

What was I gonna do? I considered going to the movies, like I did every Saturday I could. But in my current mood, I doubted I could pay attention, even to Flash Gordon. Yet I didn't want to sit at home. All that would lead to was fretting about Sean and Tom, and that wouldn't do anyone any good.

I could ride up to Delaware Park, bang on the Witkops' door, and ask, "Hey, did you all come from Poland and did you change your name?" I didn't see that as a successful strategy.

I would have to talk to Detective MacKinnon about Bridget. But I knew better than to bother him early on a Saturday morning after he'd caught a murder the previous night. Assuming he was the detective who got the case. It'd be easier for me if he was, but I wasn't too worried. Sam MacKinnon and I had built enough of a relationship that he'd slip me the dope even if he wasn't in charge.

I helped Mom wash up after breakfast, then put out a plate for Cat. Just my luck, Mom came back into the kitchen as I was about to go outside. "Elizabeth Ahern, where are you taking that saucer?" she asked.

I looked at the puddle of leftover milk and a few bits of chicken I'd saved from dinner the night before. There wasn't a story to tell about this one 'cept the truth. "It's for Cat."

"Excuse me?"

"Cat. You know, the gray stray that hangs around. We've been taking care of him, Mary Kate and I." I waited for the explosion.

It didn't come. Mom shook her head. "Betty, I've told you. We don't have enough to feed a stray. It's a cat. It'll take care of itself." She eyed me. "Then that's why there's a box of rags tucked behind the garbage cans, hmm?"

"Mom, it's ten degrees outside." I shot a glance at the outdoor thermometer. I wasn't far off the mark with my guess. "No living thing can keep itself safe in weather like that. Even the birds have left."

She tapped her foot.

"I'm not taking food that would feed us, I promise. Look." I held out the saucer. "That's the last of yesterday's milk. The chicken I took from my own plate last night."

"Does your father know about this?"

I gulped. "Yeah. He found out a couple of nights ago. He's not mad though. Just made me promise not to take food meant for the family."

"Typical." Mom sighed. "Fine, go ahead. But you listen to me. One, your father's right about the food."

"Yes, ma'am."

"Two, you'd better not bring it in the house. It stays outside."

I could hardly believe my ears. "Yes, ma'am."

"And three, if it ever brings any dead animals here, like mice, and leaves them on the doorstep, you'll be the one to clean it up. Understand?"

"Yes, ma'am. Thanks, Mom."

She sniffed and left, but I swore I saw a small smile on her face.

After I fed Cat, I went to Dot's. "Come in, it's freezing," she said when she opened the door. She had an apron on over her work clothes and a feather duster in her hand. "What's up?"

I told her about my dilemma. "I've run out of places to look."

She worried her lip. "Have you tried the library?"

"Dot, I'm not looking to borrow a book."

"No, dummy. I know that. But the librarian might have an idea of how to get the info about Witkop. I mean, when the police arrest someone, and he claims he came through Ellis Island, there's gotta be a way of checking that, right?"

She had a point. "The cops can prob'ly call direct, though."

"Maybe, but that means there might be a way for regular people to check." She pulled a loose feather off her duster. "It's worth a shot."

"I'm outta ideas, so why not? You don't look like you can join me, though." I tweaked her apron.

She groaned. "I wish. After I finish dusting, I have to wash the kitchen floor. I swear, I'm not much better than a hired maid in this place, least not on the weekends. It's like Ma saves up all the chores from the week and piles them into my free Saturdays."

I knew the Kilbrides had been less enthusiastic about Dot working at Bell than Mom had been about me. "You could tell her you've got things to do, you know."

Dot's peepers widened. "No way! I wouldn't put it past her to lock me in my room."

"Then you could sneak out the window."

She gave a rueful grin. "Face it, Betty. I'm just not as bold as you are when it comes to some things." She fixed her apron. "Tell me what you learn at the library?"

"Of course." I gave her a hug and left. Outside, I lit a cigarette. I knew Lee was working today, so no sense going to his place. I headed straight for the library.

The Buffalo and Erie County main library was located on Lafayette Square. With the stone exterior and turrets, it looked more like a rich guy's mansion than a library. Mary Kate always said it was a castle. I'd heard that Mark Twain gave the library the handwritten pages of *Huckleberry Finn.* Lee found this terribly interesting. Not me. Now, if the library had a first-take film reel of *The Maltese Falcon,* I'd be excited.

I walked up the steps to the main door and went inside. Even from the lobby, I could see oodles of books lining the walls. The library did have one thing going for it. It was warm. I approached the main desk. "'Scuse me," I said to the gray-haired woman at the desk.

She laid a finger on her lips. "Yes?" Her voice was soft, almost impossible to hear, even in the quiet building.

Mom told me that ever since I'd started working at Bell, where you had to shout to be heard in most places, I'd lost the ability to be quiet. I knew a library was s'posed to be an almost silent place. I didn't see why I couldn't talk in a regular voice at the front desk, though. All the people were over in the other room. I tried my best. "I'm hoping you can help. There's this family. I think they changed their name from the original Polish when they immigrated and I was wondering if there was a way to find out."

"Why don't you ask them?"

If all else failed I might have to, but I wasn't quite that brazen, no matter what Dot thought. "I don't know them all that well. It's more of a bet between me and a friend. Don't they keep track of that stuff at Ellis Island?"

"Not really." The woman paused to stamp a book for a mother and her little girl. Then she turned back to me. "Those who change their name often don't tell the immigration officials they've done so. They simply give the new name when they enter the country."

Rats. "But if a Polish family says their name is, oh, Smith let's say, wouldn't their accent kinda give it away? I mean, I don't see where very many Poles would be named Smith."

The librarian smiled. "You're right, but you're forgetting the sheer numbers of people who are coming in, dear. Immigration officials are so overwhelmed they take the name given, no questions. At least not if there aren't any other problems. People looking for a new life often want a new name. It's that simple."

This trip was a bust. "I don't s'pose the library keeps immigration records."

"No, dear. We're a lending library, not a records office." She paused. "Who is this family you're interested in?"

I hesitated. The Witkops had money and if I'd learned anything—from life and the pictures—it was money talked. From everything I'd learned, Mr. Witkop didn't want his original name known, if he was the one who had changed it. There could be some scary reasons he put Witkowski behind him. Could be he was Poland's equivalent to a gangster.

The librarian gazed at me, waiting for my answer.

What the heck? "It's the Witkops. See, my friend, Lee, and I were arguing about why Mr. Witkop would throw such a fancy party for the Polish government. I said maybe they were Polish and my friend said they weren't, that Witkop sounded more German. I'm trying to prove I was right, but looks like I can't. Thanks for your time." I turned to go and pulled on my mittens.

"Wait," the librarian said.

I paused and faced her.

"Come with me." She called to another woman to cover the front desk. She took some keys from under a drawer and beckoned.

I followed her through the main section of the library and eventually to a small room on the far end. Inside was a glass-covered table. The librarian unlocked the cover and lifted it. "Mr. Witkop made a donation to the library not that long ago. These books." She touched the leather covers.

I gave her a questioning look, and she nodded. Gingerly, I lifted out a book and skimmed the pages. "This looks like it's written in Polish." I looked at the inside of the front cover. In thin slanting script, it read *Witkowski*.

"Correct." The librarian nodded toward the book. "What you're holding is a book by Narcyza Żmichowska and is considered a precursor to Polish feminism. We also have books by Jozef Szujski, Adam Ansyk, and a copy of Henryk Sienkiewicz's *Quo Vadis*, which won the Nobel Prize for Literature in 1905."

It sounded very impressive. I put Narcyza's book down. "What do you mean feminist?"

"Narcyza was a nanny to Polish nobility and went with them to Paris, where she reunited with her brother. His revolutionary views and her stay in Paris changed her. She was quite the woman. She smoked cigars and thought women should have the vote."

'Cept for the cigars, she sounded like my kind of girl. "Why did Witkop donate all these books? I mean, they look original."

"They are." The librarian relocked the case. "He said he'd had them from his family, but his son had little interest in them. Since they were important works from Poland, he donated them to the library, where they could be appreciated. But he made the gift anonymously and did not want his name associated with them."

"The name inside the book I held, Narcyza's. It says Witkowski. You know, inside the cover. What about the others?"

"Yes, it's in all of them. He didn't say anything about it, and we didn't ask. Like you, I assumed the family changed their name, for whatever reason." She fixed me with a stern gaze. "I trust that you will respect his wishes and not advertise this all over Buffalo."

"No, ma'am. But why're you telling me?"

"You look like a nice girl. Also, I'm quite happy to help a woman win a bet over a man." Her eyes twinkled. "You see, my dear, we all have our ways of being feminist."

I thanked her and left. Mr. Witkop may have donated the books thinking he was breaking a tie to the old name, but he'd either forgotten, or not known, about the writing on the cover. Or he thought if he didn't mention it, no one would make the connection. But now I was certain. The Witkowskis had changed their name and Pelagia had worked for their family in Poland. Obviously, Mr. Witkop didn't want to be associated with them.

But why was it such a secret?

Chapter Twenty-Two

Sunday afternoon, I met up with Dot and Lee at his house. Cat tagged along. I think he wanted to keep an eye on us. It was too cold to stand outside, so I hid him inside my coat when we went into the kitchen. Once there, he leapt down with feline grace and checked out the digs.

"She said that, your mom?" Dot gazed in frank disbelief at me, then shifted her peepers to Cat. "Who'd have thought it? Does she secretly like cats or something?"

"No clue." I took a drag on my cigarette and looked at Lee. "You might wanna shut the door before he gets into the rest of the house."

Lee pushed the kitchen door closed.

"You shouldn't have brought him over, Betty," Dot said, disapproval stamped on her mug.

"He followed me. You try and tell a cat what to do. Go on." I pointed at her with my smoke. "It's too cold to leave him outside."

"Can we stop talkin' about the cat?" Lee sat down in a chair and rubbed his bad leg. He'd said before the cold made it ache and it was more than cold. After a warmer November than usual, we'd gone the other way. It was too cold to snow, but skin left uncovered was blue within a minute. His leg had to be giving him a lot of grief 'cause he was grumpier than he'd been in a while.

"Sorry," I said. I lit a gasper for him off mine and handed it over.

He inhaled. "Tell me again what the librarian said."

I did. "I think that's as close as we're gonna get to proving Witkop changed his name. Why else would he have all those books from Poland, written in Polish for Pete's sake?"

"Agreed." Cat jumped up on his lap and Lee obliged him by rubbing his ears. "I wonder if they'd show anyone off the street those books."

"Why d'you care?"

He shrugged. "I'd like to see 'em."

That was Lee. History buff and book fan. "And you wanted to get off the subject of pets."

"At least the books are important."

Dot broke in "You two, stop it." She put her hands on her hips. "Pets, books, whatever. How 'bout we talk about people?"

I smothered a smile. Dot didn't often take charge of things, but when she did, she was a force to be reckoned with. "Yeah, sure."

"Good." She sat down and Cat left Lee to go to her. "First up, Pelagia Brewka. Are we sure she didn't die of a plain old heart attack?"

"No," I said as I leaned against the counter. "As far as we know, she just up and died. Whatever her granddaughter says. I haven't learned anything that makes me believe otherwise."

"That could be our one coincidence," Dot said. The three of us agreed: One coincidence was kosher. More than that, and things smelled funny. "Next, Josef Pyrut."

"He was mugged," Lee said, smoke escaping his mouth as he spoke. "That's a crime. That makes his death a crime, whether it be murder or manslaughter."

She frowned. "How d'you know that?"

He shrugged. "Pulp novels."

They were my own source of info, so I couldn't argue. "I'll ask Detective MacKinnon what he thinks. But yeah, I think if the mugger beat Josef up so badly that he died, that would be murder."

Dot thought a bit, then nodded. "Okay, then there's Bridget."

"That's definitely murder," I said.

"You think there was poison in that sugar?" Lee asked as he ashed his cigarette.

"The cops sure do. Why else would they have taken it?" I laid my cigarette in the ashtray, then reached out and took Cat from Dot's lap. I'd found out that stroking his fur helped me think. He didn't mind the extra attention. "All these people have one thing in common."

Dot rested her chin on her hands. "The Witkops. Or the Witkowskis, whatever you want to call 'em."

"Exactly."

Lee sat up and ground out the stub of his smoke. "Pelagia worked for them in Poland, Josef visited with the Poles at the beginning of December, and Bridget worked for them now."

"And was more than just a maid to Paul, if the gossip is right," Dot said.

"I think it is." I ran my hands over Cat's soft gray body. "Pelagia kept saying 'he has to know' when she heard about the government visiting. That means she knew something."

Dot chewed her lip. "Well, maybe. Did she mean she had to tell him? Or she was looking for some information and he'd be the one who had it?"

"And did Pelagia talk to anyone else?" Lee asked.

"Dunno." They were good questions though. I'd been assuming Pelagia had been the one who wanted to do the telling, but maybe I was wrong. "For now, let's assume the first. That she had something to say. Did she tell Josef? Did he talk to Paul? And what about Bridget? She knew somethin'. You don't get poisoned for no reason."

We all were silent. Then Lee spoke up. "Did Pelagia ever visit the Witkops?"

I blinked. "I don't know. I s'pose I could ask the housekeeper, Mildred. There's one other person I just thought of."

"Who's that?" Dot asked.

"Mrs. Witkop. The night Lee and I saw Bridget with Paul, she didn't look happy to see her son hanging with riff-raff in the backyard."

Dot pursed her lips. "You think she was unhappy her son was fooling around with Bridget?"

"I'm sure she was."

"You might be right, but murdering the maid seems awful drastic," Lee said.

He played with Cat's tail. "Look. I think you should see if the housekeeper will talk some more. Then go see the detective. Maybe he'll spill to you about what's going on."

"Okay." Cat nuzzled my hands, clearly enjoying all the fuss. "It might have to wait until tomorrow, though. I don't know if he works Sundays and I'm sure not gonna track him down at home."

* * *

As it turned out, I didn't have to wait until Monday to talk to Detective MacKinnon. He was waiting in front of my house when I got home. "Where's your car?" I asked as I walked up.

He threw away his cigarette butt. "Based on your mother's reaction the last time I was here, I parked around the corner. She doesn't like me, does she?"

"It's not you. It's what the neighbors might think if a cop keeps visiting. But it's too cold to jaw out here. Come on inside." I led him to the door and went in. I got to the count of three before Mom appeared.

"Oh good, you're home. I was—" Her eyes narrowed. "What's he doing here?"

He doffed his fedora. "Good afternoon, Mrs. Ahern. Sorry to bother you, but I had some questions I hoped your daughter could answer for me."

She went to the living room window. "Where's your car? I didn't hear it."

"No, ma'am." He shot me a look. "I parked away from the house. I didn't want to disturb you or your neighbors."

She sniffed. "Well. I suppose I should offer you something to drink. We have a little coffee left. Tea maybe?"

I could see the war of her internal emotions on her face. She didn't want to be rude, but she didn't like having a police detective in the house. "I'll take care of it, Mom," I said. "I'm sure this won't take a lot of time. Detective MacKinnon is busy."

He twirled his hat. "Not long at all. I'll be out of your hair as quickly as I can."

She sniffed again, but I knew her well enough that she was mollified by my offer. "Very well. But talk in the kitchen, please, and keep your voices down. I'm listening to my Sunday radio program."

I guided the detective to the kitchen. "That went better than I thought it would. Are you sure you don't want something to drink?"

"Maybe a glass of water. I assured your mother I wouldn't be long. I don't want to break my promise." He laid his fedora on the table, brim up, and shucked off his coat. "It is ridiculously cold out there."

"I know you didn't come here to gab about the weather, Sam." I set the glass of water in front of him and took a seat. "What's got you edgy?"

He sat. "Is it obvious?" He moved the glass, but didn't drink. "Did you know Bridget Innes?"

I immediate went on edge. "Yeah, why?"

"Did you know she was dead?"

"I'd heard. Is that why you're here?"

He nodded. "Your name came up when we questioned the members of the household. Paul Witkop and his mother mentioned you in particular. They said you looked *shifty*."

I bristled. I did not look *shifty*. I had only been trying to talk to Bridget. "She was the maid at the Witkops' house. I knew who she was to say hello. We didn't get together regularly to flap our lips or anything." There was no sense tryin' to hide information from him. He was too good and I had a feeling he already knew the answer.

He dug in his pocket, prob'ly looking for notes. "The housekeeper..."

"Miss Janson."

He stopped. "Why am I not surprised you know her, too?"

I grinned. "I was s'posed to meet Bridget. Miss Janson came instead, to tell me Bridget had died."

"Then you were going to meet with the girl?"

"Yeah."

"What about?"

I spread my hands. "I dunno. Bridget didn't say. Miss Janson didn't know, either. I 'spect it was to tell me about Josef Pyrut." I traced my finger on the table. "I talked to her before, tryin' to get some dope on Josef. She was pretty insistent she didn't know anything. I think she did."

He leaned forward, pen at the ready. "Like what?"

How much should I tell him? He was investigating her death. "Let me ask something first. Was she murdered?"

He hesitated, maybe weighing how much to tell me. "Yes. The lab found rat poison in the sugar bowl, strychnine. It wasn't accidental, and it wasn't meant for just anyone. According to Miss Janson, Bridget was the only servant who used sugar."

Exactly what the housekeeper had told me. "Fair enough. I can't be positive, but I think she was comin' to tell me she saw Josef leave the big party early. You ever find out what he was doin' down in a Fillmore Street alley?"

"No." He pulled out a deck of cigarettes. "Will your mom mind if I smoke?"

"In here? Oh yeah."

He put them away. "This is between you and me. I've been asked to quietly look into Pyrut's death now that a second person, who was associated with the same house, is dead. One an employee, one a guest. The brass doesn't want to embarrass our foreign visitors. But if you ask me, it was no accident he was in that alley. Not that far away from Delaware Park. They want to know why and who was with him. You said you thought Bridget might have known and I'm starting to think you're right."

"Then it *wasn't* a random mugging?"

"It might have been. But why was he in that neighborhood and how did he get there? I don't believe for a second, and neither do you, he wandered there on his own." He arched an eyebrow. "Not that it's any of your business."

"It might be, if Pelagia Brewka was also murdered. She was related to a Josef Pyrut. I'm not sure it was *this* one, but it might have been. She wanted to see him and tell him something. Emmie found a letter from her. It'd been opened at City Hall."

"By whom?"

"No clue. I also don't know what she wanted to talk to Josef about or whether she did. The opened letter means someone knew that. The same someone might have passed the information on and he was killed for what he knew or what he might have known."

He paused. He hadn't touched his drink. "Miss Janson said Pyrut left around nine. Did she tell you that?"

"She did."

"What do you think?"

How much a private dick shared with the cops was always a question. But Sam had played straight with me before. "I think he left with Paul Witkop."

"Miss Janson said Paul went to bed early and never left."

"I bet she's lying. Or she doesn't know he was gone."

"She said the two of them got along."

"Maybe at first, but not by the end of the night." I got up to get the newspaper picture. I set it in front of the detective. "This is from the party. See the two of 'em? Josef is okay, but Paul isn't, not by a long shot. He doesn't like Josef, I'm sure of it. By the time this picture was taken, the two had fought, you mark my words. After this, Paul went to bed and Josef leaves, s'posedly on his own. That isn't fishy to you?"

Sam picked up the snap. "It is. My best guess would be Pyrut said something that angered Paul, and Paul lured him out to talk more."

"I think you're right, Detective." I took back the picture. "I don't know what—yet—but I'm pretty sure it was more than criticism of the food."

Chapter Twenty-Three

"Rat poison?" Dot said, her breath a cloud in front of her. Monday morning had not brought any relief to the painful cold. We huddled on the bus, mufflers wrapped tightly around our faces. But the news Bridget had died from rat poison was shocking enough that Dot's muffler slipped to expose her stunned mug.

"You heard me." I tucked my mittened hands under my arms, seeking a bit more warmth, as I stared at the brown roadside slipping by us as the bus trundled to Wheatfield.

She tugged the muffler back into place. "Why would someone kill her? Does Detective MacKinnon know?"

"No, that's why he came to see me. S'posedly Paul and Mrs. Witkop said I looked *shifty*." The statement still put my back up.

"You think it had anything to do with the Witkops?"

I stared, the image of a frightened Bridget before my eyes. "Yep. Or Josef. Or both."

"Are you sure?"

I turned to look at her. "You know the race track they opened down in Hamburg? The one for horses?"

"With the little carts?"

"That's it. Well, I'd be willing to take my paycheck down there and bet it all, that's how sure I am."

Dot's face was mostly covered by the knitted wool, but her eyes were big as dinner plates. I turned back to the window. I'd never make that bet, of course, but I was that sure. "Paul Witkop is involved somehow." The look on his face the night we'd seen him with Bridget had been that of a man in control. Bridget knew something about him, and he'd threatened her to keep her quiet, maybe with being fired. She may have fooled around with him beneath the stairs, but she'd learned something that terrified her. I had to find out what it was. Except if I was right, and Paul had killed Bridget to keep his secret, he sure wasn't gonna tell me just because I said *please*.

"If he or his mother had something to do with it, that's why they'd be looking to shift the police's attention to you?"

"Exactly. What did she call us? Those people? She'd be the exact kind of person who'd look to stick someone else with the blame, especially someone she considered beneath her."

We arrived at the factory and double-timed it to the lockers to stow our winter things and lunch pails. Emmie was there, pushing her curls beneath her bandanna before heading to the assembly line floor.

An idea struck. "Hey, Emmie."

She turned. "Yeah, Betty? Do you have any news?"

"Nothing definite, but I'm still working on it." I shut my locker door and turned to her. "I got a question."

"Shoot."

"Did your grandma ever write to Sebastian Witkop? You showed me the letter to Josef Pyrut, but if we're right, and Witkop is from the family she worked for in Poland, maybe she wrote to him, too?"

Her bow-like lips squinched together, a curl springing free from under the red fabric on her head. "I have no idea. If she did, and she mailed it, I'd never know, would I?"

"But what if she *didn't* mail it?"

"Daddy and I have been through a lot of *Babcia*'s things. I haven't seen a letter, but there are a few boxes to sort yet. Papers and stuff." Emmie's face took on a brighter and more excited look as I spoke. "*Babcia* never threw anything away, so I still might find something."

"Would you like some help?"

"Sure, but you gotta have better things to do."

"Not really. If I sit around too much, I start thinking about Tom and Sean, and I'll go nuts. You'll be helping me, too."

"Okay. Can you come tonight?"

This time I wouldn't need an excuse to leave the house. I could honestly say I was helping a friend. "Yes. Give me your address."

Emmie scrawled it on a scrap of paper from her pocket using her grease pencil and handed it to me. She gave me a rib-cracking hug. "Thank you so much, Betty, for not giving up on this. I'm right about *Babcia*, I know I am." She practically skipped out of the room.

I rubbed my side.

"Uh, Betty?" Dot asked, carefully stowing her stuff. "Don't you think you're giving her some false hope? What d'you think you'll find?"

"No clue." We exited the building and picked up our pace. "But I can't talk to Pelagia, or Josef. I can't exactly ring up the Polish government on the phone. I don't think the Witkops will invite me for dinner and spill everything. I can't just call them up and ask if they're hiding a secret from when they lived in Poland."

She looked properly abashed.

"It's a long shot, but at this point all I have is anything Pelagia left behind. Just like at the track, you pick your horse and place your bet."

"Don't gamblers lose a lot, too?"

I turned to her and stabbed the air with my smoke. "Yeah, but sometimes they win."

* * *

I hustled through the frigid night air to Emmie's house. Lucky for me, she didn't live too far from the bus stop. I knocked on the door and Mr. Brewka answered. "You must be Betty. Emmie said you'd be coming to help her."

I stepped into the warmth of the house. "Yes, sir." I took off my things and handed them to him.

"She's in the basement." He paused for a moment, like he was weighing his words. "My daughter believes someone killed her grandmother, did you know that?"

"Yes, sir." From his expression, I gathered he thought Emmie was cracked, but I didn't say anything. He didn't need to know that I'd come to believe his mother might have been involved in something before she died, even if she wasn't murdered for it.

"I appreciate you coming to help her. But please don't encourage her in these fantasies. Her mother and I don't think it's healthy. The sooner she comes to terms with Mama's death, the better."

"I understand." I did. If Pelagia had died a natural death, and I could prove that, I'd make sure Emmie knew, too. But she was right about one thing. There was something going on, and whatever was in those boxes might hold the key.

I picked my way down a set of shaky wooden steps. The basement was lit by a single unshaded bulb, a long chain dangling beside it. Laundry hung from the ceiling, but the Brewkas didn't have their own washing machine, like we did. The cinderblock walls were gray and lined with a dozen boxes. I wondered if they all contained Pelagia's belongings.

Emmie was in the middle, the contents of another box strewn around her. "Betty, hi." She pushed a curl from her forehead. She held a sheet of paper and piles littered the floor. The box was half full of yet more scraps.

I could see every kind of paper inside. Newsprint, yellow sheets from pads, the lined sheets used in schoolrooms, even sheets of white stationary. Pelagia must've been a real pack rat. "What's all this?"

"*Babcia*'s papers. Coming from Poland, then living through the 30s, she never threw a single sheet out, not unless she'd used every last bit of it. Here." She held out the piece in her hand.

I took it. It looked like a grocery list. Both sides were covered in tiny writing in both blue and black ink. "Looks like she'd write the list on one side, but then put another one on the back."

Emmie nodded. "That was her. I emptied the box, but I don't know where to start." She ran her hands through her hair.

"A big old pile isn't gonna help us. Here. First we'll sort it out." For the next half hour that's what we did. There were groups for lists, letters, notes to herself, and newspaper stories on which she'd scribbled in the margins.

Once we finished, Emmie studied the results. "What are we lookin' for again?"

"A letter, in full or maybe partial, to Sebastian Witkop. I'm thinking this was important, so maybe she wrote it a couple of times, trying to get exactly the right words."

"And since she hoarded paper, if she didn't use the whole sheet for the letter, she'd have saved it for something else."

"Right." I pushed aside the grocery and to-do lists, and the newspaper clippings. None of those would have what I wanted. I focused on the pile of handwritten notes. "Let's start with this here. If we don't find it in her correspondence, we'll start going through the others."

We read without talking, the only sound the clicking of the metal chain across the lightbulb when a draft came through. Pelagia had been a prolific letter-writer, judging by the amount of responses I read. Most of them were to her, however. Not things she'd written to others.

Next to me, Emmie sat back on her heels. "This is hopeless."

"We still have a stack to go." I pointed. "Hand it to me." She did, and I read. My heart sped up. "Emmie, I think this is it. Look." The pages had a lot of crossed out words and most weren't finished. These had to be her first drafts. But they all were addressed to Sebastian Witkop. "Listen to this. 'Dear Mr. Witkop. My name is Pelagia Brewka. I worked for your parents back in Poland. It is important that we talk about an urgent matter. Something you might not be aware of.' I guess she wasn't gonna assume Sebastian spoke Polish."

Emmie took a few of the letters and skimmed them. "That makes sense. If he came to the U.S. as a boy, he'd have learned English young. His Polish might be rusty. It doesn't look like she finished any of these, but they're all the same." She looked up. "*Babcia* couldn't have written these alone, though."

"No?"

"I don't think so. Her English was pretty broken. Somebody helped her put together these sentences. I don't know why she didn't ask me."

"She might not have wanted to get you involved." I swept up the papers. "Other than you, who would she ask? Your uncle?"

Emmie's forehead wrinkled in thought. "No. He doesn't have the patience. I'm not sure who she'd talk to. She was friends with several of the other old ladies in the neighborhood. They'd get together for cookies and talks about the Old Country. None of 'em speak real good English, but they have grandchildren who were born here. D'you think she coulda asked one of them?"

"It's possible. Even if they knew what she was writing, it wouldn't mean anything to them." I stood and brushed my hands. "Of those women, who would she most likely get help from?"

"I can think of two," Emmie said, following my lead. "Mrs. Glinka, and Mrs. Manelowa. I know their grandsons. I can ask them tomorrow if you'd like."

"That would be swell, thanks."

Emmie grabbed the chain, but didn't pull it. "Think she completed a letter and posted it?"

"I do." I glanced at my watch. "I gotta go. Here's my phone number." I used one of Pelagia's scraps to write it down. "If you find the person who helped her, all you need to do is ask if she posted a finished letter."

"I will." She pulled the chain. The basement plunged into a darkness. Fortunately, the door at the top of the stairs was open and showed us the way up. "Do you think Mr. Witkop killed her?"

I paused, my hand on the wooden railing. "I don't know, but I sure do plan on finding out."

Chapter Twenty-Four

I couldn't sit around and wait for Emmie to report back. That's not what a detective did. Also, the paper that evening was full of war news. The Germans were attempting to get supplies to their troops stuck in Russia. Served 'em right for trying to continue their invasion in the winter. Nothing major seemed to be happening in North Africa, but the Pacific was hoppin' with action between the U.S. and the Japanese. No word came from my brother or my fiancé. I could sit at home and go crazy worrying about 'em, or I could go to Delaware Park and talk to the folks there again. Maybe one of them had seen a letter from Pelagia.

I went to Delaware Park.

Dot couldn't go this time. I tried to ask Lee, but as I approached his house, I heard shoutin'. There were two male voices, one definitely Lee, the other almost certainly his pop. Every once in a while I'd hear a woman, prob'ly Mrs. Tillotson. I hastily beat feet before anyone looked out the window and saw me. Poor Lee. The Tillotsons didn't have anyone overseas, but they were having their own private war at home. I prayed for both conflicts to end soon.

I got off the bus at Delaware Avenue. Despite the persistent cold, I decided to walk through part of Forest Lawn Cemetery on my way to the Witkops. The cold and quiet gave me time to think and plan exactly what I would do once I reached the house. The grass around the headstones glittered under the streetlamp light, the brownish-green turned to sharp points by frost. I could barely make out the names on the stones. Some of 'em stood straight and proud, others were more worn around the edges. Here and there evergreen wreaths dotted the ground. Four days until Christmas.

Pelagia had finished her letter. Somehow I just knew it. What would she have done if she didn't get an answer?

She'd have visited. Not just written a second time. My steps quickened, and I headed for the Witkops'.

The house loomed in front of me. Warm light spilled out the front windows onto the frosted yard. The maples in front would be stately guardians when they had their leaves, but now they waved bare fingers against a blackened sky. I could knock on the front door. I had no doubt a maid or a butler would open it, but I would prob'ly be turned away. If Paul or his father were involved, it was almost certain.

I went around the back and knocked on the kitchen door. I'd ask for Mildred Janson, the housekeeper. She'd come to see me, so she might let me in for a second conversation. It was worth a shot.

The door cracked open to reveal the same overweight cook I'd seen the night I came to talk to Bridget. "Who are you and what do you want? We don't give to the poor directly from the house, if that's what you're after."

The words stung my pride. I didn't look that bad off, did I? My coat wasn't new, but my mittens and muffler were, and they were made of good wool. I wasn't flash, like the people this woman was used to serving, but I didn't look like some down on my luck beggar, either. I bit back a retort. "No, ma'am. My name is Betty Ahern. I'm looking for Miss Janson. She came to see me a couple days ago, and I'd like to talk to her again. If she has time, that is."

The cook sniffed. "Wait here." She slammed the door shut.

Unfriendly woman. Was she just annoyed to see a working-class girl at the door or something else? *Stop it, Betty. She's a crabby woman who cooks for a rich family. Nothing more.*

The door opened again, but this time it was Mildred. She held it open. "Come in, quick. Betty, right? Quickly, quickly, before Mr. Charles sees you. He's Mr. Witkop's valet and the butler, and he's most particular about guests." She led me to a small pantry off the kitchen. "We'll be able to talk here for a while. Mrs. Leggett, she's the cook, said you wanted to talk to me.

What for? I told you everything I knew about Bridget."

I pulled off my mittens and blew on my hands. It was warm in the pantry. Downright stuffy, as a matter of fact. I looked at the shelves. They appeared full, but closer inspection revealed the jars and boxes were arranged to give the appearance of a fully-stocked larder; however, there were bare spots. Being rich didn't get you out of war rationing.

Mildred saw me studying and snapped her fingers. "I haven't got all evening."

I wrenched my attention back to her. "I wanted to ask you about another woman. Her name was Pelagia Brewka. She worked for a wealthy family before she emigrated from Poland."

Mildred's forehead creased. "Brewka, you said? She was Polish? Why do you think she came here?"

"I think...I think the Witkops weren't always the Witkops. I think they changed their name from Witkowski when they came to the United States."

Mildred chucked. "I'm sorry, my dear, but that's highly improbable. Witkop is a German name."

A thought struck me. "The Witkowskis lived in the Prussian-controlled part of Poland. Prussia became part of Germany. I bet they picked a German name when they left. You said the house is full of Polish art, right?"

A doubtful light appeared in Mildred's eyes.

"Why would a German family have art from Poland? Wouldn't it make sense they'd have German stuff?" I paused. "I learned Mr. Witkop donated a lot of books to the library. They're by Polish authors and written in Polish. Why would he have those?"

She finally spoke. "I...I don't know."

"That's not my question, though. I just need to know if Pelagia Brewka ever came here to the house. This would have been the middle of November, maybe. She would have been an old woman with a Polish accent." I should have gotten a snap of Pelagia from Emmie, but too late for that now. Anyway, how many old Polish women could have visited?

Mildred thought for a moment. "No, I can't say as I ever saw anyone like that. I'm sorry."

Drat.

She took in my obvious disappointment. "Is it important?"

"Is it 'gonna stop the war' important? No. But it matters to a young girl." Inspiration seized me. "It could help figure out who killed Bridget, too."

"Well, if it could help Bridget..." Mildred seemed to make a decision. "Come with me." She led me to the kitchen where the cook and an older man were sipping coffee, a plate of rolls on the table between them. Maybe a post-dinner snack. They looked up as we entered.

"Miss Janson, you know I don't like you mucking about in my larder," the cook said, wagging a finger. "I'd tell you if we needed a cut of meat, just like I always do."

"My apologies, Mrs. Leggett. I needed a private place to talk to this young woman." She waved at me. "This is Betty Ahern. She was an...acquaintance of Bridget's."

Mrs. Leggett clucked. "Poor lamb. A bit fanciful, she was, and I scolded her something terrible, but she was a good girl. What a terrible way to die."

The man rumbled his agreement.

Mildred continued. "Betty here is looking for a woman, someone who may have come to the house the latter part of last month." She looked at me. "She says it may help find out who killed Bridget and why."

"I don't want to bother you—" I started.

"That's quite all right, young lady," Mrs. Leggett said. "After all the people we've had in this house, asking questions and making a mess, what's one more person?"

I nodded. "This woman was named Pelagia Brewka. She was the grandmother of a friend of mine. I don't have a picture, but she was thin, old, prob'ly wearing the traditional headscarf, and would have had a very heavy Polish accent. I think she would have asked to see Mr. Witkop. The older one, not his son."

The two servants looked at each other and thought. "No," Mrs. Leggett finally said. "I haven't seen anyone like that. I mean, I see lots of women matching that description when I go to the Broadway Market, but none at the house. What about you, Mr. Charles?"

Mr. Charles, who I took to be some kind of manservant or butler, stroked his chin. "There was a woman who came, but earlier in November than you said, more near the beginning. At least well before Thanksgiving."

A bubble swelled in my chest. "She did?"

"I have no idea if it was the woman you are referring to, but it was an old Polish lady. She came right up to the front door." Mr. Charles's disapproving tone said what he thought of that. "She demanded to see Mr. Witkop. She said she'd known his father."

"Did you let her in?" I asked, holding my breath.

His peepers flew open in a scandalized expression. "Certainly not! A total stranger, and clearly one of lower class, heavens no. I told her she must be mistaken and wished her good afternoon. As I was closing the door, Mrs. Witkop came out of the drawing room to speak to me. The old lady tried to plead with her, but Mrs. Witkop cut her off. And quite right, too. She doesn't have time for that sort of riff-raff."

The bubble in my chest deflated.

"She came back, though," he added after a moment.

"She did?" Hope wasn't dead yet.

"Yes, two, maybe three, days later. I saw her when Mr. Witkop was getting into his car. He doesn't take the car often, gas rations you understand, but he was attending an important meeting across the city. She had apparently been loitering nearby and pounced when he came outside." Mr. Charles's lips thinned. "Dreadful behavior."

"You didn't hear any of what they said, did you?" I asked. Inside my coat pocket, I crossed my fingers.

"No. The conversation started amiably enough, I suppose, but the woman grew agitated. She poked Mr. Witkop in the shoulder a couple times." Mr. Charles shook his head at Pelagia's remembered behavior. "Mr. Witkop was quite kind at first. I did hear him say something like, 'you must be mistaken.' She insisted. In the end, he pushed past her, got into the car, and left. She disappeared after that and didn't come back."

Before I could say anything, a woman appeared in the kitchen door. She was dressed in a navy blue skirt and a white silk blouse. Her hair was perfectly styled and the red polish on her nails didn't have a single chip. She reminded me of Katharine Hepburn in *The Philadelphia Story*. "Mrs. Leggett, about tonight. I—" She saw me and blinked. "Who on earth is this?"

I opened my mouth to introduce myself, but she cut me off.

"I know you. You were in the backyard with Paul and the maid that night. What, pray tell, are you doing here?"

"She's asking questions about Bridget and an old Polish lady," Miss Janson said. "Do you remember the old lady, ma'am? Mr. Charles said you saw her."

"Now just a minute," Mr. Charles said.

"I don't spend my time worrying about the help or random visitors from poor parts of the city," Mrs. Witkop said, voice icy. "Now, don't you all have jobs to do? I suggest you do them or I'll find someone else who will." She stalked out of the kitchen.

"Shrew," Mrs. Legget muttered.

"That's a bit harsh, don't you think?" Mr. Charles asked. "Her maid murdered, her house upended by the police, the poor woman has at a lot on her hands."

"Not so much she doesn't have time for her weekly manicure," Mrs. Leggett retorted. "Just like a man, excusing bad behavior if the woman is nice-looking enough. Anyway," she turned to me, "I'm sorry, that's all we have to tell you."

I looked around at the group. "Thank you all very much for your time."

"Does this help with Bridget?" Mildred asked, wringing her hands. "She was a bit of a flirt and she always had a saucy answer to any reprimand, but she was a dear child. She didn't deserve a death like that."

"It might, I'm not sure." I looked around. "Do you have a pen and paper?"

Mrs. Leggett heaved herself up and retrieved both from a drawer.

I wrote my name and telephone number, as well as that of Sam MacKinnon. "First, you should call the police, Detective MacKinnon, and tell him what you told me. He's a good guy, he'll be square with you." I handed over the slip. "If you remember anything else, please call me. I might not be available during the day, but you can leave a message at that number. I'll let myself out."

I wrapped my muffler tight around my throat, buttoned up my coat, and pulled on my mittens. Outside, the cold air took my breath away. But the trip was worth it. Pelagia had visited Delaware Park. She'd seen Sebastian Witkop and it sounded to me like they'd argued. Then there was Mrs. Witkop. She put on a good act, but how would she have known about a woman who lived in Polonia, which was definitely a cut below Delaware Park, if she hadn't seen her? Had Mrs. Witkop known Pelagia's information and killed her to prevent her husband's disgrace? Mrs. Witkop looked like a woman who liked her moneyed life. She wouldn't be nearly as happy slumming it in a less swanky neighborhood.

A male voice interrupted my thoughts. "What on earth are you doing here?" It was Paul. He was dressed in a neat suit, nothing flash, but better quality than anything I saw on a daily basis, even on Mr. Satterwaite. Despite the cold, his trench coat was open, and he held his gloves in his hand, a cream-colored scarf draped around his neck.

"Pardon me, I was just leaving." I tried to walk past him.

He grabbed my arm. "I recognize you. You were here that night harassing Bridget, you and a young man." He squeezed my arm. "I asked you what you were doing here?"

"Let go of me," I said in a low voice. There were three people on the other side of that door and if Paul thought I wouldn't scream my fool head off, he was mistaken. That would be after I stomped his foot so hard it would look like a sheet of steel coming off the rollers at Bethlehem. "I was talking to Miss Janson, Mrs. Leggett, and Mr. Charles. It's a free country, pal."

His grip tightened, almost to the point of real pain. "What about?"

"None of your business."

He squeezed harder, which I didn't think possible.

I couldn't help it, I gasped. "Let go of me."

The door opened. A portly man stood there, wearing a smoking jacket and slippers. "Paul? Is there a problem?"

"No, Father," Paul let go of my arm. "This girl was just leaving."

"Who is she?"

"No one of importance."

"Come inside. I have some business matters I want to discuss with you before tomorrow's board meeting." The man turned to me. "Good night, miss." He shut the door.

I took a few steps so I was out of Paul's reach. "Your daddy is waiting for you. You'd better get inside."

He pointed at me. "You stay away from here. If I see you again, I'll call the police and have you arrested for trespassing. No matter who has visited, you have no business here. Understand?" He stomped inside and slammed the door.

I looked after him. How'd he know I'd been asking about visitors?

Chapter Twenty-Five

December twenty-second. I had shopping to do and a case to solve. The shopping I could handle, no sweat. That was just a matter of sneaking off to Woolworth's and snapping up a new cap for Lee and Dot's much-wished-for lipstick. Easy as pie.

Solving the case might be a bit trickier.

I waited until we were on the assembly line to tell Dot what I'd learned the previous night. The racket made it harder to talk, but it also meant it would be more difficult for others to overhear us.

"What could they have argued about? Pelagia and Mr. Witkop. The same thing she was talkin' about in the letter?"

That question had bothered me all night. "I've been thinkin' about it. She worked for the Witkops, then the Witkowskis, in Poland. The family had money, despite the German occupation. Did they do something to other Poles? Maybe they were too chummy with the Germans at the time? It's the only thing that makes sense." I huffed out a breath. "I need to talk to whoever helped her write. He'd know."

"Do you think Mrs. Witkop knew?"

"Knew or suspected. She saw Pelagia, I'm sure of that."

Beside me, Florence Anderson leaned over. "Mind on your work, Betty, or Mr. Satterwaite won't let you hear the end of it."

"My mind is on my work."

She arched an eyebrow. "Which one? Makin' planes or private detective stuff?"

"How do—"

"Emmie." Florence paused to wipe off some dust from the spot where the instrument panel would go. "I had lunch with her yesterday and she mentioned how you were lookin' into her gramma's death. That's who you're talkin' about, right?"

"Yeah." I didn't particularly want to bring Florence into the case, but it didn't seem like she was gonna give me much choice.

"Emmie told me all about it. Well, as much as she knew. She said her gramma worked for this swanky family in Poland, and now they're here in Buffalo. She said they still have money, too."

I brushed hair from my forehead as I waited for the next plane to move into its spot. "Yep. The Witkops. They live up in Delaware Park."

Florence whistled.

"I know. They brought the money from Poland."

Dot piped up. "What we can't figure out is why Pelagia Brewka, that's Emmie's grandma, would write, and then argue, with Mr. Witkop. He's not that old. He can't have known her in Poland."

I thought of Mr. Witkop. He hadn't been an adult, but he'd have been a little boy. If that were the case, he would have known Pelagia, but only as a young woman who worked in the house. Maybe she played with him or gave him treats from the kitchen. But nothing more. If he and Pelagia argued, it wouldn't have been over something he did. I shared my thoughts with Florence and Dot.

Dot frowned, but Florence's face turned thoughtful. "You know, my ma did housekeeping for one of those Delaware Park families once. She told me it was a funny thing. You know how you and I would stop talking, or keep our voices low, if we don't want someone nearby to hear us?"

I looked up. "Yeah. I do it all the time. What's wrong with that?"

"Nothing." She stepped back and waited for the next plane. "Rich folks don't think the same. Oh, they do of each other. Say Mr. Swell is talkin' to Mrs. Swell, and their son comes in the room. If they don't want him to hear anything, they'll stop or keep their voices down."

"What's your point?"

"They don't do the same thing with the help." Florence looked up and fixed me with a stare. "It's like the servants are invisible. Ma heard all sorts of juicy gossip when she was workin' up there. Who was cheatin' on who, how so-and-so's dress wasn't real silk, all of that."

Dot bit her lip. "Then if Pelagia was a servant in Poland, you're saying she might have heard something like that from the Witkops, or the Witkowskis, or…I'm just gonna call 'em the Witkops and keep it simple."

Florence and I grinned at each other.

"That's exactly what I'm sayin'." Florence looked down. "I'm outta screws. Cover for me and I'll be back in a jiffy." She jogged off.

I mulled over Florence's words. "Interesting idea," I said to Dot.

She polished the front of the instrument panel and stepped back. "What is?"

"Pelagia learned something about the Witkops over in Poland, but she and her husband left the country without doin' anything about it. Years later, she sees little Sebastian in Buffalo, but now he's an adult. He's still rich, maybe even more so, and he's changed his name. She tries to get in touch with him, tell him what she knows. It can't be good because why would you blow the lid off something innocent? He won't talk to her. Then…" I trailed off.

"Then what?" Dot prompted after a moment.

"No clue."

"You think when Witkop wouldn't talk to her she went to Josef Pyrut? What did she know? Did Witkop kill her? And maybe his wife is covering for him? Or did the missus do it to protect her husband?"

I pointed a screwdriver at her. "That, my friend, is what we need to find out."

* * *

That evening after dinner, I went down to Woolworth's. I had to get my Christmas shopping done. I'd look like a sap if Dot and Lee handed me gifts on the twenty-fifth and I had nothing. I picked up a lipstick in a cheery shade of red for Dot, and found Lee a nice new soft cap to replace the one he had, which was lookin' a little fuzzy around the edges. Knowin' him, he'd keep that one for daily wear and use this one for special occasions, like church. Lee was thrifty that way.

The temperature earlier had soared, making it feel more like spring than three days before Christmas. I detoured through downtown to look at the windows at Hens and Kelley's and Kleinhan's Department Store. I paused in front of a display of smart men's clothes, the storefront dummies dressed in the newest suits. One of 'em had a fedora cocked on its head. Tom would look smashing in the navy blue. I pictured myself in a dress, maybe the red velvet one I'd seen in another window, off the shoulder, long skirt, and long white gloves. What a couple we'd be.

When the war was over and we had money, of course. I wondered what Tom was doing at that minute. According to the paper, Rommel had retreated to Tripoli, but no one thought he'd given up. As long as he had a single tank, he'd fight. I'd written Tom a Christmas letter, of course, but I didn't expect anything from him. *I miss you, Tom. Stay safe.*

My eye caught the price tag dangling from the sleeve of the suit coat and I whistled. Who had fifty dollars to spend on a single jacket? I turned to go home.

Sebastian Witkop and his son were coming out of the store. They had the cabbage, apparently, from the clerk trailing them with boxes and bags. Paul caught sight of me and stared.

I thought about saying something. No, not in such a public place. It would take longer, but I could catch the bus on the previous block and avoid them.

"I'll have these purchases loaded into the car and then..." Mr. Witkop's voice trailed off. He must have noticed his son wasn't paying attention. "Paul, do you hear me? What on earth are you staring at, boy?" He followed Paul's gaze, and a smile creased his face when he saw me. "Ah, I see. Good evening, miss." He tipped his hat. "I was wondering what on earth could distract Paul. Now I know. You're much better to look at, my dear, than a stuffy old man."

Mr. Witkop was round in the middle, the kind of shape that comes from eating a lot of good food. His clothes were quality stuff, I could tell that even from a slight distance. I suspected his black suit was gabardine wool and there wasn't a hint of shine on the lapels from wear. His wingtip shoes caught the light from the overhead lamps. If this is how he dressed to go shopping, I wondered what he wore to work. "Thank you, sir. I was admiring the windows." I waved my hand in the general direction of the displays.

"Picturing your own young man in the clothes?"

"Yes, sir. He's overseas now, of course. In North Africa. Someday, maybe. I hope."

"Ah." Mr. Witkop sighed theatrically. "She's got a man. Too bad, Paul. She'd be a lovely lady to take to the Christmas party."

"I don't think she'd enjoy it, Father," Paul said, a nasty sneer on his handsome face.

"Why ever not?" his father asked. "Who wouldn't like a party?"

"I've seen her around the house, talking to the help." Paul's chin jutted out. "I don't think she's the right...type."

Mr. Witkop wagged a meaty finger. "I've told you a dozen times, Paul. Don't be snobbish. This is America, not Europe. We don't put stock in such things." He walked over to me, winked, and took my hand to kiss it. "If you don't mind my saying, my dear, I think you'd fit in just fine."

"Thank you." I shot Paul a look. His face was dark, scowling. "Excuse me for being bold, but you're Sebastian Witkop, aren't you? I saw your picture in the paper, from that party when the Polish were visiting. It looked like a swell gathering."

He straightened. "Yes, I am. It was a wonderful evening. I was so happy to host our foreign guests. Such a sad story."

I spoke to Mr. Witkop, but half my stare stayed on Paul. "I think you know a friend of mine. Pelagia Brewka. Least she said she was gonna go see you."

The twinkle went out of Mr. Witkop's eye and his face creased in a frown. "Pelagia Brewka? No, I don't know the woman, or the family name."

"She's Polish. She swore she knew you. She told me she was gonna go up to Delaware Park and find out if you were the same family she worked for in Poland."

I wasn't mistaken. The color drained from Mr. Witkop's face. "From Poland? What an idea. No, I'm sorry, she must be mistaken. It happens with old age. I've never been to Poland in my life. Come, Paul. We should get going." He lifted his fedora. "A very Merry Christmas to you, miss." He hurried away to the shiny silver car waiting at the curb.

Paul sauntered up. He stood nose to nose with me. A rich boy trying to play a tough guy, like Jimmy Cagney. "You keep trying, don't you? First the servants, now my father directly. Just like the old lady."

I felt like a bit of ice was sliding down my back, but I stood my ground. Out of the corner of my eye, I could see shoppers and even a uniformed police officer. Paul Witkop wouldn't do anything but talk. "Tell me square. Is your family from Poland? Did they change their name? 'Cause there are a lot of Polish books at the library, and the librarian said your father donated 'em. Did he know Pelagia Brewka?"

Paul's smile didn't make him look handsome. It was a wolfish expression, more fit for a gangster than a socialite. "You stay away from my father, do you understand me? My family is no concern of yours. You look smarter than the others. Walk away while you can." He stepped back and raised his hat. "Merry Christmas." Then he went to join his father next to the swanky-looking car.

I watched the car's tail lights as it pulled away. I looked smarter, huh? "Whatever your secret is, Paul, I'm gonna find out." 'Cause I hadn't missed the fact both men knew Pelagia Brewka was an old woman, despite the fact I'd never mentioned her age.

Chapter Twenty-Six

December twenty-third. I'd started a little count-down in my head. I didn't think I'd get to the bottom of this by Christmas, not by a long shot. But maybe I would figure things out by the end of the year. I'd make more progress if I could investigate during the day. But Bell wasn't gonna close again just so I could have more time to spend as a detective. I doubted Mr. Satterwaite would give me a leave of absence, either. I'd have to make do with the time I had.

I didn't know what dirt Pelagia Brewka had on the Witkops, but I could feel it in my gut. Philip Marlowe would understand.

It wasn't until lunch that Dot demanded an answer. "Betty, what's eating you?" she asked, ignoring her food as I sat across from her. "On the ride in, you barely said boo. You've been distracted and grouchy all morning. Tell me what's goin' on."

My conscience squirmed a little. Dot was my closest friend and my partner in detecting. I had been shutting her out, but only 'cause I didn't know what to say. I told her about meeting Sebastian and Paul the previous night.

She stared, sandwich half to her mouth. "You went out alone?"

"Oh, for pete's sake, Dot. I was *Christmas* shopping. For you, I might add. I wasn't gonna take you along for that."

Her attention was momentarily diverted. "What did you get me? Better question, what did you get Lee? You said you were gonna get him a new cap, so I'm stumped. Got any ideas for me?"

"Do you want to gab about presents or the case?"

She flushed. "Both, but we'll start with the work."

"Thank you." Dot, while a dear friend and the most loyal partner a girl could ask for, would never be a detective. She got distracted too easily. "Whatever Pelagia was pestering them about, it goes back to Poland. It has to. It's not like they've been buddy-buddy in the last forty years."

She pulled the crust off her bread. "How old is Sebastian?"

"I think the paper said he's in his mid-fifties or something. Why?"

"I was thinking. If Pelagia worked for the family back in the Old Country, he'd have been a boy. She was much older, right?"

"In her seventies, yeah."

"Then whatever she's harping about, it has to be something his *parents* did, not him, right?"

I'd been mulling the same thing in my mind. "That's what I figure. Oh, he might know about it, but I'd bet my last nickel he didn't do anything personally." I pointed at her. "The same goes for Paul. I mean, he wasn't even alive back then."

"What's so awful that the secret had to be kept for three generations?" She bit her lip.

"I'm still waiting on Emmie to tell me who helped Pelagia with the letters." I took a bite. "If I don't hear from her today, I'll find her. And I told you before, quit chewing on that lip of yours. It's gonna look worse than raw meat, and how are you gonna put lipstick on it?"

She blushed. "Is knowing who helped Pelagia that important?"

"Those are the only people in the U.S. who know what happened. Oh sure, someone in Poland prob'ly does, too. I can't go there and I can't write anyone, not with the Nazis in charge, that's for sure. I can't write the government in exile. I mean, I can compose a letter, but where would I send it?" My sandwich suddenly looked unappetizing. This case might be too big for me.

Dot patted my hand. I didn't have to tell her. She knew what was going through my head. "Don't get discouraged. You'll figure it out. Hey, here's an idea. You haven't gone to Fillmore Avenue, have you?"

"No. At this point, there's no evidence."

"But if Josef Pyrut's body was found off Fillmore, maybe someone in that area would know something. You could talk to 'em, couldn't you?"

I slapped my forehead. Why hadn't I thought of that? I'd been so caught up in physical evidence, but a private detective's main tool was her ability to ask questions. "Dot, you're gold. Have I ever told you that?"

She blushed again, this time a deeper pink. "Aww, don't mention it. I'm sure you would've thought of it eventually."

"I'll go after work. Except, I have no way to tell Mom I'll be late."

"I'll tell her. I have to get home. If I don't, well, you know my folks." Dot gathered up her remaining lunch, then fixed me with a stern look. "Just be careful, okay? I know that section of Fillmore around Genesee isn't terribly rough, but keep a sharp eye out, will you?"

I promised her I would. If I remembered right, Emmie didn't live too far from there, either. I wondered if that's why Josef had been in the area, he'd been going to look for Pelagia. No, that couldn't be it. He'd never gotten her letter, which meant he couldn't have known about her. He had to have been there for some other reason.

Right as lunch was ending, and I was getting my Luckys out for a quick smoke, Emmie came up to me. "Betty, there you are. I've been looking for you."

"Do you have some names for me?"

"Better than that. I have one name." She held out a slip of paper with a flourish. "That's why it took a little longer than I thought it would. I figured I'd save you some time and ask the boys first."

I read the paper. The name Luke Manelowa and an address were scribbled on it. "This is the kid?"

"Yep. I asked the ladies, and they sent me to their grandsons. Luke said he helped *Babcia* with a letter. I told him you'd be over to see him." She beamed at me.

"Thanks, Emmie. I appreciate the help."

"Anything you need, Betty. Just let me know." She hurried off.

I tapped out a cigarette, lit it, and went outside. But was too cold to stand and puff, at least not without a jacket. I strolled toward the assembly building. I could smoke and walk.

Dot fell in beside me. "Do you want company when you go and see Luke?"

"You know I would. Not just for safety. You might hear something I miss. But you said your folks wouldn't let you."

"I don't like you going by yourself. I'm willing to risk a bit of trouble."

I blew smoke up and away and hugged her. "Don't fret. Emmie would've warned me if there was any danger. This Luke is a kid. How bad can it get? And I won't get into trouble checking the alley. You need to stay in your folks' good graces because I might need help with something really important later."

After work, I took the bus to Fillmore instead of home. The place where they'd found Josef's body wasn't even a real alley, just a space between two stores where the owners put the trash. On one side was a laundry and on the other was a tailor. This time, I'd come prepared with the newspaper pictures of Paul and Josef. I picked the laundry first.

The bells above the door jangled when I walked in. The air was damp and I could hear the racket from the machines in the back. A thin, dark-haired woman stood next to a press that let off billows of steam as she worked on a set of men's shirts, her face gleaming.

"'Scuse me."

"Yes, yes." She did not turn around, but waved toward me. "Five cents for shirts. Ten if we use extra starch."

Definitely Polish with that accent. "I'm not—"

"Take three days."

"I'm—"

"Stella be out in a minute to take care of you."

"I'm not here to have any laundry done." Pop didn't have any shirts fancy enough for this kind of cleaning and we sure didn't have the dimes to have each one of 'em laundered.

She looked up, dark eyes narrow with suspicion. "Then what do you want?"

I pulled the pictures out of my pocket. "I want to know if you've ever seen either of these men."

"Bah." She flapped her hands at me. "I no have time for that. Go away."

I watched as she lifted the press and removed a crisp white shirt. "This will only take a second."

She shook her head and muttered as she folded the shirts. I didn't recognize any of the Polish coming from her mouth, but it prob'ly wasn't nice.

I tried again. "What about Stella? Can I talk to her?"

The woman took the pile of folded shirts and stomped off to the back of the laundry.

The bells rang and a soft voice came from behind me. "You must excuse my mother."

I turned. A slim, younger version of the shirt woman, stood inside the doorway. Her voice held almost no trace of an accent. She unbuttoned her coat as she moved to the counter. "I'm Stella. Can I help you? I don't see your laundry. It's five cents for each shirt."

"And ten if you use extra starch." I grinned. "Your mom told me. But I'm not here to have clothes washed."

"Then what do you want?" Stella hung her coat and tied a white apron over her patched dress.

I put the photographs on the counter. "I want to know if you've ever seen either of these men. Take a good look."

She peered at the photos with soft brown eyes, then regretfully shook her head. "I'm sorry, no. Neither look like men who'd take their own laundry out."

"That's a fact." I put the photos back in my pocket. "Thanks."

"You might have better luck with Mr. Szmanski in the shop on the other side of our alley. He's a tailor. Those tuxedos look expensive. If either man needed alterations, and they live nearby, they'd have gone to him."

I thanked Stella and went next door. I expected Mr. Szmanski to be an old guy. The man who answered the tinkling bells was no older than Pop, his thick head of hair still dark. His fingers were scarred and calloused, prob'ly from his work, but he stood straight and tall. "Yes, miss. Can I help you?"

"I need your help."

"I'll do my best." He chuckled. "However, I must tell you right off I do primarily men's work. If you're looking for dress alterations, I'll save you some time and give you other names." He moved to the counter and picked up a pen.

I held out a hand to stop him. "This isn't about clothing, but thanks. Do you know either of these men?" Once again, I produced my pictures.

He studied them closely. "Yes. Well, I don't know the man on the right very well, and I don't remember his name, but I do recognize him. He came in with Mr. Sebastian Witkop at the beginning of the month to have his trousers shortened. The other one, yes, that's Paul Witkop, Mr. Witkop's son. I've had him in here many times for fittings. Not quite as polite as his father, but young men seldom are." Mr. Szmanski handed back the pictures.

Bingo. "Did you happen to see the two of them together, particularly on December second? It was quite a while ago, I know. It would have been at night."

Mr. Szmanski's forehead wrinkled. "I don't think so. I worked many late hours earlier in the month. I had a lot of clothes to tailor for Christmas parties. I've been here until midnight almost every night this month. I don't think I saw either of them, at least not together. May I see that picture again, the one with Paul and the other man?" He took it back and peered at it. "Yes, this is the one they found between my store and the laundry, isn't it? I understand from the police he was an undersecretary for the exiled Polish government."

"Yes. I'm tryin' to find out what happened to him. The cops think it was a mugging, but I'm not so sure."

He gave me a faint smile. "Unusual work for a young woman."

"I'm not your average girl." I took the pictures back and looked around. The shop was filled with men's clothes, some half-finished sewing on tables, some pieces hung on dummies all pinned up. "Do you do a lot of work for the Witkops?"

"For Sebastian, yes. Not as much for Paul. I believe he prefers to use a different tailor. He's a...modern young man."

I noted the pause in Mr. Szmanski's words. He didn't approve of Paul's tailor, but he was too polite to say it. "In other words, he goes to a flashy guy who doesn't appreciate old-school talent." I grinned.

Mr. Szmanski spread his hands and said nothing, but his eyes twinkled.

"Well, thanks for your time. If you happen to remember seeing the two of 'em together, Paul and the undersecretary, would you call me?" I scribbled my phone number on a slip of paper. What Mom would think of a strange Polish man calling the house, I didn't want to know.

He nodded, and I left. I had some time before the bus came, so I wandered down Genessee, looking at the shops. A few buildings down from Mr. Szmanski's was a second-hand shop, the front window displays full of jewelry and small items like plates and cups. I had a little money left to buy something nice for Mom for Christmas.

My attention was snagged by a four-piece set of cups and saucers. I knew the design on 'em. Bone white with a scalloped edge, a faint line of gold around it. The cups had a flower design. I'd seen those at the Witkops. They'd been on the washboard the day I'd talked to Mildred, Mrs. Leggett and Mr. Charles. I hurried inside.

A round man came to the front. "I'm sorry, miss. I'm closed. I must not have locked the door. Did you not see the sign?"

I hadn't, but I didn't bother with that. "Those cups in the front window. The white ones with the flower design. Where'd you get 'em?"

He blinked. "A woman brought them in last week. They are quite beautiful, aren't they? A fine Christmas present for your mother."

"Thanks, but I don't think I could afford 'em." I looked at the price tag. No, I definitely couldn't afford the set. "Whoo-ee. If this is a second-hand place, you musta paid a good price, right?"

He didn't say anything.

"A friend of mine decided to sell her grandmother's stuff not that long ago. I should send her to you. Hers are as least as nice as these. What did you give for 'em? If it was a good price, I'll send my friend to you."

It was plain he didn't want to tell me, but the thought of more business must have won him over. "She, the woman I bought the cups and plates from, said she hated to part with them, but she needed the money. I gave her three dollars for four pairs. Poor dear, she must have been hard up because she took the offer without argument. I was prepared to go as high as five dollars. They are quite fine china and I'm sure the gold is genuine. The stamp on the bottom indicates they're from France."

"This woman, what did she look like?"

"Oh, older, a little stout. Gray hair. If she hadn't been so worried, I'd imagine she'd look quite motherly."

I knew that description. Sure as anything Mildred Janson had brought in that china.

* * *

As I left the second-hand shop, I checked my watch. Almost five. My stomach grumbled, reminding me I was missing dinner. I hoped Mary Kate would save me something, and that she remembered to feed Cat, too. I spent a nickel and picked up a copy of the evening *Courier*. The war news was slow, mostly about the Germans getting bogged down in Russia. Josef Pyrut didn't even rate a mention.

I bought a hot dog and a Coke from a corner store on Genessee and wolfed them down. It was a poor substitute, but I needed something to eat and at least it was cheap. Then I walked to the address Emmie had given me for Luke Manelowa.

The house was on Frederick, a block from Genessee. Two blue stars were in the front window. *Are his brothers with you, Tom?* I walked up a cracked sidewalk and knocked. The empty window boxes gave the house a sad, neglected look, but in the summer when they were full of petunias or marigolds, they'd look pretty.

The door opened to reveal a boy no older than Mary Kate. "Are you Luke Manelowa?" I asked.

He gripped the door tight, knuckles white, and looked prepared to slam it in my face. "Yeah. Who're you?"

"My name is Betty Ahern. I—"

The transformation was instant. He relaxed his grip on the door and opened it wide. A smile spread across his freckled face. "You're Emmie's friend from Bell. She said you'd be coming to see me. C'mon in."

I entered the house. A strong smell of cooked cabbage came from the kitchen and I hoped Luke wouldn't lead me back there.

"You make planes, too? Have you ever worked on the engines? Do you fly 'em?" Luke walked backward further into the sitting room as he talked.

"Yes, yes, and no. Most of the time I install the parts, like the instrument panels and stuff. They get other people to fly the P-39s off to wherever they're going." I unwound my muffler.

"Emmie tells me a lot of 'em go to Russia. D'you think the Russians are using them against the Germans now?"

"You ask a lot of questions, you know that?"

He grinned. "My gramma tells me that. She says I should wait to ask until I know the person, but how're you gonna get to know her if you don't ask questions?"

Smart kid. "Yes, the Russians buy a lot of planes. I don't know if they are using them right now. They might be."

He plopped down on the couch and sat on his hands.

I sat across from him in an ugly brown armchair. But before I could say anything, a woman with her hair in a bun and wearing a spattered apron over a faded blue dress came into the room. I shot back to my feet. "You must be Mrs. Manelowa." I held out my hand. "I'm Betty Ahern. I wanted to ask Luke a couple of questions."

She wiped her hands on her apron and shook. "He's not in trouble, is he?"

"No, ma'am. A friend of mine, Emelia Brewka, said Luke used to do favors for her grandmother. Did you know her, old Mrs. Brewka?"

Mrs. Manelowa's face creased in a smile. "Oh, yes, Pelagia, She's a good friend of my mother's. She made the most marvelous *kolaczki* for Christmas. I'm afraid I won't do them justice." She tipped her head toward her son. "Luke did all sorts of chores for her. Is your homework done?" This last was addressed to Luke.

"Yes, Mom."

"Okay, answer Miss Ahern's questions, then you can help me in the kitchen."

"Do I get a cookie?"

"If you work hard." She turned to me. "Boys. Would you like anything to drink?"

"No, thank you. But I have two younger brothers. I know what you mean." She left us and I resumed my seat. "Luke, I'm interested in some letters you helped Mrs. Brewka with. She wrote them, but you might have helped with her English. You know, finding the right word. This would have been last month most likely." I was guessing on the dates, but the announcement about the Polish visit hadn't come until November and she'd died by the end of that month.

Luke bounced a bit more, like he had springs in his bottom and couldn't stay still. Jimmy and Michael were high energy, but they had nothin' on this kid. "What kind of letters?"

"She was writing to a man, Sebastian Witkop. She wanted to meet him."

Luke's face was blank.

"She worked for Mr. Witkop's family in Poland, she needed to meet him 'cause she had somethin' important to tell him. Does any of this sound familiar?" Maybe he didn't remember.

It came slowly, but understanding finally dawned. "Yeah, I remember. She gave me ten cents to buy some penny candy at the store."

Naturally that would be the fact he'd remember. I should've asked if she'd treated him to anything last month and why. "Do you remember what the letter said?"

"She told him who she was and she'd known his folks." He scrunched up his face. "Then she said his family had a lot of dough, but they'd done a bunch of bad things to get it. She wanted to talk to him 'cause she thought he should know. She was sure he'd want to make up for it. You know, like how when I threw my baseball and broke Mrs. Ekowski's front window last summer, Pop fixed it for her and made me help and I had to go say I was sorry and mow Mrs. Ekowski's front yard for two weeks." He said the last sentence in one breath.

The onslaught of words stunned me a sec. I recovered and asked, "I'm sure Mrs. Brewka wanted to sound good in the letter."

"She did. She asked me to help 'cause she knows I'm the best speller in my grade and I know lots of words, and—"

"I got it." How did Pelagia ever get a word in with all his yammering? "Do you know if Mrs. Brewka mailed the letter?"

He swung his legs. "Yep. She gave me another ten cents for more candy if I'd drop it in the mailbox on my way to school."

Assuming Pelagia used the right address, the letter did arrive at Delaware Park. I stood. "Thanks for your help, Luke. I appreciate it. Merry Christmas."

He bounced to his feet and held out a grubby hand. "You're welcome but aren't you forgetting somethin'?"

What had Emmie told him? "Uh, I dunno. Am I?"

"Yep." He grinned. "Emmie told me you'd give me ten cents if I answered your questions."

Chapter Twenty-Seven

After I left the Manelowas', I dropped a dime in the nearest pay phone and called home. Mary Kate answered. "Are Mom and Pop there?" I asked.

"They sure are. Pop just asked when you'd be here."

"Tell 'em..." I cast about for an excuse. "Tell 'em I met some girls when I was out and we went for milkshakes. Please?"

"Usual price?" Mary Kate's sweet tooth meant she'd do almost anything for a treat.

"Yep."

"Deal." Her smile wasn't hard to imagine. "Should I tell 'em when you'll be back?"

"No. I don't think what I'm doing will take long, but I don't wanna box myself in. You're a peach, Mary Kate." I hung up the phone. Bus or walk? I wasn't far from the Witkops' house. I could run there faster and it wasn't too cold.

I practically flew down the streets, so I was outta breath once I got to the house. I took a few moments to compose myself. There was no use showing up all red faced, sweaty, and puffing like a steam engine. Definitely not a good look for a private detective. I went around to the back, straightened my hair, and rang the bell.

The cook answered. Recognizing me, she opened the door. "Yes?"

"Mrs. Leggett, right? I don't know if you remember me—"

"Betty...I don't remember your last name, but I know that's your Christian name. What do you want?"

"Is Mildred…Miss Janson here? I need to talk to her."

"No, she isn't." Mrs. Leggett started to close the door.

I put my hand on it to stop her. "Is she at home? Do you know where that is?"

"I do not." She tried to close the door again.

Months of working at Bell had strengthened my arms. I held fast. "Did she say anything to you before she left today that might give me a clue? Please, it's important."

Mrs. Leggett huffed. "She said a lot of things before she left. I didn't pay attention to her. How dare she treat this family like her personal bank? It's wartime. Everybody is hard up, but that doesn't give her the right to do what she did."

What was she talkin' about? In my surprise, I momentarily forgot to push against the door, and she shoved it forward. Before it shut, I stuck my foot out to stop her. The door squished it against the frame and I bit off a cuss word. Mrs. Leggett tried to slam it again, but this time I put my shoulder against the wood, which was much less painful and more effective. "I don't understand. What did she do?" Then it dawned on me. *The teacups,* I thought. *They found out.*

Mr. Charles came to the door. "Mrs. Leggett! I can feel the draft all the way…what does she want?" He tilted his head toward me.

"She wants to talk to *her*," Mrs. Leggett said in a dark, ominous tone.

"Look," I said. These were honest hard-working folk who were obviously very loyal to their employers if they wouldn't even refer to Mildred by name. Maybe if I appealed to their sense of justice. "I was on Fillmore earlier and I saw some china in a second-hand shop. I swear I recognized it from the last time I was here. The shop owner said a woman sold 'em, a woman who he described as looking a lot like Miss Janson. I needed to ask her and find out."

Mrs. Leggett let go of the door. "What shop? Where?" She reached for a coat.

"You tell me what happened with Miss Janson and I'll tell you where to find the goods."

Mr. Charles frowned and Mrs. Leggett crossed her arms. They exchanged a look. Then Mr. Charles spoke. "Miss Janson was stealing from the Witkops. She has been fired."

"When? What did she take? Did she say why?"

He didn't approve of my rapid-fire questions, that was clear from his expression, but he answered. "Those china cups you saw, along with the saucers. There was a set of twelve. Mrs. Witkop noticed there were four missing when she had a large party over, discussing volunteer efforts for the war. She thought they had been misplaced, but when we started to look, we noticed other things missing, small things. A few silver spoons, some coins, things like that."

"Polish coins?" I hazarded a guess.

He nodded. "The pool of suspects was small and since Miss Janson did most of the cleaning, especially now that Bridget is gone, it wasn't hard to figure out. Mr. Witkop confronted her and she confessed."

"She said she needed the money for medicine for her sick mother," Mrs. Leggett broke in. She snorted. "It may be true, but stealing is immoral. Mr. Witkop would have given her the money if she'd asked. I know he would have. But no, she just took what wasn't hers without a by-your-leave."

"Did he tell her that?"

"I wasn't in the room when he spoke to her, so I don't know what he said. But he did dismiss her on the spot. You can't have untrustworthy employees." She put on her coat. "I'll make sure the things you saw are the Witkops' and tell them. Maybe this shop has more of the missing items."

"They're closed," I said absently. The way Mrs. Leggett talked, Mr. Witkop was generous. Then why didn't he offer to give Mildred the cash she needed once he found out about it instead of giving her the boot? She hadn't stolen out of spite, but need. Seemed to me it would be far more in character for him to forgive the theft and give his housekeeper a raise to make sure she had enough dough to make ends meet. No, for some reason Mr. Witkop didn't want the woman around any longer. That immediately prompted the question of why. Because she'd seen Paul leave early and might tie him to Josef Pyrut's death? Or was it something else? "Do you know where Miss

Janson lives?" I asked.

"I have no idea, nor do I want to, especially now." Mrs. Leggett's hand hovered over her buttons. "You're sure about the shop?"

"Yeah, I told you I was there earlier. Try tomorrow." A thought that had been dancing at the edge of my mind pushed to the front. "He said the china was French. Why would that be? I mean, the Witkops are from Poland, right? Their name used to be Witkowski."

The two in front of me said nothing, mulish looks on their faces.

I threw up my hands. "Oh, come on. Why the secret? There's no shame in being from Poland. I got lots of Polish friends at work. Heck, there's a whole neighborhood of 'em. Why're they hiding it?"

After a long moment, when they seemed to be communicating by stares, Mr. Charles spoke. "Yes, you're right. Mr. Witkop is from Poland. I noticed a particularly fine picture one day and he said his father brought it over. He, Mr. Witkop, was only a child. The only thing his father ever told him about the name change is that America was supposed to be a fresh start, so there was no point in talking about the past."

"French china, you said?" Mrs. Leggett asked. "Surely the man was wrong. It must be Polish."

"He was pretty certain," I said. "I wouldn't know, myself." Why French? More rewards from the Prussians? I shook myself. "One more thing. Do you remember a letter arriving from a woman named Pelagia Brewka? It would have been late last month or early this month."

Mr. Charles shook his head. "Miss Janson got the mail from the box, but I'd give it to Mr. Witkop. I don't remember seeing any such correspondence."

One more question to ask Mildred. "Are you sure you don't know where Miss Janson lives?"

"I'm sorry, no." Mr. Charles's voice was firm. "We've told you all we know. Thank you for the information on the china."

"Yeah, well, g'night." I turned away, and the door closed behind me.

* * *

I arrived home, intending to set out Cat's saucer with his dinner. But before I could take off my coat, Mary Kate rushed into the hallway. "Betty, you're home! You got a delivery, come see." She grabbed my arm and dragged me into the kitchen.

A square package wrapped in plain brown paper lay in the middle of the table. My name and address were written in neat printing with black ink. I checked for a return address, but there wasn't one. The postmark was Buffalo. Who in the city would send me a box by mail and anonymously at that? Dot or Lee would hand deliver. Sam MacKinnon might send me something, but he'd put his address on it. I turned it over in my hands. The heavy brown paper didn't give me any clues and neither did the thick cellophane tape holding it shut.

Mary Kate hung at my elbow. "Open it!"

"All right, hold your horses." I knew I wouldn't have much luck peeling off the tape, so I got the kitchen scissors from the drawer. I cut the folded ends of the paper and pulled out the contents.

It was a box from Wahl's. The blue shone in the kitchen light, bound neatly with a white satin ribbon. It looked familiar for some reason.

Mary Kate squealed. "It must be chocolate! Lucky, who sent you that?"

"I dunno." The only person who would give me chocolate was Tom, who was currently somewhere in North Africa. I didn't think V-mail delivered Wahl's.

"There's a card." Mary Kate held it out. "It fell on the table when you opened the wrapping."

I took it. It was plain white paper and rather heavy, not regular notepaper or ripped from a tablet. *From your secret admirer* was written on it in the same heavy block printing as the address. I put it down and examined the box again. Then I slid off the ribbon and opened the lid. Inside were neat rows of chocolate-covered globes. The label inside proclaimed them to be an assortment of liqueur-filled milk chocolates.

Mary Kate read the note. "A secret admirer." She giggled. "Better not tell Tom."

"For a secret admirer, he doesn't know me very well. I don't really like the filled stuff. Give me a slab of Hershey's or a box of Wahl's sponge candy any day."

"Then can I have it?"

Mary Kate loved any kind of chocolate. "No. Especially not before supper. Mom will tan your hide." I gathered up the paper scraps. "Speaking of supper, get the table set. I'll get changed and we can finish the cooking."

"Just one piece, please?"

"No." I slid the box back into the brown wrapping paper. "Table, plates, silverware, shoo!" I took the mystery chocolate to my room and shoved it under my bed.

The box was not V-mail. I could immediately cross Lee off the list. He knew me better than to send any kind of filled chocolate. Plus, he'd never be my secret admirer. His heart belonged to Dot, and he'd never betray his best friend. No one I knew could afford a whole box like that. One maybe, or even a Whitman's Sampler, but candy like Wahl's cost serious dough. Nobody from the First Ward would buy such a thing, not even for Christmas.

Who did that leave? Paul Witkop immediately sprang to mind. He definitely had the cabbage. But the couple of times I'd spoken to him, he'd made it pretty clear he didn't think I was worth his time. Of course, that could be a ruse. After all, if he proclaimed his affections, he wouldn't be a *secret* admirer, would he? But it didn't make any sense. We barely knew each other. Then again, it would explain why he sent a box of goodies I didn't like at all. My thoughts went back and forth for a good minute. Since I couldn't immediately think of who sent the box, I pushed it out of my head. I'd deal with that later.

I grabbed a sheet of paper and a pen, and began to write.

Dear Tom, Merry Christmas. It hasn't been that long since my last letter, barely a week, but I needed to write. Things have gotten complicated here. I didn't want to tell you in a letter, but I've taken up detective work. Most times it's not anything big, but this current case is a doozy and I need help. It started pretty simple, just a girl at Bell who thought

> *her grandma might have been murdered. But now, I don't know. Turns out the grandma is from Poland, and she worked for a family here in Buffalo when she was back in the old country, and they may have been Prussian sympathizers after the Franco-Prussian War, and...*

I stopped. I couldn't write this. I sounded crazy and poor Tom wouldn't be able to do anything to help me.

What was the Witkops' secret? Pelagia knew. So did Bridget. Josef Pyrut might have known. It had to be a big one if three people had lost their lives over it. You couldn't bury a secret that big without a cover story, right? *People tell themselves all kinds of stories to make themselves feel better,* Pop had said. I thought of the Witkops, their swell house, and their money, earned through investments. Was that their story and how had the three dead people threatened it?

I rubbed my temples. Nothing would make sense until I answered that question and Tom wasn't gonna be able to help me. I wadded up my half-written letter and stuffed it in a drawer.

As I snapped off the light, I spotted the corner of the candy box sticking out from under my bed. Secret admirer my foot. I had enough puzzles to solve. I didn't need romantic shenanigans, too.

Chapter Twenty-Eight

It was Christmas Eve, but that didn't mean much since the war started. Sean and Tom didn't get a day off, why should I? Dot and I went to work same as usual, where Mr. Satterwaite's one concession to the holiday was to say "Merry Christmas" before he snapped at us.

"Mildred was fired?" Dot repeated my words.

"Yep." I screwed in my instrument panel. "Not surprising if she was stealing from her employers."

"But it's Christmas."

"I guess that doesn't matter to the Witkops." I stood back and waited as the assembly lined chugged forward.

Dot cocked her head. "You should see your face. You still out of sorts?"

Once again, I knew better than to brush her off. "I've been working this case for three weeks. I feel like I'm running in place. Heck, I found a killer and a saboteur in less time last month."

She gazed at me, eyes full of sympathy. "They aren't all easy ones, Betty."

"You're calling last month easy?"

"Of course not. Just that you gotta think of the police and the cases they never solve." She paused. "You know…"

"What?"

"If Mildred was stealing and Bridget knew about it, maybe that's what she was coming to tell you."

I'd thought of the possibility. "Yeah, I know. Mildred knew where the rat poison was, and she knew about Bridget's sugar bowl. She coulda done it."

"I can't see Mildred as the murdering type, though. She's so *motherly*."

"Could be that she didn't know how deadly the poison would be." I pointed my screwdriver at Dot. "Mildred might only have wanted to frighten Bridget into keepin' quiet."

"C'mon, poison? You use it to kill rats, not make 'em sick. What did she expect it would do to people?"

"She put it in the sugar. People are bigger than rats. Give a smaller dose to a larger animal and you might think it would do exactly that." I finished my panel.

"She can't be that stupid."

"People have thought dumber things."

"You got that right." She chewed her lip. "Do you know what you're gonna do next?"

"I'm planning to go talk to Sam MacKinnon again right after work. He might be able to tell me more about the poisoning." I hoped the detective wouldn't get mad about me busting in on him on Christmas Eve. Perhaps I should get him a Christmas present.

We'd just sat down to lunch when Emmie came up to us. "Whew! I'm not sure old Satterwaite realizes tomorrow's a holiday."

"There is a war on." I unwrapped my sandwich. "Pop told me a story about the Great War, about how in 1914 the fighting stopped on Christmas, and the Germans and the British sang to each other across the battlefield. I don't think Adolf is keen on pausing hostilities to have a sing-a-long."

Emmie and Dot giggled.

"What's up? If you're looking for a progress report, I'm sorry to say I haven't got much to tell you."

"Luke couldn't help you?"

"Yeah, he did. He talks a lot."

Emmie leaned her chin on her hands. "I figured all boys did that. Is there a finished letter?"

"Yes." I told her about my talk with Luke and the trip to the Witkops' house.

"Then that's it?" Her disappointment showed on her round Shirley Temple face.

"No. I need to find Mildred Janson." I took a bite of my lunch, chewed, then swallowed. "Mr. Charles said she got the mail every day. Maybe she saw it, or she saw someone messing with the post."

Emmie nodded. "Makes sense. But do you know where Mildred lives?"

"Not yet, but I will. I also need to talk to Sam MacKinnon down at the Buffalo police department. I'll tell him what I've learned and see if it changes his mind at all about your grandma. I also want to see if he's made any progress with Josef Pyrut or Bridget Innes."

Emmie wrinkled her nose. "You think he'll talk to you about a police case?"

"Sam MacKinnon and I have an understanding. Least we should after everything we've been through." I turned to Dot. "I want you to do me a favor."

"Name it," she said.

"I need you to find Mildred. I don't have time to do that and see Sam."

"How do I do that?"

"Start with the telephone book and see if she's listed. If not, go up to Delaware Park and see if the folks at the Witkops' remember anything that could be helpful. What bus route she took, or if she ever talked about how long it took to get to work. Take Lee with you if you want company."

"Today?" Dot's voice was dubious.

"If you can."

She sighed. "I gotta go out for Ma later to get some things for Christmas dinner. I'll try and do it then."

"Thanks, Dot." I glanced at the clock on the wall and stuffed my sandwich in my mouth. For the first time ever, I thought about going to the infirmary and telling the nurse I was sick and had to leave work. At the rate I was goin' it would be spring before I found the answers I was lookin' for.

* * *

After work, I took the bus downtown and went to police headquarters. Sam was there, my first bit of luck in days.

When he came down, his tie was crooked, his hair mussed, and he held a lit cigarette. "Yes, Miss Ahern?"

"For the last time, I told you. Call me Betty." I presented him with a small square, which I'd hastily wrapped in the comics page of the day's newspaper. "Merry Christmas."

"What's this?"

"What do you think? It's a Christmas present."

"You shouldn't have." He took the package and ripped off the paper revealing a box containing a shiny, stainless steel Zippo lighter.

"To replace the battered one you have. I mean, unless that's got sentimental value or something." I hadn't thought of the possibility until that moment. Oops.

"No, it doesn't." He turned over the lighter. "This has a shamrock on it." He lifted an eyebrow.

"Sure. You're Irish, I'm Irish. I want you to think of me when you use it."

"Miss...Betty, it's not appropriate for a member of the public to be giving a police officer a gift."

I chucked him on the shoulder. "Oh c'mon. It's a lighter, not a car."

He glanced around at the empty lobby and slipped the Zippo in his pocket. "Thank you. Is that all?"

"Nope." I pulled Pelagia's partial letters out of my pocket.

"I should have known."

I held them out. "These came from Pelagia Brewka. They're all half-written, but they're addressed to Sebastian Witkop and they hint at some kinda secret she needed to talk to him about. These aren't finished, but I found a kid who helped her. He told me she did post one."

Sam clamped his gasper between his lips as he read the letters. "Interesting."

"I thought so, too."

"No, interesting that no one mentioned these since I've been investigating Bridget Innes's death. I asked all members of the household if anything unusual had happened in the past month, strange phone calls or correspondence. Not one of them mentioned anything like this."

"If it was addressed to Mr. Witkop, maybe they wouldn't think to."

"Possible. I can keep these, right?" Without waiting for an answer, he pocketed them.

I didn't mind. I'd kept one of 'em for my use. "Have you learned anything? Besides the fact that Mildred Janson was stealing from the Witkops and has been fired?" I figured he'd know, but my saying so made it clear I was still involved and active in the case.

His lips twitched. "I've already told you about the sugar and the strychnine. Upon further searching, we discovered a box of opened rat poison at the Witkop residence that was most likely the source of the poison. The white crystals would have mixed easily with the sugar. It was in the garden shed, however. Anyone in the house would have had access." He paused. "Have I told you anything you don't know?"

"Nothing I hadn't guessed, but it's good to have confirmation."

"I thought as much. Well, I'm sorry, but I can't tell you anything more about an ongoing investigation."

"Aw c'mon, Sam. That's not fair."

"I'm sorry. But I repeat, I can't *tell* you anything." He inhaled and blew out a stream of smoke.

I opened my mouth to protest then shut it once I recognized the way he'd stressed *tell*. "Did Bridget argue with anyone in the house?"

"People fight all the time. You should know that."

"Sebastian Witkop?"

He stayed silent.

"What about Paul or Mildred Janson? I know Bridget was carryin' on below stairs with Paul. Mildred didn't approve. Not only that, if Bridget knew about Mildred's stealing, she mighta said somethin' to the family."

"I can't confirm that." Sam gave me a wink.

I got it. "Thank you, Detective. I hope you have a pleasant holiday."

He gave me a finger-salute. "Merry Christmas, Miss Ahern. Stay out of trouble." He turned and walked away.

Before I left headquarters, I took a good look at the clock on the wall. It was five-thirty. I had to talk to Mildred and fast.

Chapter Twenty-Nine

I hopped off the bus back in the First Ward and hoofed it to Dot's house.

"Can I use your phone?" I asked as I shucked off my coat.

"It's on the hall table, same place it's always been. I'll hang these up." She took my winter things to the closet. "Lee and I will wait for you in the kitchen."

Lee and her? I hadn't expected him to be here. Did he stop by or did she ask him? "Knock it off, Betty. Stay focused," I muttered. I called home.

Mary Kate answered. "Where are you?"

"Dot's house. Tell Mom and Pop that Dot and I have a bit of last-minute shopping to do. If they say anything about us leaving it until the last minute, tell 'em we haven't had a chance because of work, but it's for Dot's folks, so it's real important."

"Sure. Anything else?"

"Yeah, feed Cat."

"You owe me two sweets for this, Betty. Two jobs means double the price."

"How about I give you a quarter and let you buy your own treats?"

"Deal."

I put the phone back in the cradle. Jimmy charged me for renting his bike. Mary Kate asked for baked goods in exchange for every favor. My siblings were businessmen, that was certain. What next, Michael would demand new model airplanes?

I headed to the kitchen. Through the doorway, I could see Dot and Lee seated at the table, a phone book next to them and a sheet of notes on top of it.

Lee was picking up crumbs from a plate. "He needs to quit or get out, and I don't know how to make him do either."

She patted his shoulder. "I know."

I stopped at the entrance. "Am I interrupting something?"

"No, we were just talking. Have a seat." Dot waved at an empty chair. "Want anything?"

"Mildred Janson's address." I fixed her with a stare. *What was that about?* I silently asked.

She shook her head slightly, which had to mean *Not now*. Dot never kept secrets from me. She'd spill when it was time. "There you go." Dot pushed the sheet of notes toward me. "We looked for any M. Janson in the phone book and found three. But then Lee said if she was married, she might be listed under her husband's name."

Lee pointed. "We found four more Jansons. Actually, we found even more, but we narrowed it down to houses in working-class neighborhoods. A housekeeper isn't going to have a flash address."

"Smart." I scanned the sheet. "This is a lot of names, though. How are we gonna find her? We can't visit all these places on Christmas Eve, no less. We can't call either. It'll take all night." It was already past six.

"Keep your shirt on," Lee said. "We didn't stop there."

"We already called them," Dot said, sweeping some stray crumbs onto the plate and taking it to the sink.

I lifted my eyebrows. "All of 'em?"

"Yep. Dot and I split the list. We pretended we were calling from the Police Benevolent Association, or collecting cans, or doing surveys...a bunch of different things." He lit a cigarette, drew on it, then exhaled. "Third number from the bottom. That's her."

I looked. M. Janson, 53 College Street. I recognized the address as being in Allentown. Not close by Delaware Park, but she could get to the Witkops by bus without much trouble. Beyond that, I wasn't familiar with the neighborhood. "Is she home now?"

"Yep," Dot said.

"You're sure she's not married?" I asked.

"Positive," Lee said. "And there's no man in the house right this minute. I pretended to be takin' a survey and asked for Mr. Janson. She said there wasn't one, so I talked to her. That's the right Mildred. One other thing. You said she stole the stuff from Witkop because she needed money for medicine?"

"That's what Mrs. Leggett told me."

"There's an old lady in the house, I'd guess pretty frail. I heard the voice over the phone. At one point Mildred broke off talking to me to tell this other lady she'd only be another minute or two, and she'd get the hot water bottle soon." He ashed his smoke. "That's your girl."

Dot, who had been drying dishes while Lee and I talked, put down her towel and turned. "What do we do next?"

"I'm gonna go to this address and see if she'll talk to me." I stood.

"You mean us. Lee and I are going too."

I waved her off. "You two have done good with this. I'm sure Lee has to get home to his sisters and I doubt your folks are gonna let you wander all over Buffalo on Christmas Eve, Dot."

Lee took one last drag off his cigarette before crushing it out in the ash tray. "Mom is home with the girls. Dad is out. I'm going with you."

"My parents are at a Christmas party for a friend of Dad's and we aren't going to church until tomorrow," Dot said as she folded the towel. "They'll never know I was gone."

I was touched by their loyalty, but I couldn't let them take the holiday time away from their families, or from themselves, if I read the tone of their earlier conversation correctly. I couldn't be with my sweetheart, but that didn't mean I was going to bust up someone else's night. "It's not necessary."

"Betty, we're coming." Lee picked up his cap and tugged it on.

Dot left and reappeared with our coats. "Mildred Janson might be a killer right? Even if she looks more like someone's mother?"

"I s'pose it's possible." I took my coat from her.

"Then we're coming with you," she said in a voice that brooked no argument. "I'm not gonna let my best friend go talk to a murderer all by herself."

"And I'm not gonna let you two go off outta my sight and get into trouble," Lee added.

I looked at them and immediately realized there was no arguing. Lee's jaw was set and Dot's expression reminded me of Mom's when she had made up her mind and that was that. I was First Ward Irish and stubborn, but so were they. I suddenly realized that's how I was different than Spade, Marlowe, and a lot of other private detectives from the movies. I had friends to back me up. I pulled on my mittens. "Well, if I can't talk you out of it, let's stop jawing and get going. We don't have all night."

* * *

We hopped on the first available bus and traveled to Allentown. We didn't talk much on the way. I spent the time trying to figure out what I was gonna say to Mildred. I knew she was a thief. What else did she know?

Fifty-three College was a modest house, clean white with a small yard. Shrubs lined the front with spaces for flowers. There weren't any Victory stars in the windows, but that wasn't surprising if the people who lived there were a spinster woman and her elderly mother. An American flag hung limp next to the door. Even in the winter, the place was tidy and well-cared for.

We approached, Lee in front, Dot and me trailing. He pushed the button for the doorbell. No answer. After a bit, he pushed again, this time leaning on it a little.

Mildred's voice came from inside. "Just a minute, give a body time to answer. Christmas Eve and visitors, unplanned at that, people's manners are going to the dogs." The door swung open. "If you're collecting, young man, I gave at my church."

"Mildred Janson?" he asked.

Her forehead wrinkled as she frowned. "Yes, who are you?"

He stepped aside so she could see Dot and me.

Her frown turned into a scowl. "You two. I have nothing more to say to you. I tried to do the right thing by Bridget and look where it got me."

I stepped. "Hey, I didn't have anything to do with you gettin' fired. I didn't know about you taking stuff from the Witkops and selling it. Not until I saw it at the shop and by then you'd been sacked. I'm sorry about that, but maybe you should have left other people's things alone."

Her formerly motherly expression turned frosty.

I continued. "I have some questions, yes. You don't have to answer them, but I expect the police will be paying you a visit, if they haven't already. Maybe I can help with that." A spot of red appeared on her cheeks and I knew I'd hit close to home. "It's about Bridget. And the Witkops. It'll only take fifteen minutes or so. Promise."

She sniffed. "I know the girl behind you. Who is the young man and why isn't he overseas?"

Lee doffed his cap. "Lee Tillotson. I'm an old friend of Betty's. I have a bum leg that kept me out of the service. It'd be real helpful if you'd talk to Betty here."

Dot piped up. "Like Betty said, we didn't know about the theft until after the fact. This is more about Bridget and the Witkops."

Mildred seemed to be battling with herself. "Fifteen minutes, no more. Don't expect coffee or snacks, and we'll talk in the kitchen. My mother is very ill and she likes to sit in the front room and listen to the radio in the evening. I won't have her disturbed."

We all promised to behave and she let us in.

As soon as Mildred closed the door, a frail voice came from the front room. "Mildred? Who is there?"

"It's nothing, Mother." Mildred went into the room. An old woman, barely more than skin and bones judging by her face, was in a big armchair by the wall. A radio in a dark brown case rested on the table beside her, tuned to some kind of music program. An announcer came on and spoke a language I didn't know. The woman was covered in multiple knitted afghans. Mildred went to her and fussed with them. "Are you cold? Do you want some tea or warm milk?"

"No, no, I'm fine. Who are these young ones?" her mother asked in her tired, thin voice.

Mildred shot a look at us. "Just some people I know. They won't be here long. You rest." She smoothed the topmost afghan and kissed the old woman's forehead. Then she came back to us, her manner going from caretaker to army sergeant with the flip of a switch. "This way." She led us to a kitchen that Mom would have approved of. Every surface gleamed. Mildred waved at a table with four upright wooden chairs, most likely uncomfortable. "What do you want?"

I pulled out the nearest chair and sat down. I was right about the comfort level. Sam prob'ly had better ones down in the interrogation room at police HQ. "Mrs. Leggett told us you'd been fired 'cause you were stealing china and stuff from the Witkops and selling it. Is that true?"

Mildred did not sit. Obviously, she wanted this conversation over quickly and hoped standing would hurry it along. After a moment, she nodded. "Yes. As you can see, Mother is not well. Her medicine is expensive. The things I took." She waved a hand. "It was never big stuff, not the important pieces. No one was supposed to know. Goodness knows the Witkops have so many knick-knacks, one or two wouldn't have been missed. Not until Mrs. Witkop's tea party."

Lee took the seat to my left. "What do you mean?"

"The cups and saucers." She huffed. "When only three people take after dinner coffee, it's not hard to hide a few missing cups. When you have a party of twelve, and only eight cups are found, it becomes a little more noticeable. She couldn't leave it alone."

Dot had sat down on my right. "She who? Bridget?"

"Yes." Mildred's voice was sharp enough to cut butter. "I suggested they'd been misplaced or packed away somewhere. 'Oh no, Miss Janson, that isn't so. I'm sure they was here. I remember cleaning them after the big to-do earlier this month.' I wasn't hurting anyone and they weren't her things. Why did she care?"

I leaned forward. "Did she figure it out or did she see you?"

Mildred paused. "The police, they haven't been here yet," she said. "Earlier you mentioned you might be able to help with that. Did you mean it?"

I knew I was on touchy ground. There was no way I could keep the police from getting involved, but it was clear to me that her mother was Mildred's primary worry. "I might. It depends on what you tell me."

In the silence, I could hear the radio program from the other room and the ticking of a clock. Mildred wouldn't look at me. She kept her gaze on the far wall, lips moving in silent speech, but I couldn't tell if it was prayer or somethin' else. I looked at Lee and Dot, neither of whom looked any more certain than me. Dot twitched her shoulders in a tiny shrug and Lee lifted his eyebrows.

After what felt like forever, Mildred spoke. "Bridget was cleaning and noticed some of the missing items. She saw my handbag in the closet, thought it looked fuller than usual, and peeked inside."

"You'd hidden the things in your bag," I said. I didn't need to make it a question.

Mildred nodded. "She confronted me and asked if I'd taken other items that were missing, a small silver frame and a porcelain figurine. I tried to deny it at first, but she wouldn't stop pestering me and I admitted it. I told her why and said I only needed to earn a little money and I'd be able to buy them back. It wasn't as though the Witkops had noticed anything missing. She didn't need to tell them. She insisted. She said she was sorry to hear about Mother, but what I was doing wasn't right and she was sure Mother would agree."

Lee leaned forward. "What did you say?"

Mildred fussed with her apron. "I begged for more time. She refused."

"I'd think she'd be sympathetic," Lee said. "What with you two working in the same house and all."

"Bridget was very Catholic," Mildred replied. "Stealing was against the commandments. She said it was her duty to inform Mr. Witkop."

I tapped my fingers on the table. "When was this?"

"The day before she died, and I met you."

Dot piped up. "Did she tell 'em? The Witkops?"

"I don't know," Mildred said. "None of them were home that evening and the next morning, well, that was when she...died."

"Pretty convenient for you," Lee said.

Mildred lifted her head and her gaze snapped to him. "What are you talking about?"

Dot leaned her chin on her palm. "Bridget was gonna blow the lid on your little scheme. Before she can, she's dead. Like Lee said, convenient. Your secret was safe, or so you thought."

It took Mildred a couple of seconds to cotton on to Dot's meaning. "You… you think I killed her?" Her chest swelled.

"It would make sense," Lee said. "Otherwise you'd have lost your job weeks ago. It's a bad time to be unemployed, even without a sick relative."

"I didn't buy your grief act when we met you," Dot added. "Just so you know."

I said nothing while all this played out in front of me. Letting Lee and Dot carry the conversation allowed me to focus on Mildred. She was pretty outraged, yes. Her face was red, her lips a pale slash from how tightly she'd mashed 'em together, and her nostrils flared. But her eyes held another look. Mildred was scared. Because she'd been discovered as a killer or because she might go down for someone else's wrong-doing?

"You had access to the poison," Lee pointed out.

"And you ran the house," I added. "It would have been easy for you to switch out some of the sugar in the servants' bowl. You knew Bridget was the only one who used it. No one else woulda gotten hurt, and you coulda switched it back without anyone knowing. I bet that was your plan, wasn't it? But the cops got there too fast."

"I did nothing of the kind," she said, trying to regain some composure. "Okay, you're right. I wasn't as sad as I pretended to be that day we met. I admit I was relieved. Bridget's death did keep me out of trouble, at least for a while." She twisted her lips. "The Witkops found out anyway and gave me the boot. If she'd have lived, they would have found out earlier. But I didn't kill her."

"If Bridget didn't tell 'em, who did?" I asked.

Mildred's stared at the wall. "I…I don't know. Maybe she did after all. I hadn't thought about it much."

Dot looked at me. "What do you think, Betty?"

"I think it coulda been exactly like Lee said." I watched the red bleed from Mildred's face, leaving it blotchy. "Then again, maybe not. I asked you once before about Paul Witkop, if he left the party. You said he went to bed. Is that true?"

Mildred's mouth worked, but no words came. She licked her lips and swallowed. "Yes, but he left shortly afterward. I saw him. He'd changed out of his tuxedo and into some plainer clothes. There's a tree next to the house and one of the branches is near his window. He used to climb down it when he was a youngster and he hasn't lost the skill."

"When was this?" Lee asked.

"Maybe nine-thirty, perhaps a little earlier."

"Which way did he go?" Dot asked.

Mildred didn't quite know which of us to look at, so she gazed at the floor. "Down the street, toward the city. I didn't follow, so after I lost sight of him I don't know."

Toward the city. That meant he could have gone to Fillmore Avenue. Then again, maybe he was just taking a stroll. There was a lot of ground between his house and Fillmore. "Is there anything else?" I asked.

She looked up. "Like what?"

"I dunno. Anything. 'Cause I talked to Mrs. Leggett. The way she told it, all you had to do was ask Mr. Witkop for the money and he'd have given it to you. That's a generous man. But he didn't even make the offer, did he?"

Mildred pressed her lips together.

"That makes me think he fired you not 'cause of the stealing, but something else. Something you knew. And I have to ask myself what it is."

Mildred's lip trembled. She looked like a woman torn between two options, deciding whether to speak up. But after a long moment, she composed herself and gave a small shake of her head. "I don't know what you're talking about. I never asked because I didn't think he would give me the money." But she sounded unconvincing, like my brothers after they'd raided the kitchen, but denied it. All the while they had milk mustaches and crumbs on their shirts.

"Suit yourself," I said. I stood. I'd give her space and try again later. Maybe time would get her to change her mind and decide to confide in me.

"Are you going to tell the police?" Mildred asked, her voice trembling.

"Tell 'em what? They already know you're a thief. Am I gonna tell 'em Bridget knew and was gonna turn you in? If you don't think they know, or they'll find out, you're wrong." I shrugged into my coat.

"I told you about Paul!" Mildred looked through the door toward her mother's room, but the old lady said nothing. Maybe she was asleep. "Doesn't that count for anything?" She asked in a lower voice. "You said you could help with the police."

"If the police haven't been here yet about the theft, they might not come. Heck, Mr. Witkop may not have called 'em, not for something like this." I reached for the doorknob as Lee and Dot prepared themselves to go. "Tell you what. I'll talk to the detective about the theft and see if it's been reported. I'm sorry about your mom and I bet the cops will take that into account, especially if you tell the Witkops how to get their stuff back. But Bridget's death is a completely different thing." I pulled the door open. "I know it sounds blunt, but the police are going to think you had a motive, 'cause she knew about your stealing and she was gonna tell your boss. You could have gotten hold of both the poison and the sugar. I'll speak to 'em, sure, but don't be surprised if a man named Detective Sam MacKinnon turns up at your door and prob'ly not long from now. I can't stop that."

We left and hurried through Allentown. Around us, snatches of song reminded us it was Christmas Eve. Lee might have a bum leg, but he also had a long stride so he kept up with me easily. Dot, with her shorter legs, had to jog to keep up with us. "Do you think she's guilty?" she asked as her breath steamed before her.

"She did confirm your suspicion that Paul Witkop wasn't in bed," Lee said.

"Which means he mighta left to meet Josef Pyrut and gotten his hands dirty for that, yeah. And maybe he knew about Pelagia. He got Mildred fired not 'cause of the theft, but so she couldn't blab about that." I tightened my muffler. "Could be Bridget knew, too and he snuffed her. But I meant what I said. Nothing we just learned takes Mildred Janson out of the picture. I do know one thing, though." We reached the bus stop.

"What's that?" Dot asked, slightly out of breath.

"I'm breaking my promise to Emmie. I'm not gonna get this wrapped up by Christmas."

Chapter Thirty

Christmas Day dawned, cold and crisp. Snow swirled down, leaving a layer of white on streets, garbage cans, and anything left outside. Today, at least, was a day of rest. For me, anyway. The Steel was open and Pop had to work, but not until the evening. We went to Mass early and planned for our big meal at mid-day. We'd done the best we could saving and trading coupons so we had a small roast, vegetables, and enough sugar for a cake. I wasn't sure what Mary Kate had used for the frosting, but it tasted good so I didn't ask any questions.

After we ate, Mom settled in the living room to listen to the radio while Pop got ready to go to the plant. Michael and Jimmy took their new toys outside, and Mary Kate sat down to do some sewing. I pulled my coat from the closet. "I'm going for a walk," I said as I pulled my hair out of my collar.

Pop didn't open an eye, but Mom faced me. "Where? And why ever would you want to do that in this cold?"

I buttoned up my coat. "I dunno, just somewhere. I might see if Dot or Lee can join me. I don't get to walk in the daylight very often. It'll be a nice change of pace."

Mom opened her mouth, then shut it. She thought a moment, then spoke. "Stay warm and out of trouble. We're going to have a light supper at six, so be home if you want to eat."

"Yes, ma'am." Outside, I paused on our front step and inhaled a lungful of crisp air. The street was eerily quiet, as though the world slept under its glittery blanket. Every so often, the silence was broken by the sound of a kid whooping over a game or as he played with Christmas goodies.

Although I'd told Mom I'd ask Dot or Lee for company, I suddenly craved solitude. I needed to think. Besides, they'd be busy with their own families. I pulled out my deck of Luckys, tapped out a cigarette, lit it, and blew smoke. I let my feet take me where they wanted. Which is how, after a walk, a bus ride, and some more walking, I ended up at Forest Lawn Cemetery.

The grounds were quiet. I wandered among the headstones, reading the names without really seeing 'em. Here and there, the white of snow and the gray granite was adorned with the dark green of a wreath and the red of a Christmas ribbon, evidence that loved ones had stopped to wish long-gone friends and family members Merry Christmas.

Just as I had concluded that I had the cemetery to myself, I spotted a figure. A man, dressed in a long black coat, stood in front of a stone, hands in his pockets. A wreath lay on the ground in front of him. A few steps more and I identified the figure as Sebastian Witkop.

Darn it. I didn't want to see him now, not on Christmas. Who was he visiting? His parents, maybe? Forest Lawn wasn't far from Delaware Park and home. If I hurried off, I could get away without a conversation.

In my haste, my foot came down on a stray twig, which snapped with a crack that was prob'ly not as loud as it sounded, but it was enough. I tried to keep going. A voice stopped me in my tracks.

"Young lady, where are you—don't I know you?" Mr. Witkop asked.

I stopped and slowly turned. "Hey there, Mr. Witkop."

He didn't twitch. "I saw you outside Kleinhan's the other night. When I was downtown with my son."

"Yes, sir." I wasn't sure whether to move closer or not. On the one hand, he might have been involved with Bridget's death, if not Josef. On the other, I didn't see a weapon of any kind on him. I decided staying a good distance away was my best bet. I was certainly faster than an old man if it came to running.

He remained still as a statue. "Mr. Charles mentioned a young woman had stopped at the house. Was that you?"

"Yes, sir. I was asking after Bridget. Well, I visited a couple of times, looking for Bridget and your old housekeeper. Your wife wasn't happy."

His eyebrows lowered, expression puzzled. "You saw Eleanor?"

"Briefly. Like I said, she wasn't pleased."

"Why on earth would you want to talk to Miss Janson?" He puzzled expression didn't change.

"I had a couple of questions."

"Mr. Charles said you identified some of our stolen items at a secondhand shop."

I nodded.

"I should thank you for that, I suppose." He exhaled, his breath loud in the silent cemetery. "But really, I have too many things, although Eleanor would not say the same. All of it with bad memories. I miss her, Miss Janson. She was an excellent housekeeper. Maybe I should have given her some money for her mother and forgiven the thefts." He chuffed a laugh. "Paul and his mother would disagree with that, of course."

Neither of us had moved. I was beginning to think he was harmless. "I gather the items were family heirlooms?"

He nodded. "My parents brought them from Poland, just like so much in the house. Too much, as I said." He waved at the headstone. "They're buried there, my mother and father. I visit them every Easter and Christmas."

"That's logical, I guess." After all, we visited the cemetery for our dead relatives on important days. "Why don't you get rid of 'em? The rest of the stuff, I mean. You gave the books to the library."

He glanced at me. "You know a lot about my household for a young lady from the First Ward."

I didn't answer. I didn't have a good one.

He paused, then continued. "Those were easier to part with. Paul doesn't care about books. Neither does my wife. I thought they should at least be somewhere they were cared for. Otherwise, they would've gone to a pawn shop, or worse, after I died. Hopefully that won't be for a good many years, but you never know. Look at poor Bridget."

I saw my opening. "You know she was murdered, right?"

"That's what the police said."

"Just like Josef Pyrut. And another woman, Pelagia Brewka." His eyebrows lowered further and I pressed on. "You know her. She wrote you a letter and she came to your house once."

He thought a moment and some of the confusion left his face. "The old woman. She claimed to have worked for my parents."

"She was telling the truth."

"I remember a young maid. I was very small, and my memories are spotty, but she worked in the house. She used to give me treats, little cakes she'd baked. She laughed a lot." The memory was a good one, 'cause he smiled. "The cakes were very good. My mother scolded me something fierce when she found sugar on my face."

It was the complete opposite of what he'd told me the last time I'd seen him. Why?

He must've seen my confusion. "You're wondering why I denied it that night outside the store. Of course. I was trying to protect Paul. Tell me, Miss…?"

"Ahern, sir. Betty Ahern."

"Miss Ahern. You seem like a sharp girl. Did you notice anything about the cups you saw in the consignment shop?"

"They were French. I did wonder why—"

"A Polish family had French china?" He looked away and didn't speak. The tortured expression on his face told me he was fighting with himself. Finally, he seemed to make a decision and faced me again. "Having French things was a mark of status in those times. Something a moneyed family would own, you understand. But with my parents, it was more. Much more and not particularly noble. May I tell you a secret, Miss Ahern? Do you promise not to tell anyone?"

"Yes, sir, of course." I wished he'd move. I had lost feeling in my toes, and my fingers weren't far behind.

He sighed. "My parents were not…well, let's just say they weren't always honorable. Do you know anything about the Franco-Prussian War?"

"A little. A friend of mine likes history. I know the Poles supported the French and the Prussians punished 'em something fierce for years after the war ended."

"Not all the Poles. Not my family." He paused. "Would it shock you if I told you my family made a great deal of money informing on their neighbors? On a few French families, too. The war ended in 1871, but resistance to the Prussians continued long after, of course."

The lightbulb clicked on. "That's why the cups have a French stamp. Your folks got 'em as a reward for passing information. What exactly did they say?"

His shoulders raised and lowered. "I don't know. As I said, I was very young. Presumably it was about the activities of other Poles, maybe knowledge obtained when my parents were believed to be against the Prussians. That's why they eventually left the country."

"When was this?"

"I was born in the 1880s. We emigrated in the early nineties." He stared at the gravestone. "When my parents' activities became known, they weren't particularly popular in the area."

"You don't say." I couldn't keep the sarcasm out of my voice.

Mr. Witkop's answering grin was a bit rueful. "I guess I deserved that. Yes, Pelagia wrote to me. I ignored the letter. Then she visited. She urged me to give away all the things from my parents to atone for their mistakes in betraying their neighbors as best I could."

"But you couldn't. Why not?"

"I'm weak, I suppose. You grow up in luxury, you get used to it." He turned to me. "This is where you point out I'm a successful businessman with my own money."

Again, I said nothing.

"I can only say these are my family's possessions, I grew up with them. Maybe I'm prouder than I believed." He headed for the path.

I followed, happy to be moving. "Does Paul know?"

"Yes, although I regret telling him. When I brushed off Pelagia, she tried talking to Paul. She said she had written to someone in the exiled Polish government as well. I don't think they could do anything, but it would be quite a to-do. Perhaps more than that." He reached the walkway and kept going.

I fell into step beside him. “It all happened a long time ago. What’s the harm in people knowing?”

“It did. But old sins cast long shadows, as the saying goes. I don’t think this is a secret that should come out. Better to let it die.”

“I think you’re exaggerating.”

“Am I? The Irish are a close-knit community, Miss Ahern, same as the Polish. They’ve had their troubles. What do you think would happen if it were known that Irish Catholics had betrayed their own to the Protestants? Or take current affairs. What if someone in your family sold information to the Nazis?” He seemed to melt into his overcoat.

I wanted to sympathize with the man next to me. But everything he’d said meant he had a motive for killing Pelagia if she’d threatened to expose him. “What about Bridget? And Josef Pyrut?”

He kept walking. “What about them?”

“Pelagia wrote to Josef. He never got the letter, but it was opened.”

That stopped him. “How do you know that?”

“Her granddaughter got it back and saw someone had resealed the envelope with tape. I don’t think Josef himself ever got his mail, but he was at City Hall. The person who opened the letter might found a way to get him the info.” I didn’t mention that the letter had been in Polish. Besides, someone could’ve translated the contents.

Mr. Witkop frowned. “Even if that were true, what could this Pyrut have done about anything? He was an undersecretary.”

I lifted my chin. “He might have told the president, old Raczkiewicz.”

We stared at each other for a moment, then a light of realization came into his eyes. “You think I killed him?”

“Maybe you thought you’d lose your stuff. Or your reputation.”

He said nothing. Then he shook his head. “You are a clever girl, I’ll give you that. You remind me of one of those detectives in the movies.”

It would have been a compliment coming from anyone other than a murder suspect.

He continued. “I suppose you’re right. Except I have an alibi. I never left the party. I was at home until my guests left around midnight. Then I went to bed with my wife. Any number of people will, what is it? Corroborate that."

"I don't know the cops put much stock in an alibi backed up by a wife. Wouldn't she lie to protect you?"

He gave a dry chuckle. "You don't know my wife."

"What about Bridget? She died right in your house. She coulda found out somehow. Maybe she blackmailed you or threatened to outright tell the cops." I couldn't see Bridget going to the police, but a spot of blackmail? Why not? If the Witkops had hidden this secret for all these years, she would believe it was important enough to pay her.

Mr. Witkop stopped, turned, and took a step toward me. I backed up, ready to run. He did nothing, his face a mask. Then he spoke. "Bridget Innes was a lovely girl. I would never have harmed one of the silken hairs on her head." Tears filled his eyes.

What employer talked about a maid that way? Why did the thought of Bridget make him cry? Unless… "You were having an affair with her, weren't you?" It was a wild guess on my part, but my gut said I was right. The servants thought the kisses stopped with Mr. Paul. Maybe Bridget had been content to let 'em believe that 'cause it kept their eyes off where the real action had been.

He blinked away the tears. "Bridget was a good Catholic girl. I'm a married man. That's all I have to say about that."

What malarkey. Like I didn't know Catholic girls and married men were capable of dallying around.

He tugged at his gloves. "It's been lovely chatting with you, Miss Ahern. But I have things to do. Good day."

"Wait a sec."

He half-turned.

"Why'd you flap your gums with me all this time?"

"I'm a lonely old man. My wife and I haven't talked in years, which is why I'm not at all confident she'd tell a falsehood to the police to protect me. Paul is too young to understand the regrets of age. Last of all, it's Christmas. I'm feeling a bit sentimental, you have a very trustworthy personality, very easy to talk to. Just like Bridget." He inclined his head. "Good bye, Miss Ahern."

Chapter Thirty-One

The next day, December 26th, work continued at Bell like it had never stopped. I filled Dot in on the details of my cemetery talk with Sebastian Witkop as we worked our tasks on the assembly line. "The problem I'm having is with the stuff the Witkops got as a payment for informing. Who cares? It's so long ago."

"But who knows what his parents told the Prussians? Maybe someone died as a result."

"Okay, but Sebastian Witkop's parents are dead. He was a little kid. No." I shook my head. "I can't see anyone making a fuss, not forty, almost fifty, years after it happened. Pelagia might've wanted him to come clean for the sake of conscience, or something, but no one was gonna take the goods. He'd know that."

"People don't always think straight. I'm more surprised about Bridget, carrying on with someone old enough to be her father."

"He's not bad looking for an old guy. And he's got cabbage. Maybe she wanted a sugar daddy."

Dot stopped, an instrument panel in her hands. "Do you think she was..." Dot looked around and mouthed the next word, although it wasn't likely anyone could hear, "...*pregnant?*"

I hadn't thought of that. It was something to ask Sam MacKinnon the next time we spoke. An affair with the household staff might be something to be swept under the rug. If the girl wound up preggers, well, that would be a different story. "I don't know. He didn't mention anything of the kind," I said.

"Here everybody thought she was carryin' on with Paul." Dot brushed hair from her forehead as the line rumbled forward, bringing the next fuselage up. "Do you think she was making whoopee with the both of 'em?"

"I s'pose it's possible. I think it's just as likely she was using Paul for a cover. Being caught with a young single man isn't as bad as it being known you're dallying with an old married one."

Dot's expression turned prim. "Nice Catholic girl indeed."

I snickered. "Dot, so-called nice Catholic girls have affairs and end up with illegitimate kids all the time. Don't be such a prude."

"What I don't understand is why Mr. Witkop didn't turn her out if she was pregnant? Isn't that what they did in the old days?"

"They did, but what if she refused to go? Or what if she meant to tell everyone who the father of her child was?" I signed the back of my instrument panel and fitted it in. "I don't think they admitted paternity back in the Old Country. Even if it was common knowledge. Besides, I think Sebastian really loved her. Unless he somehow came to believe she was also sleepin' with Paul and went wild with jealousy."

Dot's eyebrows furrowed. "Murder seems extreme, though."

"Sebastian coulda felt betrayed. Maybe he was possessive. If he couldn't have Bridget no one could. He said he was prouder than he thought. Could be he was fine with an affair, but believed a child would be an embarrassment to the family. That's real important to some folks." That would fit with Sebastian not wanting to publicly admit his parents were German informants, even if he was privately ashamed of the fact.

"Proud enough to kill?"

"Maybe." I paused. "Here's a thought. Maybe Paul found out about his pop and the maid, and *he's* the one who wanted to avoid embarrassment. He didn't want it known his father had a kid on the wrong side of the blanket."

"Or he got mad. *He's* the jilted lover and all that."

All possibilities. "But none of this explains what happened to Pelagia or Josef," I said.

"No, it doesn't. But remember last month?" Dot wagged a screwdriver at me. "That started out simple, and it turned out to be anything but." We worked without speaking for a bit, then she said, "One thing bothers me. Why'd Mr. Witkop talk to you?"

"I asked him about that. He said he was feeling sentimental, and I was a good listener, like Bridget had been."

"You don't think he was eyeing you up, do you?" Dot asked. "Could he have sent those chocolates?"

"I don't even want to consider that." I hadn't thought about the candy since the day it had been delivered. I had more important things to think about.

She giggled. "Well, don't mention it to Tom. What's the next step?"

"I gotta talk to Detective MacKinnon and find out if Bridget was pregnant or not."

"How would he know?"

"They'd have done an autopsy. At least I'm pretty sure they would."

"Eww." Dot shuddered. "Hey, did you see there's a new detective flick out? *Time to Kill*. It's s'posed to be based on a Philip Marlowe novel."

"Yeah, but the trailers said they swapped Marlowe for a different character." I stepped back and waited for the next plane. "Besides, I'm living my own murder investigation. I don't need to spend money to watch someone else's right now."

* * *

I thought about stopping at police headquarters after work, but I decided to call first this time. Sam might be tired of my surprise visits. Good thing, because he was waiting for me at the bus stop when I got back to the First Ward.

"Evening." He tipped his hat. "I hoped this was your bus."

I hopped down on the sidewalk. "What if it hadn't been?"

"I would have tried your house, but I wanted to avoid that. It would upset your mother." He glanced at Dot. "Who's this?"

"Oh, this is my friend, Dorothy Kilbride. She helps me out. I think you've met before, haven't you?" I waved at her. "Dot, this is Sam MacKinnon of the Buffalo PD."

He gave a nod of the head. "Miss Kilbride, I'm sorry. I think we have met, but I didn't recognize you."

"Don't mention it," she said. Then she looked at me. "Why do I get the feeling I'm gonna have to play messenger again?"

"Let's see what the detective has to say, first."

He looked at me. "I told you before I've been looking into Josef Pyrut's death. As part of that, I've searched the hotel where the Polish visitors stayed earlier this month." He stopped and glanced at Dot.

The look puzzled me, then it clicked. "You can say whatever you have to say in front of Dot. I'm gonna tell her, anyway. We don't have secrets."

He thought a moment, then continued. "The Polish delegation left some items behind. The hotel had been keeping them in case someone contacted the staff and wanted them back. Inside the box was this." He handed me a letter, sealed inside a bag that looked like it was made of waxed paper.

I opened the top flap to take it out, but he grabbed my wrist. "What?"

"It's evidence. You'll have to read it through the paper as best you can."

I held it under the streetlight so I could read the waxy blur. "It's from Paul Witkop to Josef." I checked the date. "Looks like it was delivered the afternoon of the second, maybe by messenger? He wants to meet with Josef at the party to discuss…" Water must have dripped on the paper and the ink had run, blurring the writing. "I can't make that out. But Paul says it's important and needs to be addressed before the Poles leave on December third." I handed the letter back to Sam. "What was it about?"

He pocketed the bag. "I'm not sure. I'm headed to the Witkop residence to talk to the people there, including Paul. I'd like you to go with me."

"Why us?" Dot asked.

Sam's cheeks were red. "I was asking Betty, Miss Kilbride. I didn't intend for this to be a group trip."

Dot bristled. "Well that's nice." She tossed her head. "You're not invitin' me? I'll have you know I've gone with Betty to some pretty dangerous places. In fact, the first time we went to Delaware Park, I was with her. So there."

I shot a look at Sam and smothered a smile. He looked like a guy who'd stood too close to the tracks when the train blew by. Dot could do that to a person. "Cool it," I told her and gave her shoulders a squeeze. "Detective MacKinnon isn't discounting your value."

"No, indeed," he said, cheeks even redder.

"It's a good question, though. You've always been pretty clear that I have no business in police matters."

He coughed. "It's a ploy. I don't intend for us to go into the house together. I wanted you to go first and talk to the staff. They already know you're asking about Bridget's death so you can say you're there for any new information. I'll show up a few minutes later to talk to the Witkops. While I'm with them, I'd like you to stay with the staff. See if you pick up any reactions or gossip."

I caught wise to his idea as he spoke. "Because you've gotten zip from them."

He doffed his hat in acknowledgement. "Correct. I'm hoping they'll be more talkative with a non-authority figure."

The idea was good. "When do you want to go?"

"How about now?"

I checked my watch. It was four-thirty. The sun had settled low in the sky and the wind swirling down the street had an edge sharp enough to cut butter. Little eddies of snow spun around my feet. "No good. If I don't have dinner with my family tonight, my mom will flip her wig." I chewed the wool of my mitten and thought.

"I could come and pick you up, tell her I need to talk to you," Sam said.

I lowered my hand. "Then she'll really snap her cap. Don't take it personally, Sam. But the idea of her daughter being driven away by a police detective is horrifying, even if you assure her I'm not in trouble. In her mind, respectable folks don't have anything to do with the police. Unless they're related, of course." I turned to Dot. "Are you up for a little charade?"

"I s'pose," she said. "What do you want me to do?"

"We'll go home, same as usual, and have dinner. You call me around six. The story will be you asked me over to compare our Christmases or something. I'll leave and go meet the detective at that coffee shop on South Park. Teddy's, it's called."

Sam's forehead crinkled. "What am I supposed to do until six o'clock?"

"Go grab a cup of joe and a sandwich. Read the evening paper or see if they have one of those dime novels. I dunno, use your imagination."

For a moment, he looked like he wanted to remind me who was in charge. But then he shook his head. "All right. Teddy's you said? I'll meet you there. Miss Kilbride, thank you for your help." He tugged the brim of his fedora. He took two steps, turned, and pointed at me. "You're a devious young woman, Miss Ahern."

I winked. "And that, Sam, is why you like me so much."

* * *

The plan went off without a hitch. Dinner was simple, especially compared to the holiday the day before. I had time to feed Cat and help Mary Kate wash up before the phone call from Dot came so I'd have my cover story. I got my coat from the hall closet and went into the living room to talk to Mom and Pop. "I'm going over to Dot's for a while. She wants to gab about our Christmases."

Mom looked up from her sewing. "You didn't talk about that this morning on the bus?"

Rats. I hadn't thought of that. "We did, but she wants to show off some of the stuff she got. You know how it is. May I go?" *Please, oh please.* I'd sneaked out before. I didn't feel like doing it right now. Inside my pocket, I crossed my fingers.

"I suppose." She resumed sewing. "Be home at a reasonable hour. By reasonable, I mean nine. Tomorrow is Sunday and we're going to church early. I'm sure the Kilbrides will have plans, too."

"Yes, ma'am." I kissed her forehead, then did the same for Pop, who was dozing in his arm chair. "I love you." I ran out the front door, their responses behind me.

I found Sam exactly where I'd told him to be, the counter at Teddy's. A partially full cup of coffee and a plate of crumbs was in front of him. "What kept you?"

"I'm only a little late, relax. I gotta be home by nine, so let's go."

He slugged back the rest of his coffee and left some coins on the counter. "I'm not the one holding us up."

Being a cop, he didn't have to worry about gas rationing, so we took his car. I leaned back into the seat. "It's nice not to have to take the bus for a change."

He laughed.

I closed my eyes, intending to take a snooze, but then I remembered my conversation with Sebastian Witkop at the cemetery. "Hey, can I ask you a question?"

"Besides the one you just asked?"

Smarty pants. I plowed on. "You would've done an autopsy on Bridget, right?"

His voice turned guarded. "Yes."

"Was she, uh…" I found myself stumbling over the idea. "Was she pregnant?"

He stopped to check for oncoming traffic and made his left before answering. "Why would you ask such a question?"

"She was having an affair with old Mr. Witkop. Sebastian." I related my Christmas talk.

"You walk in cemeteries for relaxation?" Sam asked, glancing at me.

"They're peaceful. The dead don't care." I fiddled with my mittens. "Was she pregnant or not?"

"No," he said. "You talked to Sebastian Witkop?"

I heaved a sigh of relief, unaware until that moment that if he'd said yes, I didn't know if I could continue with this case. The idea of killing a pregnant girl was too much for me. "I didn't go to Forest Lawn lookin' for him. He was there, visitin' a grave. His parents, he told me, although I didn't see the names. I didn't want to talk to him, but he spotted me. He said he was feeling sentimental, and he and his wife don't get along much anymore. He tried to give me the 'I'm a married man' line, but I could tell he was having a fling with Bridget. More than an affair, actually. I'm positive he was really in love."

He stopped at a light. "Funny, everybody swore it was Paul Witkop she was flirting with."

"Did you even suspect it was really his father? Involved with Bridget?"

"I wondered."

"It's a good cover," I said, as the light turned green and the car pulled forward. "Be seen cuddling with Paul under the stairs, start everyone's gums flapping, but you're really getting into some hanky-panky with the old man. Can you tell if she, um, had relations before she died?"

We had arrived at Delaware Park. Sam pulled to the side of the street a few houses away from the Witkops'. "There were no signs of sexual intercourse before death."

I shook my head. The things they could tell these days. "You know this gives Paul another motive."

"As far as I'm concerned, it's a motive for both men. Paul because he'd be angry Bridget led him on, Sebastian because maybe he thought Bridget was tiring of an old man and wanted to flee to greener pastures."

He had a good point. "Oh, somethin' else I thought of. That letter to Josef, the one Pelagia wrote. Somebody opened it at City Hall, which means it might have been translated. Can you find out if it was and who mighta done it? If that person gabbed, either Paul or Sebastian might have wanted to shut Pelagia up before she told anyone else."

"I can give it a shot."

I paused. "Sam, is investigatin' murder always like this?"

"What, slimy and dirty, learning the worst nature of humanity?"

"Yeah."

His face took on a sympathetic expression. "Quite often, yes. I thought you would have seen that last month."

I hugged myself. "This feels worse."

We sat, listening to the engine rumble. "You can go home," he said. "I'll take you and come back."

"No. If I'm gonna be a private dick, well, it isn't always wandering boyfriends, lost jewelry, and kittens." I steeled myself. "What's the plan again?"

"You go to the house. Get talking with the staff. I'll show up in about five minutes to see the Witkops. I want you to try and get the cook and the butler talking. See if my appearance sets off any gossip."

"Right." I grabbed the door handle, but stopped when I felt Sam's hand on my shoulder.

"You're a tough girl, Betty," he said. "You make a great detective."

The compliment made my face turn warm. "Thanks, Sam. You're not so bad yourself. Now are we gonna sit here and gab, or are we gonna find ourselves a killer?"

Chapter Thirty-Two

I knocked on the back door, breath steaming in front of my face. Would this even work? Sam had called me a good detective. I wasn't gonna let him down.

Mrs. Leggett opened it. "Oh, it's you."

"Evening, Mrs. Leggett," I said. "May I come in?"

"Why?"

"You know why. I'm here about Bridget. She didn't eat rat poison by accident. You said she was a nice girl. Don't you wanna help find out who killed her?"

The cook paused, clearly torn between two feelings.

I figured I knew what they were. "Look, I understand. The way she died, well, you gotta be thinking it's one of the family, right? Or at least someone in the household."

Her grip on the door tightened, but she didn't automatically argue with me.

"I think the Witkops have prob'ly been good to you and you feel some loyalty. At the same time, Bridget was a sweet young girl. Let me in, we'll talk, and we'll figure it out."

She clucked her tongue. "You? What can you do?"

"I've done this before. Solved a murder, I mean. There's a police detective who works for the Buffalo Police Department who thinks I'm pretty good at it." I shivered and stamped my feet. "Look at it this way. What've you got to lose? The worst case is we share a cup of tea, you give up some of your time, and all I've done is make you feel better. Best case, I learn something that will help me find out who the killer is."

Doubt clouded her face.

"Nothing you say will get back to the Witkops, I promise."

She cast a look over her shoulder. "Come in. I'll take your coat."

I stamped the snow off my shoes, handed her my coat and winter things, and followed her to the kitchen. It was considerably warmer. Two cups were on the table, a steaming pot nearby. "Did I interrupt something?"

"Mr. Charles and I always have a spot of tea before we go home in the evening." She bustled to the cabinet and got a third cup. "Milk or sugar?"

"A splash of milk if you have it is great. Black if you don't." I sat. After she poured the tea and added the milk, I wrapped my hands around the cup. It wasn't the same fine French china I'd seen in the pawn shop window, but it was a good shot nicer than a diner mug. I blew on the top. "Thanks. You haven't retrieved the other stuff?"

Mrs. Leggett took her seat. "Mr. Witkop bought it back this morning. Mrs. Witkop asked that it be washed and put away for the time being."

"He bought back his own goods?"

Mrs. Leggett gave me a disapproving look. "He explained the situation to the shop owner and reimbursed the man for the money he'd given Miss Janson."

"Speaking of that, do you know if he intends to report Mildred to the cops for stealing?"

"I don't know for certain, but I think he won't." She sipped. "Truth be told, I think he's feeling a little guilty for letting her go, especially given the circumstances. If it weren't for Mrs. Witkop, I believe he'd bring Miss Janson back."

"The missus doesn't approve of that idea?"

"No. Mrs. Witkop is..." Mrs. Leggett thought, "...rather unyielding in these kinds of matters."

I'd not given a lot of thought to Mrs. Witkop as a suspect. My focus was her son and husband. Was that a mistake? Prob'ly. I expect she'd be plenty mad if her husband was fooling around with the maid. Maybe it was *her* who didn't like the idea of her husband being known as the son of an informant, or who was afraid of losing her cushy house. I made a mental note to bring it up with Sam later.

Mr. Charles came through the door and pulled up at the sight of me. "What is she doing here?"

Mrs. Leggett waved at the third cup. "I let her in, Johnny. She's here about Bridget. As she said, it can't hurt. The police haven't got any leads, and sometimes I doubt they're even looking very hard. Who cares about an immigrant girl?"

"You'd better not let Mrs. Witkop see her."

"Oh, fiddlesticks. That woman can go sing for her supper as far as I'm concerned."

Mr. Charles's expression told me he was scandalized. "Mrs. Leggett!"

"Sit down, Johnny. I know you'd do anything for her. But you must realize she doesn't give a fig for anyone except herself, or maybe her son."

He'd do anything for her. I wondered how far that went, but didn't say anything and took a sip of tea. "I know for a fact the lead detective on the case is working as hard as he can. He's not the type to brush off a murder. Anybody's murder."

"Oh you do, huh?" Mr. Charles slumped into his chair.

"Yes." No sense gettin' into details with them. That wasn't why I was here. But I tucked away Mr. Charles's loyalty to his mistress to tell Sam. "Last time we talked, I got the idea you thought Bridget was a sweet girl. Good at her job, didn't get into too much trouble, hard worker. Is that really true?"

"Yes." Mrs. Leggett took a sip of tea. "I wouldn't have tolerated a slovenly maid or a tart. Not in my kitchen. For all her faults, Miss Janson wouldn't have either."

I turned to the butler. "What about you, Mr. Charles?"

"I didn't have as much contact with Bridget," he said. "But when we did speak, she was bright, happy, and pleasant. She was the type of person who made you smile."

"Mrs. Leggett, you said you wouldn't have put up with a tart. Yet Miss Janson told me Bridget wasn't above flirting with Paul Witkop." *Come on Sam. I can't keep up small talk all night.* Sam already knew about all this. But since I'd used talkin' about her to get invited into the house, I couldn't very well up and change the topic on a whim. "Well?"

"Honestly?" She gripped her cup. "I think that was more Mr. Paul flirting with Bridget than the other way 'round. It was always him who started it. He'd follow her when she was cleaning or come into the kitchen when she was here. I'd send her to the larder and she'd come back a little mussed. He went in after her, she said. More than once she said that was his right. The gentry often got a little free with their hands back in Ireland. She said she could handle him."

"She never complained?"

Mrs. Leggett shook her head.

The front doorbell rang. "Whoever can be visiting at this time of night?" Mr. Charles said as he dragged himself up.

That would be Sam MacKinnon, but I didn't say anything. I wasn't s'posed to know. After Mr. Charles had left the kitchen, I faced Mrs. Leggett again. "Must be something important to be ringing the front doorbell at this hour of the night. My folks would have a fit." I hoped she wouldn't point out that I'd done the exact same thing, 'cept at the back.

"It's been ghastly." She gripped her cup. "Police coming and going all the time, but no results. Mr. Witkop, bless him, hasn't been the same since Bridget died. Of course Mrs. Witkop—" She bit off her words and became very interested in the contents of her tea cup.

I tried to make my voice as sympathetic, yet conspiratorial, as I could. "I don't expect she was all that happy to have her son sneaking around with the help. I wouldn't be surprised if she was secretly glad Bridget was gone."

Mrs. Leggett pressed her lips together.

"I find that terrible, myself. After all, this is America. Aren't we supposed to be above all that class stuff?" I took a sip of tea, watching her furtively.

She seemed to tussle with her conscience for another second, then leaned forward. "Horrible, just horrible, that's what she's been. First, she was all over Miss Janson. Mind you, I don't approve of what she did, not at all."

"Of course not."

"But the poor woman was caring for a sick mother. The more I learned of the story, well, it changed my mind about it and that's a fact. Any decent Christian would feel the same. Stealing is a sin, no question about it. But couldn't a body have a little charity?"

I murmured my assent, hoping she'd continue.

"And then poor Bridget. Well." Mrs. Leggett sniffed. "Mrs. Witkop didn't even pretend to be sorry. Not her. She was more concerned about what the neighbors would think, what with the police in and out of the house. I think she even suspected Mr. Witkop of being the one who was carrying on with Bridget."

Mrs. Witkop was looking more and more like a serious suspect all the time. How could I have missed her? "She seems very fond of her house and status."

"Oh, she is. I can't even imagine what she'd do if she thought that was threatened."

Mr. Charles came back into the kitchen. "It was that police detective again, for Mr. Witkop. Blast, I wish those people would leave us alone. Mrs. Witkop will be extremely upset, poor woman. I'll check on her before I leave."

Mrs. Legget sniffed.

"Well, what do you want?" I asked. "The police will never get to the bottom of things if they don't continue to investigate."

The pair exchanged a look. "Of course we know that," Mr. Charles said, voice gruff. "I only wish they could do it without bothering Mr. Witkop. The constant visits. He has enough trouble."

I sensed a new opening. "What kind of trouble? Money?"

Mr. Charles hesitated. "No. Mr. Witkop is always very prudent with his investments. He weathered the recent depression quite well and expects that with the war, the economy will recover."

"Family issues? Does he have trouble with Paul? Mrs. Leggett was just telling me about Mrs. Witkop."

"Bernadette!"

Her cheeks colored, but she lifted her head. "She's a harridan, Johnny. You might be soft on her, but mark my words. That woman is capable of, well, almost anything if she thought she was threatened."

Mr. Charles's expression was disapproving, but after a moment, he spoke. "Mr. Paul is a good enough young man. But he's inexperienced. He doesn't understand business. I've heard him argue with his father more than once."

I sipped. "Was it always about work?"

Mr. Charles hesitated.

That wasn't it, or at least not all of it. "Something more personal, maybe. Could it have been about Paul and Bridget?"

Mr. Charles waved his hand. "Mr. Witkop was not happy about Paul keeping company with a maid, especially one in his own house."

"Not nearly as upset as his mother," Mrs. Leggett said.

Mr. Charles gave her a dark look. "But it wasn't so much the girl. No, Paul is always looking for a way to make more money, increase the prestige of the Witkop name."

"Is that so bad?"

"No, except..." He shot another look at Mrs. Leggett, who gave him a small nod in return. "Paul's ideas aren't always the best," Mr. Charles said, the words coming slowly. "He is always looking for a quick deal."

"Illegal?" I asked.

"Not that far," Mr. Charles said. "He likes to cut corners. He always stays on the right side of the law, but only just. I've heard more than one argument between the two from behind closed doors. Mr. Witkop worried that if Paul kept up his current behavior, he'd find himself in real trouble. Paul, on the other hand, believes his father is old-fashioned and needs to get with the times. 'Grandfather would understand,' I heard him say one time. 'Look how he built his fortune.'"

Sounded to me like Paul knew all about his grandparents' post-war Prussian arrangement. "What did his father say to that?"

"That you can't make money without integrity," Mr. Charles said. "Mr. Witkop's family has always been very above board in their business dealings."

Mrs. Leggett clucked her tongue. "I don't think that was always true, Johnny."

I wished I could write this all down. Sam MacKinnon would be glad he'd sent me in. "Why not?"

She paused and looked to be struggling for words. "Because more than once I heard Paul retort, 'Then why don't you give it all away?' It maybe didn't happen recently, but somewhere along the line, the money didn't come honestly. Of that I'm sure. I went into the dining room after one of the fights. Mr. Witkop was there. He looked old. Tired. I told him to cheer up. 'Maybe he's right, Mrs. Leggett. I'm a fraud. But I can't do what he wants, I simply can't.' I assured him that wasn't the case, but it didn't seem to have much impact."

I sipped my tea. "What did Mrs. Witkop say about all this?"

Mrs. Leggett snorted. "What do you expect?"

"You don't like her much."

The two servants exchanged a long look. "I've talked too much. I really shouldn't say anything else," she said slowly. But the look in her eyes said the exact opposite. She dearly wanted to flap her gums about her employer's wife and here I was, a willing listener.

The response told me I'd been right, but I still wanted to hear about it. "I told you, she'll never find out. I swear."

"Bernadette." Mr. Charles's voice held a warning note.

But Mrs. Leggett must have made her decision. "You won't tell anyone?" she asked me.

"I won't tell a soul who isn't in this house." At the moment that included Sam MacKinnon, but I doubted she thought of him. Sure, my Catholic conscience yammered at me a bit, but I was a detective. I had to stretch the truth a little sometimes to get the dope I needed, right?

She and Mr. Charles stared at each other. She raised her eyebrows, and he frowned. Finally he pushed away his cup and stood. "I won't be a part of this."

Mrs. Leggett turned to me. "I told you, Mr. and Mrs. Witkop don't have the...warmest marriage. There's no abuse, you understand, just two people who don't have very much in common. She has her society works, and she dotes on Mr. Paul. Mr. Witkop buries himself in work. They don't sleep in the same room, haven't for years. They put on a show for other people, but at home?" She sighed and shook her head. "It's a frosty house, Miss Ahern. I don't know if you understand that. I don't think she would have cared that her husband's lover was the maid, but she would very much want to keep that from being known amongst the neighbors. And if it was Mr. Paul doing the fooling around?" She shook her head. "She'd have dismissed Bridget on the spot if she'd known. I'm certain of it."

Dismissed or worse? I'd seen marriages come apart. Of course in the First Ward there was likely to be a lot of shouting, but maybe that wasn't the way it was done in Delaware Park. "Did you ever think..."

"What?" she prompted.

"Did you ever think that Mrs. Witkop had the right of it? That her husband was having an affair with Bridget?"

Mr. Charles, who'd gone to the sink, turned and his face went red. "Preposterous!"

But Mrs. Leggett was slower to respond. "Maybe not so much, Johnny," she finally said.

"Mr. Witkop would never—"

"I saw them," she said. "Oh, never anything inappropriate," she hastened to add at seeing my raised eyebrows. "To outsiders it would have looked all very proper. But there was often a look, a smile, a brushed touch. If they'd been more matched in age and class, I'd be sure they were courting. I didn't want to think of it, but..." She sighed.

"You're daft," Mr. Charles snapped. "Yes, yes, Bridget was a good girl and pretty to boot. But Mr. Witkop?" Mr. Charles barked a derisive laugh. "No matter how his personal life was, he'd never in a million years stoop to a girl of that station. Mrs. Witkop wouldn't stand it, and I can't blame her."

Which only went to show how deep Mr. Charles's prejudices ran. Mrs. Leggett was a woman, she could see it. Mr. Witkop had all but confessed to me. He'd called himself a lonely man. If he was constantly fighting with his son, and on the outs with his wife, he musta been pretty sad. And Bridget was warm, feisty, pretty and prob'ly more than willing to cheer up her employer. I focused on Mrs. Leggett. "If Mr. Witkop saw Bridget with Paul, maybe under the stairs or in a cupboard, would he have gotten angry?

Angry enough to hurt her?"

She pursed her lips. "I don't think so, no. Especially if he knew it was her way of deflecting attention."

"What about you?" I turned to him. "You said you'd do anything for Mrs. Witkop. Maybe you'd want to spare her the embarrassment?"

He sputtered. "Are you…I…never…I didn't…"

Not a good defense, as far as I was concerned. Now I had to throw Mr. Charles in the mix. What would he do to protect Mrs. Witkop? I faced Mrs. Leggett again. "What about Paul? What if he knew his father was the true object of Bridget's affection?"

Her response was immediate. "He'd be quite angry. Proud, he is. Even as a child. He'd be embarrassed to be made a fool of, and that's how he'd take it. I think it would be worse if he felt wronged at the hands of his own father."

Angry, huh? "Mad enough to dump some rat poison in a sugar bowl out of spite?"

Mr. Charles' face went red. "Never!"

But Mrs. Leggett's expression was troubled, like I'd raised an idea she hadn't wanted to think about. She turned to me. "When you put it that way, maybe."

* * *

I stayed long enough that I heard Sam MacKinnon leave. I didn't want to beat feet too early. It might look suspicious. But I couldn't stay too long, either. If Sam left me, I had no other way to get home 'cept the bus and I didn't feel like taking one late at night.

After I heard the front door shut, I waited a couple more minutes. "It's late. I should go."

"I'll get your coat," Mrs. Leggett said.

Mr. Charles stared at me. His expression gave no clue as to his thoughts.

"Thanks for the tea," I said when Mrs. Leggett returned. "And the conversation."

"Do you think it will help find who killed Bridget?" she asked.

"Yes, I do." I looked at the butler. "I can see you don't believe me. I'm not just prying or talking anyone down, honest. I appreciate you takin' the time to speak to me."

He looked like he was chewing his tongue. "Wait a moment," he said, and left the room.

I glanced at Mrs. Leggett, who spread her hands. She didn't have any more clue than I did what was up.

A minute later, Mr. Charles returned, some charred paper in his hands. "I wasn't going to give you this. But maybe...well, perhaps you're right and you can clear up this mess. Mr. Witkop is a good man. Whatever his family did before him, whatever his son may have done now, he doesn't deserve to be wronged. Mrs. Witkop is, well, she and her husband don't get along, true, but she's a fine woman. She has nothing to do with this, with either of those people."

I took the bits from him. They were the pages of a letter and the corner of an envelope. "Where'd you find these?"

"In the backyard. I went outside to dump the ashes from the fireplace and I smelled smoke. Nothing should have been burning, so I followed the scent."

"When was this?"

"Christmas Eve. Someone had started a small fire behind the shed, but they'd used green wood so it smoldered more than burned. They had walked away and must have thought it would continue to burn, but in addition to the raw wood, there was a light snow. The combination had put out the flames." He nodded at the scrap. "This bit of paper was on top of the pile."

I gingerly turned it over. Most of the paper was dirty and destroyed beyond reading. But a whole corner of the envelope remained, the corner where a return address was written in a spidery writing.

Pelagia Brewka's.

Chapter Thirty-Three

I said a couple of extra prayers at Mass on Sunday. Things didn't look that great for the war. Some French general had been assassinated. The Army was engaged with the Germans at a place in Tunis the papers called "Longstop Hill" and who knew how long that would go on. The Japanese wouldn't give up Guadalcanal. I still hadn't heard from Tom or Sean.

Also, I was no closer to finding the killer. Or killers, as the case may be.

The weather had spiked warmer again, enough for Dot to sit on her front steps while I stood nearby and smoked. Cat wandered over for some attention, which Dot was happy to give. "I thought old Mr. Witkop said he threw the letter out."

I'd told Dot all about our venture to Delaware Park last night. Sam had been happy with the outcome. I'd given him the scoop, along with the remains of Pelagia's envelope, when he drove me back to the First Ward. "He did," I said, blowing smoke into the spring-like air. The snow was gone, leaving scattered wet spots in the street.

"So how come you, or that butler, found the envelope?"

"I see three possibilities. Sebastian lied, kept it, and then got rid of it, or someone stole it from his desk or whatever, or someone fished the letter outta the garbage, read it, and burned it. Detective MacKinnon agreed with me."

"But why do it now? Pelagia died, what, a month ago? Why not burn it then?"

I ashed my cigarette. "Dunno. Could be whoever had the letter felt safe as long as nobody was looking into Pelagia's death, but now questions are being asked and he wanted to get rid of it. Or he stashed it and forgot he had it. The point is, Pelagia wrote to Sebastian Witkop and *someone* in that house read it. Maybe just him, maybe someone else as well."

"And the staff really didn't know about Sebastian and Bridget?" She scratched Cat under the chin and he stretched his neck up.

"Not for certain, no. But from what the cook, Mrs. Leggett, said about the state of the Witkops' marriage, I'm not surprised. Sounds like things were pretty frigid between 'em."

"What did Detective MacKinnon say about Mrs. Witkop as a suspect?"

"He said it was a good thought, but Mrs. Witkop has an alibi for the death of Josef Pyrut. She never left the party and a lot of people can say that. We also don't have proof she ever met Pelagia."

"What about Bridget?"

"She has an alibi for that, too. Sam said the servants' sugar bowl would have had to be doctored the night before or at the very latest, that morning. Otherwise Bridget would have died earlier. Mrs. Witkop went to visit her sister in Niagara Falls the morning of the day before Bridget's death and didn't return until late the next afternoon. Otherwise, he agreed she'd be a good candidate. But he's gonna check into Mr. Charles, in case he did it 'cause of his loyalty to Mrs. Witkop." I took a drag off the gasper. "What are you looking at?"

Dot's attention had wandered from me to the end of the street. "Her," she said and pointed. "Isn't that Mildred Janson?"

I turned around. It was Mildred. She was consulting a paper in her hand and looking at house numbers, prob'ly tryin' to find a house. I flicked away the stub end of my cigarette. "Miss Janson! Who are you lookin' for?"

She looked up, folded her paper and picked up the pace. "Oh, thank heavens. You do live on this street. I hoped I wasn't wrong."

"How'd you find me?"

"The phone book. I knew you lived in the First Ward, so I looked for every Ahern with an address in this neighborhood. Fortunately, there aren't many of you." She cast a look at Dot. "Good morning, Miss Kilbride."

Dot didn't stand. "Hello."

"What do you want?" I asked. "It's a nice day, but it's kinda out of the way, Allentown to here. Can I help you with something?"

"Perhaps." She shifted. "I don't suppose there's anywhere to go and sit."

"Not really. It's Sunday and our families are home," Dot said. "We could go to the diner, but I get the feeling you wanna talk in private."

"That's true." Mildred crossed her arms over her chest. "It's about Mother. And Bridget."

I leaned on a nearby light post. "Go on."

Mildred bit her lip. "I told you I stole from the Witkops because I needed to buy medicine for Mother. She has a weak heart. The medicine isn't terribly expensive, but last month I had to buy it twice."

"Why?"

"It disappeared. I go to the pharmacy on the first of the month. That way, I always have the new bottle at least two weeks before Mother runs out. Last month, when I went to get the new bottle, it was gone."

"Maybe you forgot where you put it," Dot said.

"No. I have to get other things on the first, and I always put the entire bag on the shelf where I keep my bed linens. In November, the bag was exactly where it was supposed to be, but the medicine bottle was missing," Mildred said.

"Did you go anywhere after you left the pharmacy?" I asked.

Mildred shook her head. "I always stop in the morning and from there I go to work. That way I don't get to the pharmacy after it closes if I'm tied up at the Witkops' with something. And I went straight home that day, I know I did. It had to be taken while I was at the Witkops'."

I frowned. "I don't see how this figures in. Bridget was killed with strychnine."

"I thought you'd be interested in the missing medicine, that's all. I'm sure someone in the house took it. Perhaps that person tried to kill her with Mother's pills. When that didn't work, the killer used the rat poison."

It was possible. "Did Bridget complain of being sick or something last month?"

"Not to me, but she might have kept quiet about it or talked to Mrs. Leggett. Or it could have happened overnight. Remember, none of us except Bridget lived there," Mildred said.

"Okay, I'll bite." I glanced at Dot, who gave the tiniest shrug and focused on Cat. It looked like I'd have to go back to Delaware Park to talk to Mrs. Leggett. "What kind of medicine does your mother take?"

"It's called digitoxin," Mildred said. "They are little white tablets that would be easy to crush. And easy to hide in something, or so I'd think."

I immediately thought of Pelagia's heart attack. "When I visited your house, you looked like you wanted to tell me something."

Shutters closed behind Milred's eyes. "I told you about the theft and now the medicine. What more could there be?"

"You tell me."

Mildred stared at me for a long moment. Then she licked her lips. "No, nothing."

"Okay. Well, thanks for letting me know about your mom's pills. I'll keep it in mind."

Mildred looked at me, then Dot, then back to me. She nodded and bustled off to the bus stop.

I picked up Cat and scratched underneath his chin. "That woman knows something."

"Like what?" Dot asked.

"I dunno. But it's important and it has to do with one or all of these murders. I'm sure of it."

* * *

After Mildred left us, Dot and I stood on her steps discussing this new bit of information. "Medicine for a bad heart," Dot said.

"And Emmie's grandma died of what they said was a heart attack." I tapped out a fresh cigarette and lit it. I thought better with something in my hands. "But are the two connected?"

Dot shifted her seat on the step and Cat returned to her lap. "What happens when you take those pills and you don't have a heart problem?"

"Dunno. The library is closed, so we can't go look it up. It'll have to wait." I hated waiting.

There was silence for a few minutes, then Dot snapped her fingers. "I got it. Come inside." She got to her feet and dumped Cat on the ground. He yowled and flicked his tail in feline annoyance. "Oh, sorry, kitty." He stalked off, tail held high. "You gotta put that smoke out first."

"I just lit it."

"Mom will have a fit."

I carefully rubbed out my gasper and slipped it back in the pack. I wasn't gonna throw away a perfectly good cigarette. I followed Dot into the house. "Where are we going?"

"Just follow me." She led me to the living room, where she knelt in front of a bookshelf. "It's here somewhere."

"What's there?"

"Another one of those Agatha Christie books. She uses a lot of poisons and I know I just read one where the old lady died from an overdose of her medication. It's the same one, digitoxin. I thought it sounded familiar when Mildred told us. It makes sense it's a poison. Heck, it even has the word *toxin* in the name."

"You're reading? Since when?" I'd never known Dot to be a reader of any kind, much less mysteries.

Her cheeks pinked. "Mom got me hooked. Some of 'em are really good, Betty. I think you'd like the ones featuring her Belgian detective. He's not as physical as Spade or Marlowe, but he's smart." She skimmed her fingers over the titles. "Here it is. *Appointment with Death*. See, in this one, the old lady takes digitoxin for her heart, but she's really awful to her family and she's killed. Everyone thinks she's been injected, but Poirot, that's the Belgian, figures out it's an overdose of her heart medicine." She held out the paperback.

I took it and thumbed the pages. "Dot, this is fiction. How d'you know this Christie woman didn't make it up?"

"She worked in a medical dispensary in the Great War. She knows all about poisons." Dot sat on the armrest of a chair.

"Is digitoxin a pretty common treatment?"

She shrugged. "The story makes it sound like it is."

I skimmed the book. If Dot was right, and an overdose of digitoxin would cause death in a person with a bad heart, that could be what killed Pelagia. "What would it do to someone who had a good ticker?"

"I dunno for sure, but it makes sense it wouldn't be good, right? Maybe Detective MacKinnon would know."

"I guess." If the medicine could cause a heart attack, then yeah, maybe that's what had happened to Pelagia. "This is no good, though. Mildred said she thought her mother's pills went missing while she was at the Witkop place, right? If that's so, how did it get to Pelagia?"

Dot had no answer.

I slapped the book against my palm and thought. I liked the idea of someone pilfering the heart stuff and giving it to Pelagia because it was a clean solution. It explained why she died and it covered why Emmie had been so surprised. But I couldn't get past the problem of how the thief got the drugs to Pelagia. Emmie had never mentioned a guest of any kind, much less a swell from Delaware Park. Such a person would have stood out a mile in Polonia, another one of Buffalo's working-class neighborhoods. I'd talk to her again. Of course, it was also possible Pelagia had been invited in when she went to the house. One of the family could have crushed the pills and sprinkled them in her tea or on a cookie. But how fast would it kill her? Was this medication so slow that it'd take days to do any harm? "Can I borrow this?" I held up the book.

"Yeah, I'm not reading it and neither is Mom. Why?"

"If it has information on digitoxin, I figured I might skim it and see if I can get any other clues."

Dot raised her eyebrows. "You? Read? By choice?"

I threw a needlepoint pillow at her. "Don't get excited. No matter how good this Christie woman is, she can't be better than the pictures."

Chapter Thirty-Four

Monday the twenty-eighth, I spent the ride to work talkin' with Dot and tryin' to figure out where I stood. I kept thinkin' I was a step closer, but to what?

"Did you finish the book?" Dot asked.

"What, *Appointment with Death*? I borrowed it yesterday, for cripe's sake."

"But if it was good, you mighta kept reading."

It had been interesting, but I didn't feel like admitting that to Dot. "I got far enough. In the book, the killer gives the old lady the poison in her medicine, some little tablets she took. That goes along with my idea about Pelagia getting it from what Mildred bought for her mother. What it doesn't explain is how medicine from Delaware Park, 'cause that's where Mildred thinks it went missing, got to the lower East Side."

Dot thought about it a bit, then said, "I'm stumped."

"So was I. Then I remembered. Emmie said her grandma got a box of candy a couple of days before she died. The old lady said it was a gift, but Emmie couldn't think who'd give her a box of store-bought candy."

"So?"

"Well, what if the pills, this digitoxin, was in the candy? The killer stole it from Mildred, bought a box of candy, mixed it in, then delivered the box to Pelagia."

"That's a pretty far-fetched idea."

"It's the best one I got." The thermometer outside our kitchen window that morning read nearly forty degrees, but I could feel snow in my bones. It was as if winter was determined to pour something cold on any progress

I might make. I didn't need Dot to be skeptical, too. "I called Emmie last night and asked her to bring me the box, if she still had it."

We got to Bell and went to hang our coats up. Emmie was waiting for me, holding a blue box with a white bow. "Good morning, Betty."

"Morning, Emmie." I stuffed my things in a locker and turned to her. "I'm real sorry I don't have this case wrapped up. I know I told you by Christmas, but it's takin' longer than I thought."

"It's okay. I know you're doing your best," she said.

"Is that the box?"

"Yes. The candy is gone. *Babcia* must have eaten it all. She had such a sweet tooth."

I took it. It was a box of peppermints, at least that's what the sticker said. Inside was a crumpled sheet of white paper and a lot of dust that gave off the minty scent. "You didn't eat any?"

"I don't much care for peppermint. It was one of *Babcia*'s favorites and she was always tryin' to give me some, but I didn't have the heart to tell her I hated it. I generally took the candy and threw it away." Emmie blushed. "She didn't try to give me any of these, though. After you called last night, I was afraid Daddy had thrown away the box, but it was still in her room. It had fallen on the floor and someone kicked it under the bed."

A box under the bed. I had a box like this, too. In the same place. What were the odds? But mine was full of expensive chocolate, not peppermint. And it had come with a note. I couldn't let myself be distracted by made-up connections. I nudged the paper around, but I didn't see anything except the white dust. If the candy had been wafers or dry tablets, that was to be expected. "You're sure she didn't tell you where she got 'em?"

Emmie shrugged. "Nope. The label on the box says Wahl's. Maybe they'd know who bought them." She looked at the clock. "I gotta run. Catch you later."

After she left, I scoured the box for a clue. I even replaced the lid and ran my nail around the edge on the off chance I could find something underneath the paper. But it stubbornly remained what it looked like. A plain blue box from a popular neighborhood candy store.

"Do you really think someone coulda stolen the digitoxin, mixed it with the candy, and poisoned Pelagia?" Dot asked, voice doubtful.

"I dunno." I placed the box in my locker. "I'll take it to Sam MacKinnon. Maybe the police can run some kind of test to be sure. But if Pelagia was indeed poisoned, this could be how it was done."

* * *

After work, I went to police headquarters and asked to talk to Detective MacKinnon. Sam appeared not long after, shirt sleeves rolled up, tie loosened, and a lit cigarette hanging from his lips. "Betty, what can I do for you?"

"I brought you something." I held out the blue box.

He took it from me. "What is this?"

"It was s'posed to be a box of peppermints."

He opened it and sniffed. "Smells like exactly that."

"Oh, I'm sure there were real peppermints in there. But I think some of it was heart medicine."

He looked up and removed his gasper. "Say that again."

I told him the story of Mildred's mother, how Pelagia got the box of candies, and my suspicions. "Pelagia died of a heart attack. But remember how her granddaughter kept sayin' it was impossible?"

"Yes, you told me."

I pointed at the box. "I think Mildred's missing tablets were in that box. That's what killed Pelagia."

"How do you know what taking heart pills does to a healthy person? You're not a doctor."

"I read it." I didn't tell him the book had been a novel.

"Pelagia ate them by mistake, thinking they were candy, and died. Is that your idea?"

"Exactly. If she ate more than one at time, she would have tasted peppermint. Or maybe she didn't and just wondered why that particular piece tasted funny. She may even have thought it was just a mistake. Who knows?" I crossed my arms. "You can find out, right? If it was something other than peppermint?"

"Yes. I'll send the box to our lab. They can test the dust. If they find anything other than peppermint, I can ask for Mrs. Brewka's body to be exhumed and we can test the corpse for the poison." He took a drag off his smoke. "But who would want to kill the old lady?"

I pointed at the box. "My money is someone from the Witkops' place. That's where the medicine disappeared. The candy is from Wahl's. That's over on Losson, in Cheektowaga. It wouldn't take but an hour or so to get there by bus and it's a good way to throw off suspicion, buying the stuff from a store in a different neighborhood. If we want to be sure, we'd have to go there and ask."

Sam inspected the label. "For that matter, it could have been Mildred Janson. After all, it's her mother's medicine we suspect of being in here. She'd have the best opportunity to lace the box. We only have her word that the pills were stolen." He looked at me. "What's the motive?"

"Sebastian Witkop has two. What if Pelagia knew about his affair with Bridget and was threatening to tell? It's one thing to have a secret affair with the help. It's another if it's public."

"How would Mrs. Brewka know about that?"

"I dunno, maybe she saw them in public or something."

"It's a stretch."

"All right, how about this? Sebastian as good as admitted to me when I talked to him at Forest Lawn that his folks didn't come by their money honestly. Pelagia might have known about *that* and said she was gonna tell. Heck, she kinda did."

"I find that motive more compelling, especially in light of the letter to Josef Pyrut found at City Hall." He pulled out a pack of cigarettes and offered me one.

They weren't my brand, but I took it and he gave me a light. "Did you find out anything about a translator?"

He exhaled a cloud of smoke. "The letter wound up in the mayor's office, because they coordinated the visit. I've learned there are two people in the office who could have translated the Polish. One recently shipped out for the Pacific."

"That'll make him hard to get in touch with."

"The second is an older lady who works there as a secretary. I'm planning to talk to her later." He tapped his smoke against the tray in the corner. "However, I had it translated here at HQ. It's not very specific and only says Pelagia has some important information to give to the Polish government regarding the Witkops, especially in light of the party."

"We already know what that is." I puffed. "Do you think someone at City Hall coulda killed Pelagia to cover up what she knew? Then they offed Josef in case he knew?" Josef had been mugged and hit over the head. Could a woman do that? Maybe, if she was strong and used something heavy, like a rock or a pipe.

Sam shrugged. "Always a possibility, but it's pretty late in the investigation to start multiplying suspects. Who else in the Witkop house has motive?"

I thought for a moment. "Paul Witkop for sure."

Sam's narrowed his peepers. "I can see him wanting to kill Bridget because he'd feel betrayed by the affair, but Pelagia?"

"Paul's proud, his pop told me. So did the servants. If he thought Pelagia was gonna blow the old man's reputation and maybe cost the family its dough, he might take steps. I was thinking Mrs. Witkop, but you nixed that. Have you looked into Mr. Charles?"

"I'm working on it," Sam said. "That leaves Miss Janson. I suppose Pelagia might have become suspicious of the theft, especially if she saw the goods in the secondhand shop. She might have threatened to tell Mr. and Mrs. Witkop."

I crushed out my cigarette. Sam's brand definitely had a harsher taste than my Luckys. "Maybe, but how would Pelagia know the stuff belonged to the Witkops? No, I like someone in the family for all of this."

"You're leaving someone out." He jabbed his finger at me.

"Who?"

"Bridget." He watched me a second. I must have had quite the expression 'cause he laughed. "Just because Bridget herself was murdered, doesn't mean she isn't also a killer. Pelagia could have found out about her and Mr. Witkop. For that matter, Bridget might have wanted to protect her lover's fortune and keep him safe."

"That's an awful thing to say."

He sobered. "But true. You want to be a detective, you have to learn to face the possibility that anyone can be a crook given the right incentive."

I swallowed hard. I hadn't thought of that. I wondered about myself. Could I kill to protect my family? Absolutely, if they were in danger. Could I do it in cold blood? I'd like to think not, but then again, I hoped I'd never find out. Sam said nothing, letting me come to grips with that fact. "All right," I finally said. "Now what?"

"Looks like I have to take a trip to Wahl's." He ground out his cigarette under his foot. "Are you up to coming with me?"

I paused, then made up my mind. "Yeah. I'm game. Let's go."

Chapter Thirty-Five

Sam and I didn't say much on the way to Cheektowaga. Once again, I thought about how nice it was to drive. The lights in the store were on when we arrived. Wahl's had opened in the middle of the Great Depression, but hard times hadn't stopped them from becoming one of the most popular candy shops in Cheektowaga or even Buffalo. Mary Kate loved their jellybeans. I was a sucker for their sponge candy, light spun sugar covered in smooth chocolate.

The sign on the door said *Closed*, but that didn't stop Sam MacKinnon from walking right in. "Hello?" he called.

I followed and eyed the cases full of sweets. Good heaven, Mary Kate would die of sugar overload if I let her loose in this place.

A tubby balding man came from the back of the store. "I'm sorry, didn't you see the sign? We're closed."

Sam showed his badge. "I need a few moments of your time."

The man paled. "Oh, um, yes, of course. What can I do for you, officer?"

"Detective." Sam smiled. "Detective Sam MacKinnon, Buffalo PD." He noticed the man's gaze drift to me. "This is my associate, Betty Ahern. I gather you work here. For how long?"

"I've been here for five years."

"What's your name?"

"Milton. Milton Carle."

"Mr. Carle." Sam took the box of peppermints from his pocket, holding it with a handkerchief. "Is this from Wahl's?"

"It looks like one of our boxes, yes." Milton reached for it. "May I have it?"

"I'd rather you don't touch it. Fingerprints, you know." Sam removed the box lid and held out both for Milton to examine.

"Yes, that's one of ours, the smaller size. It holds about a quarter-pound of chocolate. We also use them for smaller products." He indicated a display of jellybeans and other small candies.

"I see a lot of chocolate in your cases," I said. "Do you sell other things?"

Milton transferred his gaze to me. "Oh yes. Not as much as the meltaways or the sponge candy or jellybeans. But Mr. Wahl likes to keep a variety, something for every customer." Milton waved to the glass case to his left.

I moved to examine it. There were several trays of multi-colored candies of different sizes. At the end of the row, a tray of round, white tablets labeled "peppermint" was marked with a label claiming you could get half a pound for twenty-five cents. "Can I see 'em?"

Milton shot a glance at Sam, who nodded. Milton came over, scooped up some peppermints, and handed them to me. I picked one, turned it over in my palm, then popped it in my mouth. Then looked at my hands, now dusted with a white powder. "I'd say it was the same as was in the box," I told Sam. I held up my hands.

He nodded. "You said these aren't as popular as chocolate," he said as Milton replaced the tray. "I don't suppose you can tell me when this box was sold."

Milton closed the case and returned to the detective. "Not off the top of my head, but it had to have been this Christmas."

"How can you tell?" I asked.

"The color. We used it for the season. We thought the pale blue went with the image of the Nativity."

"But you don't remember selling a box of peppermints about that size? This would have been at the end of last month, maybe as early as Thanksgiving. I don't know when you'd start using Christmas stuff," I said. Mildred told us she noticed her mother's medicine missing the week before Thanksgiving. Pelagia had died not long after. The timing fit.

"I believe we began using them after that." Milton frowned. "But if you're asking me to remember a single sale, and a small one at that, from almost a month ago, that's a pretty tall order."

"Try," said Sam. His voice was friendly, but it was definitely a command, not a suggestion. "Perhaps you have receipts you can look through?"

"We might," Milton said, his words coming slowly. "I don't think we've gotten rid of last month's records. I suppose I could look and you could come back."

"Why don't you take a peek and we'll wait?" Again, Sam's words were a suggestion, but his tone said it was more of an order.

Milton sighed. "Our shop girl, Caroline, is still here. Let me get her and we'll do what we can." He hurried off to the back.

I strolled around looking at the displays. "My sister would go nuts in this place. She loves sweets of any kind."

"Buy her something while we're here," Sam said.

"I don't have the cabbage on me."

He tossed a dollar bill on the counter. "My treat. After all, I didn't get you anything for Christmas." My surprise must have shown on my mug, because he laughed. "I'm not pulling your leg. Pick out her favorites. And yours."

A whole dollar for candy? I'd never seen such riches. I got so caught up in thinking about all the options, I didn't notice Milton had come back, slips of paper in his hand.

"You're in luck," he said. "We were able to find several slips from the time period you're interested in." He spread them on the counter. "These two are for more than the box would hold, and these three are for less. We would have used a much smaller box. That leaves these four."

I returned to Sam's side. The receipts all described sales of the white peppermints. "Not these two," I said, pushing away two slips. "The goods were bought after Pelagia died."

"Do you remember either of these sales?" Sam asked, pointing at the papers.

Milton picked them up. "Let me see. Yes, this one is old Mrs. Hildebrand. She bought the mints plus chocolate for her grandchildren. I remember because we had to wrap every box in a different paper because the gifts were supposed to be from Santa Claus and the children would be suspicious if the paper was the same. It was quite a to-do. I had to get Caroline to wrap because Mrs. Hildebrand didn't think I did a fancy enough job." He gave us a wry smile. "This one...I don't remember. This isn't my handwriting. One moment." He went to the door to the back. "Caroline, please come here."

After a moment, a younger girl with a spotty face appeared, wringing her hands in a white apron streaked with brown, prob'ly chocolate. Her mouth was slightly open. My first uncharitable thought was this girl was gonna have a tough time snagging a boyfriend when the war was over, with her plain face and a gap in her front teeth. "Yes, Mr. Carle?" She lisped, too, her "yes" sounding more like "yeth."

"This is your handwriting." Milton held out the receipt. "Do you happen to remember this customer? It was a very small order, only peppermints. It would have been rather unusual, so I thought you might recall some detail about who bought it."

Caroline frowned, obviously concentrating. Then her expression cleared. "No, sir, I'm sorry. We get so busy. I plain don't remember."

"You're sure?" I asked.

The girl frowned, a bit of her tongue sticking out. "No, miss. If you'd asked me the next day, maybe, but not now."

Drat. I crossed my arms and stalked back to the chocolate displays.

Sam shot me a look. "Thank you very much for your time. Sorry we delayed your closing."

Mr. Carle and Caroline both assured us they were happy to help the police. Sam took my arm, and we left.

"Well, that was a bust," I said. I stared at the dying grass as a bitter breeze stirred my hair. I hadn't realized how hopeful I'd been about finding an answer from Wahl's.

"Cheer up. That's part of detective work. Not every lead pans out. Let's go." He took a step, then stopped. "Wait, you forgot something."

"I did?" I didn't have any other questions. What was he talking about?

"That dollar is still on the counter. You didn't get your chocolate. Hopefully they'll let you back in."

Chapter Thirty-Six

The next day, I told Dot about going to Wahl's. "Well, that wasn't much help," she said. "I am jealous of the treat though."

"You didn't think I'd forget you, did I?" I gave her a square of chocolate. "I decided it didn't matter. I'm convinced Bridget bought that candy."

Dot popped the square in her mouth, closed her eyes, and savored it as she ate. When she was done, she looked at me. "How do you figure that?"

"Let's think on this logically. It's a gift box, or at least it looks like one. Who buys a gift box?"

"Well, the only man who buys a fancy box is one who is buying something for his sweetheart. Least that's my experience. Like your secret admirer."

"Dot, will you give it a rest?" I nudged her. "No guy is going to buy a cheap box of peppermints. He'll buy the good stuff. Okay, so it's a woman and one without a lot of money."

"Why couldn't it be one of Pelagia's friends, like Emmie said?" Dot asked.

"An old Polish grandma doesn't buy a cheap box of mints either. It has to be Bridget. She's a maid, so she doesn't have a lot of dough. I s'pose you could argue Mrs. Witkop might buy the box as a gift for a servant or someone like that, but she prob'ly wouldn't go to the store herself, she's too good for that. Who would she send?"

"Bridget."

"Right." My hands went through the motions of assembling P-39s, but my mind was miles away. "Detectives work with assumptions all the time. So let's take it for a fact that it was Bridget who bought the mints."

"Okay," Dot said. "But why would Bridget want to kill Pelagia?"

"No reason, but listen. Bridget goes to Wahl's to buy the candy. She could have been buyin' them for Mr. Witkop. They're cheap and it's not a flashy present, but I can believe a girl buying her guy, even a sugar daddy, a box of candy for Christmas. Heck, maybe they were a childhood favorite of his. Who knows."

"I s'pose we could ask Mr. Witkop, but yeah, I don't have a problem with anything you said."

"For now, let's assume that's the case. Bridget takes the box to Delaware Park and gives it to her beau. While it's there, someone notices what a swell copy the mints are of the medicine, steals the bottle from Mildred, and dumps it in."

"Are we sure the heart pills were in the box?"

I finished with my instrument panel, stepped back, and waited for the next fuselage. "Sam's gonna run the box through the lab and tell me. For now, that's another assumption so I can keep makin' progress."

"Okay, but why do that? Dump in some of the tablets?"

"I can see two possibilities." I held up a finger. "The first is the person wanted to poison Bridget and thought the candies were hers. That means it coulda been Mildred, if she was afraid of losing her job. Or it coulda been someone else at the house who wanted to get rid of Bridget."

Dot chewed her lip. "Was she...you know?"

I shook my head. "No, Sam told me. But we still have the possibility Paul was jealous of his pop, or the other way around."

"You said Mr. Witkop loved her."

"I believe he did. But that might just make him extra mad if he thought she'd dumped him for Paul. Crime of passion and all that. Although this kind of poisoning is hardly what I'd call a spur of the moment thing. It could take Bridget days to eat the medicine, or eat enough to kill her."

"True." A new fuselage stopped in front of us and we worked for a moment. "I can see where someone at Delaware Park might want to bump off Bridget. What's the other possibility?"

"Bridget was never the intended victim of the candy. The killer stole the heart pills and used the candy as a way to deliver them." But the more I talked about it, the more doubts I had. It was so chancy. Bridget's poisoning was way more direct. Sending medicine disguised in a box was sloppy.

"Then the killer has to be someone connected with the Witkops, whether Bridget was the victim or if that person stole the box to send to Pelagia."

"Yep."

"But how does the stuff get to Emmie's grandma?"

"That's what's tripping me up." I signed my name to the back of the instrument panel and attached it. "I gotta talk to Emmie. She has to tell me where her grandma got that box of candy."

"It's not a very good plan, you know. I can see a lot of things that would go wrong and I'm not exactly a criminal mastermind."

"I never claimed we were looking for a professional killer." In fact, if the culprit was someone in the Witkop house, it was most definitely an amateur. That could explain the hokey plan, but if the same person had killed Bridget and Josef, those had been clean enough. Maybe I was looking for two killers.

I tracked Emmie down at lunch and buttonholed her. "Those candies. Where did your grandma get them?"

"I told you, I don't know," she said, unwrapping her lunch.

"Think hard. It's important."

She crinkled her face and thought for a minute. "I came home from work. *Babcia* had the box on the table next to her chair. She offered me a piece, but I reminded her I don't like peppermint. I noticed the label from Wahl's and I asked where they'd come from."

I leaned forward. "What'd she say?"

Emmie paused, and her eyes lost focus as she remembered. "A boy brought them to the house."

"A delivery boy?" Dot asked.

"No." Emmie drew out the word. "A boy from the neighborhood. In fact, it might have been Luke. She said they were a gift." She blinked. "That's all I know. She didn't say who from and that's why I assumed it was a friend." She stared at me. "What's so important about the box?"

"I'm pretty sure it had tablets in it that were heart medicine," I told her.

"You said your grandma died of a heart attack. Well, s'pose she got medicine intended for someone with a bum ticker. I'm not a doctor, but it couldn't have done anything good for her."

"You think that's how she was killed? How can we be sure?"

"I got a friend who can hopefully tell me if there's any medicine left in the box, in the dust or something. And yeah, I think it's possible."

Emmie's excitement was tempered with doubt. "Do you know why someone would want her dead?"

"I think your grandma had some dirt on a prominent family here in Buffalo, one she used to work for back in Poland," I said. "What she knew, well, it wouldn't get them into real trouble, least I don't think so. But they might be embarrassed. You and I wouldn't think it was a big important secret. But I guess the size of the secret depends on the person. For example, pretend you grew up telling yourself your family was one sort of people, the nice kind. One day you find out they weren't, but it's okay, no one else knows. Then bam, someone shows up who knows the secret and you're afraid it'll get out, that maybe folks will think less of you because of it."

Emmie gave a half-hearted laugh. "You think someone would commit murder just cause of some dumb secret that isn't even that big of a deal?"

I stared at her. "I think people have killed for a lot less. In the pictures, murder happens for all sorts of reasons. We may think it's dumb, but to the killer it's the most important thing in the world."

Emmie stared at her food. "I'm not hungry all of a sudden. I think I'll take a walk. Talk to you later, Betty." She put her lunch back in its bag and left.

Dot cocked her head. "Do you believe that? What you just said?"

"I do." I picked at my sandwich. "Who we are, and where we come from, is important. To us and to others. It affects how we're seen and thought of. I wouldn't want to be known as the granddaughter of someone who sold out his neighbors for some dough and shiny trinkets, would you?"

Dot paused. "Why would this Luke, or any boy really, deliver a package for a stranger?"

"I'm guessing he was paid." I took a bite. "But that's exactly what I intend to find out."

* * *

We went to the Manelowas' house immediately after work. Luke was on the sidewalk, counting the cans in a battered red wagon. Engrossed in his counting, he didn't look up.

"Hi, Luke. Remember me?" I asked.

He paused and looked at me. "Sure do. You're Miss Ahern. You came to ask me about old Mrs. Brewka and whether I helped her. I already told you about that." He went back to his task.

"I have some different questions, if you can spare a moment."

He broke off and looked up, a gleam in his eye. "I do if you got any cans to give me."

I spread my hands. "Sorry, I don't have anything. I came from work."

He jerked her head at Dot. "What about her?"

She crossed her arms. "We don't carry scrap metal around in our purses. Sorry."

"If you don't have anything to give me, then I don't have any time." He tossed the last can in the wagon and picked up the handle.

I pulled out my change purse. Dot grabbed my arm and tugged me aside. "Don't tell me you're gonna pay this kid."

"I need info, Dot. All of 'em are businessmen these days. Cost of being a private detective, I guess." I searched around in my change purse to find a couple of nickels. I went back to Luke. "The only kind of metal I have is this." I held up the coins.

He looked and held out a grubby paw. Once I dropped a nickel in his hand, he stuffed it in his pocket and said, "What do you wanna know? I know lots of things. Math, and spelling, and—"

"None of that," I said. I'd forgotten how fast he talked. "Emmie told me you might have given old Mrs. Brewka a box of candy. It would have been blue, with a shiny white ribbon on it. It came from Wahl's."

His lips turned down. "That was a long time ago. Mrs. Brewka died last month. I can't be expected to remember that far back for only five cents."

Beside me Dot huffed. I bit back a sigh and handed over the other nickel.

He brightened. "Nope, don't remember nothing like that. But thanks for the money. G'bye."

Dot swiped at him. "Why you little—"

Luke danced away from her, a mischievous grin on his face.

I held her back. Luke had miscalculated. He'd skipped away from Dot, but closer to me. And he'd failed to take into the account I had longer arms and legs than she did. With only a step I was able to reach out and snag his collar. "Come back here, you thief."

He yelped. "I ain't no thief. I did exactly what I told you I would."

I let go of his jacket. All I needed was his mom to look out the window and see me rough up her kid. "No, you didn't. Let's try this again. Think. Last month. Blue box, white ribbon. Box was from Wahl's. Maybe someone paid you to make a delivery?"

He wrinkled his forehead, this time in what looked like genuine thought. "Yeah. I remember now. Mom bought it because Mrs. Brewka had given us a batch of her homemade *kolachkes*, which is the best cookie ever, and Mom didn't have time to bake anything so she bought the candy because she knew Mrs. Brewka has a sweet tooth. Her favorite candy is peppermint from when she was a young girl and the first time she came to America, but she doesn't get it very much."

"Your mom?" I could see my theory going right down the drain.

"Yep. Bye." He turned to go.

I wasn't leaving with nothing. Pelagia had gotten two boxes or something. It had to be that way. "Luke, you're a smart kid. I bet you see a lot that goes on in this neighborhood."

His chest puffed up. "I sure am. I've got the best math grades of everybody in my class. I'm outside all the time collecting cans and stuff. Ask me anything and I prob'ly know it."

"I want you to think back to last month, either right before or right after Mrs. Brewka passed away. Did you see *anything* out of place? There's another nickel in it for you if you did." I held up the shiny coin.

He made a grab for it.

"Uh-uh." I held it out of his reach. "You gotta give me something first."

He stomped his foot. "Last month? Nothing exciting ever happens here. I never see any strangers."

"You sure about that?" Dot asked. "Maybe someone visiting around Thanksgiving?"

Luke's scowled and his eyebrows came down over his eyes.

I tilted the nickel so it caught the last rays of sunlight. "Nobody gave you anything? Maybe you delivered another box or something?" The seconds ticked on and I closed my hand around the coin, ready to put it back in my change purse.

"Hey wait a minute." Luke's face cleared. "Now I remember. A man came around and said he was looking for Pelagia Brewka and did I know her. I said sure, I know most everyone in the neighborhood. He asked where she lived so he could go say hello and he gave me a whole fifty-cent piece just for telling him, but I wasn't to let anyone know about him 'cause it was a surprise for her. You wouldn't believe the candy I bought with a whole fifty cents, it was more money then I'd ever seen. I even got some licorice for Mom. She likes the black kind, but—"

"Right, thanks." I shot a look at Dot, who merely looked heavenward. "Did you tell him where to find Mrs. Brewka?"

"Yeah, the cemetery 'cause she was already dead, but I told him where she was buried in case he wanted to leave flowers or anything at the grave. Mom sometimes leaves flowers at my grandpa's grave that is when she can afford—"

I cut into the flow of words. "What did he say? The guy?"

Luke thought, then shrugged. "Nothing, I guess. He said he was sorry and I could keep the fifty-cent piece. Then he left."

Dot shot me a look. "This man, was he old or young? What can you tell us about him?" she asked.

"He was rich, I can tell you that. He had on swell clothes, shiny black shoes, and a tan coat that was long and had a belt right about here." Luke patted his tummy. "His hair was slicked back, the way fancy guys in the pictures wear theirs. And his shirt was white, but the tie was dark and not like my dad's ties but made of something awful soft looking. When he took the fifty-cent piece outta his wallet, I could see loads of greenbacks in there. Yep, he was rich all right."

"You didn't say whether he was young or old," I said.

Luke thought a moment. "He was old."

Dot looked at me. "Sebastian?"

Unlike Dot, I had little brothers. To them, anybody older than me was old. "How could you tell he was old? You said he had slicked hair. Gray or another color? Was he fat, or did he have wrinkles or anything?"

Luke shrugged. "Naw, nothing like that. He had dark hair, no wrinkles that I could see. He had a scar on his mouth, right there." Luke tapped his upper lip. "I guess he was younger than my dad, but older'n you." A cunning look came onto his face. "I can tell ya something else, if you give me another nickel."

"Betty, don't you dare," Dot said.

But I had already dug a fourth coin out of my change purse. I held it up. "It's yours, but you gotta tell me first."

Luke pouted. "His shirt, around the wrists, it didn't have buttons. It had those shiny things on the end to keep it closed."

"Cufflinks?" I asked.

"Yeah, those. Anyway, they had an M on 'em, so I asked if it was for his name 'cause my cousin's name started with M, and he said yes, but not his first name his last. I told him my name started with M, Manelowa, and he just smiled and walked away. But I'm sure of it. His name started with M. That's helpful right? Isn't it?"

Dot and I exchanged a look. "Very helpful. Thanks, Luke. Try not to spend the money all at one time." I handed him the nickel.

As Dot and I walked away, we could hear Luke rattling on about how much candy he could buy once he turned in all the cans. The kid was in for a serious stomach ache.

"That wasn't an M, you know that, right?" Dot asked.

"Yeah, I know. It would have looked like an M 'cause it would've been upside down. It was a W."

A young, rich guy asking questions about Pelagia Brewka. It had to be

Paul Witkop.

Chapter Thirty-Seven

From Polonia, we hopped a bus to Delaware Park. On the way, I tried to think of what I was gonna say when I got there.

"Let me get this straight," Dot said. "You thought Bridget bought the candy at Wahl's. Someone at the Witkops' stole the medicine that was for Mildred's mother and put it in the box. But it turns out the box Luke delivered was from his mother. How does that help us?"

"It doesn't," I replied. "But we also learned that a rich stranger was hanging out asking about Pelagia. I'm sure it was Paul. How many guys with slicked dark hair and a scar on his puss are involved in this mess?"

She grumbled in response. "My head hurts."

"I know the feeling." I nibbled my thumbnail. With the sun on the way down and the temperature falling, part of me wished I'd worn my mittens, but chewing wool wasn't particularly tasty. "Maybe he came to scope out the neighborhood and find Pelagia. Or he came back to check on his dirty work and he got the medicine to her another way."

"Aren't you making a lot of guesses, Betty? We don't even know if Paul knew Mrs. Brewka." Dot chewed her lip.

I snapped my fingers. "He did know her. Remember I told you? When I talked to him outside Kleinhan's he knew Pelagia was an old woman. How would he know that if he'd never met her?"

"You're sure he said that?" Dot worried her lip some more.

"Positive." I swatted her hand. "How many times I gotta tell you to stop turning your lip into minced meat?"

"You chew your nails."

"Not the same. I can file a ragged nail and I can't have long ones with my work at Bell anyway." I waved my hand. "Back to business. Here's what we know. Paul left the party early. He'd been talking to Josef and that picture, the one where Paul's all stiff, tells me they had an argument. I'll bet you anything he knew about the contents of Pelagia's letter, either the one to his pop or the one she wrote to Josef. For all we know, he has a friend at City Hall who tipped him off. So he goes to check on Pelagia and finds out she's dead. That's one threat gone. Now all he has to do is deal with Josef."

Dot pointed at me. "But that means Paul didn't kill her. Who else would?"

"No one. Could be Emmie's family is right and she just died 'cause she was old and her heart gave out."

"You don't have proof of any of this."

"Look, if Sam's tests find there's heart medicine in that box, we'll know that somehow, some way, it got from Delaware Park to Pelagia and she was murdered. Until that happens, our best bet is talkin' to Paul. Maybe he'll crack and spill his guts, and the case will be over." I glanced at my wristwatch. It was almost five o'clock. "Don't you have to get home? Your folks won't be happy."

"Yes, but I'm not letting you go to meet Paul Witkop on your own." She thought a minute. "You gotta tell this to Detective MacKinnon, too."

"I will. After I leave the Witkops. Wish I knew where Sam lives. This hour of the day, he prob'ly won't be at work." I could always check the phone book. Would a police detective be listed in the white pages?

We got off the bus in Delaware Park and hoofed it to the Witkops' house. Somebody had turned the lights in the front room on, but the curtains were drawn and I couldn't see any shadows that would give a clue about people. To be safe, we went around back. I could hear raised voices. I held my finger to my lips. "Shh."

"I don't know who sent it out," a woman's voice said. It sounded like Mrs. Leggett. "A girl showed up at the door and told me she had a delivery. What was I going to do, send her away without a word?"

"Yes," a man said. Mr. Charles. "She made a mistake. There was no reason to let her in the house. At least you didn't pay her for a shirt."

I knocked on the door.

Less than a minute later, Mr. Charles yanked it open. "What on earth do you want now? It's the dinner hour. Have you no decency?"

"Sorry to interrupt," I said. "I want to ask you about something else, but I couldn't help but overhear. What's this about a laundry delivery? Is that unusual?"

"It's none of your business. Good evening." He pushed the door.

This time I knew better to stick my foot out, and I used my shoulder to keep it open. "I'm actually here to talk to Mrs. Leggett. I'd appreciate it if you'd tell her she has company and let her make her own decision about who to talk to before you slam the door in my face."

Mrs. Leggett came into view. "Who is it, Johnny?"

"It's that girl again. She wants to talk to you. About what I have no idea."

I nodded at the cook. "Evening, Mrs. Leggett. It has to do with Bridget, but not what we talked about last time. I promise I won't take you away from your dinner."

She glanced at Mr. Charles. "Very well, come in."

"Bernadette, Mr. and Mrs. Witkop are at the table," he said.

She tossed her head. "I'm not proposing I take Betty and her friend into the dining room. The police have been here how many times? They still don't seem to be any closer to catching Bridget's killer than you are. If these girls can help, it's our duty to give assistance."

He muttered under his breath, but let us in.

"Thank you very much, both of you," I said. "I have a couple questions, but first, where is Paul Witkop if he isn't eating dinner with his folks?"

The two servants exchanged a look. Mr. Charles shrugged, and Mrs. Leggett responded. "Two days ago, Mr. Paul and his father quarreled something dreadful."

"About what?" Dot asked.

Mrs. Leggett wrung her hands. "I don't rightly know. They were in Mr. Witkop's study and I didn't hear exactly what they were saying, but they both sounded terribly angry. All of a sudden, Mr. Witkop threw open the door and said, 'Get out, right now, and don't come back. I'll never forgive you and that's final.' Mr. Paul stormed out, packed a bag, left, and no one's seen hide nor hair of him since." She sniffed and dabbed at her eyes with a handkerchief. "Mrs. Witkop was furious. 'You have no right, no right at all, not after what you've done,' she said. Then she shut herself up in her room. I've been bringing her meals to her. Tonight's the first night since the argument they've dined together."

Huh. Could Sebastian Witkop have found out his son was a murderer? But then why didn't he call the cops? "I also heard something about a laundry delivery?"

Mrs. Leggett seemed to calm down. At least she stopped sniffling. "Earlier today, a girl showed up with a package. It was from a laundry down on Fillmore, next to the secondhand shop where you found the Witkops' things."

"I know it. Go on."

"Well," Mrs. Leggett continued, "the girl said she had a shirt to deliver. It had been at the laundry for quite some time, but no one had gone to pick it up. I told her she must be mistaken. One, we don't use that laundry and two, all of the family's clothing was accounted for. I'd made the trip myself not two days ago. She was very insistent."

"It was a mistake," Mr. Charles said, breaking into the conversation. "She didn't need to get so huffy about it. Paying her for her time. We didn't tell her to come all the way up here."

"Was the shirt Mr. Paul's?"

"I don't know," said Mrs. Leggett. "When we wouldn't pay her, she left. In quite a huff, I might add."

I glanced at Dot. "What I came to ask you about is this. I talked to Mr. Sebastian Witkop at Forest Lawn Cemetery on Christmas."

Mr. Charles nodded. "He always goes to visit his parents' grave on Christmas and Easter. Never any other time. He's always very somber when he returns, too."

Maybe because the visit reminded him that his folks weren't very nice people, I thought. That would explain why he was so talkative when I saw him. I'd caught him when he was feeling reflective and vulnerable. "Right. Anyway, when we talked, he admitted he'd met Pelagia Brewka. What I want to know is this. Did Mr. Paul ever meet her?"

"Not to my knowledge," Mrs. Leggett said.

Mr. Charles was silent. After a few seconds under my patient gaze, he relented. "I believe he did," he said. "Either right before, or right after Thanksgiving, I'm not sure which. I want to say afterward. She was standing in front of the house, just staring. I tried to shoo her away, but she wouldn't go." He stopped.

I waited a moment. "Go on."

He was quiet and looked to be fighting with himself, but eventually spoke. "Mr. Paul came out and asked what was going on. I told him the woman, this Mrs. Brewka, wouldn't leave. Mr. Paul told me not to worry, he'd take care of it, and I could go back inside. As I walked to the house, I could hear them speaking."

After another pause that felt longer than it prob'ly was, I prompted him again. "What did they say?"

"I didn't hear all of the conversation because I went inside. Mr. Paul told her she had the wrong house. Pelagia said, 'I knew your father. If he won't do the honorable thing, then you must.' After that, I'd entered the house, so I didn't hear anything further. Mr. Paul came inside a minute or so later. When I asked him if everything was all right or should I call the police, he told me not to bother. It was all a mistake, and he and the woman had worked it out."

"Did he say anything after that?"

"No." Mr. Charles slumped. "He didn't say anything and I didn't ask."

"The last time I was here," I said, "you told me you thought you saw something between Bridget and Mr. Witkop. The older one."

"Yes," Mrs. Leggett said.

"If Paul had found out about that, how would he have reacted?"

Mrs. Leggett's expression turned serious. "Oh, he'd have been quite angry, I'm sure of it. He would have been personally insulted, of course. What young girl would choose his father over him? Not only that, but because of how it would look to others. His father having an affair with a girl young enough to be his daughter, and a servant to boot? Plus Mr. Paul is devoted to his mother. He couldn't bear the shame it would cause her."

"I thought Mr. and Mrs. Witkop weren't all that good together," Dot said.

Mrs. Leggett looked at her. "They aren't. They don't get a divorce because of how it would look to their friends. If it had been known that Mr. Witkop had been carrying on with the help, well, Mr. Paul would have been mortified, just as his mother would. I'm sure he'd also fight to have Bridget dismissed immediately."

"Also? Who else wanted Bridget fired?" I asked.

"Mrs. Witkop," said Mr. Charles. "I was upstairs, putting clothes away, when she came storming up the steps. It must have been right after the argument you heard, Bernadette." He nodded at Mrs. Leggett. "Mrs. Witkop said she'd had enough and she intended to tell Bridget that night that her services were no longer wanted. Mr. Witkop absolutely forbade his wife to say anything of the kind."

"Then she did find out," I said to Mrs. Leggett. "Last time we talked you weren't sure."

"Yes, I suppose she did," she said.

"What about you, Mr. Charles?" I fixed him with a look.

"Me? Why would I do such a thing?"

"You're pretty loyal to Mrs. Witkop. I think you'd do anything for her. Where were you when Josef Pyrut was killed? You were here the morning Bridget died, weren't you?"

He gave me a dirty look. "I never left the party. I served all night long and didn't go home until midnight. As for Bridget, no, I wasn't here. I generally don't come to the house until nine-thirty or ten. By the time I arrived, Bridget had already drunk her blasted tea and I would have had no opportunity to poison it. I left the previous night right after supper, because I had an errand to run. Bridget usually has a cup of tea before bed. As you may recall, the police have determined the sugar had to be poisoned the night before or that morning. If I'd done it before I left, she would have died during the night."

"He's telling the truth," Mrs. Leggett said. "I'll say the same to the police."

Dot and I exchanged a look. She seemed dubious, but I'd heard enough.

"Thanks for your time," I said.

Outside, the sun was almost gone and the whole neighborhood had been thrown into darkness. The streetlights had come on, casting pools of yellowish light on the browning grass at intervals along the street. We headed for the bus stop.

"What are you thinking?" Dot asked.

"I'm thinking Paul Witkop looks more and more like a suspect."

Chapter Thirty-Eight

I said goodnight to Dot in front of her house.

"You think you'll find Detective MacKinnon tonight?" she asked.

"That's my plan." My breath trailed off into the chilly night sky. "I'll let you know how it goes."

When I got home, however, a different problem confronted me. Mary Kate sat on the back step, scratching Cat behind the ears. He meowed at me, a definite warning. "You're in big trouble, Betty," she said, not rising.

I checked my watch for the time. Almost seven o'clock, way past dinner. Shoot. "They say anything?" I didn't have to identify *they*. I could only be talkin' about our parents.

"Nope, and you know that means it's bad," my sister said. "Good luck."

"You aren't gonna go in with me?"

"Not on your life."

"Coward." I reached for the door. Behind me, Cat meowed again, his own form of well wishes.

Inside, the kitchen was tidy, not a spot out of place. No food had been left on the table for me. I was smart enough not to check the fridge. Not only had I missed dinner, I hadn't dropped a dime to let my folks know. Or to tell 'em where I was or when I'd be home. *Not a bright move.* I hung my coat in the closet and took a step down the hallway.

Pop's voice came from the front room. "Elizabeth Anne, come here. Now."

I winced. He didn't thunder, or swear, or come barreling out of the room after me. But he used my full name. I was used to Mom doing it. That wasn't good, but that calm tone from Pop, added to the baptismal name, was beyond bad and I knew it.

I steadied my nerves and went to the front room. "Yes, sir?"

Mom and Pop were seated in their usual spots, Mom sewing, Pop puffing on his pipe. Next to them, the radio was tuned to the evening news, but the volume was barely audible. Mom's lips were a thin line and a spot of red showed on each cheek. But she didn't speak. She left it to Pop.

This was real bad.

He puffed his pipe a couple times, then removed the stem from his mouth. "Where have you been?"

The idea of lying didn't crossed my mind, not once. "I went to Polonia, up near Fillmore Avenue. Then I was over to Delaware Park, to the Witkops' house."

"Who?"

"Mr. and Mrs. Sebastian Witkop. They have a son, Paul. That's the family that hosted the big party for the exiled Polish government when they were in Buffalo at the beginning of December."

"Why?"

Oh boy. "I'm investigating a few murders."

He lifted an eyebrow. "A few?"

"Yes, sir." I paused, but he didn't say anything, so I went on. "First, there's Josef Pyrut. You read about him in the paper. He's the undersecretary attached to the Polish government who went missing and was later found in an alley up on Fillmore. Then there's Bridget Innes. You might remember her, Mom. She came to Ladies of Charity at least once."

My mother didn't move.

"She's an Irish girl and was a maid for the Witkops. She's dead. Poisoned. Lastly, a girl at work asked me to investigate her grandmother's death."

Pop said nothing for a moment and smoke trailed from his pipe. "I see." He paused. "And why would you do this?"

"I think all the deaths are connected. At first Emmie, that's the girl from Bell, asked me to look into her grandma's death 'cause Emmie was suspicious, even though the rest of her family wasn't. That led to Josef and then Bridget. Now I think Mrs. Brewka was murdered, just like the other two."

"You're investigating," he said.

"Yes, sir."

"Why?"

I rolled the dice. "'Cause Emmie paid me. I've been doing private detective work on the side, ever since the incident last month with Anne Linden."

"I'll ask you again, why?"

A year, heck, six months ago, I think I would have snapped under that calm, firm, gaze. But almost a year of working at Bell made me bold as brass, as my grandmother would say. "I'm good at it, Pop. And I like it."

Mom finally spoke. "I knew letting you go to all those movies was a mistake." She bit off a thread, still not looking at me.

"Mary, I said I would handle this," Pop said, his gaze never leaving my face. "You like being the hero of the story, is that it?"

"No!" I had to make him understand. "It's not about me, Pop. Honest. Sure, I like solving the puzzle and that's kinda fun and all, but mostly it's about helping folks. You know, things the cops won't do." I swallowed. "I've even made a friend at the police department. That detective who's been here, Detective MacKinnon. I've helped him out."

Mom's head snapped up. "What? You've been gallivanting around Buffalo with a police detective? An older man?"

"I wouldn't call it gallivanting, Mom," I said. "He asked for my help and I said yes."

"What would Tom think of all this? Hmm? Your fiancé?"

"I think, well, I think he'd be proud of me." Least I hoped so.

"You think he wants to be married to a—"

"Mary." Pop held up his hand, stemming what would have been quite the flow of words. "Elizabeth, have you done this all by yourself?"

Here, I fibbed. I couldn't get my friends into trouble. "Yes, sir."

"And tonight? It didn't occur to you that your mother and I would be worried when you didn't come home after work or for dinner?"

"I'm sorry about that. I should have found a pay phone and called you."

"No." He pointed at me. "What you should have done is come directly home." He studied me for a long second. "I'm very disappointed in you,

Elizabeth. You may be a working girl, but you live under my roof and you will abide by my rules. For now, you will go to your room. Tomorrow, you will go to work and come straight home afterward. What happens after that, we shall see. Good night."

I thought about arguing some more, but one look at Pop's face told me I needed to cut and run. "Yes, sir." Before I went down the back hall to my bedroom, I grabbed the phone book from the table in the hallway where the telephone was. If I was banished to my room, least I could do is look up Detective MacKinnon's address and phone number, or try to.

In the room, Mary Kate lounged on her bed, flipping the pages of a magazine. "Bad?"

"Worse than bad. You know how Mom yells, but Pop has this terrible quiet voice when he's real angry?"

"Yeah."

"That."

She winced.

I flopped on my bed and opened the phone book to the M's. Just my luck, there had to be a half a page of MacKinnons listed. "Shoot," I said under my breath.

Mary Kate sat up. "What's wrong?"

"Nothing. It's a research project."

She shook her head. "You get in trouble over everything you've been doing and you still can't let it go. I don't know if that's determination or stupidity."

I didn't know which it was either. But it might be time for me to think about getting my own place.

* * *

I stayed up late working on my project. I rejected all the listings with first initials that weren't S. There were several Samuel MacKinnons in the book. Sam was too old to be living at home. I tossed a couple of names with addresses I thought were unlikely, either too swanky or too poor for a police detective who prob'ly made a good buck. It left me with a round half-dozen options, two right here in the First Ward. The rest were in other neighborhoods.

I looked at the clock. Almost eleven. Mary Kate had gone to sleep a couple of hours ago and snored gently from across the room. The boys' bedtime had been much earlier. I heard Mom and Pop wrap up their nightly routines and settle in to their room. All around me, the house slumbered, quiet and still.

Except for me.

I'd met Sam MacKinnon in October, when Mr. Lippincott was murdered up at Bell. I thought back to that meeting. He'd said I reminded him of his sister, another good Irish First Ward girl. I laid my money on one of the two addresses and crept to the telephone in the hallway.

The cord was just long enough for me to hide in the front closet. I couldn't afford to be busted. Making a phone call in the dead of night was unthinkable. But I had to.

I cracked the door just enough so I could read the numbers I'd scribbled on a scrap of paper and dialed the first one. A woman's sleepy voice answer. "Hello?"

I pressed down to disconnect the call quick as I could. Would the woman call the cops? I found that unlikely. I'd hung up so fast, she'd think it was a simple wrong number. Or that's what I hoped. Unless she was Sam MacKinnon's wife. Wait, did he have a wife? How did I not know this? I tried to visualize his left hand. I was almost positive he didn't wear a ring. I dialed the second number.

The man who answered didn't sound sleepy at all. "MacKinnon."

I kept my voice as hushed as I could and still be heard over the line. "Is this the Sam MacKinnon who works as a detective for the Buffalo Police Department?"

"Who is this?"

"Sam, it's me. Betty Ahern."

"Betty? What in God's name...it's the middle of the night. What's wrong? I can barely hear you. Are you in trouble?"

"No trouble, well, none that requires the cops. I gotta see you tonight, as soon as possible."

"Can't it wait until tomorrow?"

"No. I'll explain later. Can you meet me at that coffee shop? Where you were before we went to go see the Witkops?"

"What's so urgent I have to meet you now?"

"I told you, I'll explain when we meet. Can you?"

His sigh whooshed over the line. "This better be good. Give me twenty minutes to get dressed and I'll see you there." He hung up.

I eased the receiver back into the cradle. I pushed open the closet door, which gave off a squeak so loud I swear it coulda been heard at the Tillotson house a block away. I froze. Nothing. I put the phone back and tiptoed to my room.

Thank goodness Mary Kate slept like the proverbial dead. I threw on a pair of work pants, a shirt, and some shoes. But I couldn't go out without a coat, not in the middle of a December night in Buffalo. Back to the closet I went, avoiding all the spots on the floor I knew creaked. I grabbed my coat and mittens. So far, so good.

Noise from the kitchen was less likely to wake my folks. I unlocked the door and pulled it open with excruciating slowness. Out the storm door I went, onto the back step, and tugged the door shut. Stage one complete. I turned to go down the steps.

And trod on Cat, who'd been nosing for who knows what. He screeched and rocketed between the garbage cans, knocking them over in a cacophony of falling metal.

Pop's voice was distant, but clear. "What the devil is going on?"

I didn't bother to stay and witness what came next. I bolted down the street and ducked behind the first shelter I saw, a light post. I sucked in my breath and stood sideways. I still wasn't as skinny as the post, but hopefully if Pop looked out the windows he wouldn't see me in the distance and among the shadows. I waited for what seemed like forever, but was prob'ly closer to a couple of minutes. No one appeared from my front door or from around the back of the house. I didn't hear the sounds of slamming. With any luck,

Pop had looked out the back window, seen the toppled garbage cans, and chalked it up to the nighttime activities of some animal, not an escaping wayward daughter.

As time passed and nothing happened, my breathing slowed. Taking care not to step on anything else that crossed my path, I hustled down the street and to the diner for my meeting with Sam.

The place was open all night. True to his word, Sam walked in almost exactly when he said he would. His hair was mussed and he wore an old trench coat over clothes that weren't nearly as sharp as what he wore for work. He stopped inside the door and looked around.

I waved. "Over here. I got you a cup of joe."

He headed to my booth and slid in. "Thank you." He dumped in some sugar and milk. "Now what in God's name is so important that you had to see me at eleven-thirty at night?"

I told him all about my visit to Luke Manelowa, his description of Paul, and my trip to Delaware Park. "Paul Witkop got that poison to Pelagia somehow, I'd bet anything. And I don't care what Mr. Charles said, I'd lay dollars to donuts that was Paul's shirt. Did your lab guys run their tests?"

"Yes. There was nothing in the box except for powder from a chalky peppermint candy, like the one we saw at Wahl's."

"Darn it."

Sam chuckled. "Cheer up. I told you, not every lead pans out. You have to learn to accept that if you're going to be a detective." He sipped the coffee. "Tell me more about this shirt. It was delivered from a laundry on Fillmore, you said?"

"The one right next to where you found Josef Pyrut's body." I was too hyped up to drink my own java. "There had to be something on it, maybe blood from killing Josef. Heck, maybe he told Bridget to take it out, then he decided she knew too much, and that's why he killed her. He either forgot about the shirt or figured if nobody claimed it, it would be thrown away. Too bad we can't ask Bridget about it."

"It's a little crazy, but I guess it's possible. It's more likely that if there was blood or other incriminating evidence on the shirt he'd have thrown it away. Then again, he's not a professional killer so he might not have been thinking clearly." He stared at the brownish contents of his mug. "We can always question the laundry staff and see why Paul had the shirt cleaned."

"Then he's our killer."

Sam made a see-saw motion with his hand. "Maybe, maybe not. I can't rule out the possibility he was acting under orders."

"Those would most likely come from his pop." I thought. "Sebastian was in love with Bridget."

"So he says."

"No, he was. There's a look men get when they truly love a woman and you can't counterfeit that."

Sam shook his head. "You watch enough movies, Betty. You know men kill the women they love all the time."

"You're right, they do. Stabbing, or strangling, or even shooting, I get. But with rat poison?"

Sam wouldn't back down. "Both men had a run in with Pelagia Brewka. Both men were in love with Bridget Innes, and both knew Josef Pyrut. I think the fact Sebastian has been less than honest about his parents all these years means keeping the family name clean is just as important to him as to his son. Maybe even more so."

"Protecting the secret only needs to be important to him." I ran my finger around the rim of the mug. It was what I'd told Emmie and Dot. If Mr. Witkop or his son and told themselves a story about who they were, and something, or someone, threatened that story, it just might end in murder.

"It's more than that, Betty. I thought you understood."

I looked at him. His eyes were dark and face serious. I knew he would take murder, for whatever reason, seriously. But from his expression, I could tell I was missing something important. "What?"

"Think about it." He leaned forward. "Sebastian Witkop's parents were Prussian sympathizers. So much so, they were willing to rat out their neighbors, at least that's your idea. In exchange, they were paid off. You think with valuables from the families the Prussians punished during and after the Franco-Prussian War, correct?"

"Yeah, so?"

"Who are we fighting now?"

The lightbulb in my head flickered on. "The Germans. And if I remember my history lessons correctly, the Prussians were the ones behind the big push to German unification. They created the modern Germany, at least you could look at it that way."

"Right." Sam waved his spoon at me. "Now, if it got out about Sebastian's parents, don't you think it would be logical that people might think he was a modern German supporter?"

"I guess."

"And if you back Germany these days, who are you tacitly and sometimes not-so-quietly, supporting?"

"The Nazis." The light from the mental bulb grew stronger. "It's treason."

"Correct. If Witkop is perceived as a traitor—"

"People would stop doing business with him. He might be shunned socially, he'd lose his money, and that would really set his wife and son off." His reputation would take a hit, and a big one.

"Precisely. His family could be attacked and his house damaged. Now do you understand why it's not just an old secret? It's a big deal. If Pelagia knew about the past, and Josef Pyrut found out, they'd have to go. Even Bridget wouldn't be safe."

I thought a moment. "What if it's his son who is the Nazi-lover?"

"I would imagine the consequences would be much the same," Sam said. "Whatever Paul does is going to reflect badly on his father. Mr. and Mrs. Witkop are still targets, as is the family house. How much damage there is to the business probably depends on how closely Paul is involved, but I can easily see where others might be reluctant to engage in any dealings with the father until they were sure he wasn't of the same mind as the son. It isn't the 1930s any more, but things are hardly so good that Sebastian Witkop can afford to lose his business."

"That might be why he threw his son out of the house."

"You could be right. The elder Witkop might no longer be able to turn a blind eye and is trying to distance himself and protect what he has." Sam finished his coffee. "At least I understand why you wanted to meet tonight. Why the subterfuge, though? Unless I'm off my game, you were trying not to be heard when you called me. You snuck out of the house, didn't you?"

"What are you, a detective?" I told him about the fight with my folks.

He frowned. "This isn't worth getting yourself into trouble, Betty."

"You let me worry about my family. It'll be okay."

"If you say so." He finished his coffee. "Oh, I found out about that letter at City Hall."

"You did?"

"Yes. They did open it since the Polish government had left, but once they saw it was in Polish, they simply sealed it up and sent it back to Pelagia. No one thought it important enough to translate the contents."

"That's dumb."

"Perhaps, but I'd lay odds the person who opened it was a secretary who had other things to do." He looked at the clock. "Come on, it's late. I'll walk you back to Mackinaw, to make sure you get home safely."

He held out my coat, and I slipped it on. "What are you gonna do with what I told you?"

"I'll be visiting the Witkops to question them again. You?"

"I'm gonna go to work, but I'll be stopping by a certain Polish laundry on my way home."

Chapter Thirty-Nine

The house was dark when I returned. I learned my lesson from earlier and looked for Cat before I approached the back door. He was gone, prob'ly off hunting or sleeping. I unlocked the kitchen door and eased inside, taking care to make as little noise as possible.

"You should turn on the light so you don't trip over anything."

Doggone it. I flipped the switch and turned. Pop sat at the kitchen table, hands folded and resting in front of him. A glass that was only a quarter-full of water told me he'd been sitting there for a while, maybe even since I'd left. So much for hoping he'd go back to bed. I gave a weak wave. "Hiya, Pop."

He gestured at the chair across from him. "Have a seat."

I did as instructed. "You're up late. Can't sleep?"

"It was the oddest thing." He gazed at me. "I was woken up by the most god-awful racket. A cat-fight that knocked over the garbage cans, or so I thought. I looked into your bedroom on the way back to my own. There was Mary Kate, sound asleep. And your bed was empty."

I kept my lips zipped.

"Where have you been?" Pop's voice was level, calm even. A stranger might have thought he wasn't that upset, or maybe he was being respectful of the sleepers in the house.

I knew better. When Pop was this quiet, he was beyond mad. "I went out to meet Detective MacKinnon at Teddy's."

"Why?"

"I had some information I had to give him and it couldn't wait until tomorrow."

"What could be so important that you snuck out of the house, against my direct instructions, at eleven o'clock at night?"

I tried not to fidget under his steely-eyed stare. "It's about the case I'm working. I would have had to wait until late afternoon tomorrow 'cause of work and that would've been too late. He had to have the info now."

"Ah, your case. The one where you're involving yourself in police business?"

"Well, sort of."

His eyebrow twitched.

"Okay, yes. See it's like this." I explained what led to that night's meeting with Sam MacKinnon. "You could say that I'm helping the cops out."

"Is that what you think?" Pop leaned back. "Elizabeth, what in the world has gotten into you?" He held up a hand. "I know what you're going to say. You did this last month. That was different. I can understand being curious about a situation that directly affected your job. But this? Who do you think you are, Miss Marple?"

"I'd prefer if you compared me to Sam Spade or Philip Marlowe. They're more my style." I tried for a joke to at least make him smile.

It didn't work. "This isn't funny."

"No, it's not." I studied my hands. "Pop, look. I'm sorry I snuck out and I broke the rules. But I'm not gonna give this up. I told you. I'm good at this. I like being a detective. See, ever since last month, the girls at Bell, they bring me their problems."

"What kind of problems?"

"All sorts of stuff. Missing items, lost pets, one girl even asked me to follow her guy 'cause she was afraid he was going out with other girls before he shipped out. Sowing his wild oats, you might say."

Pop looked like he might be fighting a grin but, if so, he beat it back. "Was he?"

"No, he was out shopping for an engagement ring." I twisted my own. "I guess Tom and I aren't the only ones who want to get hitched just in case, well, you know."

He nodded.

"Most of the time, the problems aren't big. Not like Emmie's grandma. Which wasn't s'posed to be a big deal, actually. It just..." I spread my hands. "Well, it got a little more complicated."

"I can understand helping out with little things, even the possibly straying boy. But this? Elizabeth, why? If the police are involved, why not stay out of it?"

"Because the cops aren't looking into Mrs. Brewka's death. Far as they're concerned, she died of natural causes. And maybe that's the case. But Emmie asked me for help and I can give it to her." I paused. "And because Detective MacKinnon thinks I'm good. At investigating, I mean. I just told you, he even asked me for help. You always say to me that if I can do something, I should. So I am."

"Breaking the household rules in the process."

"I'm sorry about that, I really am." Did I dare say what I was thinking? It might be now or never. "I'm not a kid anymore, Pop. I'm eighteen. I got a job, a good one. Not the detecting, I mean at Bell. Don't you think I deserve a little more freedom than Mary Kate?"

"My house, my rules, Elizabeth."

"Then maybe I got to get my own place."

He paused. "You wouldn't."

"I don't want to, but yeah, I would." I watched him. "The world's not the same, Pop. You said it yourself. You can't expect things out there to change and everything in this house to stay the same."

He studied his hands. Big and strong, callused and burned from his work at the steel mill. Those hands had protected me for eighteen years. I knew part of the reason he was mad was 'cause he still saw that as his job and I loved him for it. But he needed to know I wasn't going to accept protection when it came in the form of smothering.

Finally, he looked up. "What happens after the war?"

I hadn't thought that far ahead, but the answer wasn't hard. "God willing, Tom gets home, and we get married, and we figure it out." I crossed myself. "Until then, he's over there and I'm here. He's gotta know it won't be the same for either of us when he gets back, least I hope he does."

Pop nodded. "You've said your bit. I have to think on it. For now, go to bed. And for heaven's sake don't wake your mother or your sister." He stood.

"Pop—"

"I said I'd think on it. Good night, Elizabeth."

I sat by myself in the kitchen for a few minutes. Then I got up, shut off the light, and made my way to bed. All things considered, I s'posed it was the best I could hope for. At least he hadn't thrown me out.

I changed into my nightclothes and snuggled down in bed. I didn't want to leave. But if it came down to it, maybe Dot would want to be my roommate.

Chapter Forty

On Wednesday morning, I determined my plan of action for the afternoon. Pop and I hadn't spoken before he left for Bethlehem, but he hadn't laid down the law, either. Mom was off with her church work and wouldn't be back until six. If I wanted to be treated like an adult, I had to act like one. That meant getting my work done, building planes and detecting, and getting home to do my part for the family, too.

Dot pulled a doubtful expression when I told her my plans. "I dunno, Betty. You really think you can handle it all?"

"I gotta. Otherwise, I have to start looking for another place and your folks might have to put me up in the meantime. I can't afford to stay in a hotel if I get thrown out."

"You don't know my parents if you think they'll take you in."

"Then I'll ask Lee. He'll do it." I stared out the bus window at snow-flecked brown grass. "The other option is staying home, like a good girl, and giving up the detective work." With any luck, Pop would come around. I couldn't give up my new profession. Not when I had just started and certainly not after Sam MacKinnon said how good I was.

After work, we went straight to the laundry on Fillmore. Dot insisted on going with me. "You need someone to keep you out of trouble," she said. "If nothing else, I'll remind you when to leave so you're home by dinner time."

"What about your folks? What will they think?"

"I have no idea. But if we both get kicked out, maybe we can live together and share the rent."

I hugged her. "Dot, you're the best."

She blushed. "What are friends for?"

We walked into the store and the bells above the door jangled. A moment later, Stella came out, drying her hands on her apron. "Can I help you?" She cocked her head. "Say, don't I know you?"

"I was in here before, looking for a guy," I said.

"That's right. I'm sorry, but I already told you everything I know."

"It's about something different this time." The shop air was hot and damp, prob'ly due to all the machinery involved in washing, drying, and pressing clothes. "Yesterday, you made a delivery to the Witkop residence in Delaware Park." I gave her the address.

"Yes. One man's shirt, white with a black monogram, cleaned and pressed, light starch," Stella said.

"That." I unbuttoned my coat. "I have two questions. One, who dropped it off and two, how hard was it to clean? I mean, what kind of stains?"

Stella narrowed her peepers. "Why do you want to know?"

"I'm still looking into the death of that joe, the one from the alley. The shirt might be a clue."

She sniffed. "It's been more trouble than it was worth. The actual cleaning and then those people insisting I had the wrong address. As if I didn't have it written on the slip, plain as day. It's not my fault the girl never came back to pick it up."

"Whoa, slow down. One thing at a time." I glanced at Dot. "What girl?"

"The girl who dropped it off, who else?"

"What did she look like?" Dot asked.

"Young, fair skin, like she doesn't see a lot of sunlight, but she had a lot of freckles. Her hands were those of a working girl. Callused, like she does a lot of scrubbing and manual work."

Not for the first time, I wished I had a notepad. "Let me guess, she had long red hair, green eyes, and an Irish accent?"

"Yes. Do you know her?"

"Slightly."

Stella tossed her dark hair. "Then you can ask her why she didn't pick up her order. It cost time and money for that delivery, and the family didn't even pay me for it."

"We would, except she's dead. That's prob'ly why she didn't come back," Dot said.

The indignant look faded from Stella's mug. "Oh. I didn't know that."

"We didn't expect you to." Gosh, the air was warm. I fanned myself. "What was wrong with the shirt?"

"It was stained." Stella reached under the counter and pulled out a box of order sheets. "Hold on." She flipped through them. "Here it is. There was ground in dirt and dried blood on the cuffs. Blood is hard enough to get out of a white garment. But whatever was in the dirt must have been oily. We had to treat the stains twice to remove them. I was of a mind to double-charge for the work, but Mama said no, you never made a rich customer mad. They might not come back."

Blood and oily dirt. Josef Pyrut had been bashed on the head and that alley was none too clean. It was easy to see where his attacker would have wound up with soiled clothes. "Was she s'posed to pick it up? The red-headed girl?"

"Yes. We deliver, but only in the neighborhood. The address she gave was too far away. Normally customers pick up their clothes in a week or less, but this shirt sat on the shelves forever." Stella replaced the slip. "I was ready to discard it, or give it to the church closet as a donation. After all, it was a high-quality garment. But Mama insisted on delivering it. I'm sure she made an exception to the rules because the family lived in Delaware Park. I tried to tell her that rich folks from up there weren't likely to patronize a laundry like ours, way down in Polonia, on a regular basis but she wouldn't hear of it."

"Did you tell them all this when you dropped off the package?" I asked.

"Of course I did." Stella brushed back her hair. "I may not have finished high school, but I'm not stupid."

"This girl," Dot spoke up. "She gave her name or the family's name?"

Stella pursed her lips and looked at the slip. "Hers. I assumed she was a maid or something, sent to take out the laundry."

"She didn't mention the family's name?" I asked.

"No, just hers."

"And you don't know the name of the family who lived there?"

"Haven't a clue. I told you, we don't do a lot of business up with the rich folks. This girl," she glanced at the slip, "Bridget Innes, brought in the shirt, asked if we could take care of it, and that was that." She looked from me to Dot. "Is there anything else I can help you with? I really should be getting back to work."

"Thanks, that's all." I headed for the door, then turned. "You said it was monogrammed, the shirt. What were the initials?"

"P-W-R," Stella replied.

"Thanks again." I nodded to Dot, and we left.

The cool air outside was a welcome change. "Paul's shirt. He pops Josef and gets dirty in the process. Maybe he doesn't notice until he gets home."

"He wads up the shirt and gives it to Bridget to take out for laundering. But why? Why not just toss it? That would make more sense," Dot said.

"He may not have told her to take it to the cleaners." I thought it out. "It could be he just said for her to take care of it. He assumed she'd throw it away, but being a poor girl from Ireland, she tried to save it first." My steps slowed. "She prob'ly didn't think twice about giving the address 'cause she always intended to come and get it."

We reached the bus stop and Dot sat. "Then Josef really did get the letter."

"Maybe, maybe not. Both Paul and Sebastian talked to Pelagia, right? When neither Witkop gave her a good answer, she could have said she intended to talk to Josef. Then when he showed up, something led one of them, or both, to believe Josef knew about their secret and that's all it took. He had to die."

Dot shivered. "It makes me wonder. Did Bridget make the connection between the shirt and Josef being mugged? We already think she saw him and Paul leave the party. Maybe she realized that the dirty shirt, the mugging, and the early exit all happened on the same night. She might have put two and two together and threatened Paul."

"That's what I was thinking." I tapped my fingers on my lips. "Or she didn't really have a clue, but it got her curious and she asked him. Paul killed her just to keep himself in the clear."

The bus pulled up and belched a cloud of dark, smelly smoke. "That's really awful," Dot said.

"I get the feeling that Paul Witkop is a pretty nasty piece of goods." We took our seats. "What I can't figure is whether he's in it with his old man or if he acted alone." I told Dot about what Sam had said.

"Are the Witkops really Nazi sympathizers?" Dot asked.

"I don't know, but if I understand Detective MacKinnon correctly, even the hint would be bad enough. Businesses would drop Sebastian like a hot potato. Mobs might attack first and ask questions later. By the time the truth came out, it would be too late."

"If that's the case, both Paul and his father have a reason to kill Josef. My vote is still Paul as the villain when it comes to Bridget, though. Especially if he really was jealous of his dad."

"Could be." My heart couldn't square Sebastian Witkop killing the woman he loved. But if that woman threatened his money and safety?

Maybe love didn't conquer all.

* * *

I had just put a plate with a bit of margarine on it on the table when Pop came through the door. "Evening," he said and leaned over to give me a kiss on the cheek.

I wrinkled my nose. "It must have been a particularly dirty shift, you really stink. You'd better wash up or Mom will be unhappy. Dinner is about ready."

He grasped my shoulders and held me at arm's length. "That's all you have for your old father?"

"Welcome home."

"You did this all by yourself or did your mother ask you?" He let go.

I dried my hands and hung the towel up. "I did. Well, Mary Kate helped. Mom is in the living room and the boys are doing their homework."

"And?"

"And what?" I faced him.

"Nothing." He stared at me with suspicion, but eventually gave up and went to wash.

When the after-dinner cleanup was finished, I went to the living room where I knew I'd find Pop in his chair, reading the paper, listening to the radio, and smoking his pipe. I sat down at his feet and watched as the smoke curled around his head, filling the room with its sweet scent.

He read for a moment, then looked up. "What is it you want, my darling girl?"

"Who said I wanted anything?" I put on my best innocent look. "Can't a girl sit with her father after supper?"

He lowered his paper. "Betty, don't try to fool me. You haven't sat at my feet for no good reason since you were a wee girl. And maybe not even then. You always had a reason up your sleeve. What is it?"

I knew he'd see right through me. I'd counted on it. I wanted to talk things over, but I didn't want him to shut me up before I started. "I was thinking about my case."

"The one that caused you to sneak out of the house in the middle of the night to meet with a police detective?"

"That one."

"There's no reason for you to be thinking about that."

I rubbed my finger on the carpet. "I know. I'm trying not to. But it was a tricky problem and I can't help wondering how it's all gonna work out. When Detective MacKinnon solves it, of course."

"You'll probably read about it in the paper." He snapped his up.

"I s'pose. But I can't stop thinking about it. It was getting very interesting."

He looked over his paper. "How so?"

"I couldn't get the right combination."

"What do you mean?"

I ticked off the points on my fingers. "Well, Mildred Janson, she was the housekeeper, had a motive to kill Bridget, but not Josef Pyrut. Sebastian Witkop might have wanted to bump off Josef to protect his family's secret, but I can't see him killing Bridget, even if he did think she'd left him for his son. He loved her. He'd fire her, maybe, to get her out of the house. But dose her with strychnine? That's horrible."

"I agree. A man with a broken heart doesn't poison the girl. He might shoot or stab her, or even more likely strangle her. Besides." His eyes twinkled. "In all those movies you've seen, don't they always say poison is a woman's weapon? It could have been Mr. Witkop's wife."

I stuck my tongue out at him. "She has an alibi. Anyway, Paul had a motive to kill both Josef and Bridget. He'd get rid of someone who could reveal his family's past and someone who might turn him in to the police."

Pop pointed at me with his pipe stem. "What about your friend's grandmother?"

"I don't know." Try as I might, I couldn't make Pelagia's death fit. "I s'pose Sebastian or Paul might have killed her to protect the secret, but how? My last idea, that those peppermint candies were poisoned, was a bust."

"I'm sure there are other poisons that would look like a heart attack, or cause one. The police will figure it out."

"Yeah, but they'll have the same problem I did, which is figuring out how she got the poison. No." I shook my head. "I think the police will find out that Pelagia's death is exactly what it looks like. An old woman who had a heart attack. She may have started this whole mess with her letter writing and I don't have any doubt Sebastian or Paul would happily have gotten rid of her to keep the truth from coming out, but I think she died before they could do anything."

"What about Paul's visit to see the Brewkas?"

I went back to tracing patterns on the carpet. My plan to talk to Pop was workin' out better than I thought. "Could be he went to scope the place out, see how hard it would be to get close to Pelagia. While he was there he found out she was already dead and no longer a threat." I pressed my hands into my eyes until lights popped. "The men are involved somehow. It doesn't make any sense otherwise. Tell me." I uncovered my eyes and blinked to get rid of the spots. "You were close to your father, right?"

"Extremely," Pop said.

"Would you have done anything he said?"

Pop examined his pipe. "Me? No. But there was a boy who lived next to me when I was growing up. Jimmy Fenwick. He loved his old man, or so we thought. If Mr. Fenwick had asked Jimmy to hold up a store or beat someone up, Jimmy would have done it, no questions asked. He was too afraid not to." He turned his gaze to me. "Why do I get the feeling I've been had? All these questions. You've always been a curious cat, but this seems a little extreme. The police will solve it all, Betty. It's none of your concern."

I stood and kissed his cheek. "You know curiosity, Pop. You can't turn it off like a light switch. I'll prob'ly wonder about it until it's over. Mind if I go for a walk?"

Pop glanced at the clock. "Don't leave the street."

"Promise." I went outside and took a deep breath of crisp air. Mr. Witkop had always seemed real friendly to me, but that might have been an act. I was pretty sure Paul knew exactly what had happened to Bridget and Josef Pyrut. Was he keepin' quiet 'cause he was guilty? Or because he was afraid of the killer?

* * *

The cold air cleared my mind. Pop was right. Sebastian and Paul's relationship was key. When I'd seen them outside Kleinhan's, I hadn't thought about how they interacted. Now that I thought back to that night, I realized there'd been sort of a suppressed anger in Paul. His father hadn't quite rolled over his opinions, but Sebastian did sort of assume Paul would agree with him. Mr. Charles reported he'd heard the two Witkops fight quite a bit. Perhaps Paul had tried to assert his independence and Sebastian had knocked him down, even threatened him in some way. If Paul was involved in any of the murders, could it have been because his father ordered him to and he was too scared to resist? It was an idea worth exploring.

I hung up my coat and called out, "I'm back. I'm gonna be in my room writing a letter to Tom." I heard Pop respond, but I didn't stop to chat.

Mary Kate lolled on her bed, reading a magazine. "Hey, Betty. Have you eaten any of those chocolates yet?"

I sat at the desk, pulled out my crumpled letter, and stared at it. I'd been concentrating so much on my case, I'd clean forgot about the mystery box of candy. Trust Mary Kate to remember chocolate. "No. Why would I eat something I don't like?"

"You might have tried one." She sat up. "Can I have 'em? I don't mind the filling. I mean, those have to cost a pretty penny. Seems a shame to let them go to waste. You know, Mom always says—"

"Yeah, yeah. Go ahead, they're yours." Anything to shut her up. I couldn't concentrate on my letter-writing with her yapping in my ear. If giving her a crummy box of candy would buy me a few minutes of peace, it was well worth it. "I think the box is under my bed."

From my seat at my desk, out of the corner of my eye, I saw her get up and get the candy. I focused on my letter and chewed on the end of the pen. I knew what I wanted to write. But how could I tell Tom about my detective work in a way so he wouldn't worry about me? Once again, the thought occurred to me that Pelagia had gotten a box from an unknown source. A box of Wahl's candy. True, hers had been cheap peppermints and mine were fancy filled chocolates, but this time, the thought refused to be shoved aside. I half turned in my chair.

"These are stinky," Mary Kate said. "What do you s'pose they're filled with? Ew, this one's leaking. It's all thick and black, and it doesn't smell very good. Does candy filling go bad?"

"What are you talkin' about?"

"The chocolates." She poked at one. "Whatever they're filled with smells awful."

"How do you mean?"

"Almost like medicine. And look. This one has all sorts of black goo around it. What on earth would smell like that?" She reached for the chocolate.

Alarm bells rung in my head. "Mary Kate, stop. Do not touch those. Let me see." Two mystery boxes, one which ended in death. I had to have been sleeping. Why hadn't I connected them before? Because I hadn't thought it important, that I'd been seeing things where nothing existed. But when you're investigating a murder, everything is important. Any detective on the silver screen would tell you that.

"C'mon, Betty."

"I mean it. Give me the box."

Reluctantly, she handed it over. I held it under my desk lamp. Just like she said, the filling from the chocolate in the bottom corner had leaked all over the little tray. A thick, black puddle had formed around it, almost like a jelly. I sniffed. The scent was sharp, like the liniment Grandma Ahern had used for her arthritis. I pried up the chocolate with a nail file. It came away from the tray, but the black goop stuck fast. "Mary Kate, who delivered this box?"

She shrugged. "I dunno. It was on the table when I got home from school. I thought Mom had brought it in with the mail."

Holding the box as though it were a bomb, I went to the living room. Pop was still in his chair, now listening to the radio with his eyes closed. Mom sat opposite him, sewing a patch on a pair of Michael's pants. "Mom, did a package come in the mail for me right around Christmas? A small box wrapped in brown paper. I don't think it had a return address on it."

She paused in her stitching. "Why, yes. I thought it rather odd, you getting something like that. But I figured it was a present from someone. I knew it wasn't from Tom. Anybody else would have put their name on it. I always meant to ask you about it. What was inside?"

"A box of chocolates from Wahl's. The note with it said it was from a secret admirer."

"Elizabeth Anne. Accepting gifts like that is hardly appropriate for a young woman who is engaged," Mom snapped, setting down the trousers.

"I know that. I didn't know what the box was until I opened it." I looked at her. "Do you remember if it had a postmark?"

"What on earth are you talking about? Why wouldn't it?"

"I wanted to know if it came through the mail, or if someone left it in our mailbox."

Pop reached over and turned the volume down on the radio. "You look funny, Betty. What's wrong? Do you know who sent them?"

"No, I don't." I held out the box. "But I'm pretty sure they're filled with poison."

Chapter Forty-One

The next day was New Year's Eve. Pop insisted I call Bell and tell them I wasn't coming to work. I didn't fight him much on that point. After my statement the previous night, Pop had called the cops. A uniformed officer showed up, asked a lot of questions, and took the box of chocolates. Most of them I answered with "I don't know." I didn't know who dropped off the box, or who had bought them, or who might want to poison me. Well, that last one wasn't quite true. Sebastian or Paul Witkop, even Mildred Janson—if any of 'em had killed Josef Pyrut or Bridget, they might have gotten nervous with me poking around. I no longer thought Pelagia had been murdered, but I hadn't been quiet about letting folks know I was interested in her letters and activities regarding the Witkops. After the police officer left with the box from Wahl's, I scrubbed my hands with the hottest water I could stand and more soap than I usually used in a month. All I could think of was Grandma telling me to stay away from her liniment 'cause it would make me sick if I spilled it and accidentally swallowed some.

Mom's reaction the previous night had been quiet, but she let me sleep until I awoke at eight o'clock on the 31st. She never let me do that when I had the day off. I followed the scent of eggs and bacon to the kitchen. A plate was waiting, covered with a napkin. She'd made me breakfast, even giving me the last bit of bacon.

Yeah, she was unsettled.

I ate, washed up, and got dressed. Pop had left for work, but Mom was in the living room, dusting. "Betty, are you all right? Did you sleep well?"

"I'm fine, Mom. Thanks for breakfast."

She came over and brushed hair off my face. "After last night, well, you deserved a little treat." She sniffed, then dropped her feather duster and clutched me to her. "Oh, Betty! If anything had happened to you, I don't know what I'd have done. I told you this detective work was dangerous."

I patted her back. "It's okay, Mom. I'm all right. Really. I wasn't even in much danger. I wasn't ever gonna eat those things. Now if whoever it was had sent a box of sponge candy laced with that stuff, that would be different. It smelled awful, though. I think my nose would have warned me long before I ate anything." I didn't say Mary Kate would have bolted half the box if I hadn't stopped her. She would've thought it was a funny filling for chocolate, but that wouldn't have put her off. Mom was already distraught. She didn't need me to add to her worry.

I held her for a couple of minutes while she cried. Eventually she pulled away and wiped her nose with a handkerchief from her apron pocket. "Look at me, I'm a mess."

"You're fine. Are you sure you don't know who left that box?"

"No. I told the policeman last night, it was in our mailbox with the rest of the post. I saw it was addressed to you and put it on the table. I assumed the mailman had left it. I didn't even notice if there was a postmark." She bent and picked up the feather duster. "Are you up to helping me tidy up a bit before tonight? I've invited the Tillotsons and the Kilbrides for a party for New Year's, and I want the house to be clean."

The doorbell rang. "Sure. I'll answer that and be back in a minute." I went to the door and opened it. "Detective MacKinnon! What brings you here?"

"Good morning, Miss Ahern. May I come in?" All formality. Uh oh.

I stepped back and motioned for him to enter.

Mom came out of the living room. "Did I hear you say detective? From the police?"

Sam took off his fedora and held out his hand. "Good morning, Mrs. Ahern. I'm Detective Sam MacKinnon from the Buffalo police."

"Haven't I met you?"

"Yes, ma'am. Your daughter, Betty, and I have crossed paths a couple of times."

Mom glanced at me. "I assume you're here about last night?"

"Among other things."

I caught his eye. "Detective, would you like a drink? Maybe a cup of coffee or tea, or a glass of water?" I turned to my mother. "Mom, why don't I take the detective to the kitchen and talk to him. I'll come back to help you when I'm done."

She nodded. "That's a good idea. I'll be in the living room if you need me." She hurried away.

"This way." I led him to the kitchen. "She must be really upset. The idea of having a police detective in the house didn't even bother her. What would you like to drink?"

"Just water, thank you." He set down his hat and took a seat. "I heard you had some excitement last night."

"Yes." I put the glass in front of him and took the opposite chair.

"That's part of the reason I'm here. You must have riled up someone, Betty. According to the report, no one could say where the chocolates came from. Well, we know they were bought at Wahl's, but you have no idea who delivered them?"

"Nope." I repeated Mom's story. "Personally, I don't think they came with the mail. It seems more likely someone would have slipped them in our box. But you'd have to ask all the neighbors if they saw a stranger. I don't think you'll have much luck with that. Even with the holiday, a lot of folks would have been at work, or up at the church, or some charity. Unless the person walked through here wearing a clown suit, I don't think he or she would have been noticed."

"Damn. And I suppose the paper wrapping has been thrown out?"

"Yes. I didn't think it was worth saving." I paused. "I feel so stupid. I should have connected it with Pelagia immediately."

"Don't be too hard on yourself. We can't be perfect."

"Do you know what was in 'em? The chocolates?"

"The lab is still working on it. But given what they have observed, our head scientist thinks it was some kind of syrup that contained aconite."

The word meant nothing to me.

It must have showed on my puss because he said, "Aconite is also called monkshood. It's a flower. You sometimes find it in lotions or liniments for arthritis or joint pain."

No wonder it had smelled like Grandma Ahern's stuff. That had prob'ly also contained aconite. "Is it poisonous?"

"Very." He sipped his water, expression grim. "If you or your sister had eaten even a tiny bit of one of those chocolates, well, let's just say your family would be having a very sad New Year's."

A shiver ran down my spine. No one had ever wanted me dead before.

"But that's not the only reason I'm here."

"Oh? Have you found out anything about our killer? Was it one of the Witkops or was it Mildred?" I tried to push away the sting of not solving the case myself. The important thing was the killer was caught, not who did it.

"It wasn't Mildred Janson."

"How do you know?"

"Because she's dead." He set aside his glass.

I felt my jaw drop. "Dead? When? How?"

"Yesterday. That's why I didn't respond to the call here last night. I was at the Janson house, talking to Mrs. Janson." He looked at me. "Mildred's mother."

"How did she die? Was she killed?" I'd been right. Mildred had known something. Now I'd never find out. Drat.

"She also received a box of chocolates from Wahl's from an anonymous giver. Unfortunately, her nose wasn't as sharp as yours."

I swallowed hard. Two boxes, both containing aconite-filled candy, and both from a person or persons unknown. I'd seen enough detective pictures to know it was no coincidence. "Could her mother tell you anything useful?"

"I haven't asked her. She was too upset last night to talk to me. I thought I'd go back today." He stood. "Would you like to come along?"

I didn't even think about it. "Just let me tell Mom I can't help her and then I'll get my coat."

* * *

Sam and I didn't talk much as we drove to Allentown. I was too busy going over my mental notes. With Mildred gone, the only two suspects left were Sebastian and Paul Witkop. Did they work together? Were they alone? Were both of them guilty, but they'd acted independently?

Mr. Charles said they argued, and Mr. Witkop had been upset with his son. What if it hadn't been about business? If the Witkops were willing to cover the fact that their ancestors were traitors to the Poles all those years ago, would the elder Witkop be willing to cover up murder?

It seemed like no time at all had passed when we pulled up in front of the Janson home. "What time is it?" I asked.

Sam checked his watch. "Nine-thirty."

"D'you think we're too early? Will she be up?" I nibbled my thumbnail. "Are you sure she's still home? Mrs. Janson seemed pretty frail when I was here before. Maybe she's gone to another relative."

"She doesn't have any other family in Buffalo." Sam turned the car off and we got out. "A neighbor is taking care of her. And while it might be too early for a social call, we're making inquiries about the murder of her daughter." He rang the doorbell.

A minute later, an unfamiliar woman answered the door. She looked like she was Mom's age, maybe a little older. I could see threads of gray in her brown hair, but her eyes were kind. "May I help you?"

Sam showed his badge. "Detective Sam MacKinnon, Buffalo police, homicide. I was here last night about Mildred Janson."

"Oh yes, Detective. I'm so sorry, I didn't recognize you." She held the door open. "It's been a long night and Mrs. Janson, Mildred's mother that is, hasn't slept well." She glanced at me, obviously curious, but she must have been too well-mannered to ask who I was.

"This is Betty Ahern. She's a friend of mine. You're Mrs. Turner, correct?"

"Yes, Addie Turner. I live next door."

Sam checked out the rooms to either side of the narrow entryway. "Is Mrs. Janson able to speak with us? I hate to bother her, but it is important we talk to her as soon as possible. Time is critical in cases such as these."

"Mrs. Janson is in the front room." Addie led the way. "Harriet? The police detective is back. He'd like to talk to you, if you're up to it."

The woman in the chair by the window was bundled up with afghans, but it didn't hide the bird-like structure of her hands and face. Her hair was snow white and her tiny face was etched with so many lines it looked like a wrinkled apple. There was no color in her cheeks and if I hadn't seen the afghan fringe under her chin waver with her breath, I'd swear she was dead.

"Harriet?" Mrs. Turner patted one of the spindly hands.

Mrs. Janson's eyelids fluttered. Her eyes were slightly milky, but must've once been a warm brown. "Addie?" she breathed.

"Yes, dear. The police are here. They want to talk about Mildred."

Mrs. Janson blinked and struggled under the afghans. Mrs. Turner reached for her and I went to the other side. Together we repositioned her against the chair. "Thank you," the old lady said. "I don't think I've seen you before. Are you a friend of Mildred's?"

"Good morning, Mrs. Janson. My name is Betty." I gave her my best smile. "I don't know that your daughter and I were friends, but I knew her. I'm real sorry to hear about her passing."

Mrs. Turner walked over to Sam, whispered something, and left.

"Mildred talked about a Betty recently," said Mrs. Janson in a whispery voice. "Was that you?"

I shot a look at Sam. "It might have been. I visited a couple of weeks ago, right before Christmas. And she came to see me a couple of times."

"Yes, you must be the right girl. She talked about visiting you just the other day."

At Sam's nod, I answered. "She did? Last time I saw her, I didn't think she had anything more to tell me."

"Oh yes, my dear. She did." The faded eyes closed and I thought she'd fallen asleep, but then she opened them. "It was about her old job at the Witkop house. She said it was very important. Now, what was it? My memory isn't what it used to be, I'm afraid."

I was right. Mildred had known more than just about Paul leaving the house. Now the knowledge rested with an old woman who looked like a good sneeze would blow her away.

Sam cleared his throat. "Mrs. Janson? About Mildred and what happened last night. We found a box of chocolates from Wahl's in the kitchen. We think they may have been poisoned, and that's how she died. Did Mildred buy those?"

"Oh no. She didn't spend money on fancy treats like that. Everything she earned went toward keeping the house and taking care of me. I often wished she'd spend a little on herself, but she would laugh and say it was too late for that."

"Then where did they come from?"

Mrs. Janson stared past Sam. "They were a gift, I think. Yes. Mildred came home the other day. She'd been out looking for work. I believe she said the package had been left in the mailbox."

"There was no name on it?" Sam asked as he wrote in a little notebook he'd taken from his pocket. I had to get myself one of those.

"I don't…no, there wasn't. It was a box wrapped in plain brown paper. Her name and address was on it, she told me, but no postmark and no return address."

I shifted so I could study the old lady's face. "She ate something from a stranger? That doesn't seem right."

Mrs. Janson looked up at me. "Oh, I don't think it was a stranger, dear."

"Oh? Why d'you say that?"

Mrs. Janson patted my hand. "She said something about how it made for a nice apology, that maybe she'd have her old job back soon and he must have forgiven her."

It had to be Sebastian Witkop. He had sent poisoned chocolates? But that would mean he prob'ly sent them to me, too. I hadn't pegged Sebastian as a poisoner. It felt wrong. I was so caught up in my thinking, I almost missed Mrs. Janson's next words.

"She said maybe it wouldn't matter after all," Mrs. Janson said.

"What wouldn't matter?" Sam asked. "Mrs. Janson?"

She looked like she'd fallen asleep again, but woke as soon as I touched her shoulder. "I'm sorry," she said. "Sometimes I can't keep my eyes open, I'm so tired. What did you say?"

"Mildred said something wouldn't matter," Sam said. "What was it?"

"Oh, something she'd seen at the Witkop house." Mrs. Janson frowned. "Something about Mr. Paul coming out of the shed with a box of rat poison. And she said how she'd have the chance to return it, now. You know, that might have been what she wanted to tell you."

Sam and I looked at each other, baffled. "Return what?" I asked.

"Mr. Witkop's great coat." Mrs. Janson pointed a wavering finger at the closet. "Mildred had brought it home to clean. She'd found it stuffed in the back of the closet. It was all muddy, she said, and it smelled like smoke. Great streaks of ash on it, there were. But she got it all out. She was always quite a hand with cleaning things, my Mildred."

Sam went over to the closet and opened it. "This one?" he said, removing a man's overcoat from the rack.

Mrs. Janson nodded. "That's it. She said he'd be ever so pleased to have it back. She offered me a chocolate, but those things are much too rich for me. My stomach would be upset for days. I told her to enjoy them. Such a good girl, my Mildred. Always looking after others." Her voice faded away and this time she really did fall asleep.

I made sure she was snug under her covers with a pillow supporting her head and eased away. I went over to Sam. "Those chocolates would have given her way more than an upset tummy," I said. "I'd bet the same person who sent the package to me sent another one to Mildred and for the same reason. To keep a secret."

"Yes. To stop you from uncovering it and prevent Mildred Janson from talking. Here. Do you recognize this?" He held out the coat.

It was definitely quality goods. The dark wool had been brushed so it practically shone, the brass buttons polished until they gleamed. I'd seen this coat before, on a man standing in front of Kleinhan's Department Store. "I do." I touched the soft fabric. "It's Sebastian Witkop's." As I ran the fabric through my hand, I heard a crinkling sound. "Something's in the pocket." I fished out a crumpled piece of paper. I read it, then cleared my throat. "Sam, listen to this." I read.

Dear Mr. Witkop,

You won't remember me, but I knew your parents. I worked for them in Poland when you were a boy. I'm sure you think they were good people, but they weren't. I'm sorry to tell you this, but much of their money, and many of the things you must still own, were gifts from the Prussians. Your parents were informers. Even after the Franco-Prussian War, they gave the Prussians information about their neighbors in exchange for money. I saw this with my own eyes. I know it is true.

My husband and I came to America, and I did not know what happened to your family, the Witkowskis. Then I saw your picture in the paper and I knew you must be the little boy I took care of all those years ago. And I knew I had to talk to you.

You must return the things your parents got. You must put it right, for the sake of the Poles and all the people they wronged. I tried to tell you this when I visited, but you refused to listen. So I am writing this letter.

I know from the paper that the Polish government will visit Buffalo next month. If you do nothing, I will speak to them. I believe I have a relative in the government, a man named Josef Pyrut. If you will not listen to me, an old woman, you will listen to him.

I hope you will do the right thing.

"She ends it with the usual stuff," I said. I folded the letter and handed it to him.

Sam let out a low whistle. "Well, she was going to blow the lid on Witkop and his past. And she did speak to Pyrut."

"Well, she was *going* to. She wrote a letter, but it never got to him. Sebastian didn't know that. Neither did Paul." I pointed at the paper. "Pelagia died, but they had to make sure there wasn't a threat from Pyrut."

Sam slipped the letter in his pocket. "That tells us where we go next." He looked up.

I met his gaze. “Delaware Park.”

Chapter Forty-Two

We raced through the streets of Buffalo, Sam expertly dodging pedestrians and the random delivery truck. "They were in it together."

I drummed my fingers on the door panel. "Seems so," I said. "But, I dunno."

"What don't you know?"

"I can't figure Sebastian as a killer. Well, not by poison. He'd straight up shoot a man and sure, I guess he coulda clobbered Josef in a back alley. But he's spent his whole life hiding his family's secret without hurting anyone. Why start now?"

"Perhaps the hiding wasn't working any longer." Sam laid on the horn and shot through an intersection. "The stakes have gotten higher, remember. To be seen as a Nazi supporter? Even if it isn't true, the fallout from the rumors could be catastrophic. I'd imagine that's been the case since the war with the Kaiser, but especially now."

"I get it, I get it. It's just...I keep coming back to Bridget. Sam, he *loved* her. The kind of love that a man would give up a whole lot, maybe everything, for." I glanced at him. His face was puckered as he processed my words. "Look, I know you'll think I'm just naïve—"

"No, I don't."

"Good. Think about it. Sebastian Witkop is in a loveless marriage. Here's this charming young girl, she's pretty, she makes him laugh, maybe he hasn't felt this way since when he was first married. Heck, maybe *ever*. So to keep this secret, he bumps her off with rat poison? Or tells his son to? 'Cause it was Paul that Mildred saw, not his pop."

"You've got a point."

"Then he sends poisoned chocolates to two women, one of them another young girl. That'd be me, in case you missed it."

Sam shot me a dirty look. "I am well aware of your age, Miss Ahern. Frankly, if I didn't agree with you, I'd be insulted."

"You do? You think I'm right?"

"Yes. On the surface, the facts point to Sebastian Witkop pulling the strings. But the psychology is wrong. Not that I don't think he'd kill a man. But three women, two of them young enough to be his daughters and one he's desperately in love with? No. At least not with poison."

I snorted. "Psychology? You sound like a character in a book I read. Some French detective named Hercules."

Sam's mouth twitched. "You are clearly not an avid reader. If you are referring to the novels by Agatha Christie, his name is Hercule, and he's Belgian."

I was trapped in a car with a book critic. "Where are you goin'?"

"My plan was to confront Sebastian Witkop."

"He threw his son out of the house."

"I'm aware of that."

"My gut says we gotta find Paul. With Mildred dead, I bet Daddy went to confront his boy and Paul wouldn't have answered a summons to come to the family home." I watched the buildings zip by. "Problem is, I have no clue where Paul might be. I can't imagine Sebastian threw him out then gave him an allowance, so where would he be living?"

"I know where Paul Witkop is." Sam made a right at the next corner. The street would take us into Buffalo's North Side, outside Delaware Park, but still where the rich folks lived. Maybe Sebastian *had* given his son some dough before kicking him to the curb.

"How do you know that?"

The question earned me another look. "As I am constantly reminding you—"

"The police have resources I don't. Gotcha." I needed to find a way to tap into these "resources" if I was gonna make it as a detective.

"We've had a tail on Paul Witkop for days. He's taken rooms at an apartment building not far from his former home. Here we are." Sam parked the car across the street from an elegant four-story stone building. Stately elm trees lined the street, leaves long gone and the branches stark against the blue winter sky.

"Say, hold it." I stopped to look at a silver car parked in front of the building. I'd seen it before, parked in front of Kleinhan's the day I'd talked to Sebastian and Paul. The car's body gleamed in the sun and the light winked off the curved blue fenders. The whitewall tires were spotless and the silver hood ornament shone. "I'm pretty sure this is Sebastian's."

Sam circled it. "I think you're right. He owns a 1930 Cadillac."

I glanced up at the building. "Which means he's inside. You know which apartment is Paul's?"

"Fourth floor at the front. You stay here."

"Aw, no way. You brought me along."

"Yes, to talk to Mrs. Janson. We did that. Now it's your turn to wait while I do my job." He dashed off.

I watched him go into the building. If he thought I was gonna wait by his car, he was nuts. I took the stairs two at a time. The hallway was quiet, but that only served to highlight the angry men's voices coming from behind the door to apartment 4A.

Sam was outside the door. "I thought I told you to stay by the car." His whispered voice held as much frustration as if he'd shouted.

"Did you really think I'd do that?"

He sighed and held a finger to his lips. "Shhh." We leaned closer.

"...totally out of control." It was Sebastian's voice, loaded with anger. "I told you to take care of matters, not go off like a half-cocked maniac."

"If you hadn't noticed, I did exactly that. No one can trouble us now. Not that foreign secretary, not the Irish bitch, not the old lady."

"Don't tell me you killed the old Polish woman as well."

"Not that one." Paul's voice dripped scorn. "I might have, but she was dead when I showed up in Polonia to check on the situation. No, I meant the housekeeper. You know, the one who *stole* from us and you actually talked of hiring her back."

"Bridget never would have betrayed me. As for Miss Janson, if I'd helped her with her finances, she would have been grateful. Enough that she would have held her tongue, I daresay. And the Polish undersecretary, do you understand that you could have caused an incident? One big enough that all our secrets would have been brought to light? You didn't even make sure he knew anything."

Paul laughed, a scornful, ugly sound. "There you go again, bleating like an old granny. Don't you get it? The possibility was just as threatening as fact, maybe more so. My way was much more secure. Grandfather would have understood. Your problem is you're a coward, Father. You've grown soft. You only have to look at the past to see that Grandfather knew the value of being decisive, even if what he had to do was somewhat ugly. God, I can't believe I'm your son. I should have been his!"

Sam grabbed the doorknob. "Stay in the hallway," he whispered. Then he drew a revolver from his shoulder holster, turned the knob and entered the apartment. "Good evening, gentlemen. Hope you don't mind, but I stopped by for a simple conversation and maybe a cup of coffee. I would have knocked, but when I heard what you were discussing, I felt compelled to let myself in."

Despite my instructions, I slipped in and saw a scene right out of a detective flick. Paul held a wicked-looking switchblade, waving it between his father and Sam. The detective trained his gun on Paul. Sebastian completed the picture, face red, hands clenched, his expensive overcoat open to show his tailored suit and crisp white shirt. As far as I could see, he was unarmed.

Paul glanced at me. What happened next was a blur. I'd come too far inside the apartment or his reflexes were quicker than I thought because next thing I knew, he had my left arm twisted behind me and the tip of the knife pricked my throat. *You're so dumb, Betty. Spade and Marlowe would not be impressed.*

Sam didn't flinch. "Let her go."

Paul sneered. "No, I don't think so. You're going to back away, Detective.

You and my pathetic excuse for a father are going to give me a clear path to the door. The girlie and I are going to leave. When I get to the street, I'll leave her and be off. In Father Dear's car, of course. You left the keys in the ignition, I assume, like you always do when you drive yourself? God, you can't even function without a servant to take care of you."

Sebastian's face darkened from red to almost purple. "You aren't going to get away with this, Paul. I'll make a clean breast of it and tell the detective everything. They'll be looking for you before you even get past the Buffalo city line."

"That won't be necessary, Mr. Witkop." Sam's face coulda been carved from the stone at the bottom of Niagara Falls. "I've already heard enough out of both of you to support the evidence I have." He pointed the gun at Paul. "Let go of the girl, drop the knife, and put your hands up."

"I already told you, no." Paul jerked my arm up. "She's my get out of jail free card. You let me go, she walks. If not, well..." He pushed the knife against my skin.

My eyes were watering from the pain in my arm. My neck stung where the knife had nicked me and I felt a trickle that had to be blood. *Now what?* I'd told my folks I wouldn't be in danger. Showed what I knew. All this time I'd be worried about us getting a telegram about Sean or the Flannerys getting one about Tom. I should have been more worried about myself. Drops of sweat dripped off my face and my thoughts raced. What was I gonna do?

In the pictures, Spade or Marlowe could fight their way out of a mess like this. But I wasn't them. I wasn't that big, and I'd seen enough to know Paul's knife meant business. I didn't know how good he was at street fighting, but in a case like this, he didn't have to be.

Wait, what about Nick Charles? Smooth talking, crafty Nick Charles, the Thin Man. He didn't fight. He might spill his drink. He'd talk his way out. "It's not gonna work, Paul," I said.

His voice was a snarl in my ear. "Shut up."

"The minute we're outta here, Detective MacKinnon is gonna pick up your telephone and call his buddies at the station. Your pop is right. The cops will close the city limits before you can say boo. But if you let me go now, well, it's not your fault, right? You were just following orders. That's gotta mean something, right, Detective?" *Play along, Sam,* I silently urged him.

"Maybe," Sam said. "I'm pretty sure I can talk to the district attorney. After all, if it was Witkop Senior calling the shots and his son was merely a puppet, well, that should be considered. But if Paul leaves without talking I'll have no choice but to accept his father's story."

"It's not a story!" Sebastian's gaze flicked to Sam. "Yes, okay. The old woman, what was her name? Pelagia Brewka. She worked for my parents years ago, before they left Poland. When she was there, she knew of their collaboration with the Prussians after the war. They informed on Poles who were sympathetic to the French. The Prussians rewarded them handsomely for the information, with money and things taken from the French, including that tea set Miss Janson stole. She found Pelagia's letter in my coat pocket before I fired her. She tried to use that information to keep her job."

I shifted and the tip of the knife poked my neck. Paul held my arm in a steel grip. "Don't s'pose you could ease up on the arm twisting, could ya? My shoulder is killing me."

Paul's hot breath tickled my ear. "Something else is going to be killing you if you don't shut up."

"Well somebody's feeling a little out of sorts," I said. *Think, Betty.* There had to be a way out of this that didn't end with my dead body.

He jerked my arm tighter and I let out a yelp.

"Pelagia said she saw your picture in the paper," I said to Sebastian.

Sebastian ran his fingers through his hair. "Yes, the society pages," he said. "The name was different, but she remembered my face. Even though the last time she'd seen me I was a child, she recognized me."

"I gather she hadn't approved of your folks' behavior," I said.

"No. She called them traitors." Sebastian's gaze flitted around, first to me and Paul, then to Sam, and back again. "She came to the house and said I'd made my fortune. I had been a child back in Poland, and not responsible, but it was time to right the wrongs of the past. I'd have the perfect opportunity with the Polish government in town. With the war on, it would be impossible to return everything that had been stolen to the rightful owners. She knew that. I think she believed I had a guilty conscience and giving it all to the exiled officials would help."

"I have a funny feeling your conscience didn't bother you much," Sam said. He didn't even glance at Sebastian.

"Father, you've held your tongue for years," Paul snapped. "You can hold it a bit longer."

Sebastian waved him off. "I told Pelagia to go away. Then she wrote that stupid letter and said she would write the exiled government and tell them what my family had done. I didn't believe she would, but the night of the party that young man, the secretary, asked to speak to me."

"Josef Pyrut," I said.

"He said we needed to talk, but he wouldn't say about what. I assumed the worst." Sebastian looked a little wild about the eyes. "Don't you understand? It isn't safe to be seen as a supporter of the Germans. I don't hold with the Nazis, not at all, but if word had gotten out…it would have been a disaster."

"So you killed him? Isn't that a little extreme?"

He shook his head. "No. I…I told Paul to take care of him, find out what he wanted." He glared at his son. "Take care of him, not kill him, you dolt!"

"Oh, please." Paul sneered. "He was a minor functionary in an exiled government. No one would miss him and our secret would stay safe."

"Except it wasn't," I said. I moved again, but his grip was still solid. Sam had to be thinking along the same lines I was. How could I distract Paul long enough to get free? "Who saw you, Bridget or Miss Janson?"

"Both," Paul spat. His spittle landed on my cheek. "Bridget saw me leave that night. The next day, the stupid bitch found my shirt and took it to the cleaners. She said at first she thought the blood was from a cut or something, but when she read in the paper about the mugging, she knew I was involved. She told me I had to turn myself in or she'd go to the police. I had to silence her."

Sebastian moaned and buried his face in his hands. When he lifted his face, his expression was ravaged, but a new light was in his eyes. Anger. "I loved her!"

"She was a trollop," Paul said. "Running around with me, leading you on, if you only knew how embarrassing it was. Mother knew all about it, but you were too besotted to do the right thing. I thought things were in the clear after I got rid of her, but I found out the Janson woman also knew I'd left. Then she found that letter. Stupid, Father. You should have burned it along with the envelope."

"And she saw you with the rat poison," Sam added. "Don't forget that."

"Suddenly you had all these bodies," I said. "I bet that was pretty inconvenient."

I couldn't see Paul's face, but his body twitched and I could feel the hand holding the knife tremble. If he thought he could get away, he really was dumb. Not only had he brought a knife to a gun fight, Sam was a trained cop. Paul was an amateur. No doubt who my money was on in this one.

"Dead people usually are, especially when you made them that way," Sam said. His gaze flicked to the side, then back to me. He did it again.

I risked a quick look. With all my squirming, Paul and I had moved just enough that the space to my right was empty. If I could twist outta Paul's grip, Sam would be free to make his move. "Let's not forget me, since we're talking about people who knew things." I said. I gave Sam a tiny nod to let him know I understood. "You thought you were home free and here comes another person asking questions. So you sent me those poisoned chocolates. It might have worked. They were mighty nice candies. But can I give you two pieces of advice?" I wiggled a bit to my left and felt Paul's ribcage under my elbow.

"Like I need advice from a girl who didn't finish high school," Paul said.

"In the first place, if you want to kill someone with poisoned chocolates, make sure you send something she likes to eat." I locked eyes with Sam.

I pulled my right arm forward and drove my elbow into Paul's midsection. His breath whooshed out of him and I dove into the free space. The switchblade clattered to the floor. Sam sprang forward and punched him in the jaw, knocking him to the ground. Paul cried out and stumbled back.

I clambered up from the floor. "By the way, I did finish high school, so there."

Sam knelt on Paul's back and wrestled him into handcuffs. "Paul Witkop, you're under arrest." He looked up. "Sebastian Witkop, don't move. Betty."

"Call the cops. Got it." I took a step toward the telephone in the hallway. "Oh, before I forget. Second piece of advice. If you're gonna restrain someone, make sure you take care of both arms."

"And here's a third tidbit for you." Sam heaved his prisoner to his feet. "Don't mess with a First Ward girl."

Chapter Forty-Three

Uniformed officers showed up to slap cuffs on Sebastian and haul both prisoners away. As they hustled outside, Sam turned to me. "I know I drove you here, but I really should go downtown while the Witkops are processed. If you need a ride, I can ask one of the officers to take you to the First Ward."

I waved him off. "I'll take the bus. My mom would flip her lid if she thought the neighbors saw me getting out of a cop car."

"Are you sure?"

"Positive. If you wanna help, you can give me the bus fare." I grinned.

He flipped me a quarter. "Good job, Betty. Again."

"Thanks, Detective. Be seein' ya."

It bein' New Year's Eve, I traveled to Polonia first. I needed to let Emmie know I'd fulfilled my promise to her.

"Ma is sick," she said. "I hate to lose the holiday pay, but someone's gotta watch the little ones. Come to the kitchen."

Over a cup of hot chocolate I told her all about the case and the resolution, including the Witkops' big secret and her grandma's role in exposing it.

"Then she did write to Josef Pyrut," she said.

"Seems that way. He never got the letter."

"But they didn't kill her? The Witkops?"

"Nope." I swirled the cocoa. "I know you couldn't believe it, but looks like she really did die of a heart attack."

"But you said Paul Witkop came to the neighborhood looking for *Babcia*."

"He did, and if he hadn't learned she'd already died, I have no doubt he woulda killed her. They may not have been Nazi-lovers, but neither Witkop wanted any hint of a German connection to be public." I finished my drink and stood. "Happy New Year, Emmie."

"Happy New Year, Betty. And thanks."

As I rode home, I breezed through a newspaper someone had left on the bus. The war in Europe was quiet for now. With Rommel pretty much done in North Africa, I wondered where Tom would be sent next. He sure wasn't coming home, not as long as the Nazis and the Italians were rampaging through Europe. I needed to finish my letter.

When I arrived home, Cat greeted me at the back door. *Meow.*

"Thanks, Cat. I think I did a pretty good job with this one."

Meow.

"Now I have to convince Pop to let me continue. Could be a rough fight."

Meow. Cat blinked at me and swished his tail. Then he disappeared behind the garbage cans.

"Fat lot of help you are," I called after him. I let myself in.

Mary Kate was peeling potatoes for dinner. "Who were you talkin' to?"

"Cat. You need help with that?"

"Sure." She sidestepped to make room for me at the sink.

"Let me hang up my coat." I did, returned, and picked up a spud. "Pop home yet?"

"No, why?"

"I gotta talk to him."

She eyed me slantwise. "About the detective stuff?"

"Yeah." I focused on the potato in my hands.

"Good luck with that."

Pop arrived home at his usual time and complimented us on the smell of dinner. It wasn't until much later I cornered him in the living room, where he'd retired with his pipe and evening paper as usual. "Pop, we gotta talk." I looked around. "Where's Mom?"

"She went to the church." He puffed. "Talk about what?"

I took a deep breath. "My detective work."

He laid down the paper. "What about it?"

I'd rehearsed my speech a hundred times while I cooked. Why was I hesitating now? "The thing is…I'm not gonna stop. I can't. I told you last night. I'm good at what I do and I'm helping folks."

Pop didn't speak.

"I understand it's not ladylike, even less than working at Bell. And sometimes it takes me away from family time, and it means I have to break the rules, and yeah, it can even be dangerous. I went with Detective MacKinnon and he arrested a couple of criminals today in my latest case. The one I talked to you about last night." I told him all about the Witkops.

"Did they admit to supporting the Germans?"

"In the current war?" I shrugged. "No. I don't think they do. But they needed to cover up what Sebastian's parents had done with the Prussians, or else they might have been *believed* to be traitors. They couldn't risk it."

Pop made a *hmm* sound.

"The point is, I solved it. Detective MacKinnon said I did a good job. You've always supported me and I hope you can do that now."

He removed the pipe from his mouth. "And if I tell you I absolutely forbid you to carry on with it?"

"Then I'm gonna move out. I don't want to, Pop. I really don't. But you gotta see this is important to me. Would you want me to give up on something that would make me really happy just to be a 'good girl'?"

Pop tapped out his pipe. "You're a stubborn one, you know that?"

"Didn't you raise me to be that way?" I lifted my chin. "Never give up and all that?"

He laughed. "I did indeed." Then he sobered. "It's not about having you at home. Someday, you're going to get married and leave. I know that. Betty, this is dangerous work. What if you get into trouble?"

"I have Dot, and Lee, and Detective MacKinnon, Pop. I'm not looking to get hurt." I caught his gaze, his forget-me-not blue eyes filled with concern and worry. "I promise, I'll get help if I need it."

"Nothing I say will talk you out of this, will it?"

"Nope."

He sighed, and a cloud of smoke washed over me. "I expected you to say that. I wasn't keen on Sean signing up for the Navy, and he did it because he thought it was the right thing to do. Why would you be any different?"

I pulled myself up to kiss his forehead. "Thanks, Pop."

"Just promise me one thing."

"What?"

He snapped his paper. "Next time you sneak out of the house, watch out for the cat."

I laughed.

* * *

I went to my room and pulled out the crumpled letter to Tom. After reading it, I wadded it back up, threw it away, and pulled out a fresh sheet.

Dear Tom,

I read in the papers Rommel is on the run. Good job. I knew the Germans were no match for good old American boys. Any chance they'll send you home now? Never mind, I know they won't. That's just me being hopeful.

I've been keeping busy. Not only am I working at Bell, I've picked up another job. I'm sort of, well, I'm a detective. Mostly it's for the girls at work. They bring me their problems and I figure them out. I'm pretty good at it.

I paused. Just how was I gonna word this without worryin' him half to death?

My last case was a thorny problem all right, but I worked through it and found the truth. Dot and Lee helped out. We're a regular team. You could come home and find yourself engaged to a real live private dick. How would that feel?

Cat is still hanging around. You know how cats are.

Wherever the war takes you, stay safe. I can't wait for the day this is all over and you come back to me.

Until then, I'm always your girl.

Love,

Betty

A Note from the Author

The Polish Government in Exile did visit Buffalo, NY, in early December of 1942. Buffalo had then, and has now, a vibrant Polish community, which made the city an excellent stop for political speeches and fund raising.

Similarly, the Polish people did side with the French during (and after) the Franco-Prussian war. Poland was divided into three "zones"—Prussian, Austrian, and Russian. The Prussians did punish the Poles severely for their support of the French, including stripping their lands and possessions.

Of course, no undersecretary named Josef Pyrut was part of the Polish delegation and no murders resulted from the Buffalo visit. Nor do I know of any Polish families that truly were Prussian sympathizers and who wound up fleeing to America as a result of their actions. But this, after all, is why I write fiction. These things *might* have happened—and that's what makes for a good story.

Acknowledgements

As always, thanks go out to my critique group—Annette Dashofy, Peter W.J. Hayes, and Jeff Boarts—for keeping me honest, never letting me shirk the hard work, and spotting my historical gaffes.

Also thanks to my father, Gary Lederman, for helping me with the research into Buffalo's past.

A million thanks to Kathy Deyell, for providing stellar proofreading services on extremely short notice.

A shout-out to Ramona DeFelice-Long and The Sprint Club for holding me accountable to my daily goals.

Thank you to all the readers who have embraced Betty and her friends. I'm glad you enjoy reading these stories as much as I like writing them.

And last, but certainly not least, thanks to my husband, Paul, for his encouragement and unwavering support. I love you.

About the Author

Liz Milliron is the author of **The Laurel Highlands Mysteries** series, set in the scenic Laurel Highlands of Southwestern Pennsylvania, and **The Homefront Mysteries**, set in Buffalo, NY, during the early years of World War II. She is a member of Sisters in Crime, Pennwriters, and International Thriller Writers. A recent empty-nester, Liz lives outside Pittsburgh with her husband and a retired-racer greyhound.

http://lizmilliron.com

Lightning Source UK Ltd.
Milton Keynes UK
UKHW010631110221
378620UK00001B/54